A Caine & Ferraro Novel

ENDURING
Caine

JANET OPPEDISANO

Enduring Caine

ISBN Digital: 978-1-7778856-8-7
ISBN Paperback: 978-1-7778856-9-4

For everyone who's endured
the ups and downs life brings us
on the way to happiness

Free Novella

To instantly receive the free romantic suspense novella *The Phoenix Heist*, with cameos by Samantha and Antonio and introducing the Reynolds Recoveries heist crew, claim your copy at https://bf.janetoppedisano.com/smbari40im.

Chapter 1

Samantha

No matter how comfortable the quilted seats of first class were or how flat they folded for the overnight flight, I couldn't sleep. Every time I closed my eyes, I was staring down the barrel of a gun again. Watching Antonio slump to the floor. The dizzying strobes of flashlights and all the voices yelling different orders when the police arrived.

And the bodies.

Nothing I'd ever done, including my training at Quantico, had prepared me to watch two people die in front of me—let alone to think the love of my life would be next.

Antonio groaned quietly in his sleep, like he'd been doing since he got out of the hospital. His seat was on a slight recline, the only way he could doze off with the damaged arm slung against his chest. Per his doctor's orders, it was loose enough to accommodate the changes in pressure, but that meant every time he moved, he risked hitting it on something.

I sat up to watch him, wrapping myself in the plush duvet the airline had provided. He wore the black first-class loungewear, sleep mask over his eyes. Not being able to hold him when we were both hurting threw my world off-balance.

It was only Sunday night—or maybe Monday morning, depending on the time zone—and he'd been shot on Friday. I'd tried talking him out of flying back to Naples so soon, but he waved it off like he waved off everything. Said he wanted to get his team started on their new conservation project in Pompeii. The sooner they started, the sooner they'd finish, so he could come home to sleepy little Brenton, Michigan—and me—for good.

A flight attendant made his way slowly through the small cabin and paused next to me. He whispered, "Can I get you anything?"

The lights were off, save a few safety reminders. Most of the others were asleep, but a man in the row behind us hadn't stopped working on his computer since we were in the air, the rhythmic clicks of the keyboard tempting me into a sleep I didn't want.

What I wanted was to redesign the plane so there wasn't a barrier between Antonio and me. Our privacy wall was down, but our seats were still separated and those few inches were too much. If I could be closer to him, maybe the memories would fade. Maybe they'd be replaced by how wonderful our New Year's Eve had been Thursday night, before I was drugged, kidnapped, and nearly killed.

I nodded slowly at the flight attendant, with his kind and patient professional face. "Sparkling water, thanks."

As much as Antonio should have stayed home, I needed this two weeks in Naples with him. Away from the prying eyes and probing questions of family, friends, and co-workers.

My hand drifted to my tender, bruised neck.

You're fine, Sam.

The flight attendant returned, carrying a bottle and a glass with ice. "I apologize for the intrusion, but I have a message from another gentleman on the plane who asked if you're awake." The man leaned closer to whisper. "He's law enforcement and asked me to pass along that E wants to talk to you."

I sat up straighter. Elliot Skinner, my former boss and mentor from the FBI Art Crime Team, had boarded the same flight as us, heading to Rome on Bureau business.

"Would you like me to tell him you're sleeping?"

"No." I pushed the button to raise my seat and stood, folding the blanket and stacking the pillow on top of it. "What row is he in?"

"Thirty-seven."

I cast one last look at Antonio and resisted kissing the side of his head. He needed recovery time, not to be woken up by my need for comfort. "If he wakes up while I'm gone, let him know I'm talking to E."

The flight attendant nodded and I slipped on my airline slippers to make my way through first and then business class.

Pulling aside the curtain into the rear cabin, I spied Elliot in the front row. No window to call his own, but extra legroom and the emergency exit. His tray table was out, laptop casting an eerie glow against his warm brown skin in the dark plane. When he saw me, he removed his suit jacket from the seat next to him and offered me the spot.

I sat, keeping my voice down to not disturb the other passengers. "Do you have a seatmate somewhere?"

"No. I hit the airline jackpot." He scanned me and my outfit. "You look comfortable."

"Far more comfortable than the last time I made this trip." That time, I'd been in coach, wearing jeans and a leather jacket, too freaked out at the prospect of seeing Antonio again to get a wink of sleep.

"But tired?"

I leaned back in the chair and nodded. "Can't sleep."

"That's normal after what you went through."

This wasn't news. Both Antonio and I had spoken to a counselor after the events of New Year's and she told me all the *It's normal* lines, but that didn't make things better. Time and a distraction were the best remedies. "What do you need?"

"Straight to business, as always." Elliot chuckled quietly and returned his focus to his laptop. He lowered his voice further. "I told you in the airport I couldn't give you any more details about the smuggling case, but I just received an email with something you need to know."

I straightened, my eyes drifting to his laptop screen, but it had a filter preventing people from catching a glimpse from the side.

"You remember we talked about Antonio's uncle last week?"

"Yeah." At my insistence, Elliot had told me about a mysterious uncle, one neither Antonio nor his father wanted to speak of. Between that conversation and several revelations from Antonio afterward, I'd learned the uncle was Giovanni Ferraro and that he and his son, Cristian, were involved in smuggling stolen art and cultural heritage items.

"The TPC has someone in place within his organization, living at his estate." The TPC was the Italian Carabinieri's art crimes squad, similar to the team Elliot worked for with the FBI. "His communications have been sporadic the last few months, but he got a message out last week which included reference to a plan for Antonio."

My eyes shot to the curtain between classes, toward the front of the plane where Antonio was sleeping. "A plan? For Antonio?"

"That's all the information I have." Elliot patted my forearm. "But don't be surprised if his uncle reaches out to him while you're there."

My heart screamed in my chest. Antonio told me he'd gotten involved with them a decade ago, only leaving when he'd been shot and nearly killed. I leaned in closer. "Could this be related to what I told you about Antonio being recruited by Parker's boss?"

Parker Johnson, the other man who'd tried to kill us—the one I wasn't having nightmares about—had told me the people he worked for wanted Antonio. It sounded like a pitch to bring him into their organization, but no one knew why.

Elliot used his touchpad and keyboard, the light reflecting against his face shifting as his screens changed. "I thought the same originally, but I'm fairly certain Parker isn't linked to the uncle."

"He's linked to the man you're really targeting in your smuggling investigation?" Talking in vagaries was fraying the ends of my nerves, but most of this discussion was privileged intel. If the wrong ears overheard something on the quiet plane, it could ruin Elliot's entire investigation into the smuggling ring. But people like that wouldn't usually fly back here. They'd be on private jets or on enormous yachts, like the man Antonio and I thought might be behind all of it.

Maybe it was the fatigue hindering my judgment or an overwhelming need to put it all out there as clearly as possible, but I reached a hand to Elliot's keyboard and touched five letters: F-I-O-R-I.

He paused, staring at the keyboard. Antonio and I suspected Pasquale Fiori was behind most of the crimes we'd encountered over the last half year. A stolen painting at an auction, a stolen fresco from Pompeii, more stolen paintings hidden away in Parker's girlfriend's house in Brenton. But he'd also been the man who took us onto his private yacht when I twisted my ankle while hiking. Who insisted Antonio could *pay him back later* for that kindness.

When Elliot finally nodded, my heart slowed. That meant Antonio's uncle, despite the wiretaps and undercover operative in his estate, wasn't the centerpiece of the investigation. It shouldn't have mattered. Antonio and his immediate family had little contact with Giovanni, but still, they were family, and that was important to him. Plus, his cousin Cristian had been the one Antonio called when he needed help, not just in Naples in September, but over the last couple of weeks in Brenton.

"What should we do, Elliot?" I was so tired. Bone-weary tired.

"Be yourself, Sam." A smile creased his face, his eyes crinkling at the corners. "Keep your eyes open and your brain engaged. You and Antonio make a good team, so lean on him and let him do the same with you."

Be yourself. What did that even mean anymore? Should I be the skittish woman who jumped at every loud noise since the first shooting two weeks ago? Or the woman who wanted desperately to work with Elliot again, solving the world's art crimes? Or the woman who wanted nothing more in the world than two weeks of peace and quiet with her injured boyfriend?

"Can I tell Antonio about this? Warn him if nothing else?"

"Only if you think he won't tip them off."

"He wouldn't." I gave him the best smile I could, the muscles in my face protesting the entire action. "I don't know how much more of this chaos I can handle."

He closed the laptop lid and stared at it for a moment before turning to me. "Did your mother tell you she was the one who secured your internship with me after college?"

The same twisting feeling skittered through my stomach as it always did when she and the FBI came up in the same breath. Her urging reinforced my desire to join, while her death was the reason I left. "She said you two worked together on a case."

He covered his mouth, hiding his reaction. In my experience, Elliot rarely displayed emotion other than pride in a job well done or the encouragement his team needed to accomplish those jobs. As quickly as whatever he was hiding came over him, it was gone, and the hand fell to his armrest. "She told me you put your whole heart into things, but your brain tries to hold you back."

My mom, state prosecutor and apparently amateur psychiatrist. That about summed things up. My brain and heart had been battling over my relationship with Antonio almost every day for the last five months.

"I expect that's what you're going through now." He squeezed my forearm. "You watched two people die after they'd drugged and kidnapped you. You had a friend turn his gun on you and Antonio. Your brain is trying to reconcile anger over what happened with the respect and faith in humanity you have inside you. Until that happens, your heart can't grieve or heal."

Maybe he was right. Which part of the event bothered me more? Watching the Scotts die or knowing that my old friend—a cop—was the one who killed them, just before he shot Antonio? And how much of my panic was the lingering fear over watching Antonio being whisked away by paramedics, then having to wait for him to come out of surgery?

"But here's the hard truth. You don't have to reconcile those things. You can be angry about what they did, but still regret the outcome. You haven't been dealt an easy hand, Sam. The question is: What are you going to do with it?"

"Right now, I want to focus on two quiet weeks in Naples." My gaze drifted to the curtain into the next cabin, to the seatbelt signs above, not really focusing on anything. "I should get back to Antonio."

"I'm just a call away if you need me."

I leaned over and gave him a hug. Not sure why I did—maybe it was him using my mother's memory, the fatigue, or simply an appreciation for how much he always supported me, while still nagging me to come back to the FBI. He hugged me back.

With all my thanks stuck in my throat, I stood and made my way to first class in the dark.

CHAPTER 2

SAMANTHA

I reached through the too-small opening in the privacy wall to stroke a gentle thumb over Antonio's shoulder, my eyes crawling down to the sling and his damaged bicep underneath. The bullet had pierced the muscle and nicked an artery, but the doctor said he'd be good as new—at least, that's what Antonio told me. More likely, it would be six to twelve months of physiotherapy and the potential for pain and stiffness the rest of his life.

But neither of us were dead. And that counted for a lot.

Someone in our cabin opened their window shade and the orange light of daybreak shone through.

"Wake up, sleepyhead."

"No," he murmured, leaning his head toward me but leaving his sleep mask in place. "I want to cuddle longer."

"Worst cuddle of my life."

He pushed the mask to his forehead, eyes fluttering open, and a soft smile formed. "Perhaps, but your face is the most wondrous view to wake up to."

Warmth curled in my belly at the sight of those gorgeous brown eyes with their little golden flecks dancing in what little sunlight came through the window. "I thought you might want to change before they announce the descent and whatnot. We only have a couple of hours in the airport in Rome before our connection leaves for Naples, so we need to be ready."

The corner of his mouth twitched, like it did so often, and his irritatingly sexy smirk emerged. "Never late, sì?"

I hadn't dozed off for more than a minute or two and was looking forward to the end of our journey. If everything continued per schedule, we'd arrive at Mario's in just under six hours and I could collapse onto Antonio's bed. With his arms around me, I'd finally be able to sleep.

"We're in first class and can leave before the rest of the passengers. Neither of us checked any bags, so we only need to deal with the shuttle to the terminal and passport control. Is this flight currently on time?"

I nodded.

"I'll get changed and brush my teeth." He sat up and yawned. "Care to join me?"

"That's not a group activity on a plane."

He leaned closer to me, into the tiny open space between our seats, a slight grimace as his arm touched the chair-side ledge next to him. "I have a different group activity in mind."

I pulled my head back to frown at him, but whispered, "I'm not joining the Mile High Club."

"No?"

"And your breath stinks." My mock-frown slipped a little. "Go brush your teeth."

He chuckled low in his throat. "Perhaps the next time we cross the Atlantic together, I'll rent a jet. Far more—" He winked at me, causing my smile to break free and a flash of heat to travel through me. "—private."

"Just go." I gestured to the ledge between us, to the black leather toiletries bag. "I got your things out for you."

"I see you're taking your role as nurse seriously?" He'd been shot point-blank protecting me. There was very little I wouldn't do for him.

"As long as you continue to play good patient and follow my orders." I flicked my fingers toward the bathroom.

"On one condition, Samantha." He let my name trip off his tongue, so slow, the way he knew gave me goosebumps. His thick Italian accent added a musicality to everything he said, but the way my name danced from his lips was a favorite of mine. "Say the words again."

My arms folded and eyes rolled, years of denying feelings for anyone but my family taking hold. But who could deny this amazing man? "I love you, Antonio."

"Ahh, music to my ears. Perhaps I'll have to record you, so I can use your declaration as my morning alarm once you go back to the States."

"Oh my god, you get cheesier by the second."

He puckered his lips and blew me an air kiss as he stood with the toiletries bag. It took him two trips with a single functional arm—one trip to freshen up, one to carry his clothes and get changed. I offered to help navigate the shirts, but he cracked more jokes and waved me off like it was nothing but a flesh wound. It was *only* three hours in surgery, he said. He'd had worse, he laughed.

But he paused and winced every time he shifted the wrong way or he tried to do something with his right arm, like he'd forgotten the injury. For all his claims otherwise, he was not only in pain, but was likely biting back the frustration at being so limited physically. He was tall, with broad shoulders that dinged off surfaces in the cabin that felt somehow smaller when I watched him move.

The saving grace of his injury was that he was left-handed, so he wasn't fighting against natural inclinations to do everything with the bandaged arm.

Once he finished, his dark wavy hair was as perfect as always, short on the sides and longer on top, with a hint of intentional messiness. He'd skipped shaving and sported some facial hair part of me wanted to drag my nails across. Paired with a light wool navy suit and white button-front that highlighted his olive skin, he was back into the Italian supermodel look he favored while in his home country.

· · · · ·•·•· · · ·

"How long are you planning to wear the scarves?" he asked as we flowed with the foot traffic through the airport.

I walked to his right side, hand on his back, creating a buffer around his arm. "Until the bruises fade."

"You know you're the only one who can see them, sì? To anyone else, it looks like a shadow crossing your neck."

Every instinct told me to reach for my neck, to rip the scarf off, but between holding onto Antonio and pulling my bag behind me, there was nothing I could do but sigh. It was silly, but whenever someone's eyes landed anywhere near my neck, all I could think about was Olivia, choking me into unconsciousness. It made me feel... *lean on him, like Elliot told you to.* "I don't know. It's embarrassing."

"I have a thought." Antonio inclined his head toward the passport control area. "How about we promise to put all of that out of our minds for the next two weeks? Focus on us—on being together. How does that sound, amore?"

"Like paradise. But first I need to tell you what I found out on the plane."

"Found out?"

"I had a chat with Elliot while you were asleep. The FBI received intel that your uncle Giovanni is planning something related to you. They don't know much more than that, other than it sounds like it'll happen soon."

He strode with his head high as we approached the customs area, appearing unconcerned, other than a tick in his jaw. He veered into the much longer non-EU line with me instead of using his Italian passport. "I liked my suggestion far better."

"Me, too, but at least we've been warned. You don't think they'd hurt you, would they?" Was there a chance they'd contact him during our two weeks? As far as he'd told me, the last time he saw his cousin was when I visited in September. What if they approached him again? Would they do it while I was there or avoid me, like they had last time?

Elliot's words hung in my mind: *Be yourself.* Maybe he meant curious. Maybe he even meant seize whatever opportunities presented themselves to get more information. Help the FBI. Build that portfolio Elliot and I had discussed a few times—the one that would secure me a contract position with the Bureau, allowing me to work from wherever I wanted.

"If there's one thing I know about my uncle, it's that family has always been as important to him as it is to the rest of my family. He'd never hurt me." We reached the end of the line and stopped. "At least not intentionally."

CHAPTER 3

ANTONIO

"You see, bella?" I raised my chin toward the "Nothing to Declare" exit ahead of us. "In and out in just over an hour. Plenty of time to make our connection."

Samantha had grown increasingly restless the longer the normally quick line took. Once we'd finished with passport control and were on our way again, she finally stopped fiddling with her necklace and tapping her foot. "Is this the part where you tell me it's time to relax?"

"I might mention that once or twice this trip." I leaned over to kiss her temple, a feat made more difficult by the frustrating sling around my arm.

Asking her to join me as my nurse was supposed to be a flirtation, but she continued offering to do things for me. Carry my bags, help me dress, get out my toiletries. The injury was to my bicep, not my head.

But this was how she showed her love—terrible with words but eloquent with actions.

As we neared the door to proceed to the next terminal and our connection to Napoli, so too did a trio of customs agents.

Odd. Each of them asked random people for their documents, smiling and nodding, letting them move past.

"Documents?" said one of them to me in Italian. He stood a few inches shorter than me, roughly Samantha's height and twice her breadth. Pale skin and hair, with a thick beard.

I slung my bag off my left shoulder to the floor and withdrew my Italian passport for him.

He opened it to the photo, held it up to my face, and nodded. "I noticed you were in the non-EU line. Why go through there with an Italian passport?"

"My girlfriend is American." I gestured to Samantha, who held out her passport, which he ignored. "I wanted to go with her."

"Did you present this passport when you went through?"

"Sì, as always."

"Are you a dual citizen?" His face remained impassive.

I couldn't tell if these were standard questions or not. What I *could* tell was that he was holding us up longer than the other random checks. "I am. Would you like my American passport as well?"

"Where were you born?"

"America."

"And how did you obtain Italian citizenship?"

These were not standard questions. "My parents are from here and I lived in Roma for thirteen years when I was younger."

The customs agent's eyes traveled to Samantha and back to me. "Any intention to marry or have children here for her to obtain faster citizenship?"

Marry and have children with her, sì. But not for citizenship. My mouth opened and closed, no words coming. I was tired, on painkillers, my arm hurt, and I wanted to get to Mario's for a nap.

"No," said Samantha.

Her short yet firm word elicited the first show of emotion from the agent. Likely surprise that an American understood what he was saying.

He recovered quickly and pointed to my brown leather duffel. "Only the one bag?"

"Sì."

"Pick it up and follow me, please." He tucked my passport into his belt and waited while I lifted the bag.

I let out a small grunt with the effort. Not that the bag was heavy, but leaning over let my bad arm swing away from my body. The twinge of pain was a far cry from how I'd felt the last two days, but it was an unpleasant experience, nonetheless.

"We have a connection in an hour," said Samantha, in her beautiful, flawless Italian, with a Roman accent.

The agent gestured to the exit. "Follow the signs out there."

"But..." She glanced from him to me and back again. The tension from earlier gripped her once more. It was possible she hadn't slept at all on the plane. She looked as tired as she had that day in August when she showed up on my doorstep in Napoli. Sharp words would come next, which wouldn't help our cause.

I leaned closer to her and whispered, "Wait for me outside the door. I'll be quick, I'm sure."

She blinked several times, jaw clenching and releasing, before she nodded and left. No kiss, no *I love you*. It was appropriate for the moment in front of the agent, but felt empty. The words were so new from her and caused my heart to leap every time she said them.

"No checked bags, you said?" the agent asked.

"No, just the carry-on."

The agent gestured for me to join him and walked with me in silence until we arrived in a small private room. Two chairs at least six feet away from a metal table at the center of the room, a desk with a laptop, and testing equipment against the far wall.

"Place your bag here," he said, standing behind the table. "And then take a seat."

I did as he asked. I'd been through this before with American customs, but this was the first time in Italy. The best thing to do was follow his instructions and remain quiet unless asked questions.

He unzipped my bag and removed the clothing, laptop bag, toiletry bag, and the book—a brilliant treatise on cultivating a positive mindset, whose lessons all seemed to escape me at the moment—I'd purchased in the Detroit airport. His fingers danced about the bag, opening the interior zippers, checking seams, inspecting the corners.

Twenty minutes ticked away without him sparing me a glance until he pulled out the bottle of painkillers I'd been given at the hospital. His eyebrow rose as he opened it, retrieving the radio from his belt. "I need a dog and another agent."

• • • • • • • • • •

I left through the "Nothing to Declare" door, wanting little more than to punch it open. An hour to go through a single duffel bag?

A hint of the rage left me as my eyes fell on Samantha, sitting in a bank of chairs along the wall by the door. Hunched over her phone, she scrolled through an app.

"Ciao, bella," I sighed and dropped into the seat next to her.

She slipped the phone into her purse. "What happened? You were in there for over an hour. We missed our connection to Naples."

I leaned my head against the wall. "He said traveling over Christmas to the States without any checked bags was a red flag."

"Seriously?"

"And that the codeine bottle was suspicious."

Her lip curled, and she glared at the door I'd come through, as though casting an evil spell at the customs agent. "You have a prescription for that."

"I can't even talk about it."

"Alright." She brushed her palm across mine, intertwining our fingers. "Call your travel agent and book us on another flight?"

I brought her hand to my lips and held it against my chest. "We'll get there sooner if we take the train from Termini. I'm not in the mood for more airline security today."

"Fair enough." She pulled her hand free and stood to give me the smile I normally gave her. The one that went with the wave of my hand to dismiss things she stressed over. "Which direction?"

I pointed to the exterior doors down the hall. "We'll grab a taxi."

"Perfetto!" she announced through a yawn.

Before retrieving my bag, I got up and stepped close to her, into the circle of calm she was attempting to exude, and kissed her forehead. "Grazie mille."

She stroked a hand down my cheek and smiled. "I just want a nap."

"You didn't sleep at all on the flight?" I knelt to pick up my bag, more comfortable than leaning over.

Samantha hummed aloud. "Did you already call a car?"

"No," I said as I straightened. "They had my phone in the room."

"Because..." She shifted so her body was between me and the exit doors. "There's a driver with a sign for Dr. Antonio Ferraro. That would be an awfully big coincidence if he was here for someone else with the same name and title."

I looked over her shoulder and spotted the man with the chauffeur's sign in his narrow black suit. A rock settled deep in my gut. I didn't recognize the man, but things clicked in my brain. Elliot's warning about my uncle having plans for me, the supposedly random search, and the agent's ridiculous production of going through my bag.

It was all a delay so I'd miss our connection.

My cousin Cristian asked on innumerable occasions when I would visit him and Zio Giovanni in Roma. Each time, I said *later*. Last week, I'd told him I was in the States. They must have had one of their men ensure there would be no more laters.

"I suspect he works for my uncle Giovanni."

Samantha's eyes shifted to the side, as though wanting to turn around to look at him. "You think this is what Elliot—"

"Sì, this is exactly what he was talking about."

The driver hadn't seen me yet. Samantha and I could bypass him and take our own transport to Napoli. But Gio's machinations would ruin my time with her and no doubt he'd attempt something again if he wanted to see me so badly he'd go to these lengths.

"I need to go with him. Do you still want to ride the train or would you rather we get you on a later flight?"

She tightened her lips and lifted her eyebrows, conveying how silly an idea she thought that was. "I'm not going to visit Mario while you're dealing with this. I'm going with you."

"I don't want you to spend any time with these people. I don't even want you to meet them."

"Antonio, I'm not just here for a random vacation in Italy. I'm here to spend time with you. I don't care who they are." She moved closer, her hand drifting up my injured arm. "Partners, remember?"

"Again, I'm a lucky man." I stared down into her stunning—almost glassy—exhausted eyes. Where there had once been fear and nervousness when she looked at me, there was now confidence, support, and love. I couldn't have her anywhere near that side of my family. They were my greatest shame and would exert too much stress on my relationship with her—let alone on my health. I had healing to do. "And yet no, bella. We'll go to Mario's and I'll deal with them later."

CHAPTER 4

SAMANTHA

Be yourself, Elliot had said. *Eyes open and brain engaged.*

This was my in. The TPC agent inside Antonio's uncle's organization was only getting rare communications out. I could help with that.

No matter what my job title was, I was an investigator at my core. And this was an opportunity I had to seize.

I looked up at Antonio, trying to figure out the face I was seeing. Anxiety, worry, and fatigue were all over him. "What do you mean, *No*?"

His bad arm flinched, like it had so many times since the shooting. If he was alright, his fingers would have glided up my jaw until he cupped my face, thumb brushing over my cheek. If he'd let me carry his bag, he still would have had one hand to do that.

"C'mon," I said, inclining my head toward the driver. "It'll be an adventure."

"You were right—we're here to spend time together. Whatever Giovanni wants, it will consume too much of my attention. It will prevent me from being with you, from making love to you, from simply enjoying your presence." His head shook slowly.

"The next two weeks are about us and about me getting the team started in Pompeii. The sooner we start, the sooner we finish, and the sooner you and I can be together again."

These were all good points.

"Did we not just agree to put everything else in the world aside?"

I feigned a glower, one of the most common reactions I had with this man. Second only to the eye roll. *He took a bullet for you. Let him win, for once, Sam.* "Okay, fine. But you owe me two dinners at Vista dell'Ovo."

A smile lit up his face, and he leaned forward to kiss my forehead. "And two nights at the hotel next to it?"

"Deal." I refrained from huffing out a breath or turning around to check out the driver. "Do you recognize him?"

He shook his head. "I've not been to visit Giovanni in nine years. I don't know who's still there, other than my cousin Cristian?"

"Do you think he knows what you look like?"

His eyes flicked over my shoulder and back. "No doubt my uncle gave him a picture. But we have one important thing in our favor."

I cocked an eyebrow.

Antonio shifted his weight and tucked his head down to hide behind me. "He'll expect I'm traveling alone."

"You don't think the customs agent told your uncle about me?"

"Of course." His head fell back, gaze flying to the ceiling. "He would have reported I have a traveling companion. It's possible he even sent your passport photo."

That wasn't right—being tracked as I went from place to place. "So, the question is: Does the driver know about me yet?"

"I'd rather not wait to find out."

"Turn," I said, grasping his good arm and pivoting the two of us so his back was to the driver. As we moved, I scanned the open area. A throng of people milled behind the driver, reading the overhead signs, pointing this way and that, consulting phones. The man was located between us and the door to the taxis.

Antonio stood out everywhere we went. If the driver had any idea what he looked like, there'd be no chance of slipping past him.

"Have you calculated the square footage yet?" he chuckled. When I gave him another glower, he frowned back at me. "Alright, bella, do you have a plan?

A steady stream of travelers exited through the customs doors and moved past us. We were off to the side from that flow and could use it as a cover.

"You're too tall and handsome to be good at sneaking. You know that?"

He winked at me. "It's a good thing I'm with such a beautiful woman. Surely no one will notice me."

Excited voices caught my attention, and I turned to see a group of seven twenty-somethings coming through the customs door. Three young women and four men, speaking English and dressed in winter jackets.

We were in luck. Two of the men were taller than Antonio.

"This is it," I said, hauling him into step behind them. I kept him between me and the driver. "If you can, hunch over a little and turn your face toward me."

He did as I asked, letting out a quiet laugh. "This is fun."

Antonio's focus was too zoomed in on me, and he jostled one of the men.

"Back off!" The guy lifted a hand as though he were about to shove Antonio.

I shuffled to the side and swatted the arm away before he could. "Sorry, our mistake."

"Get your hands off—" started another man in the group.

Antonio sidestepped as the women stopped instead of running into them. "Bella—"

I grabbed the back of his jacket, pulling him around the group. I glimpsed the driver, who—like everyone else in the vicinity—was looking in our direction. "Shit. That was the worst sneaking ever. Let's go."

The first man and two of the women hollered curses at us and resumed their pace. They weren't nearly as good a cover as they should have been.

My legs were no match for Antonio's long strides, but he slowed, so I didn't have to run and make more of a scene. There was still a chance he'd lose us in the airport crowds, as people walked between gates and doors, from shops and cafés.

We were nearly at the exit when the driver appeared with his 'Dr. Antonio Ferraro' sign.

"Dr. Ferraro," he said in English, looking from Antonio to me. "Ms. Caine?"

Well, that answered that question. He knew who I was.

"I'm sorry, you have us confused for someone else," said Antonio, pushing me toward the door.

"I was told you might say that." The driver fished in a pocket and pulled out his phone, showing Antonio's photo. "Your uncle politely requests your company."

Antonio's face flushed, sweat collecting at his hairline. From stress or the injury? He'd been like that several times after getting out of the hospital.

I touched his good arm. Maybe we could get the visit over with quickly. He could find out what his uncle wanted, I could find the TPC agent and offer to help deliver some messages, then we could get to Mario's and resume our wonderful vacation. "It's fine, Antonio. We can go with him."

"I'm sorry, Ms. Caine," the driver said. "The invitation is for Dr. Ferraro only. I've been instructed to drop you off at the train station. Your ticket to Naples has already been purchased."

Son of a—

"I'm not going to see him." Antonio's voice rose, and people walking through the doors gave us a wide berth. "Tell him I'll be there later. On *my* schedule."

"Anton—"

He tossed his bag over his shoulder instead of holding it in place and used his free hand to nudge me toward the doors. "No. I'm sick of these men interfering and ruining everything."

Ruining? He'd called Cristian last week for help and information about who was after us.

"Samantha and I are going to the train station. You can tell my uncle if he ever tries something like this again, he'll never see me, for as long as I live."

The driver remained calm, as though he dealt with outbursts like Antonio's all the time. "I'll pass the message along. Let me drive you to the train station."

That was too easy. "Thank—"

"No." Antonio urged me toward the exit. "You and I both know if we get in that car, you'll take us nowhere near the train station."

The driver stepped in front of me, blocking my path. "I'm sure you don't want to inconvenience all the people at Termini with a delay?"

Antonio stopped, easing his shoulder forward to drop his bag into his hand. "You're kidding me."

"I'm sorry, sir, but I've been sent here to bring you to see your uncle. I apologize if you don't want to go, but I'm sure you can appreciate I need to do my job. We can drive Ms. Caine to the train station, but if you choose to get out there with her, I will have to ensure you don't make it out of the station."

What could possibly be so important to go through all this effort? To disrupt the train's schedule?

I turned to face Antonio, blinking slowly at him. Being myself meant pressing my desire to visit his uncle. Showing him I wouldn't be scared off by men who issued threats and broke laws. Proving I loved him by standing by his side when things got difficult.

He stared down at me, breaths rapid and more sweat beading on his forehead. Hopefully, it wasn't an early sign of infection or some problem from flying with the arm in the sling.

"I'm worried about your health," I whispered.

Antonio swept his upper arm across his forehead, his leather duffel flailing about. "Don't worry. I'm not going anywhere without you, bella."

Score one for Samantha. I addressed the driver, "There you have it. If you want him to go, I'm going with him."

"Call my uncle," said Antonio. "Tell him that's the deal."

The driver nodded and took a few steps away, keeping his eyes on us.

"Fool woman," muttered Antonio.

I grinned at him. "I have to be, to be so in love with a fool man like you."

"I *am* serious, Samantha. I don't want you there." His shoulders flagged and he rolled his bad shoulder, fighting off a grimace.

"Amore," I said, resting a hand on his chest. "You've already given me the details. I know I didn't react well when you told me originally, but I can handle it. Don't worry. I love you and I'm going to continue loving you after this."

"The reality is very different than whatever picture you've painted in your head, bella."

"If we can get through this, we can get through anything, right?" I had a dozen lines I could feed to him, even if they preyed on his optimism about our relationship. But they were all true. "Honesty and truth. Partners. Stronger together."

Antonio let out a sigh, his resistance falling. "Visiting them will test all of those things."

"Every muscle needs to be broken before it can heal and become stronger?"

"That's a ridiculous analogy." He chuckled, then resumed the serious tone. He stepped closer and whispered, "But I need to warn you, there will be rules that challenge your natural inclinations. The walls have ears and eyes there. No snooping, no matter what you see. No searching for Elliot's contact. Pretend you don't know what they do and don't let them know your ties to the FBI."

I wanted to debate his assumptions about what I'd do there, but he'd never believe me. My inner detective was too busy doing cartwheels to be convincing. "I understand."

"And I hate to say this, but it's very important for you to know—there will be many lies and secrets while we are there, and some of them may come from me."

At the word *lie*, my stomach tightened and a tremble ran through me. We'd finally gotten past hiding things from each other. Diving back into a world of deception could be devastating for us.

"But I promise, on my heart, that I'll explain everything once we leave."

I blinked slowly, not as intentionally this time. Was I ready for this? "Okay. I trust you."

The driver returned, tucking his phone into his pocket. "Ms. Caine, you're welcome to join us at the villa."

"Excellent." How long would we be there? The afternoon? A day? A week? How much could I accomplish in that amount of time?

And could I convince Antonio that I was doing this for us? Not just for this moment in time together, but longer term. Would it be enough to prove to the FBI that I could work as a consultant from anywhere in the world so I wouldn't have to leave him to pursue my dreams?

In the end, this was about *our future*.

CHAPTER 5

ANTONIO

The town car turned from the coastal highway, passed through the immense gate, and drove onto the pebbled driveway that wound its way to the top of the hill where Zio Giovanni's estate stood sentinel over the Mediterranean. Tall cypress trees lined the driveway, with umbrella pines soaring to the heavens closer to the buildings.

In my mind's eye, I saw the gardens overflowing with reds and purples and whites, the nearby vineyard, the beaches crowded with tourists. But in the midst of winter, the colors were muted and the beaches bare.

It had been nine years since I last made this drive. A young man, full of increasing anger and confusion, who fell too deep into this world of money, power, and influence. Mario whisked me away to Napoli when I got out of the hospital all those years ago, after being shot on a job for my uncle. I swore never to return.

Now here I was once more, under their influence.

"Wake up, bella." I squeezed Samantha's hand which I'd held while she drifted off against my shoulder on the two-hour drive from Roma. Quiet whimpers invaded her sleep, as they had since New Year's. Each time, I shushed her, and they faded. "You'll want to see the view as we get closer."

In the distance, the small town that supplied everything the estate needed, no more than a half-hour walk away, nestled against the water. "There's a wonderful bakery in Cittavera—the town—that also sells gelato. They make the best tartufo in the world."

She stretched through her spine, gaze sweeping out through my window to the crumbling remnants of a Roman-era villa below us. It led to a cave and ancient sculptures that remained from when the villa was inhabited. Blinking to clear away the sleep, she sat up straighter. "Are those the ruins you told me about?"

"Sì. The villa belonged to a wealthy merchant who had it built in fifteen C.E. We'll squeeze in a visit down there before we leave. You'll love it." To the left, the hill rose, blocking our view of all but the trees and top of the estate's tower.

"And maybe a detour to the bakery when we head to Mario's." The smile spreading across Samantha's face reminded me how beautiful Gio's home was. But the prospect of her meeting this part of my family sat like a lead weight in my stomach. They stood for everything in this world that she wanted to fight—primarily art and antiquities trafficking.

We reached the top of the hill, and the magnificent view of the sea stretched before us. A light rain fell, obscuring the island down the coast. The final turn led us under an archway and into the open-roofed auto court at the front of the three-story main building. Marble stairs to our left led up to a courtyard and then the dark wood double-doors. The villa was covered in white stucco, while more marble decorated a half-dozen columns which rose to the courtyard's roof.

Ahead of us, another archway led to the driveway that circled the hill and would return the vehicle to the highway. To the right, a garage with four large black SUVs for transporting my uncle and cousin.

From here, only the top of the seven-story stone tower at the other end of the villa was visible, and none of the smaller buildings with apartments for Gio's staff.

A row of men lined the stairs at the edge of the courtyard. Among them, my cousin Cristian and my uncle. The rest were no doubt bodyguards, their hard faces and matching outfits of black cargo pants with black T-shirts and light jackets melding together, despite the array of skin tones and hair colors. Two of them sported automatic rifles. Another two carried umbrellas and followed Cristian and Gio as they left the covered courtyard to approach our car.

Samantha's face hardened, an almost perceptible switch flicking her into professional mode.

"Remember what I said," I whispered. "You can't do that here."

Her nostrils flared as she swept her gaze across the area. She took in the men, their positions, guards posted outside the arches, security cameras watching every move. Knowing her, she was measuring distances, recording exits and entrances, calculating how long it would take to get to the cliff and the sea.

Her mental mapping finished as the car came to a halt and she let out one slow breath. "You may need to remind me of that a few times."

The driver—who hadn't said a word since we left the airport—pulled an umbrella from the passenger seat and got out to open Samantha's door. He offered a hand, which she stubbornly refused, but he dutifully shielded her from the rain.

She moved to the side as I joined her, and my uncle stepped forward with his arms wide. Like Cristian, Giovanni was closer to Samantha's height than mine. His mostly gray hair was cropped short and he wore a brown suede jacket over black pants. I held up my arm and tapped it lightly on his back while he gave me a loose hug.

Gio stepped back, maintaining one arm around me, and smiled at Samantha. "Who is this beauty you bring to my door?"

Surprisingly, he spoke in English.

"Zio, things will go far more smoothly if you don't treat me like I'm stupid. No doubt your man in the airport told you I was traveling with a woman. I'm also sure the driver alerted you that I insisted she join us." I gestured to my love. "Even though I'm sure you already know her name, since your driver did, I would nonetheless like to introduce you to my girlfriend, Samantha Caine."

Samantha held out her hand and replied in Italian. It was either an attempt to impress him or more likely a statement of power—that she was not just some beauty but possessed brains. "It's a pleasure to meet you, Mr. Ferraro."

Giovanni smiled, no comment about the language, then continued in his native tongue. "Mr. Ferraro was my father—my name is Giovanni. I'm sure you've heard Dominico's joke about Dom Perignon? Sadly I have no catchy nickname to offer a pretty young woman like yourself, except perhaps Gio. But I *can* offer you my home and my hospitality."

Cristian stepped forward next, his umbrella carrier moving with him. He stalked over to Samantha in a way even Mario never did, looking her up and down in a far too predatory way. "I've heard a lot about you, but Antonio failed to sufficiently describe how beautiful you are."

The pleasant face she'd attempted for my uncle fell dramatically. "That's probably because Antonio's more focused on my important qualities."

"Like a sharp wit, I see." Cristian took her by the shoulders and kissed the air by both of her cheeks, which she accepted while flicking her eyes to me. Then he turned to give me a half-embrace. "Cugino, you've chosen a firecracker."

Once upon a time, my cousin had been my hero. Powerful, charismatic, and with overwhelming self-confidence. But once my eyes cleared and I saw him and his father for who they truly were, all I saw were petty men chasing an easy euro.

Perhaps not easy, but they certainly did not play by the rules. That fact had fractured my family when I was fifteen years old, and my father hadn't spoken to this brother since then. I happily would've finished my time in Pompeii and left Italia in much the same way. My grandfather crossed enemy lines during World War II to help save the antiquities in Napoli. Now these men—my uncle and cousin—sold them off to the highest bidder.

These two were a stain on our family's name.

I pulled Samantha closer, wrapping my good arm around her shoulders, to fend off Cristian's leers. "So, are you going to tell me why I'm here?"

"Tell you?" The only thing Gio had going for him at this moment was his resemblance to my father. The salt and pepper hair, the broad smile, the aura of joy that spread out from him—no matter how fake it was. "No, no. I want to show you. But that will have to wait for tomorrow. You'll be my guest for a few days so we can have some important conversations." He gestured to the trunk of the car and two of the men retrieved our bags. "For now, I have duties. I'll see you for dinner."

With a wave, Gio departed, his umbrella man walking with him.

Cristian gestured one of the other men forward, a small metal case in the man's hands. He opened it. Empty, save for a black fabric lining. "While you're here, I'm sure you'll understand that we have certain protocols and security measures in place. I'll need your cell phones, laptops, and any other electronics you brought with you."

"I'm not—"

I interrupted Samantha before she could react in a very *her* way. "Mario is expecting us in Napoli later today. Let me call him first and then we'll hand everything over."

Samantha's face hardened further. I gave her a quick look, silently conveying, *Not now, bella*. This was going to be a difficult few days.

· · · ● · ● · · ·

Cristian entered the bedroom on the villa's second floor, strolling to the center and throwing his arms wide. "Your old room! We thought you'd be most comfortable here."

The man who carried my bag placed it on the red and gold covers of the king-sized bed, under a white chiffon canopy. They'd changed the colors since I used to stay here, but the cream-colored wing chairs remained by a window next to the single door leading out onto the large terrace. Through the glass door with its ornate metalwork, one of the cypress trees was visible, and then the sea beyond.

"Grazie, cugino." I led Samantha to the terrace door to see the view. It was mid-afternoon and balmy outside, but the rain kept us inside. In January, the weather just south of Roma was more akin to Michigan in the early spring. "I think we'll take a nap before dinner. It's been a long day."

"You misunderstand, Antonio," said Cristian.

The man with Samantha's bag hadn't joined us.

"This room is for you. Our lovely Samantha will be staying in a guest room in the tower."

"No." I'd invited her to join me for two weeks in Italia as a couple, not as individual travelers crossing paths in the night. "As I told your driver, the only way I would come is if she joined me. I'm not leaving her alone in a separate section of the villa."

Cristian shrugged but didn't invite the man with her bags inside. "Mi scusi, but these are Papa's rules now. No ring, no shared bed."

This was a dramatic departure from the last time I'd been here.

I held up my left hand, showing the black ceramic promise ring I wore. "I have one of those, as does she."

"Antonio, it's alright." Samantha laid a hand on my arm. It most certainly was not alright. She'd deny it if I asked, but it was clear the woman could barely sleep an hour without me next to her. Hopefully the nightmares would fade by the time she went home, but it wouldn't miraculously happen by tonight.

I eased my injured arm across my body, placing my hand atop hers. It was instinct, and the jolt of pain screaming through my bicep reminded me that my instincts were sometimes wrong.

Cristian shook his head. "Unless you wish to have them blessed by a priest and start introducing her as your wife instead of your girlfriend, those don't count."

"Fine." I stepped to the bed, a thousand memories of staying here flowing over me. Sneaking in study time, late nights drinking and talking with Cristian, and women who weren't a fraction as perfect for me as Samantha. I threw the duffel over my shoulder. "Then put me in the room next to hers. I never liked this bed."

Chapter 6

Samantha

The family dining room was opulent. Overdone, even. A huge carved table that could sit ten comfortably, five-foot long gold-framed paintings on two walls, tapestries on the others. Sixteen-foot coffered ceilings decorated with pale blue and white paint, gold leaf covering the coffers. Double doors into the kitchen and more to the courtyard out front, plus two sets of doors leading to a garden at the side of the house.

And a giant carved fireplace with gargoyles on it.

If the separate rooms hadn't pissed me off, or if there weren't so many guards wandering the villa and tower with a mix of sidearms and the occasional semi-automatic rifle, I would have been excited to explore. The small globe security cameras which appeared in every single room eliminated any excitement that might have survived.

Fort Knox had nothing on this place.

Added to all that, it was well past sunset at eight o'clock in the evening, and I hadn't gotten any sleep. The best I could manage was a shower to wash off the long day of travel.

All I could make out through the glass doors and the rain that had been growing progressively stronger all day were bushes and trees. When the weather warmed up and the flowers bloomed, Antonio claimed it was one of the most magical places he'd ever been.

He sat next to me, gentle light from the ornate three-tiered chandelier highlighting his cheekbones and sharp jaw. His handsome face was pinched, betraying how much the ordeal we'd been through had affected him.

Giovanni sat at one end of the table, Cristian at the other end. Leonardo—Cristian's friend and head of security—sat across from Antonio. Gio's fourteen-year-old daughter Francesca—who politely asked us to drop the 'Fran' and call her Cesca—sat across from me.

"You truly live in a campervan?" Cesca said, eyes wide and speech as rapid as it had been since Giovanni introduced her to us. She spoke in English, which we all did since sitting at the table, and she wanted to know everything about the States.

"Not since last summer. It's been parked since June." I scooped a spoonful of minestrone. "It's different from camping over here, I think. I tow it with my truck."

She leaned forward. "How big is the truck?"

Antonio laughed. Spending time with his little cousin shook some negativity off him. "It's a behemoth."

Leonardo muttered, "How very American."

"I think it's cool," said Cesca. "I want to visit America and meet my Aunt Valentina and Uncle Dom. Antonio's the only one of my cousins I've ever met!"

Over Christmas, I witnessed some of the bitterness remaining between Dom and this brother. It was easy to be angry with Gio for what he did for a living, but Cesca was an innocent victim in all of it, denied a connection she longed for.

A man with warm beige skin and light brown hair entered through the open doors behind Cristian, pushing a serving cart. He wore a white chef's jacket and busied himself with clearing our bowls.

I'd counted at least two dozen inhabitants of Giovanni's estate, between family, bodyguards, and other staff like the chef. Elliot said the TPC had someone inside, so one of them was an undercover agent. The question was, who? Not Giovanni, obviously, nor Cristian, Cesca, nor Leonardo. Everyone else was a candidate.

But no snooping, right?

"Speaking of cousins..." Antonio handed his bowl to the man, continuing to speak to Cesca. "Where are your mother and sister?"

Giovanni answered for her. "They went to Paris for New Year's, to a spa and to do some shopping."

Cesca made a vomiting face at me. "They asked me to go with them, but there was no way."

"You don't enjoy spas?" I asked. A girl after my own heart.

"I wanted to see Antonio again! It's been so long, I barely remembered him."

Antonio's eyebrow cocked and I shifted my foot to tap his. That answered the question—this visit was planned in advance and the delay at the airport *was* what Elliot had heard about.

Leonardo clasped his hands together, focusing on Antonio. "And what do you think, Cesca? Is your American cousin all you hoped for?"

A darkness crossed Antonio's features as his eyes slowly traveled to Leonardo. The bodyguard had barely spoken since we met him. Antonio didn't answer, an uncomfortable silence stretching between them.

Cesca's eyes fell to her empty place setting.

There was history between these men. But what? Had Leonardo been here when Antonio was working for his uncle? And what about Antonio's aunt and other cousin? Why hadn't they stayed? Was there bad blood since Antonio left the first time?

Gio cleared his throat. "What do you have next, Henri?"

"Pistachio-crusted salmon with a light salad of arugula and beets." The server, with a French accent, collected Cristian's dishes last and smiled at his boss, who nodded.

Once Henri left, Gio looked at me. "Our chef joined us last year. I'm sure you'll agree he's wonderful?"

"The food is quite good, thank you."

"So tell me more about this job, Samantha," said Giovanni. "You told us you live in the camper because you're an insurance adjuster? Is this common in America?"

"For some types of adjusters, yes. I travel a lot."

"That must make your relationship difficult."

I turned to Antonio, who smiled at me. "I should say I used to travel a lot."

Antonio sat to my left, an unfortunate direction, since his injured arm faced me. It twitched, as though he was instinctively reaching for me. He gritted his teeth, the smile faltering for a moment. "Her boss offered her a permanent position in Brenton."

My turn for my smile to falter. A week ago, I'd been offered a job with the Special Investigations Unit at the insurance company and was supposed to be mulling it over. My boss—who was also my ex-husband—had told me the company might fold if I didn't take over the role. It was a tremendous weight placed on my shoulders, but one I'd barely thought about since New Year's. "I haven't decided yet."

"You'll do well no matter what you decide, bella." Antonio winked at me. "You're too clever to do anything but succeed."

"Speaking of clever..." Leonardo took a sip of the dry red wine we'd all been served. "I understand you're also an investigator, Samantha?"

Undercover 101: The fewer lies you tell, the fewer you risk being exposed over. "That's a core part of being an adjuster. Sometimes you have to dig a little deeper to be sure the person identifies the right losses."

Leonardo scrutinized me, not appearing to be satisfied with that answer. "And what about this auction a few months ago? And the items that were stolen from Pompeii when Antonio arrived? Neither of these are insurance—"

Giovanni knocked on the table, cutting off the discussion with a pointed look at Leonardo. "You'd be wise to remember she's our guest. If you can't, you can eat with the others."

Leonardo's face flushed, his shoulders tightening. This man was not happy about our visit. "Mi dispiace, signore."

"And in English at the dinner table, so Cesca can practice."

"Of course, sir."

Gio turned to address someone who entered the room from the door behind me. "All arranged?"

I picked up my wineglass as the man—dressed in the black pants and T-shirt outfit all the guards wore—approached Giovanni from the side. In my periphery, he didn't stand out, at home with the other men at the table with their rich olive complexions and variations of short to medium black hair.

The newcomer leaned down to whisper in Giovanni's ear. I made out snippets of the conversation, about a half-hour drive, a studio, and Antonio's name came up a few times. The context was lost on me, but it seemed to be about what they were doing tomorrow.

I took a sip and swallowed, placing my glass down as the man straightened. The motion caught my attention and I looked at him.

Oh, god. My stomach clenched and all the breath rushed out of my lungs.

The man's gaze locked on mine.

This was not happening. He was not here.

"I'm tired." I tugged, dragged, forced my eyes to move over to Antonio. To my rock. My words tumbled out too fast, but my brain was fuzzy and heart raced. "I think I'm going to skip the rest of the meal."

"Of course, amore." Antonio stood from his chair and pulled mine out, leaning close enough to whisper, "You look rather gray. Are you alright?"

The man was Vincenzo Romano.

We'd gone through art crimes postgrad together ten years ago. Threw our coins into the Trevi Fountain. Spent every waking moment in each other's company—and beds—for months.

He'd sworn he loved me and would move to the States to be with me. Memories of Vin's empty promises had made me doubt Antonio's feelings for far too long. And here he was. Inspiring a rapidly shifting series of emotions, from shock to anger to sadness and back to shock again.

I was going to be sick.

"I can't…" I swayed closer to Antonio, inhaling his vanilla and amber cologne, feeling the heat of his body next to me, searching for calm. "I don't feel well. I think I need to get to bed."

The other men all stood.

Gio spoke to Vincenzo. "Escort her up to her room."

"No, I—" I gripped Antonio's good arm. "I can go myself."

Vin's eyes bored into me. There was no hint of surprise on his face. Someone must have told him I was here. "I'd be happy to."

I needed to run. Get away from the room, from him, from all the attention on me. I slipped my fingers off Antonio's arm, rubbing them together to combat the pins and needles shooting up my arm.

Antonio took my elbow. "I'll take her and come back to finish the meal."

"This is why I have staff, Antonio." Giovanni's smile slipped from his eyes, the pleasantries obviously neither an offer nor a request.

"I insist." Antonio's hand traveled down to mine and he gave it a squeeze. He knew my numb fingers were a sign of panic. "She's not feeling well and I'd be remiss in my boyfriend duties if I didn't."

"Indeed you would." Giovanni nodded. "My man will take you both up and ensure you don't get lost on your way back. We have a great deal of catching up to do."

CHAPTER 7

ANTONIO

The reflection staring back at me was almost a stranger. Haggard and beaten. The bandages around my right bicep sported a hint of blood, a consequence of over-exerting myself with my bag, plus sleeping on it on the plane, not to mention every damn thing I dinged it on.

I looked down to my left hand braced on the white marble bathroom counter, to the black ring I wore as a symbol of my promise to love Samantha—and my unspoken promise that someday I would replace it with a wedding band. Had I known these new rules about no shared rooms, I would've told her we would pose as married for this visit. We'd done it over the last couple of weeks while investigating a stolen painting.

But Cristian knew the truth, so it wouldn't have worked. The man knew too much about my life, despite barely being involved in it.

There was a knock at my door.

"Who is it?" I called out. I'd been preparing for bed and was shirtless. Wrangling one back on was more effort than I wished to endure.

"Your favorite cousin!" Cristian most certainly was not my favorite cousin. That would have been Mario, whose house I should have been at, already in bed asleep with my girlfriend. But we decided to come here and suffer through the visit to get it over with.

The rooms of the tower were similar to those in a standard hotel. Four per floor, each with a private bathroom near the entry. These were new since I'd worked here, when the original tower cells had housed many of the guards. This remodel must have required a great deal of construction.

I stalked out to the door and pulled it open. A wide quarter turn staircase dominated the eastern and northern wall of each floor. The guest rooms were all on the south and west, providing a view of the water from every balcony. We were on the fourth floor, with Samantha's door opposite the top of the staircase and mine next to it. The center of the space opened upwards and down, with a view from the thick stone railing of the common room and the monstrous fireplace on the ground floor.

One key difference between a hotel and being a *guest* in my uncle's home was the sheer number of armed guards walking the hallways—one of whom was making his way to our floor from the one above.

I raised an eyebrow at Cristian rather than snapping 'What?' at him.

He looked me up and down. "Keeping up with the exercise, I see?"

"Of course." When I first arrived in Roma for my master's degree, I'd weighed a hundred pounds more, so much that my friends called me Fat Tony. When I moved into Cristian's apartment in Roma, he helped me change that. Mental discipline I'd known, but he showed me a physical one that transformed me into a different man.

That was the first step on a long path he and I took together. I slept around, got into fights, and railed against my parents' expectations. It was not until I was shot collecting money from someone and nearly died that I realized which of the lessons I learned from Cristian were the good ones—healthy living—and which were the bad ones. Literally, everything else.

"Good man." He gestured to the door, as though requesting access, but I didn't move.

"I'm tired and want to get some sleep. It's not time for a visit."

Cristian bowed his head in acquiescence. "We're going out tomorrow. Like Papa said this afternoon, he wants to show you something important. It's a half-hour drive and we'll be leaving before noon."

"And Samantha?"

"Will stay here. This is for you, not her."

"How long are we expected to stay?" I folded my arms, which caused a stab of pain, and hastily unfolded the good one, leaving the bad one in place. Samantha's suitcase was full of what she'd brought for ten days at my condo over Christmas. The trip to Italia was a surprise to her, so she hadn't had time to repack. I only had one change of day clothes for travel. "Neither Samantha nor I have clean clothes."

"A week at most."

A week? I'd lose half my time with Samantha to this ridiculous visit?

"I'll loan you some of my things and we can launder hers."

Henri, the chef, crested the top of the staircase, wearing a large blue tote bag across his body. He smiled warmly at me. "I'm going to close the kitchen soon. Did you need anything? Water, snacks, wine?"

Cristian put a hand out. "Sparkling, please."

Henri unzipped the bag and withdrew a glass bottle, handing it to Cristian. He moved to Samantha's door, hand raised to knock.

"She's sleeping," I said.

"Is she alright?" asked Henri. "She left so suddenly after the soup. Did it disagree with her? Are there allergies I should know about?"

"No, no, I—"

Her door whipped open, and she appeared, dressed in the loungewear the airline had provided. "Did I hear wine?"

"Bella, what are you doing up?"

"Of course." Henri unzipped a different compartment, producing a small bottle of red wine—no doubt the red bottled from Gio's vineyard—and a glass. "Snacks? I have a few items with me, but can prepare something in the kitchen and bring it up."

"No." She hadn't spoken to me or our escort the entire walk to her room. Only gave me the tiniest peck on the cheek and a whispered *I love you*, before locking the door behind her. "But what time is breakfast?"

"Ten o'clock."

She ran a hand over her face, the sign she was frustrated. "I'll need something earlier than that."

Henri nodded. "We can arrange it, but I'm heading into town around seven to purchase ingredients, so it will be after I return."

"Antonio told me there's an excellent bakery in town. Do you mind if I tag along?"

Cristian spoke up. "I'll have one of the men escort you."

The corners of Samantha's mouth turned down as her face tilted toward my cousin. "I don't need an escort."

"I'll go with you, bella."

"Ahm, no," said Cristian, in much the same way he'd informed us we wouldn't be sharing a bedroom. "You can go with her, but one of the men will join you."

Despite the tension, Henri continued to smile. "You'll barely notice them. I'm still escorted everywhere I go outside the estate."

Samantha's frown found Henri. "Wonderful. All I need is to be here a year in order to be allowed to walk from one room to another on my own."

"Amore..."

"If you'll excuse me." Henri gave a slight bow as he zipped his bag before leaving.

"This separate room thing is ridiculous." Samantha's look fell to me next, easing from a full-on glower to mere irritation. She left her doorway and approached me, her hand whispering across my bandages. "You're supposed to see a doctor about this."

Cristian cocked his head to see the spot where she'd stopped tracing, at the edge of the red bloom. "We have a doctor on staff."

I waved my hand, brushing their concerns away. My surgeon had prescribed fourteen days' worth of painkillers and I simply needed to replace my bandage. "My follow-up is in a week. We'll be in Napoli by then." Hopefully.

Her hand rose and brushed across my cheek. Quite unlike herself, Samantha stepped closer to me, touching her lips to mine. The fresh, citrusy scent of her, the touch of her warm body as she kissed me, the soft sigh that escaped her when we parted—I wrapped my good arm around her, not wanting the connection to end.

But she backed away, the frown resuming for Cristian. "Good night."

Once she was in her room, I let out a long breath. "Cristian, she and I were through hell only days ago. Why this silly rule to separate us when we need each other?"

He tightened his lips. "I can't tell you everything—Papa wants to save it for tomorrow. But, the truth is, he had a stroke a couple of years ago."

My stomach twisted, a wave of unexpected regret shooting through me. "I never heard that."

"Of course not. He's not spoken to your father or Zio Andrea in years. This rift between them..." He looked heavenward, shaking his head. "You saw Cesca at dinner? How excited she was to see you again? She was, what, five when you saw her last?"

"Sì, it's a sin she's a stranger to so many of her relatives."

He nodded. "Papa received excellent care, but a few hours afterward, he had a heart attack."

"Marone, seriously?"

"He died on the table. Ten minutes he was gone. And he swears upon all that is holy that he met Saint Peter."

Near-death experiences could change a person—it was what inspired me to leave this life behind. But actual death?

"They conversed before the gates to Heaven, where Papa was denied entry. Saint Peter told him he was living his life in direct opposition to everything it would take to get inside."

When I'd seen Cristian in September during Samantha's visit, he'd mentioned that Zio Giovanni was changing business models. He wouldn't explain, and it made no sense at the time, but now it did. "And tomorrow he's going to show me how he's shifting the business?"

"Exactly." Cristian inclined his head toward Samantha's room. "And this is why your girlfriend can't come with us."

Samantha was a woman of action who craved movement.

"She'll go stir crazy in that room alone," I said.

"I'll have someone take her on a tour of the estate. Do you think she'd prefer the cinema, kitchen, library, or the ruins?"

I chuckled. "Definitely the ruins. She loves art and history."

"I'll tell Papa. We can take her on a tour to see the artwork around the house when we get back."

"Good." I grimaced. "Just don't have Leonardo playing tour guide. He's as foul as when I left, and I'd rather make this as pleasant for her as the circumstances allow."

Cristian grinned. "He was always jealous of you and the attention Papa and I gave you. Family first, Antonio. He never understood that."

"Family," I muttered. "Is that why you watch every step we take?"

"What do you mean?" He was either playing innocent or had grown too accustomed to the eyes lurking everywhere.

"Not allowing her to walk upstairs on her own, the cameras in every room." Every room? I peered toward Samantha's door. "No one's watching her sleep, are they?"

"Security is higher since Papa got sick." Cristian frowned and pointed toward the top of the staircase.

Inside the elaborately carved finial, a flash of reflected light told me there was a camera hidden inside. Watching our doors.

"That one sees the entire floor," Cristian continued. "But the additional eyes are to protect our guests, not watch them. The bedrooms are not monitored, but all public areas are."

Perfetto. If she chose to snoop, despite my warning, she'd be caught on camera. I had to ensure she didn't.

CHAPTER 8

SAMANTHA

"Heya, Sammy!" My old friend Jimmy Slater sauntered out from behind a tree, dressed in his police uniform. "How's the doc doin'?"

We were on the Michigan State University campus in early spring, the magnolia trees in full bloom around Beaumont Tower. Sun drenched my skin from behind the trees, but it couldn't pierce the cold crawling up my spine.

"Still in surgery, but they think he'll make it."

"It's a shame what happened, David Scott trying to kill him like that." Jimmy shook his head slowly, pulling out a lit flashlight. It was the middle of the day. Why would he do that?

The bells of the carillon in the tower chimed, a slow, sad song that told me I was alone. Antonio died. Again. And again.

Blood began trickling from Jimmy's left eye and his nose. His lip welled up. "He kinda deserved it, though."

"What?"

Jimmy tossed the flashlight to me and I scrambled to catch it, while he grabbed his service pistol and—

I shot up from my pillow, gulping in air.

My heart hammered against my ribs, screaming to escape, like the noises caught in my throat.

The room was dark, a faint light spilling in from underneath the door, illuminating a desk across from the burgundy monstrosity of a bed. I pressed a hand against my chest, soaking up sweat with the waffle-weaved cotton of my pajamas.

My fingers found the diamond at my neck and I held on, sipping on slow breaths to calm myself. He was fine. I was fine. Just another nightmare.

What time was it? They'd taken my phone, so I grabbed my watch from the bedside table and hit the button to turn on its light. Two in the morning.

How long could I go on like this, unable to close my eyes for more than a few hours without Antonio next to me?

I slipped out from under the covers and went into the bathroom to splash water on my face. Maybe I could sneak next door. When I'd come out four hours ago, Antonio and Cristian were talking, but there was a guard stationed on the other side of the landing around the open staircase.

Maybe I should have gone straight to Mario's. At least I wouldn't be stuck so close to Antonio, but so far away.

I dried my face and walked to the wall adjoining our rooms, pressing my forehead against it. My hand rose to the wall, palm flat like I could touch him by touching his room. He needed his rest. Knocking to wake him up was a bad idea. I curled my hand into a fist, laying it against the wall, battling my need to be next to him.

I was strong. I had work to do here, and I could get through this.

A clunking noise came from his room, like from a glass or something being put on a table.

I pressed my ear to the wall. The sound came again.

Along with faint voices and music. Gunfire. Explosion.

He was awake! Watching a movie.

Damn the guards. They wouldn't shoot me for visiting him. I opened my door as casually as possible and headed for Antonio's room.

A man in black pants and shirt interrupted his patrol of the floor to approach me. "Is there something I can help with?"

"He has my sleeping pills." I knocked once, and the man grabbed my arm. When I yanked against his grip, he held firm. Before I could smash a palm into his sternum or knee him in the groin, Antonio's door clicked open.

"What are you doing?" Antonio snapped at the guard. "Take your hands off of her."

The guard did exactly that. "Sorry, Mr. Ferraro."

"The title is Doctor," Antonio sneered. He wore the lounge pants from the airline. We must have made quite the pair in our matching outfits. He glowered at the man a moment longer, until he stepped back, then Antonio's gaze fell to me. "Are you alright, bella?"

"You have my sleeping pills."

He stared, brows turning down. It was a lie, but he said, "Sì, of course. I forgot them in my bag."

I walked in through the open door, Antonio's broad form just behind me. So close I could feel his presence, already calming my heart more than the breathing exercises did. The door didn't shut, though, so I looked back and saw the guard holding it open. There'd be no sneaking around like teenagers.

I flicked on the bathroom light as we entered.

"We'll just be a moment," said Antonio as he closed the door, ensuring the guard wouldn't follow us. He turned me to face him and pulled me to his chest, groaning as he slid his injured arm around me.

"Sorry if I woke you."

"All this flying from Italia to America and back again has my body clock rather confused." He kissed the side of my head. "Plus, I rolled onto my arm and it woke me up."

No matter how many times I watched him die in my dreams, or had someone tell me he was gone, or just felt his presence leave the world, it ripped a hole in my heart every time. Having his arms around me, my cheek pressed to his, and having a moment to simply breathe together centered me.

"Did you have another bad dream?"

"I have a balcony attached to my room that I haven't explored yet. Does it link up with yours?"

"No, but they're close enough to talk from."

I pulled back from him. "Give me a couple of whatever pills will convince him, then meet me outside?"

"Of course, bella."

· · · ● · ● · · ·

I stepped out onto the small balcony, bundled in my winter jacket. "Holy shit, it's a lot colder than I was expecting!"

Antonio chuckled, wrapped up in his blankets. He sat on the thick stone railing, leaning against the wall. "Warmer than Michigan."

"By a long shot." We were four very tall stories up—lit by the half-moon and security lights on various buildings—and ten feet apart. Once the sun rose, I'd have to inspect the wall. Maybe the rough exterior would have hand holds and I could climb across. Note to self: pack climbing gear next time. "A bit cooler than my winters in southern California and Texas, but nowhere near as warm as southern Florida."

"You should tell Cesca some stories about all the places you've lived. I think she'd appreciate that."

"She's kinda cute. I like her."

"Her older sister was away at boarding school while I was here, so I didn't know her well. But my Zia Giulia—I'm surprised she didn't stay. She's much like my mother. Smothering."

"Probably for the best, then." I leaned over the edge, unable to see anyone else outside, other than a guard patrol on the ground. "You never told me this was a fortress."

He placed a finger to his lips, reminding me of the eyes and ears he warned me about. "It's a very safe place."

"What's the plan for tomorrow?"

"Have you ever noticed—" Antonio's head rested against the wall, rolling toward me like he was talking to me from a rather hard pillow. "—how often you touch the necklace you swore you didn't want?"

My hand froze, unconsciously wrapped around the diamond pendant he'd given me for Christmas. His mother's necklace, that she and his father wanted me to have. I pulled it up to see it reflecting the silvery light of the moon. I turned my hand over to admire the trinity ring on my left hand, with its bands of black ceramic, white gold, and a white gold channel of diamonds.

I don't want stuff, I'd said to him over and over again. Yet still he bought me things. "They're not just stuff."

He smiled, a peaceful look on his face, despite the insanity of our predicament. "No, they're not."

I held tight to the necklace and that smile. "I love you."

"Good," he said with a smirk, his eyes fluttering closed.

"Jerk." I did my best to scowl at him, but let out a chuckle—he wasn't looking at me anyway. For months, he'd told me he loved me, while all I'd say in response was 'good.' Now he liked to say it in return.

"Do you want to tell me what happened at dinner? Why you ran out in such a hurry?"

I settled on the railing closest to him, mirroring his posture. Vincenzo hadn't spoken to either of us while he escorted us up to my room, but he obviously hadn't told Antonio the truth about our history on Antonio's way back to the dining room. To Antonio, it would have seemed like he was focused on his job as a bodyguard. There was no reason to suspect more.

"Do you remember my ex from my time in Amelia? I told you about him before I left Naples in September, just after you gave me the ring."

His eyes flashed open and he sucked in a quick breath. "He's not..."

I nodded slowly. "He is."

Antonio stood, his features falling into shadow. He had an enormous jealous streak, so part of me hadn't wanted to tell him. But we promised honesty, so there it was. He leaned forward on his railing and whispered, "Do you want me to punch him out for you? Have him fired?"

I whispered back, "How about tar and feathers?"

"This is a good idea." He sat again, far calmer than I'd expected. "How dare he treat the love of my life that way?"

Warmth spread through me at the sound of those words. He'd told me he loved me within a month of meeting me. I'd taken longer, the scars of my past weighing heavily on me. Vincenzo had been a powerful scar that took a lot of getting over. But Antonio and I had clawed our way to each other, and here we were. "No jealous reaction?"

He waved that silly hand of his. "Pfft. He's part of your history that made you the amazing woman you are today. I should thank him for being blind to how wonderful you are."

I let out a yawn, which was cut off by a shiver. "Back to my earlier question. What's going on tomorrow after we go for breakfast?"

"My uncle is taking me somewhere. I don't know the details, but it's why I'm here."

"Taking *you*?"

"Sì, unfortunately you can't come."

I zipped up the collar of the jacket. "Probably for the best. I'm having a difficult time controlling my temper around these men."

"No one noticed." Antonio's shoulders shook with quiet laughter.

Another yawn prevented me from insulting him again.

"But one of the men will take you on a tour of the ruins. I'd hoped to do it myself, but it appears I'll be busy while I'm here."

"Not Leonardo, I hope?"

"I specifically requested not." He stood, stretching his neck from side to side, blinking slowly. He was so tired. "Do you think you can sleep now?"

"Hopefully."

"Un momento," he said and vanished into his room. He returned a few minutes later without his blanket around him, but with something in his hands. "Think fast."

He threw a wadded up piece of fabric at me.

I caught it and held it up. It was his pajama shirt from the airline. I pulled it to my nose and inhaled, the comforting scent of him washing over me.

"You may be too stubborn to admit it, but I know you're having nightmares. I also know when I speak to you in your sleep, they fade. Perhaps having that will help."

"Just what every big girl needs. A security blankie."

"Whatever works." He shrugged. "And if it doesn't, tomorrow we construct a bridge between our balconies."

CHAPTER 9

ANTONIO

At seven thirty the next morning, Samantha and I were finishing breakfast in the bakery café I'd told her about. She'd deviated from the chocolate hazelnut cornetto she ate every morning in Italia and had indulged in one filled with cherries and mascarpone cheese. She savored her cappuccino while I sipped my espresso.

We'd originally joined Henri on the trip, but one of the other guards saw him to the market, while the miserable Leonardo hovered ten feet away from us. To the outside observer, it might seem Leo was there to protect us, as though there were some danger in this small town outside the estate. But those privy to what went on inside the walls knew it was the other way around. Samantha was an outsider—so was I, in some ways—and Giovanni was protecting his business by ensuring she didn't speak to the wrong people or see things she should not.

I placed my small cup on the table and reached for her hand, bringing it to my lips. If I angled my seat properly, I couldn't see the scowl from Leonardo. "This is more like what I'd planned."

Samantha smiled, the most glorious smile she'd shared since I woke on the plane. "I feel like I've been missing out by only eating one flavor all these years."

"Sì, you have. Perhaps we can come back tomorrow and we can try their lemon?"

"That sounds perfect." She sat up straighter, eyes scanning the café, its bank of glassed-in pastries, the gelato counter. "I don't suppose they have a bathroom?"

"I'm not sure."

Leonardo approached the baked goods counter, where a woman with medium olive skin and bright blond hair was sliding a tray into the display—freshly made cannoli, dusted with powdered sugar. He whispered something to her and turned to us, hooking a thumb over his shoulder. "Back there."

Samantha frowned at his curt words, but stood, gave me a peck on the cheek, and stepped around the end of the counter. On her way past the cash register, she nodded to the woman and said, "Grazie."

Leonardo fell into step behind her.

Samantha paused. "What are you doing?"

"I have to check the room, then I'll wait for you."

Her eyes clamped shut and her jaw clenched. She took a deep breath to compose herself, then looked him square in the eyes. "It's a bathroom. I don't need an escort to a bathroom."

"Giovanni's rules," he said as he pushed past her and disappeared through a doorway into the back. As the head of security, it was unlikely Leonardo was simply following anyone else's rules. These were no doubt his and were aimed solely at pissing me off.

I'm going to kill him, she mouthed to me before following.

The dining section contained only four small tables. Outside, there were over twenty more, but it was far too cold and the sun's early morning light barely made it over the hills to the east. The scent of baking breads and pastries was thick in the air. I stood and passed the gelato counter, continuing to the pastries.

The door to the café opened and closed behind me and the blond woman smiled briefly before returning to the back.

A tray of maritozzi, sweet buns sliced in half and filled with whipped cream, caught my attention. Then the biscotti next to them. I should buy some of those and bring them back for Samantha. She'd like that. That woman loved her Italian sweets.

Like me, her Italian sweet.

I shook my head at myself. That might have been too cheesy, even for her.

The new patron stopped next to me, his deep voice quiet. "We need to be fast."

I looked up, startled he'd spoken to me, let alone in English. Warm brown skin, short goatee with gray highlights, navy blue jacket and pants. Special Agent Elliot Skinner. Samantha's FBI mentor.

"Are you alright?" he asked.

"Speci—"

He put a finger to his lips, eyes darting to the door Samantha, Leonardo, and the staff woman had exited through.

"Sì, we're alright."

"Why is Sam being followed like that?" Elliot knew things about my family—had revealed some of them to Samantha last week—but how much did he know?

How to answer this question without revealing things I shouldn't? "Long story."

He lowered his voice, so quiet I could barely hear him above the sounds from the kitchen. "Is your visit related to the rumors about your uncle getting out of his business?"

"My what?"

The woman returned with a tray of zeppole and slid it into place. The fried dough balls were covered in powdered sugar, with dollops of lemony curd on top of them, which should have caused my mouth to water. Should have had me thinking to buy them for Samantha. Instead, I was half a step behind the conversation, my brain—and tongue, apparently—a whirl of questions.

Cristian had said Zio Giovanni was *shifting the business.* Did that mean getting out of the smuggling trade altogether? Or did this FBI agent and my cousin mean different parts of the business? Extortion? Bribery? Interfering with local elections to ensure his businesses carried on without challenge?

Elliot leaned closer to the display and whispered, "I need to talk to her. Have her call me."

"She can't." I pointed to the biscotti, as though he and I were having a debate on what to order. "They took all of our electronics."

"Then I definitely need to talk to her. I'll be here at ten and two every day. Come as soon as you can."

"They're watching her like a hawk, Ell—"

He put the finger up again, but it drifted across his face like he was brushing something away. Was this an undercover job?

He'd silenced me on his title and his name. So clearly, it was. "You'll have to provide some sort of diversion."

What could I possibly do to keep Leo's eyes off of her? A female guard I could have distracted, but not him.

The woman closed the back of the display and ran her hands over her white apron, mouth opening as if to speak.

Before she could, Elliot shook his head and said to her, "I'll be back later."

As he vanished between the tables outside the café, Samantha and Leonardo returned from the washroom in the back.

"There's not even a window in there," Samantha hissed. "What *exactly* did you think I was going to do that required a bodyguard?"

"Maybe choke on your venomous tongue," Leo shot back.

I pulled Samantha to me, providing Leo with my most patronizing smile possible. "Just as successful at charming the ladies as ever, I see."

"She's a harpy. Just what you deserve."

Samantha cocked her head, a smirk crossing her face. "Not used to a woman who stands up for herself?"

"I'm used to women who know their place."

It was wrong to insult him so much, but perhaps if we pissed him off enough, he'd insist on another guard taking over for him. "Do you know your place, bella?"

"I do." She wrapped her arm around my waist and looked up at me. "It's wherever the fuck I want to be."

I kissed the tip of her nose. "So long as I can be there with you?"

"Icing on the cake." Her spirits had made a turn for the better so quickly, Leo returned to the background of our lives.

"Speaking of icing…" I pointed to the maritozzi. "A few for the road?"

Samantha craned her head toward Leo. "What does Cesca like?"

His frown hardened, but he said, "She prefers the cannoli with chocolate."

Behind him, through the glass door, the brilliant blue of the morning sky pushed the darkness back. The bakery sat on the edge of a grand square with other restaurants and shops. In the warmer seasons, a thriving market of fresh produce battled with the scent of the fishmongers, all while musicians shared their songs and children played football.

At the far edge of the square, a short wall of stone and stucco marked the transition from town to beach. In a few months' time, the beach would be clogged with blue umbrellas shading tourists who came for sun and laughter.

While I pined over the better half of my memories of this town, Samantha finished her order, receiving a white box tied with a string, and said, "All done."

Leonardo left ahead of us, scanning the square for anyone who looked out of place.

No sign of Elliot. I'd have to tell Samantha about his visit and his request soon, but when? Those details were not ones I could risk someone overhearing. Not quiet words while we ate, nor in the car back to the estate, nor even across the gap between our balconies. The risk of someone finding out the FBI was in town—let alone the Art Crime Team and that Samantha once worked for them—was too great. Her relationship with me may have provided her protection if they found out her past, but if they also knew a Special Agent was nearby, she could be in grave danger.

Henri and his pale blond guard appeared from one of the shops, each of them carrying several bags. He waved to us, and we convened on the stairs up from the square, heading to the SUV to take us all back.

"Did you get everything you needed?" asked Samantha.

Henri opened the car door and slipped into the third row. "I did. Antonio told me last night you love Grana Padano cheese, so I picked some up and will stuff ravioli with it tonight."

"That sounds wonderful!" She smiled at me as she settled in her seat. "I also picked up some extra pastries. Would you like anything?"

"No powdered sugar in the car." Leo looked at me in the rear-view mirror, as though I would control her.

The other guard, sitting in the passenger seat, turned around. In a German accent, he said, "You didn't get any of their little apple cakes by any chance, did you?"

"I did." Samantha opened the box and handed him one. "Don't worry, Leo, no powdered sugar on them."

The German guard resumed his position, head on a swivel as we drove. But each time he took a bite of his cake, he smiled. Perhaps if we were lucky, this man would be our town guard going forward.

Samantha dusted the sugar from one of the cannoli into the box and handed it to Henri. "Based on your French accent, I'm assuming you're not from anywhere near here. Where are you from?"

"Quiet," said Leo.

"Merci," said Henri, who simply bit into his cannolo, seeming unphased by Leo's hostile attitude.

Samantha inched herself closer on the seat and intertwined her fingers with mine. She closed her eyes, the sunlight barely penetrating the dark tinted windows, but she turned her face toward the sun hanging low on the horizon.

Leo's orders could hardly stand, despite Samantha and Henri finding peace in them.

I tapped his shoulder. "Are you coming with Giovanni and me this afternoon, Leo?"

"Of course. There's important business to discuss."

"Should be a fun trip."

Samantha bit down on her bottom lip to stifle a laugh.

"That was always your problem, Antonio." Leo glanced at me in the mirror, from behind his dark glasses. "You're incapable of taking anything seriously."

"Perhaps if I had as narrow a perspective of the world as you do, I'd be equally incapable of enjoying the beauty of life." I ran my thumb over Samantha's knuckle, the simple contact with her centering me. "Fortunately, I've seen enough to know how fleeting joy can be. And how important it is to find as much positive as possible in each moment."

Leonardo's jaw flexed, but he said nothing more, nor did he glower at my reflection. All I had to do now was listen to my own words for the rest of this visit.

CHAPTER 10

SAMANTHA

When we got back from town, Antonio headed off with Cristian to choose some clothes to borrow. Leonardo's plan was to lock me in my room—like a princess in a tower—but the apple-cake loving German guard, Johann, offered to take me on a tour of the property.

With the sun fully up, the air was warming, much like a nice spring afternoon, so I left the jacket behind and wore my favorite white Foster Mutual sweater.

"You can see all of Cittavera from here. Can you spot the square where the bakery is?" Johann pointed to the north, coming close enough I could use his arm as a sight.

Why did he bring me outside? Did the apple cakes buy me a shred of kindness? Did Antonio have a word with him? Or maybe...

What if *he* was the TPC agent?

"Cittavera?" White buildings crammed together on a low hill by the water. Between trees and bushes, terracotta roofs popped up here and there. I couldn't make out the bakery, but a square by the water's edge with a short white wall stood out. "Town of Vera?"

He nodded and continued the stroll. "The town's named after the merchant, whose ruins are below the hill. It was a small fishing village, but close enough to the Via Appia—the main Roman road across the country—that he took an interest and built it into a market town. It was never as successful as some of the other towns nearby, but it makes a pleasant home now."

"You know the area well?"

"I've been here four years. Giovanni loves to talk about the region and history, plus an understanding of the local geography can be critical in my job." He shrugged. "The tower and the site of the main villa were originally a small medieval monastery, which housed forty monks."

"I imagine the rooms were smaller back then?"

He laughed, pointing up to the tower's peak. "From what I'm told, the seven stories you see today were originally nine."

"What happened?"

"Earthquake, they say." He guided me toward a vine-covered archway. "The coast here is at lower risk than much of the rest of the country, but still high enough to show evidence of quakes over the centuries."

The pebbled walkway opened into a vast garden with squared hedges, round bushes, and edged flowerbeds that were little more than dirt and pruned stalks. "Do you live in town?"

"No, in the—" He turned, walking backward, gesturing to a pair of low stucco buildings near the tower. "—we call it 'the village.' Leonardo and Henri have rooms in the villa, of course, since they're needed so often. But the rest of the staff live there. Twenty of us, some with families, some not."

"Twenty? Is there really that much to do here?"

"It was thirty-five when I started. Giovanni's cut back in the last two years."

Cut back? Why would he do that? Decrease in business? "Why's that?"

He made a playful grimacing face, eyes wide. For such a big and intimidating man, carrying a pistol at his waist, he was very easygoing. "I don't get into the business, just do what I'm told."

We continued around a dry marble fountain, ten feet across at its base, with a carved angel holding a lyre in one hand, reaching to the heavens with the other. It would be beautiful here in the summer.

"Yeah, Leonardo seems to enjoy giving orders," I said.

Johann slowed to swipe some leaves from the edge of the fountain. "He's the head of security. It's expected."

"Do you like working for him?"

"The pay is good. The winters are easy." He knelt as we passed a stone bench, and a calico cat appeared from between some bushes. The cat looked up at him, purring when he picked it up and resumed his walk. "I get along with the other staff."

"You're from Germany?"

He nodded, stroking the cat's back as it settled against his chest. "A small town north of Hamburg. So far north it's practically in Denmark."

The TPC wouldn't have a German on their payroll, would they? Elliot had told me their man inside the estate was with the TPC, specifically. Johann could be lying about his background. Or Elliot could have meant that their man was with Interpol, coordinating with the Italian authorities.

How deep did the smuggling investigation go? How many people were on it?

Nathan Miller, one of my best friends—and Antonio's nemesis—was involved in the investigation, too. I'd tried getting information out of him, but only found out a few minor facts. Everything else came from Elliot, whether or not he was supposed to tell me.

And if I wanted the full details, I'd have to join Elliot's team.

He'd dangled a very large carrot in front of me last week. Giovanni had some role in a smuggling ring that was going to move the most expensive painting ever stolen, *The Concert*, by Johannes Vermeer. At least, that's what the chatter was pointing to. Maybe the FBI was reading too much into it, maybe they were misinterpreting the codes the smugglers were using, or maybe it was a red herring.

Much of me wanted to quit my job, rejoin the FBI, and go chasing after it. But that would take me away from my sister before she finished her radiation treatments and from Antonio. And from Foster Mutual, where my ex-husband, the acting president, was offering me a full-time job to save the company after I'd discovered the former president was taking bribes.

I ran a palm over my forehead. *Quit thinking about it and focus.*

Johann came to a stop at the top of the hill and turned around, waving a hand in front of him. We faced away from the Mediterranean, looking back at the entire garden. "Most people like the water view, but I prefer this one. Roses, lilies, poppies, narcissi, peonies, and a dozen other flowers. In summer, it's the most peaceful place I've ever visited."

Unless there were hidden cameras in the plants or the fountain, we were all alone. Cautiousness won over curiosity. Instead of asking if he was the undercover agent, I asked, "How did you end up here when you're from so far away?"

"My sister got sick and I was her entire support system. I needed some extra money, so I..." He scratched under the cat's ear and looked up toward the tower. "I made some poor choices, got in with some people I shouldn't have, and wound up here."

I understood the toll of serious illness too well. My own sister had been diagnosed with breast cancer in June, and I moved home to help her. She was lucky for the support she had, particularly my brother-in-law. She was even planning to return to work in a few months. "How is she?"

His eyes trailed down the tower, sweeping across the buildings that made up Giovanni's estate. "She'll be fine, but I still send her money regularly."

"Any plans to go home?"

He shook his head. "Things are improving. My job has changed over the last couple of years and with the decrease in staff, my pay's gone up."

Another comment about changes two years ago. I had to talk to Antonio about that and find out the details. "It's surprising to need so many guards when the place has so many cameras."

"True." His gaze returned to me, a warning flashing in his eyes. "They record everything across the grounds and inside the main buildings, including here. There's little privacy."

The hairs prickled at the back of my neck. Johann was a tall, broad, overwhelming German who looked like he could snap someone's neck without a thought. But he cradled stray cats and seemed to be warning me about the security. He had to be the agent.

And if he was, did he know who I was? Were the warnings general or specific? I angled my body so my back was to the buildings and whispered, "Why did you bring me out here?"

Another cat appeared from behind a bush, and Johann exchanged the one he was carrying for the new one. He scratched the new cat, gray with flashes of white, which purred in his arms. He didn't lower his voice at all. "Cristian's spoken of Antonio many times. He sounds like a good man, which means you're probably a good woman. I didn't think it was fair for you to be locked in the tower all morning."

Was that an honest answer or a cover? "Do you have guests often?"

"Regularly in the warmer months. Not so much this time of—"

"Samantha!" Cesca appeared at the far edge of the garden, from under the arch, hurrying in our direction—spoiling any chance of getting more information out of Johann. "Henri said you bought cannoli!"

I called back, "Leonardo said the ones with chocolate are your favorite."

"She's a good kid." Johann leaned over to let the cat jump out of his arms and whispered, "Talented, but lonely."

What must it be like to grow up surrounded by armed guards and spies? I smiled at her. "Do you want to come up to my room, Cesca? I got a whole box full of sweets. We'll eat at least the cannoli."

Chapter 11

Samantha

"It's so good!" said Cesca as she licked the chocolate crème off her fingers. "Thanks for thinking of me."

Antonio was still picking out clothes with Cristian, so Johann had escorted Cesca and I upstairs. She and I sat on my bed, eating too many of the treats I'd brought from the café.

Must have been nice to have free rein of the estate like they did.

"When do you go back to school?" I asked before popping the last zeppola into my mouth.

Her shoulders caved in and she mumbled, "I'm home-schooled and my teacher lives here, so I don't get time off."

"Same teacher for all subjects?"

"Yes, one teacher my whole life." She rolled her eyes. "She also taught Cristian, but my sister got sent off to boarding school because she didn't pay attention. Her entire goal in life is to shop with my mom."

"And that's not what you want?"

"Papa says all Ferraros go into finance or the arts, like him and Cristian."

Did she know what kind of arts they were actually in? The illegally traded kind?

"That's what I want to do." She leaned forward, her eyes sparkling. "When I told Papa that, he agreed to have one of his men teach me art history, because he knows more than my teacher."

A weight settled in my stomach. I was pretty sure who she meant.

"Vincenzo knows so much about art." Cesca sighed dreamily and I could have shaken her. She was a kid and he was a two-faced asshole, but who could temper the teenage heart? "He's the one who walked you and Antonio upstairs last night. Isn't he gorgeous?"

Thankfully, a knock at the door rescued me from having to formulate a polite answer.

"One sec." I pulled the door open and the weight sloshed around in my stomach as I laid eyes on a hard face. "Leonardo, what a pleasure."

"Francesca," he called over my shoulder, like I wasn't even there. "Time to go."

She groaned and stomped across the floor, stopping next to me. "How'd you find me?"

"Johann told me he brought you two up here. And you're supposed to keep your phone on you at all times." Leonardo handed her a smartphone.

"What teenager leaves their phone behind?" I smiled down at her—she was roughly half a foot shorter than me.

"The kind that only gets messages like these." She woke the phone and showed me the lock screen, with five messages from

Cristian, all telling her it was class time. "Gotta go. Thanks for the food. Maybe it'll get me through math."

"Good luck," I said as she hit the top of the wide staircase.

Leonardo watched her go, but didn't budge from my doorway. Once her footsteps were no longer audible, he turned to me. "Sucking up to the family, I see? You and Antonio are quite the pair."

"We are, as a matter of fact."

"I couldn't help but notice last night at dinner..." He stepped closer, his broad frame and the four or five inches he had on me inspiring the instinct to retreat. "You left when our handsome Vincenzo arrived."

I held my ground. "Antonio and I finished an overnight flight to Rome, had to endure two hours at customs, and then the surprise drive here. I was tired and needed sleep."

"Still, the way you looked at him..." He ran the back of his knuckles across his jaw, telegraphing that he was trying to bait me.

"Plus, I think your cologne was making me nauseous."

"Tell me, my pretty little investigator..." His eyes eased down the too-short T-shirt Cesca had lent me from her sister while my clothes were in the laundry, angling to the side as his gaze skimmed over my hips. "How much has Antonio told you about our business?"

This was one of Antonio's rules from the airport. Don't let on that I know what they do.

"He didn't have to tell me anything. We were greeted at the front door by men with automatic rifles in their hands and SIGs at their waists. Then we had to deposit all of our electronics into a Faraday case for security measures. It really doesn't matter what you do, because it's clear you're not men to be trifled with."

"Clever observations." He stepped close enough his chest was almost touching mine, a dark scent of musk and sweat enveloping me. "You recognize the model of pistol so easily? And the Faraday case?"

"Hollywood movies."

He snorted a derisive laugh. "Just because Signore Ferraro and Cristian see you as nothing but the brunette on Antonio's arm doesn't mean I feel the same."

Back off, Sam. This is a dangerous game. "What's your goal here, Leo? Intimidate me? Fine, consider me intimidated." The wise part of my brain forced my stubborn body to step away, although it couldn't convince my voice to sound scared, like it should have. "Now can we move on with our day? I'm apparently getting a tour of the ruins while you boys are out playing your mysterious games that I really don't care about."

"Oh, don't you worry. You'll get your tour, just as Antonio requested." He stepped into the room, taking up the space I'd conceded.

Shit. Not good.

Footsteps sounded on the stairs behind Leonardo—*please be Antonio.*

"Leave her alone," Antonio said in his deep voice that sent a different shiver through me than it usually did. One of relief.

"We were only chatting, weren't we?" Leo's smug smile lingered until Antonio's hand appeared on the shoulder that was too close to me.

"I said—"

Leo shrugged out of Antonio's grip. "What are you going to do with only one arm? Run away like you did the last time someone challenged you?"

"Making wise choices isn't running away." Antonio shook his head, like he pitied Leo for his anger, which he probably did. "That's something you've never been able to understand."

Leo turned his face toward Antonio, squaring up against him. "A word of warning—and I don't care if you tell Cristian: You can't just come back here and think you have a place in this new world. There are too many wolves at the gate for a soft man like you." He shouldered his way past Antonio, ramming against his injured arm.

Antonio held his breath, eyes and lips clamped shut.

"What the hell was that about?" I asked, watching Leo's retreating form.

Once the footsteps on the stairs had faded, Antonio let out a slow, "Cazzo Madre di Dio, but that hurt."

"Are you alright?"

"Speaking of wise choices, I think we should stop taunting him." He stretched his shoulder backward, holding the arm tight to his body. "I should have put the sling on before I thought to argue with him."

"And maybe hide some spikes in it for the next time he tries that."

Antonio laughed and groaned. "Remind me to never get on your bad side."

"You've already been there." I pulled close, wrapping an arm around his neck. "You just got the silent treatment."

"Punishment suits the crime?"

"More it suits the criminal." I lifted on my tiptoes to kiss him, but he shook his head.

"We can't." He whispered, "Did you spot the camera?"

I scanned the square floor that surrounded the L-shaped staircase. Nothing on the walls or the ceiling here. "No."

More footsteps sounded from the floor below, two pairs.

"It's in the finial at the top of the staircase. Three-sixty. They see everything outside of the bedrooms."

What would that have meant if I'd backed down with Leonardo? "So if Leo had pushed his way inside my room…"

"He'd threaten you, but he wouldn't—"

"Cugino!" Cristian appeared on the stairs with Johann at his side, both of them carrying bags. "It's time to go."

Antonio's gaze remained locked with mine for a moment before he nodded. "I need to grab my jacket and sling."

Cristian approached me, while Johann took Cristian's bag and followed Antonio into his room. The leering gaze he'd used on our arrival was gone, replaced by an almost casual friendliness. Either he recognized the first one didn't work or Antonio might have had a talk with him about it.

"Will Johann be taking me down to the ruins?"

"No, Antonio said you have a passion for this sort of thing, so I picked the man who knows the most about the ruins and the cave," said Cristian. "He's busy right now but will be up within the hour."

Maybe if I pretended I was some ultra-wealthy woman who had her own staff, I could sink into this experience and enjoy it.

It wouldn't get me closer to Antonio, but I could release a little of the pent-up energy. "Thank you."

"And I spoke with Leonardo. I explained to him the concept of *guest* once more." Had Cristian been watching that exchange? Nothing happened in this villa without him knowing about, did it? "If he tries something like that again, please let me know. He takes his tenure too seriously at times and forgets his place."

What was going on? He was being so... nice. Polite. Courteous, even. But he was an antiquities smuggler. He was the embodiment of what I wanted to fight.

Antonio came out of his room with Johann, wearing a navy blue V-neck and jacket with jeans that didn't quite fit him, but he still looked amazing. He smiled and came over to press a kiss to my cheek.

"Can I have Henri bring something up for you while you wait?" asked Cristian.

"No," I said, squeezing Antonio's hand. "But thank you."

Maybe Cristian and Leonardo were playing some kind of good cop bad cop.

If that was it, why?

CHAPTER 12

ANTONIO

"You need to use your imagination, Antonio." Giovanni stood in front of the double-doors leading into a dilapidated building in the town of Terracina.

The twenty minute coastal commute from his estate was a more enjoyable one than the short drive to and from Cittavera earlier in the morning. Leonardo was with us again, but Cristian's stern eye fell on him the moment he began mumbling some insult.

The building was a single story with white stucco walls and corrugated metal boarding up all the windows. Graffiti decorated most of the exterior. Why on Earth would he bring me somewhere like this?

"It's not much to look at yet, but..." Giovanni pointed over my shoulder, away from the building. "You can see the Temple of Jupiter Anxur from here."

We stood on a point between two marinas where boats of various sizes moored. A ferry motored by, on its way down the coast or out to the islands nearby. High on the hill overlooking the city, one of the terraces of the temple he pointed out was clear, its arched arcades a Roman hallmark.

"Sì, Zio Gio, but why are we here?" And more importantly, why was I here without Samantha?

A second SUV full of guards emptied onto the street behind us, two walking the length of the building's exterior, two more settling next to the doors—including Johann, the German guard who'd gone into town with us, took Samantha on a short tour, and helped carry my borrowed clothes to my room. This armed presence was more than Gio used to travel with. Perhaps it was related to the business change.

Cristian had told me in the fall that there were those who sought to take Gio's place. That must have been the reason for the extra guards.

My stomach tightened. How much danger were we in here? What had I brought Samantha into?

Surely if our lives were at stake, Elliot would have said more at the bakery. He wouldn't have asked to speak with her—he would have told me to get her out of there. What was it he said about rumors? That my uncle was getting out of the business?

Leonardo opened the building's door and flicked on a light switch. Giovanni, Cristian, and I following him in. Two guards remained outside—the others likely patrolling the perimeter.

The building was spacious, slivers of sunshine peeking around the window coverings. Dust and debris littered the space, and stalls which looked like they were used for purchasing tickets stood off to one side, while banks of plastic chairs were affixed to the floor in the center.

"I bought this." Giovanni spread his arms wide, a gleam in his eyes. "For the family."

"Scusi, but why?" As far as I could tell, it had once been a ticket collection office, possibly for the ferry. I knew little of the town other than having visited the temple several times for my building restoration studies.

Giovanni beckoned me forward and encouraged me to stand next to him, placing a hand upon my back. He waved the other hand in front of himself like he saw something completely different when he looked at this space. "The work tables will go over there. We'll section off a room for imaging, another for carpentry, and another for storage. On that side—" He turned with me, so we faced the rear of the building. "—there's a rolling door which large pieces can come in through. Perhaps even a mechanical lift for working on particularly grand paintings and sculptures."

"Wait..." I stepped away from him, searching his face. He was describing a conservation studio.

"Sì." He nodded, before I could form the words. "I'm not growing any younger, Antonio. I've squandered my life and want to make up for it. This is three times the space of the Ferraro's studio in Roma."

"You want Zio Andrea to move his business here?"

"No!" He raised his hands, as if in surrender. "My father and uncle founded that company in Roma. The building survived a world war. Occupation by the Nazis. I would never ask he close that shop."

"So what is this? You want to start your own company?"

His hands fell slowly to his sides, a vulnerability coming over him like I'd never seen my entire life. "I tried to speak with your father and uncle, my nieces and nephews and cousins in the family business, but they've all shut me out. You were always more open to change than the rest of them, so I knew your time in Napoli would be the key."

"The key to what?"

He gripped my good arm. "To a reconciliation."

That would take more than a miracle. More than intervention from Saint Peter himself.

"Like you, I was born into a certain wealth. I took that and built an empire out of it." He shook his head slowly, raising a fist to the heavens. "But none of that wealth means anything in front of the gates to Heaven. After I'm gone, what does it even mean to my family? What consolation will they take from a bank account?"

"A comfortable life is some consolation."

"Antonio, you're part of the legacy my father built with his brother." His voice dropped to a whisper. "I want to be part of that, too."

It was not so simple, though. Giovanni had spent decades destroying everything that legacy represented. How could he think buying a building would repair any of that?

"You should see Cesca's artwork. She's talented. Our family always excelled in two things: money and art. I thought for a time my branch of our tree was blessed only with the first. But she's like you, like both of my brothers, and so many of their children." He turned, bringing his hands together as if in prayer. "I want to build this for her. For you. For all of us. I know the company does well enough you have to turn away work. Why not expand? Why not here, where we can look out at the sea or up to the ruins?"

This was the same man who had me collecting money from those under his protection. Thought I would take a job after my graduation, authenticating works of art to help him achieve top dollar in his underworld transactions. He was a master liar, manipulator, and all he wanted in life was to collect power.

There was no way this was true. There was an angle. Perhaps he meant to have a place where he could deconstruct pieces for transport or repair them after being smuggled into the country.

But still, I wanted to believe him. He and Cristian had once been so important to me. He'd been my favorite uncle when I was small.

"I told you this was a waste of time," muttered Leonardo.

Giovanni snapped his fingers—his true self shining through for a moment—and Leonardo clamped his jaw shut.

I turned slowly around, architectural sketches forming in my brain. He was right about the location of each part of the studio, so he must have spent a lot of time thinking it over. The rolling door, the windows that would open to allow the sun to shine through. No tall buildings on the point to block out the view. Anyone working here would have easy access to restaurants, the shore, transportation.

It could be a place of inspiration.

I took a slow breath, angling my shoulder forward to ease some of the ache in my arm. "It's a lot to take in."

Cristian joined Giovanni and me. "That's what I said when he first told me last summer."

I said, "This is why you've been asking me to visit? To see this?"

"Sì," said Giovanni. "I was hoping you'd ask to see the plans."

"You have plans drawn up already?"

Cristian said, "The blueprints are back at home. He wanted to bring them, but I'd prefer we do that at the villa."

I dragged a hand through my hair. "You organized all of this—practically kidnapped my girlfriend and me at the airport—when you could have simply emailed me the plans? Told me all of this on the phone?" For once, I could have had a conversation with them across a distance that didn't require a burner phone.

Leonardo scoffed, which was met by a silencing glare from Cristian.

Giovanni's features clouded over. "Be honest, Antonio. If we'd done that, you would have hung up or deleted the emails. I have big plans and this was the only way."

It was always about him. About what *he* wanted and what *his* business needed. Nothing with him was truly about the people around him or his family, save his wife and children.

But he'd had blueprints drawn up. What if that meant there was some shred of honesty behind all this?

I'd have to at least look at the designs. Perhaps there would be some clue there.

Chapter 13

Samantha

Noon. The sun had passed over the top of the tower, warming my skin as I stared out to the aquamarine Mediterranean Sea three hundred feet away. My balcony was tiny, barely as wide as the double-doors leading out to it with a small metal chair wedged to the side, but the view was spectacular. A band of cumulus clouds drifted along the horizon, leaving an open sky over the land.

Above me, stonework protruded from the tower, supporting a roof of terracotta tiles, just like all the other roofs below me. Four guards walked their separate routes around the estate, and no doubt more were stationed in other buildings or were hidden away monitoring the security feeds.

I scanned the space above me, searching for more of the near-invisible cameras. Was someone listening to our conversation last night? Did they know I wasn't sleeping? Or how much I missed being with Antonio?

If they were, I couldn't spot them. It would make more sense to have microphones closer to the ground, where people could attempt to gain access. Cameras belonged at the top of the tower but positioned to view as much of the property as possible, not to watch the balconies.

No wonder the TPC didn't hear from their undercover agent often. The security was intense.

I ran my hands over the stone wall, identifying several places I could grab onto. All I needed was space to get my fingertips and shoes in, although my climbing shoes would have been more useful than anything I had with me. The fifty-foot drop made it a risk not worth taking, no matter how much I wanted to sneak into Antonio's room.

But if I had a rope...

Back in my room, I searched under the bed, in the bathroom, the closet. Checked the television cable. The sheets weren't long enough, but maybe if I tied them together, I could make it across.

Stupid, Sam. I collapsed on the bed, letting out a long sigh. We'd only be here a few days, then we'd be at Mario's together, without a wall between us.

Damn Antonio Ferraro.

I scrubbed my hands over my face. It hadn't even been six months since we met and he invaded too many of my thoughts. My focus should have been on seeing the ruins or figuring out how I could help the authorities with any antiquities smuggling going on here.

Instead, I was thinking about Antonio. About crazy tactics to cross a ten-foot divide between our rooms. About being in his arms, against his skin. Nuzzling my nose in his neck and smelling that delicious amber and vanilla cologne. His soft lips on mine. Hot breath brushing across every inch of my body.

One hand trailed down my neck, imagining his tongue tracing its way to the neckline of my long-sleeve T-shirt. It continued to the waistband of my jeans and I popped the button, sliding my hand down to—

There was a knock at my door, and I sat up with a start, like I'd been caught red-handed.

The last knock had been one of the staff returning my freshly-washed clothes. They were probably back with something they missed. I shook my head, rebuttoned my pants, and headed for the door.

And once it was open, I was overcome with a deep need to rewind time and ignore the knock.

Vincenzo.

I should have known.

He was teaching Cesca art history because he knew it the best. Of course he'd be the one who knew the most about the ruins.

Vin wasn't as broad as Antonio or the bodyguards. Not as tall, either. A thick head of black hair with more curl than Antonio's swept down to his shoulders. He had a dimple in his chin that I remembered deepened the more he laughed, but he'd grown a short beard that covered it.

I hated beards.

My ex-husband had too much facial hair, too. I should have seen the trend.

Before I could slam the door in his face, he mouthed, *Cameras*, and pointed toward his chest. Likely signaling the one I knew was in the finial.

"So what?" I whispered.

"Good afternoon, Samantha," he said, his voice not betraying the look on his face, the way his brows pulled down, nor the way he clasped his hands together in prayer. "My name is Vincenzo, and I'll be your guide this afternoon. We'll be going to see the ruins of the villa of Lucius Verus and the cave next to it."

What was he doing? Why was he talking this way?

"I understand you're an art lover? There are several statues—in various states of repair—commemorating moments from the Odyssey, which I'm sure you want to see, as well." His voice was light and conversational, as though he didn't remember me. There was a silent message underneath his words. He didn't want Giovanni's staff to know we knew each other. That also explained why he hadn't told Antonio anything when he escorted us up to my room yesterday.

The desire to slam the door was nowhere near as powerful as my curiosity. I'd go along with his game. For now. "That sounds nice, thank you."

• • • • • • • • • • •

"This area was the kitchen, including the wood-fired stove which still remains." Vincenzo gestured to the stone structure, rising one foot higher than the remaining outer walls. Irregular white lava stone made up the building's remnants, while the oven was red rectangular bricks, completely level to the ground. Grass fought against the dirt where the ancient floor had once been.

The villa's remains stood on a flat area two hundred feet wide and long, nestled against the base of the hill which Giovanni's estate crowned. It jutted out into the water with a stone sea break protecting the edge of the building, allowing for a natural pool to form at the shore.

"It's beautiful." They were the first words I'd uttered since we left my room, despite Vincenzo talking the whole way. Telling me the history of the area, pointing out the islands in the distance, sharing stories about his favorite spots in town. My throat had remained tight through the entire experience, bracing for the moment he'd say something real.

"Wait until you see the best part!" He gave me a smile which had grown progressively weaker the longer we walked. This tour was a game. We had to get to the point, eventually.

A stone walkway bordered the natural pool and when we reached the midpoint, he pointed to the cliffs at the edge of the hill. With a few more steps, the entrance to the cave Antonio told me about came into view.

The mouth opened to the Mediterranean, canted so it would be visible from the beaches of Cittavera. The sea break protected it from the open sea, allowing water to flow through a small channel then into the cave.

"Antonio didn't tell me it was full of water."

"It's not completely full." Vin grabbed my hand, and I yanked it away. "Sorry."

"Vin, it's about time you—"

He pulled closer and I stepped back. Still, he lowered his voice and leaned toward me. "Wait until I give you the okay."

The okay? *Something is definitely going on.*

I followed him along the six-foot wide stone path edging the pool. Once we got closer, the statues he'd mentioned became visible. The inside of the natural cave was practically a round room, and its ceiling soared fifty feet above us. The walkway we were on ran along the edge of the cave, providing a view into the surprisingly deep water.

The cave wasn't just a round room; it was like a hollow sphere, with water filling the bottom half.

Five alcoves dotted the walls, each with a marble statue inside. But the most breathtaking statue stood on a platform in the center, a twelve-foot reclining giant, surrounded by men with spears.

"The blinding of the cyclops Polyphemos," I said.

Vin chuckled. He pressed himself against the wall by the second alcove, placed one foot next to a status of Venus, launched himself up to grab a handhold above her, then reached in behind her head.

When he hopped down, his whole body relaxed. "I can't believe it's you, Sam."

"What?"

He fiddled with his watch and spoke rapidly. "The camera's off. We can speak plainly for now. They'll dispatch someone when any camera's malfunctioning for more than ten minutes, so that's it."

I scanned the cave and spotted the camera above the Venus statue. The damn things were everywhere! "You were in a blind spot against the wall?"

He gave a quick nod. "When did the FBI get involved in this?"

Was this a test? Leonardo had asked about me being an investigator, so maybe he'd enlisted Vin to do some snooping. Antonio said it was critical they didn't know my link to the

Bureau. Vincenzo was one of Gio's employees, so I gave the most non-committal answer I could. "FBI?"

"They didn't tell you about their agent on the inside, did they?" He sighed, dropping his head to chuckle. "Sam, I'm with the TPC."

He was what?

Vin looked at me, those narrow gray eyes I'd once thought were so piercing and gorgeous danced with excitement. "I've been trying to figure out how to talk to you in private since I saw you. But you've got Antonio wound like a coil and he won't let you out of his sight. So when Leonardo assigned me to take you down here, it was the perfect opportunity."

He couldn't be. Couldn't be the one Elliot was talking about. It wasn't fair that this man, of all the people at the villa—in the entire fucking world—would be the one I was excited to find.

"You've changed." He tucked his hands into his pockets, the smile slipping. "You used to be so chatty. I expected a stream of comments about the ruins, let alone the view from the top of the cliffs."

"Yeah, life does that to a person. Changes them." *Like changing you from swearing you'd move to the States to be with me, you son of a bitch, then not bothering to tell me you decided against it.*

Vin turned away from me, walking along the outer edge of the pool. "We don't have time to rehash old wounds."

"Then explain what you're doing here."

"I couldn't tell you back then, but the job I took..." He checked his watch. "It was a special force within the TPC tackling art smuggling. I'd been undercover for a couple of years before I landed my spot here. But Giovanni's clamped down lately and it's been difficult to get in touch with my handler. A hidden phone gave way to dead drops, which eventually stopped going both ways. I was afraid they'd left me to the wind, except someone was picking up my messages."

It made sense. He did the same art crimes training I did. When we'd first met, I wanted to join the FBI's Art Crime Team, while Vincenzo had wanted to join the Carabinieri TPC. Why didn't he tell me?

"But here you are." He turned back to me, checking his watch again. "So the FBI is working with the TPC? You're here to, what? Get me out? Take a report of what I've found? Or are you staying?"

"I'm not with the FBI." It was the truth, even though it felt like a lie.

"But that's all you talked about. It was your dream since you were a kid." How dare he remember that?

"I'm an insurance adjuster and Antonio Ferraro is my boyfriend." I lifted my left hand, showing him the ring. "This isn't an undercover role. I'm in love with a good man who's crazy about me."

He checked his watch again. "Two minutes."

"What's your job here?"

"Bodyguard." He smirked, which quickly faded when I didn't react the way he must have been hoping. "The real one? Gather intel on Giovanni's network to find the man behind it all. Maybe catch a deal that's big enough we can use it for leverage to have him help us."

I needed to talk to Elliot. I was in such a perfect position to help. "And... have you found a deal like that?"

"Something's been in the works for a while and I'm hoping it'll arrive soon."

"What is it?"

"Come here." He returned to the alcove and I joined him. He pulled me in close to the statue, pointing to the device he'd used to turn off the camera. "It'll be less suspicious if I'm standing on the other side of the pool when the camera comes on."

Following his unspoken request, I stepped on the ledge and pulled myself up so I could reach it. "How did you get this here?"

"The security camera primarily monitors the entrance, so there are a lot of blind spots. My handler managed to smuggle it in for me so we could conduct short meetings in here."

I nodded, reaching for the device.

"My phone's monitored, so maybe you could get a message to him..." He paused as he crossed to the other side of the pool. "No, I can't put you in danger. I have other ways of contacting them."

My finger hovered over the switch. Our history was part of my past, just like Antonio said. I couldn't let the anger still sitting at the back of my brain ruin this opportunity. Elliot reminded me on the plane that my mother said I threw my whole heart into things, but my brain always held me back. What was I doing now? My heart wanted to continue being angry, but my head was the one telling me to push through and help the TPC do good work. My life was all upside down. "I don't know how long we're here, but if there's anything I can do, just say it."

He stopped in front of another alcove, with a statue which had once been a man, with only the legs remaining. His finger rose and he craned his neck around with a broad smile. "Thanks, Sam. Now hit the switch and let's pretend we're finishing the tour. Remember how quiet you were, or it'll give you away."

I flicked the switch and looked up, no discernible change in the white bullet camera to tell me it was or wasn't working. It didn't move back or forth, just stared straight toward the entrance.

Vincenzo picked up as though he were in the middle of an explanation. "—of the legs and the tunic, they believe this was originally Ulysses."

He continued talking, while I meandered around the walkway edging the cave, sweeping my hands along the rough walls. Dips and curves in the wall created smaller offshoots, one looking large enough for a person to walk deeper into the heart of the hill.

I'd promised Antonio I wouldn't snoop. No investigations. Was that because he was protecting his family or me? Was offering to help putting us both in danger?

CHAPTER 14

ANTONIO

The SUV slowed as it progressed up the pebbled driveway, toward the arched entryway into the auto court at the front of the villa. A path meandered past the swimming pool and between a row of hedges which would border a sea of roses in various shades of pinks and reds once the temperatures warmed again.

Samantha and Vincenzo walked up the path at the same time, yet not quite together. She was a few paces ahead of him, his gaze locked on her form.

The day was not as cool as it had been yesterday, so she'd forgone her winter jacket, and sported her favorite white Foster Mutual sweater. Far from the sexiest thing she'd ever worn, but still, the woman took my breath away.

Her long hair was back in the braid, as she normally wore it, instead of letting the strands play in the sunshine, like I preferred. Perhaps she was concerned about me being jealous of her past with Vincenzo. I'd been clear she had no need to worry, but she apparently thought she knew me better than that.

"Who's that?" Leonardo leaned forward in his seat next to me, looking out my window at them. "Is that your girlfriend with the charming young Vincenzo?"

Leo likely arranged for Vincenzo to be her guide, either knowing their history, or guessing from her reaction to him at dinner that his presence might irritate me. Samantha had been right that morning, that Leo was not used to women like her—at least, he hadn't been when we'd worked together. My aunt and no doubt her older daughter would have spoken their mind to him clearly, but it was his job to listen and obey their words. He wouldn't have baited them like he did Samantha.

I bit back a chuckle at the pace she kept, her tremendous stride an indication of her foul mood. Memories of taking her to Pompeii and the museums in Napoli came over me. The excited look on her face, the joy which radiated off of her. That should have been her reaction to seeing the ruins. We'd have to take another trip to the shore together before we left, so she could appreciate it.

"It looks like my rather pissed off girlfriend. I don't suppose I can spend some time alone with her to help cheer her up?" And to talk to her about Elliot finally. We'd been apart all day and had already missed his afternoon visit to the café, so we'd have to try for tomorrow. *If* we were going to try to see him. Perhaps simply seeing her and receiving a wave and a smile would be sufficient. What would happen if Leonardo insisted on joining us and found her talking to an FBI agent? Nothing good.

"No, no, you're coming to look at the plans." Giovanni stared out his window toward Samantha and Vincenzo until the car rolled through the archway and into the court, concealing them from view. "I need my architect nephew to advise me on whether or not we have everything covered."

"I'd like it if she can join us."

Giovanni rose a hand to wave the suggestion off. "Family and trusted staff only."

"Zio Gio," I sighed. "She *is* my family and I *do* trust her. Marone, it's just floor plans. There's nothing to hide in that. She's come to Italia to spend two weeks with me before we're apart for another four months. The separate rooms are bad enough—"

Leo scoffed, but wisely said nothing.

"It's only right," said Giovanni.

"You want my help, but you concede nothing—give me nothing in return. All you do is ask."

"I give you my hospitality."

Hospitality? Food and drink, a roof over my head, and a guard to follow her every step if she left her room. I'd have the same if I tried to leave the property. We weren't prisoners, but we certainly were not free.

How far could I push my uncle? How much could I demand in return for doing as he asked?

How much, indeed. The truth was, I couldn't push. I never could.

"I'm going to say hello. Then I'll come with you." I fumbled with the door, reaching across my body to use my opposite hand. As I got out of the vehicle, the second SUV pulled in, turning into the garage across from the courtyard and front doors.

Samantha walked through the archway. Our eyes met and her pace slowed, shoulders relaxing. There was no rush to meet me. Only the barest hint of a smile. A person had to know her to understand what all the tiny clues added up to. I was fortunate she'd let me into her heart so I could learn what many of them meant.

She gave me a slow blink. This was her *I'm so relieved to see you, you hot stud* blink. Perhaps the last part was my own addition, but close enough.

Vincenzo appeared, his voice buzzing in the background, but she didn't react.

I was her entire world at that moment, every bit as much as she was mine.

We met halfway between the arch and the SUV, coming so close our bodies nearly touched. She looked up at me, her jade green eyes alight in the sun, and intertwined her fingers with mine.

"How was the tour, bella?"

"Interesting."

Vincenzo passed us, hailing my uncle and the other men.

Samantha whispered, "Would have been better with you."

"Maybe tomorrow."

"How was the drive?"

A question I was not prepared to answer. I should have been, but I hadn't expected even this brief moment of near-privacy, and too many guards were within earshot. Giovanni said she couldn't join us, so I couldn't tell her what we'd done, either. "Not interesting. He's having the pool redone. We drove to a quarry nearby to look at some limestone slabs for the deck."

Her grip on my hand faltered and she mouthed, *That's what you're here for?*

I raised an eyebrow at her, hopefully clear enough this was one of my lies I'd explain later.

"Antonio!" called Giovanni.

"Going off with the boys again?" She squeezed my hand, jaw tightening. "More... pool talk?"

"I'm afraid so, amore."

"Awesome. I guess I'll go sit in my room like a good little girl. Maybe stare out my tower window and sing to the birds."

I released her hand and cupped her jaw. "I'll see you at—"

Gravel crunched underfoot behind me, and Giovanni arrived next to us. "Samantha, I was going to take Antonio to the game room and show him some floor plans I want his input on. It won't be particularly interesting, but if you'd like to join us, you're welcome."

"Floor plans?" She produced her professional smile for him and snaked her arm around the crook of my elbow. "With the Ferraro men? There's nothing I'd enjoy more."

CHAPTER 15

ANTONIO

We all stood around a carom table—Samantha, Zio Giovanni, Cristian, the horrific Leonardo, and the German bodyguard Johann—with large sheets of vellum paper covering the table. Two copies of the floor plan, along with plumbing, electrical, and a project plan. The company he'd contracted had done an excellent job.

While my profession in America and the training I received from my father was in art conservation, my schooling focused on architecture and then on architectural restoration. Reviewing the blueprints for a conservation studio combined two of my passions.

"You're missing a meeting room," I said.

Giovanni frowned at the sheet in front of us. "To meet with whom? The workers can just talk to each other—it's a large, open space."

"To meet with clients."

"I can do that here." Gio shook his head as though it were an obvious answer to a silly question. He was too accustomed to the way he'd been doing things with his less than legal pursuits.

"No, when you're working with clients, they'll expect to meet with you in your office. It's the professional way to do it."

My uncle leaned his hands on the table and stared at the plan. Cristian pulled closer to Samantha, looking at the sheet in front of her. Leo and Johann drifted off to the darts board. As much as Leo attempted to seem like he was crucial to Gio's operation, he remained a bodyguard in the end. Even if he was the head of security, he'd looked bored the entire time.

It may have been a step too far, but I appealed to Gio's past. At least, to the past I was told he had. "Do you remember when you worked for the International Monetary Fund? You would have had a space to do your work and if you had meetings, there was separate room for that, sì?"

He hesitated but nodded. "There was."

"Similar to that, you'll need an office manager who schedules the pieces that will come in, discusses price and handles contracts—"

Samantha added, "That's what Sofia does in Brenton. I deal almost exclusively with her."

Giovanni finally looked up. "You work with the family company?"

Samantha's eyes flicked to me in question. I nodded, and she continued. "Sometimes I handle artwork claims for the insurance company. Ferraro's is the first place we go for everything like that."

I smiled at her, remembering the first time she'd come into my office. It was only two days after we'd made a toast to go out if we saw each other again within a month. "That's how we met. She had a ruined Chagall."

She smiled back, giving me the slow blink again. The *I love you* blink, which likely held a hint of *It wasn't a real Chagall, but we probably shouldn't say that around Giovanni*. "I also suspect the storage area is too small. This studio is larger than the Brenton office, but the storage is a hair smaller."

I'd only shown her the storage room once, but it shouldn't have surprised me she'd know its exact dimensions. "Excellent point."

A dart hit the board at the end of the room, and Leonardo said, "You seem to know a lot for someone who only deals with the office manager."

Samantha turned to look at him, and she lifted one hand to drag it over her mouth. There was a battle raging inside her, one that demanded she snap back at him, but she held her tongue.

"Samantha's worked for insurance companies around the country, which included claims for large galleries that have their own conservators," I said. How much of that was true? I didn't know, but she didn't contradict me, and it would keep Leo's accusations at bay. "I also took her to the research lab in Pompeii a few times, which operates differently. So she has a great deal of experience."

Leo frowned and threw another dart. Why was he so focused on her? Cristian had asked me several times late last summer, when she was visiting, whether or not she was with the authorities. Had he shared those concerns with Leonardo? Had Leo been the one to search out information on her in the first place?

A door by the dart board opened, and Henri appeared. "Dinner will be served soon."

Cristian nodded, waving a hand at the chef.

Henri approached the table, leaning over to look at the plans. "Making changes?"

"These are not for your eyes." Giovanni flipped two sheets over. "We'll head to the dining room soon."

"I can recommend several changes to the kitchen and pantries—" Henri cut off at a glare from Giovanni.

Samantha straightened from inspecting the floor plans. "I'm actually tired and I think I'll skip the meal."

Henri's brows rose in concern. "Would you like me to bring up a sandwich, some antipasti, or anything?"

"Not tonight, thanks. I still have a few items left over from the bakery this morning." She yawned. "I don't suppose we can go back for breakfast tomorrow? There were a few things I want to try."

That could give us a chance to see Elliot, even if I didn't get to warn her about it ahead of time. "I'd like that."

Henri shook his head. "I'm not scheduled to go."

"Johann," I said, catching the guard's attention. "Can you take Samantha and me to the bakery tomorrow?"

He looked at Giovanni, who nodded. "As long as I can get one of those apple cakes?"

"We can arrange that." Samantha chuckled, then gave me a peck on the cheek. "Knock on my door when you come up, so I can say good night if I'm still up?"

I returned the kiss and nodded.

Johann escorted her out, and Henri followed them.

I let out a sigh. "Why is she being monitored so closely, Zio? What could she possibly do between here and her room that's such a problem?"

"What I told you earlier about our family's legacy and expanding is only part of the story. I—" Giovanni leaned on the carom table and let his head fall forward. "I don't want to help spoil our cultural heritage anymore. I want to bring things back home and make up for the sins of my past."

This was the reason he didn't want Samantha here. He didn't want her to hear the truth behind it all.

I said, "Cristian told me you'd been ill and it changed your perspective?"

His head rose, and he frowned slightly. "It did. Between that and how Cesca's love of art is developing, I can't do anything else. I want this—" He tapped the plans. "—to be her sixteenth birthday present in two years. Up and running."

"How does this lead back to a guard tailing Samantha everywhere?"

"It's a slow and treacherous path to get out of my business. Some of my competitors rejoice, some fear I'm putting them at risk."

Cristian flipped the plans back over so we could see them. "Dead men tell no tales."

Leo scoffed, raising fingers as he neared us. "Your girlfriend identified a stolen painting at an auction in your hometown last summer. Then, she tracks down the thieves who stole items from your workplace in Pompeii. Finally, she's the target of several shootings and is responsible for a smuggler being locked up only last week."

Cristian had known about the auction painting, a man in their employ was involved with the Pompeii theft, and I'd called Cristian about the shootings. How did they know about the recovered paintings? My cousin always said he knew things, but that was between Samantha and the FBI.

Leo continued, "All four events had two things in common. One, your girlfriend, who seems very adept at interfering with the free movement of artwork. And two, the same man was behind each of them."

I gasped. "Pasquale Fiori?"

Fiori had been a kind man who picked Samantha and me up after she'd been hurt on a hike in Napoli. He took us to his boat in Capri, had his doctor look after Samantha, and then his helicopter delivered us to the mainland. Afterward, we discovered he was behind the theft from my worksite in Pompeii, a fresco of yellow flowers and a tiny matching pot containing an ancient pigment.

Last week, Cristian had told us Parker Johnson—one of the men who tried to kill us and whose smuggling of three stolen paintings we'd intercepted—was under consideration by an old associate of Zio Gio.

It all made sense. Fiori, for how helpful he'd been, was behind everything.

Cristian moved to my side and rested a hand on my shoulder. "Leo and I insisted on the increase in security after Papa's illness. It came on after a special dessert was prepared for him one night. No proof that it was intentional, but we took care of the chef and made some security changes."

Took care of? What were the odds that chef continued to breathe? "And you suspect Fiori is behind that as well?"

"Can we trust your girlfriend?" Cristian raised a hand before I could respond. "I know what your answer is. But even if we can trust her, what if Fiori finds out she's here and decides it's a perfect opportunity to silence both her and Papa at the same time?"

I stared off in the direction where she'd left with Johann and Henri. Was she safe with them?

Cristian continued, "Add to that what you told me about the rumors someone was looking to recruit you? She becomes another liability. Based on how you look at her, it's clear you'd do anything if someone took her."

"That's why she was kidnapped on New Year's Eve," I said. "They thought I'd pay to get her back."

"And would you have?"

My eyes drifted closed. Could any of this be true? Or were they manipulating me into compliance by claiming they were protecting her? If she was in danger from someone inside these walls, I had to keep her away from Elliot—Leo would have a field day if they suspected she was working with the FBI. But if she was in danger from someone else, someone like Pasquale Fiori, I needed to get her to Elliot as soon as possible.

"I would have done anything." I stepped in front of a bullet for her. Money was nothing. "She and I should leave."

"No," said Giovanni. "She's safer here, where my men can watch out for her, like I trust them to watch over my family."

Parker seemed to have acted out his own vendetta against Samantha, not one instigated by Fiori. And if he'd been behind it all, why help us in Napoli?

Of course—because the auction was the only crime we'd stopped by then.

"Plus, I've arranged for a special surprise for you." Giovanni's eyes and smile grew wide again, signaling that the discussion of danger was done. "I got word earlier today that it will arrive on Friday."

I stepped away from the table, out of Cristian's comforting grip. "Friday? It's only Tuesday. We've looked at the new studio. I've provided my feedback on the blueprints. It's only two hours away. I can come back later."

"Friday?" Leonardo began straightening the blueprints, an almost happy energy coming off of him. He seemed excited for this surprise, which didn't bode well for me.

Giovanni knocked on the table—another of his signals that he was to be listened to and obeyed. "Antonio, you've been telling us you'd visit *later* since September. We need to speak more of your father and how you're going to help everyone open up to my changes."

I clenched my fist, rather than dragging the hand through my hair. I was taller than him, stronger than him, smarter than him. I could have walked Samantha out the door and never looked back. Not talked to Papa about this, not spared a second thought for these wild conservation studio plans, not subjected Samantha to being followed day and night by some muscle-bound meathead or by her ex-boyfriend.

"You said I was not conceding anything." Giovanni folded his arms, still smiling, as though he were making an honest invitation and not a commandment. "How about we change your girlfriend's security detail? So long as you're not leaving the grounds, you can be the one to accompany her. No other guards."

Cristian leaned a hip against the carom table. "Cesca wants you to see her artwork. It would mean a great deal to her if you'd stay for that."

"Excellent idea!" said Giovanni. "I'd like to show your girl-friend the estate, as well. You said she likes art and history, so I thought we could take her on a tour of our artwork on the upper floors of the villa?"

Giovanni had been my favorite uncle once upon a time, just as Cristian had been my idol. I'd only ever said no to them once, when they invited me back after I graduated from my master's degree. Even with all the times they asked me to visit after arriving in Napoli, I'd always said I'd come later.

I never declined. But I could now.

"No, Zio, I need to get back to Pompeii and—"

He knocked on the table again, and my chest constricted. "This is not up for debate, Antonio."

"I can take care of her."

"Sorry, cugino, but you can't." Cristian's hand landed on my bad shoulder this time. When I winced, he squeezed—a jolt of pain radiated from my stitches, causing my bicep to flex, which sent another wave of agony through my arm.

"Stop," I said, trying not to sound like the pathetic man-child I'd been when I first moved in with him.

In the background, Leo chuckled as he placed the floor plans on my uncle's desk.

"You're not at full strength." Cristian let go of my shoulder and resumed his easy stance against the carom table, no malice on his face. Not even pity. Just a frustratingly fake smile, like his father. "This visit is in both our best interests. Your family wants you to stay, and it gives us the time to ensure Fiori isn't coming after Samantha."

I looked at him, then back at my uncle. Their methods were deplorable, but these men had been looking out for me for months.

Leo flopped into a chair by the wall, a devilish smile on his face.

There was no way Leo would see me weak.

I swallowed hard, intentionally not cradling my aching arm. "You're serious about the guard detail?"

Giovanni's smile spread. He knew he'd won. "I am."

This was not what I wanted. But what choice did I have if there was even a shred of truth about the danger to Samantha's life? "Alright, we'll stay until Friday under those rules, but I need to call Mario and let him know."

Giovanni gestured for Cristian to hand over his cell phone. I accepted it and made to step away for privacy, but my uncle shook his head and inclined it to where I'd been standing.

I stood still a moment, the throbbing in my arm a reminder that I was not in control here. For all of Giovanni's claims that he was changing business models, some things remained the same.

Among those things, I still couldn't stand up to them.

I dialed Mario's number.

He picked up immediately, his voice cautious. "Ciao."

"It's me," I said.

"How's your family?" he asked.

Watching me, I thought into Mario's brain. "We're going to be here longer than expected. How's the team progressing?"

He was silent a moment, hopefully catching the seriousness in my tone. "Océane and Bianca get back this afternoon, Thomas was shadowing another team instead of—"

"I need you to start on the garden wall conservation," I snapped. "We don't have the time and funding for everyone to be slacking off like that."

Mario huffed, but Giovanni's smile grew a fraction more genuine.

"You need to take over for the week, Mario."

"So, you're having a fun time?" he said, sarcasm dripping off his words. This was why *he* was my favorite cousin, and not Cristian, nor any of the others. He understood I couldn't speak plainly and that I was miserable here.

"Just see that they're focused. Tell Bianca to write up the changes she proposed, since that will go in the publication. And have Océane check her bacterial cultures. We need to scale that up."

"Of course, boss." Mario liked to tell me he was actually the boss, since he was the project manager and filed all of our reports to the Pompeii Archaeological Park's Board of Directors. Everyone else treated me like the boss, since it was my dissertation forming the basis of our work, and I was instructing. This concession was in case I was on speaker, no doubt.

"I'll see you Friday."

"Or Saturday," said Giovanni.

I added, like an obedient dog, "Or Saturday."

Giovanni clapped me on my good shoulder after I hung up, a genuine smile spreading across his face. "My nephew, the man in charge. It must make your father so proud."

"It does." Proud was an understatement. If he had his way, Papa would be traveling to every conference and symposium, bragging about it. But it was a different type of pride than what Gio meant. It was not pride that I was in charge. "He's proud of the difference my team is making and that we're advancing the science of conservation."

"Whatever that means," muttered Leonardo.

Giovanni glowered at him. "This is what I want my new conservation studio to do. Push the boundaries. Learn and teach."

All of this was too much. Could the conservation studio, the floor plans, his intention to have it up and running in two years—could it be real? Giovanni had used the Ferraro name in the past to gain credence with his buyers and suppliers. This new enterprise could simply be him doubling down on that. A legal front for his activities.

I had to talk to Samantha about this. Had to find some private place for us. We'd sort out a plan together.

Chapter 16

Samantha

I had to talk to Antonio. Had to tell him about Vincenzo and the TPC.

If it was even true.

Of course it was true. That's what Vin wanted to do after postgrad and Elliot told me they had a TPC agent inside. Fuck. Of all the men in Italy, why did it have to be him?

It was barely five o'clock and the sun had already set into the sea. Once it was down, the temperature fell sharply. Despite the chill, I sat on the small metal chair on my tiny balcony, staring into the distance.

How could Vin not have told me he'd joined the Carabinieri all those years ago? He'd just called it a *job* that was keeping him in Italy. He knew my life's goal was to join the FBI's Art Crime Team, so why not tell me the truth? It would have cushioned the blow because I'd have understood the drive to do something like that.

Then again, maybe I'd have continued to be the naïve young thing I was back then and moved to Italy, thinking we could be together while he did great things.

That would have been a wasted life.

There was a knock at my door and I sprang up from my chair and dashed inside. It was hours before I expected Antonio, given the timing of dinner, but I said a little prayer, all the same.

I swung the door open, and there stood Antonio, all six-foot-one, wavy-haired, chisel-jawed Italian with his slung arm. My heart leaped, but then crashed immediately. He was missing his ready smile, which was a bad sign.

He mouthed, *I need to speak with you.*

Me, too, I mouthed back.

"I'm glad you're still up, bella. I thought you'd be asleep from how you looked downstairs." His calm words didn't match the anxious look on his face.

"I was waiting for you to come up, so I could say good night." I forced out a yawn. If Antonio was mouthing to me, there was either a guard somewhere nearby or the microphones on the security camera were that powerful. "Are you going down to dinner or turning in early?"

"Shower and bed, I think. The jet lag and my medication are taking all the strength out of me."

"Good night, then." I slid a hand around his neck and lifted on my tiptoes for a moment to kiss his cheek, allowing me to spot Johann across the open space, where the stairs began to the fifth floor.

Antonio mouthed, *I'll distract him and the camera, you sneak into my room?*

I nodded and spoke just above a whisper, as though trying to be private, but ensuring the guard would hear me. "I'll see you in the morning."

Antonio kissed my temple and left for his room.

I let my door close over, click shut, then immediately opened it a fraction, so the sound of both actions melded into one. And then I waited. Patiently. What was he going to do? It wouldn't be something from his room, and I couldn't open my door enough to peek out, so I listened carefully.

Not five minutes later, Antonio's door opened. "Mi scusi, Johann, but I need some help."

"Ja?" came the voice from much farther away.

"My arm is hurting quite a lot and I can't open my pill bottle with the one hand. Can you do this for me?"

"Of course." His footsteps grew nearer, and I heard a popping noise followed by a rattle of pills. "Is that everything?"

"No, it's not," said Antonio. "I wanted to say thank you. Samantha is having a difficult time here and you've been very kind to her."

Making small talk had to be the signal. I inched the door open until I could peer out. Antonio stood against the staircase finial, blocking the security camera. And he'd stopped there so Johann was angled with his back to our doors. Clever man.

"It's part of my job, sir."

I opened the door only as far as I needed to slip out and eased it shut behind me.

"I know, but it's also part of Leonardo's job, and small moments like you asking for the apple cake or taking her on a tour of the gardens—"

I tiptoed next to the wall, thankful the floor was all stonework, so no creaky floorboards could give me away. Antonio's door was wide open.

"—those helped relieve some of her discomfort. He even followed her to the washroom and waited outside it this morning. Did you know that?"

Maybe that was another hint, so I snuck into the bathroom and hid behind the door, just in case.

They spoke a few minutes longer, and I held my breath as slow and steady as possible, despite the blood pounding in my veins. It wasn't like I was risking my life coming over here, but I needed a private moment with Antonio badly. Between Vincenzo, the TPC, being separated from Antonio, seeing the pain in his eyes when Leo hit his arm... If they caught me, they'd likely confine me to my room, and I'd have to content myself with visits from Henri with food.

"I'm going to shower and turn in for the night. I only had surgery last week and Samantha has been lecturing me about getting my rest. Please see that no one disturbs me."

"Of course."

"And the same goes for Samantha. She slept poorly last night and was yawning so much she could hardly speak to me just now."

"Certainly. I'll pass the message along to my replacement."

"Grazie mille," said Antonio, and his door clicked closed.

I clamped my lips together, waiting, barely able to control my breathing.

The door moved, and Antonio appeared, pressing a finger against his lips. As he turned on the water in the shower, I locked the bathroom door. I closed the distance between us, and pressed my face against his back, wrapping my arms around his big, warm frame.

"Stay quiet or someone may hear you." He turned in my arms, groaning quietly, causing me to shift so I wasn't touching his bad arm. The good one slid around my shoulders and we both exhaled deeply.

The entire world slowed from its normally manic pace, and I melted against him. There were so many sides to him, each one my favorite depending on the moment. But here, in the den of an antiquities smuggling empire, surrounded by men with guns and all the questions of what was really going on, gentle Antonio was what I needed most. The one who whispered *I love you* instead of shouting it from the rooftops. Who held me without making me feel weak. Who gritted back whatever pain he was feeling to comfort me. I would have done the same for him—and had in the past—but the best part was I didn't have to ask for any of it. He just knew. He understood me like we'd known each other our entire lives.

"I love you, Antonio," I whispered against his neck.

"I hope there are no other cameras," he sighed. "Because I don't want to give this up."

"Then let's take advantage of our time." I withdrew from the embrace, keeping my eyes on his, and pulled my shirt off, revealing a utilitarian black bra. "You can shower by now, right?"

His eyes narrowed, a smirk spreading across his lips, but it rapidly turned into a shaking head. "Elliot was at the bakery this morning."

I gasped, throwing both hands over my mouth, for fear of how loud I was.

"Sì, I told you I needed to speak with you," he whispered.

"What did he want?"

"To know if we're alright. I told him we were, but he wants to see you."

My hands rose to my forehead and down my cheeks, trying to scrape the layer of surprise and confusion off myself. "Elliot said he was coming to Rome for meetings. A touch-base with the team. It may be close, but this isn't Rome. So, what's he doing here?"

"This is not a coincidence."

"No, it isn't." I clasped my hands together and pulled them against my heart. How was Antonio going to take *my* news? "Vincenzo's an undercover TPC officer."

He took a half-step back, head turning slightly like he was unsure if he'd heard me clearly. "In my uncle's house?"

"I probably wasn't clear about this in the airport, but Elliot said the TPC had a man inside. I just never would have thought—"

"That it would be your ex-boyfriend?" The tick in his jaw and the way his pitch flattened told me the jealousy wasn't as firmly packed away as he claimed. But who could blame him? This wasn't just any old ex—this was the ex who almost prevented me from dating Antonio at all. Plus, I'd spent hours with Vincenzo earlier doing something I loved, and now he was an undercover agent spying on Antonio's family.

Any less reaction and I would have questioned if they'd swapped out my Antonio with a sexy imposter.

"Alright," I said, stepping closer to eliminate the space he'd created between us. "How are we going to see Elliot again? Or does it wait until we leave here? How long are we staying?"

"Giovanni has another surprise for me, which is arriving on Friday. I told him we'd stay until then." His gaze fell to my chest, his thumb tracing the edge of my bra. It was a quiet moment, not about sex, but about intimacy. "Elliot will be at the bakery every day. Ten and two."

"Good thing I mentioned wanting to go back?"

He nodded, the hand drifting down my side, then to my stomach. "He wants to know you're alright."

I snuck my fingers under his shirt, echoing his movements, brushing along the dip of his obliques. "Vin said he's had problems communicating with his handler because the security's so tight. I wonder how closely the FBI and TPC are working together?"

Antonio's hand left me and extended over his head to his back. He pulled his shirt off in a slow motion, careful to wind it around his injured arm. "Did Vincenzo ask you to contact anyone?"

"No." I pressed my lips to his bare shoulder, catching sight of a few stitches on his back which hadn't fallen out yet. My stomach clenched at the memory of the gunshots and shattering glass that caused them. *He's okay. We both survived.* "I need to talk to Elliot."

"Sì." His large hand splayed across the small of my back and he held me tight against him. "But you also need to be extra careful. They know about your involvement in the auction, the fresco in Pompeii, and the paintings in Brenton. Leonardo's suspicious of you already."

That explained some of his attitude. He thought I was a spy. "So we don't have to keep my past a secret?"

"I think it's wise to hold as much back from them as possible. Let them make their guesses and assumptions, rather than accidentally offering more than they know." He exhaled slowly. "He said Fiori was behind all of those crimes."

"That makes sense, since Parker was involved with the auction painting and the ones we found last week. But why would a wealthy Corsican thief be funding operations in tiny little Brenton?" I sucked in a quick breath as it dawned on me. "Of course! Detroit!"

"Detroit?"

"All of Parker's paintings came through a pawnshop in Detroit. And the doctor on Fiori's yacht told me that's where he's from." I'd asked him to distract me with stories while he worked on the ankle I'd injured on a hike. "And he told me they were planning a trip up the St. Lawrence River this spring. Detroit must be one of their hubs."

"You're as brilliant as you are beautiful." Antonio's hand swept up to the middle of my back and down again, gliding over the curve of my ass. "They must be delivering pieces to that pawnshop to filter through the States, picking things up, or both."

"Except Elliot told me—in the airport, before we left for here—that they shut the pawnshop down." I bit down on my lip. Elliot needed to hear about the trip Fiori was planning if he didn't know already. He'd need to have people ready—watching—for the yacht to deliver or take out stolen goods.

"I see that look in your eye. Before you sneak out of the villa and into town, you should also know they're claiming they've stationed guards around you are because they fear Fiori will come for you."

I pulled back, unable to control my frown. "Hardly."

"I'm just reporting what they're telling me, bella." He gave a half-shrug. "The only other news I have is that we didn't go to a quarry. We went to see the building he's converting for the new conservation studio."

"Why did you lie about that?"

"In the car—" He pressed a kiss to my temple, and I let out a little sigh. "—Zio Gio said you couldn't be told about his plans. He said family only."

"I don't understand. He showed me the blueprints."

He cupped my chin, gazing into my eyes, the silent *I love you* filling them. "I told him very clearly you *are* my family."

I swallowed hard, searching for moisture in my mouth, pins and needles shooting up my fingers. The invite to Vegas. Joking about celebrating the new year as newlyweds. Giving me the necklace his father gave his mother and telling me he wants it to hang around my neck for the rest of *our* lives.

Vin swore he'd move to the States, then abandoned me for this job. Matt said "I do" and abandoned me for someone else.

Everything was temporary. Nothing—

"Stop." Antonio leaned closer and kissed me, his tongue easing into my mouth. Slowly, so slowly. Like he was savoring each taste and touch, showing me how precious I was to him.

Heat poured through me, filling my heart as much as my core. I loved him with every ounce of myself. And my fears were not strong enough to hold me back from him anymore.

"We'll finish this conversation later." He separated from me and tugged at his belt, then the button on his jeans, his cock straining at the fabric. "Right now, I need your body naked in this shower."

I clenched my inner muscles hard and hauled off my pants and underwear. "Good idea. But what about your arm?"

"Dr. Steve said to keep it dry for forty-eight hours. After that, just no soaking."

"We could use the bed."

"Too far," he growled, ripping the tape holding his bandage while I tore off my bra.

"Let me." I moved to his side and began unrolling the bandage for him, so he could slide his pants and underwear off.

He stroked his ready shaft, watching me work.

I'd dealt with a lot of injuries in my day, but when I saw the small, round wound under the gauze, a lump caught in my throat.

He could have been killed.

More than once.

His blood on my hands.

Pacing the waiting room while he was in surgery.

"I'm here." He took my hand and placed it against his hard pectoral, over his heart.

"The way you fell—" My breath hitched. "—I was so scared, Antonio."

He stepped backward into the shower, over the low lip of pale blue tiles, holding my hand against him. "Vieni qui, bella."

The spray hit his back, creating a fine mist that floated around us.

I could have lost him that night.

"We slept alone last night. We were separated by the airline seats the night before. The night before that, I was propped in the chaise in my room, because I couldn't lie down comfortably." He turned us to press my back against the cool tiles of the shower. "Tonight, we make love again. And then we sleep in each other's arms. And I guarantee..."

My leg rose to latch around his hips, his cock rubbing against me. The heat pushed aside the other worries, and I guided him to my entrance. This would distract me. This was what I needed.

"You'll feel better tomorrow." He sank his full length deep inside me, stretching me, filling me. Completing my world. "As will I."

My head dropped back against the wall, and his mouth found my neck as our hips moved. Months ago, I thought my feelings for Antonio made me weak. But they didn't. They made both of us more than we were alone. "Stronger together, amore."

CHAPTER 17

ANTONIO

"Is it okay like this?" Samantha asked, nestling her back against my chest under the covers of my bed. The television played in the background, some action movie with enough gunfire and yelling that it would mask our restrained noises.

Her head lay on my good arm, and my injured one rested around her waist. "The physiotherapist said to do stretches to ensure the muscle heals properly."

She chuckled. "How far can you stretch it?"

"A little farther, I think." I couldn't hold back the groan as I extended the arm until it was nearly straight—and not the good kind of groan I should have made when nestling my hand between her thighs.

"Don't hurt yourself."

"Shh, you." I nipped her shoulder, eliciting the rare Samantha giggle. "Doctor's orders."

"Just keep it there." Her hips rolled against my hand, and she pressed my middle finger down to stroke against her clit. "Is that okay?"

"I'll tell you if it's not."

"No, you won't, you stubborn man."

My cock sprang to life, realizing it lay against her bare ass, which was far more interesting to it than the pain screaming up and down my arm. "Orgasms are a natural analgesic."

A noise somewhere between a chuckle and a gasp escaped her lips.

I let her guide my hand lower, maintaining pressure against her most sensitive spot, until she nudged two of my fingers inside herself.

"Oh, god," she breathed, riding my fingers, grinding slowly.

I lifted enough to kiss her ear, running my teeth along the shell.

"More," she whispered, arching her back to invite me inside her. "If it's okay."

I removed my fingers and tilted my hips, burying myself in paradise. Our visit should have had more of this and less of the rest of the chaos. More of us. And of love. And of laughter.

Her inner muscles clamped down hard while she held my fingers against her clit.

"It's more than okay. It's perfect." My orgasm built tortuously slowly, the agony in my arm holding me back. The need to speed up was strong, but that would hurt more. I was not so foolish to risk things ending prematurely.

She stretched, pushing her shoulders against me, her hand trembling over mine. Tiny gasps of "yes" and "please" burst from her and I tucked my face against her neck.

Her climax broke with a whimper instead of a cry. A quiet noise to match our quiet pace. But it ripped the last shred of my control away and I followed her, tumbling over the edge with a groan muffled in her hair.

I held her against me for long minutes, our breaths slowing together, not wanting to separate from her. "I love you, Samantha."

"Do you think he heard us?"

"That's three orgasms so far tonight." I chuckled. "It hardly matters now if he heard us."

"It does." She rubbed her foot down the length of my calf. "I don't want the bedroom police to burst in and kick me out."

"Nor do I." My bicep shuddered as I attempted to move my hand.

She interlaced her fingers with mine and guided my hand to her stomach, where it was most comfortable. "Of course, that raises the question of how I'm going to sneak back to my room in the morning."

"A good question. But one we should deal with—"

"Tomorrow." She hooked the foot around my leg. "I know."

"Now sleep, amore," I yawned. "For tomorrow shall be a far better day."

She yawned with me. "Do you think we'll be able to see Elliot?"

"I'm not sure how many diversions I have in me." I shrugged my right shoulder, the arm not as comfortable as I'd hoped.

Samantha squirmed out of my grasp and turned to look at me, her face pinched. "Lie on your back and I'll prop some pillows under that arm."

"Is this where you call me stubborn again?"

"I don't have to." She rolled off the bed and took two of the extra pillows, helping me find a bearable position before rejoining me under the covers. "I remember the last time I broke a bone and everyone tried telling me not to do things."

"That must have pissed you off."

She laughed, stifling it and turning to look at the door, waiting for a knock that didn't come. "It did. And I may have done some of those things I was told not to, then paid for it in the long run."

"So you're saving me from myself?"

"It was my ankle and I had a five-day whitewater rafting trip scheduled down the Colorado River. Pushed myself too hard getting ready for it and ended up having to cancel after the first day."

"That must have been fun."

She snuggled in next to me and lay her head on my shoulder, running her fingers up and down the length of my nearly immobilized forearm. "It sucked."

"Did it teach you a lesson?"

She was quiet a moment, continuing to stroke my arm. Her head grew heavy and she let out a long yawn. "What was the rest of the story about your uncle?"

"He claims he wants out of the *shipping* business."

She pushed up sharply to look at me. "Seriously?"

"This is what he says."

"Do you believe him?"

"I don't know. Cristian says Gio had a brush with death two years ago that changed him. He does seem different, but the two of them are masters of manipulation." I encouraged her to lie down. "He claims the Ferraro's expansion is about giving back and reconciling with my father and Zio Andrea."

"Johann mentioned the staff's been cut almost in half over the last couple of years and that his job's changed in that time." Her hand rose to her mouth, fingers tapping against her lips. "What else could it be?"

I wrapped my good arm around her, pulling her against me. "A restorer could just as easily conceal a painting for illegal transport using our tools as they could repair it. They could cut apart a looted krater and prepare it for shipping in multiple containers, then have another company put it back together at its destination. No one would catch them. What if that's what he's doing?"

Her head snapped up to look at me again. The switch had flicked so soundly in her brain I could have heard it if something had not been exploding on the television. My investigator was back. "Or switching *what* he's smuggling? What if the conservation studio is a front to hide drugs inside frames or sandwiched between layers of canvas?"

I sighed. "Or what if he's simply telling the truth?"

Samantha's eyes twinkled in the dim light and she slowly lay her head down again. "Elliot in town, an undercover TPC agent inside the villa, and your uncle wants to get out of the business."

"*If* he's telling the truth." My eyes drifted closed. Elliot said that's what the rumors were. How wonderful would it be? If my family could be whole again and the mention of Giovanni didn't send my parents into a rage?

"Why would Vin lie about that, though?"

I tapped her back so she sat up again, and I could see her face. "I meant my uncle. But I'm guessing you have doubts about Vincenzo, as well?"

She stifled a laugh. "Who am I not suspicious of?"

"Your sister, her children, and your ridiculously sexy boyfriend?"

Rolling her eyes, she leaned over to the bedside table and used the remote to turn off the television. "I guess we'll just have to—"

"No snooping," I whispered as she settled onto my shoulder once more.

"Vincenzo's got a device of some sort down in the cave to disable the security camera."

"I don't believe this is Samantha-speak for, 'Yes, my love, I understand and I will not snoop.'"

"Yes, my love, I understand." She let out long, slow breath, her body growing heavy against me.

The rest of the words didn't come.

Not that I'd expected them to.

I couldn't blame her. Because I wanted to snoop, as well. I wanted to discover whether Giovanni was telling the truth or simply using me for some other purpose.

Chapter 18

Antonio

An earth-shattering boom rocked the bed and my eyes shot open.

Samantha bolted upright, eyes scanning the dark room. "What the fuck?"

A brilliant white light lit the room from around the curtains over the terrace doors. It flashed three times and the world shook again. A light rain pattered across the glass in the doors, growing stronger and fiercer until it was the clatter of hailstones.

Another flash of lightning and tremendous crash of thunder.

"Welcome to January in Roma," I yawned. "Just be happy you got sun yesterday."

She rose from the bed and tiptoed first to the main door—she'd sworn far too loud, but anyone outside likely thought it came from her room—then to the terrace doors. As she pulled one curtain aside, the lightning flashed again, illuminating her naked form. Long and lithe, with subtle curves and strong muscles I'd memorized months ago. My rock climber.

"Marone, you're gorgeous," I whispered, my brain waking enough to remember to keep my voice down since we were secret lovers.

Mmm, secret lovers. I liked that.

The curtain slid shut, but her silhouette was burned into my brain.

"That's quite the storm out there. The trees look like they're all going to snap off." The bed dipped on my right side and she adjusted the pillows propping me up. "Do you need your medication?"

"I can get it."

She ran a hand over my cheek and kissed my forehead. "So can I."

"Bella, I don't actually need a nurse." In the dim light, I couldn't make out her face; and with the hail pelting the door, I couldn't hear any change in her breath. The silence told me little.

Before the shower last night, she'd had a moment of panic, like she had too many times early in our relationship. Samantha Caine was a strong woman, in control of herself, but at the mercy of certain fears. And one of them was that she would lose me, like she'd lost so many others.

I'd thought she showed her love purely through actions, but it was becoming clearer that it was not just actions but acts of service. Chasing down a man who tried to kill us was not merely any reaction but done specifically *for* me and those she loved. "But I suppose this one time, I'll allow it."

Without a word, she went to the bathroom, busied herself with my codeine and returned with a bottle of water from the selection on the desk. "Since I don't have a phone, I can't check... any idea how long these storms normally last?"

I sat up, cradling my arm, and accepted my nurse's attention. "You're thinking about Elliot?"

"It would seem awfully suspicious if we went to the bakery in this weather."

"True." I tossed the pills back and handed the water bottle to her. "It may pass by noon—he said he'd be there at ten and two every day."

"Vin might have loaned me his phone, but he says they're monitored." She took a swig from the bottle, throwing his nickname around too easily for my comfort. "What about Cesca's? They wouldn't monitor her phone, would they?"

"Knowing Leo, anything's possible." Giovanni would have balked at that. Depending on how accurate their concerns about everyone's safety were, he may have conceded. Would they have told her? Told my aunt?

"He brought Cesca her phone yesterday, just before that incident with him at my door."

"Stronzo," I muttered. How dare he treat Samantha like that. If my arm were better... but it was useless. Cristian was right. I couldn't even protect her from my uncle's employees.

"Leo told her to always keep it with her. I bet they at least have a GPS tag on her."

"Elliot's a professional. Whether we talk to him today or tomorrow makes little difference, I'm sure. Leave Cesca out of this."

"Maybe..." She placed the bottle of water on the bedside table, but it was too dark to tell her expression, which would have given me a clue as to whether she'd listen to me or not. "What time is it now? When's breakfast?"

"It's still dark out and there's a naked woman in my bed." I urged her closer, until she slung a leg over to straddle me. No matter how injured I was, there were still things I could do to her that no other man could. "I don't care what time it is."

Her eyes widened as my cock hardened underneath her. "Well, good morning."

"What do you say, bella. Shall we... ride out the storm?"

She made a humming noise, low in her throat, and slid her sex along my shaft. "Wonderful idea."

· · · · ● · ● · · ·

I strode out of my room a few hours later, went to Samantha's door and rapped on it. "Time to go for breakfast, sleepy head. You can't stay in there all day."

Nine o'clock and the hail had returned to rain. The thunder and lightning continued sporadically, but it had moved down the coast or further inland. My goal was to approach the staircase finial with its hidden camera, block it off, then distract the guard as I had last night.

But there was no guard. Since we arrived two days ago, there had been at least one in Samantha's vicinity at all hours. Either they were making a poor shift change, on another floor, or my uncle had decreased her security, as he'd promised.

All I had to do was stand in front of the finial and our plan was in motion.

"I slept so—" she said from behind me, as she emerged from my room. "Oh shoot, I forgot something."

She ducked into her room, and I left the camera to stand by her door. It was a simple switch, but she was still wearing her clothes from yesterday, so was making a quick clothing swap.

Without someone watching us, it was easy. Hopefully, it would continue this way every night, rather than having to come up with new ways to distract a bodyguard.

She swung her door open, breathtaking in skinny black pants, a pale cream blouse, and a brilliant smile. Her long hair hung loose down her back, just the way I preferred it—although slightly damp since I didn't have a hair dryer in my room for her. "Did you hear the thunder this morning?"

"Did it wake you? There was hail, as well." No matter how sore my arm was after our late night escapades, it was the first time we'd made love and slept in each other's arms since the shooting. The fractured nap in the hospital bed hardly counted, nor did snuggling on the couch. And her face showed a magnificent difference for it. I produced my good elbow for her, and she slipped her hand into it.

We stepped out from her room and made it as far as the top of the stairs before Giovanni, Leonardo, and Johann appeared further down.

"Are we going to the bakery now?" Samantha asked.

Giovanni crossed his hands over his heart. "I'm sorry, but I fear the weather is too severe. We called and with the tornado watch on, they're closed today."

Her smile fell, a more dramatic response than was necessary. "I'm sure Henri has a wonderful breakfast prepared."

"He does," said my uncle. "We were coming to get you for the meal. Then, I have a special surprise."

"What sort of surprise?" I asked. And where was Cristian?

Giovanni reached the top of the stairs, the two guards waiting halfway to the third floor, and produced his own elbow for Samantha. Had they discovered we spent the night together? Were we avoiding the bakery because they knew the truth about Elliot? Had they found out about Vincenzo's deceptions?

Calm down, Tony. This was not a smart game we were playing.

Samantha looked at me, forcing her professional smile into place before turning to him. "I love a good surprise."

This was not true. She hated surprises. Preferred to be in control of every moment.

Giovanni began down the stairs with her in tow. "Henri prepared a full American breakfast for you, including bacon and eggs and—" He looked to Leo. "—what are the potato things called?"

"Hash browns?" I said.

Samantha's favorite breakfast was Italian—cornetti with cappuccino. Although she also loved frittatas and breakfast burritos filled with onions and peppers. "That's so sweet."

"And after we eat, I want to take you on a tour. The weather's not scheduled to clear until tonight, so we'll be confined to the estate today. But I thought you might like to see the gallery?" He waved his free hand as he spoke. "Cesca will join us for breakfast and the tour. She wants to show both of you her artwork."

Samantha peered over her shoulder at me, raising her eyebrows. Zio Gio had mentioned showing her the semi-public artwork on the upper floors of the villa. His private gallery was a different story. It would be one of the worst places in the estate to take her, second only to his storage room. How many stolen pieces of art would still be in there and how much self-control would she need to expend not to catalogue every piece and report back to Elliot?

Unless Giovanni was so committed to this story he was telling about changing his life that he'd cleared everything out of there?

Either way, this was the first step on our non-snooping non-investigation.

CHAPTER 19

SAMANTHA

Breakfast lasted an hour. Sixty minutes of listening to rain alternating with hail bashing at the terrace doors of the dining room. True to Giovanni's word, Henri had prepared a full savory breakfast, which inspired more than one muttered comment from Leonardo as he ate.

After a couple of days in his company, his attitude continued grinding on my nerves, but he was becoming easier to ignore. Or maybe the calming influence of having spent the night with Antonio made the difference.

Not a single nightmare.

The group of us—Antonio, Giovanni, Cristian, Leonardo, and Cesca—walked out of the dining room together, through the grand hall with its soaring marble columns and balconies ringing the floors above, past sculptures and display furniture, over lush rugs with vibrant colors.

I counted four cameras before we entered the short hallway that led to the game room, sure there were even more hidden from sight. We headed in the opposite direction from yesterday's blueprint review and ended in front of a large carved wooden door, with its own camera trained on it.

"Samantha, Antonio tells me you're family," said Giovanni, as he stopped. A burst of cold struck through my spine and another rumble of thunder sounded in the distance. Antonio's mother had said essentially the same thing the night she showed me into the small private art gallery in her home. I told Antonio I never wanted to see him again after what I'd seen that night.

Antonio's hand snuck into mine. Was he thinking about that night? Or did the 'family' word have him focused on *us*? Focused on all those threats and teases he kept making about proposing to me someday?

Giovanni continued, "Last night, I let you see my plans for the future. Vincenzo said you quite enjoyed his tour of the ruins and the statues in the cave at the shore. So today, I wish to share more of the past we are fortunate enough to possess here."

"What about a movie?" Antonio used our held hands to point back the way we came. "Or we could show her the view from the top of the tower?"

Cristian—standing behind Giovanni, with Leonardo ever-present at his side—furrowed his brow at Antonio. "The top of the tower in a storm like this? All you'd see is the rain."

Cesca said, "I want to show you some of my paintings. Papa says you're an amazing artist and could give me some advice. Maybe if you stay long enough or visit again before you leave, you could teach me?"

"Sì, but of course." Antonio's forced smile was unlike him. He didn't want to go into this room. Why not?

Cesca reached for the number pad next to the door.

"Remember, tesorina," said Giovanni.

She moved closer to the pad, shielding the numbers from both our view and that of the camera. Why did their gallery have a keypad door lock that had to be kept secret? Anyone coming here had already gotten access to the house and everything else in it.

I looked at Antonio from the corner of my eye, watching a muscle flex in his jaw. He noticed me and raised both eyebrows. The *no snooping* sign. That's why he wanted to go anywhere but into the gallery. He was afraid I'd find something inside.

Cesca pushed the door open, revealing a room with terracotta tiled floors and rich Oriental rugs in whites, blues, and browns. An inset bookcase dominated the far wall with Doric columns dividing it into three, showcasing a few books, several small sculptures, and one painting I couldn't make out any details of. The walls were a pale coppery color, a perfect background for the six antique chairs at the perimeter, upholstered to match the rugs. A crystal chandelier hung at the center of the room, over a narrow inlaid wood table with a vase of white flowers.

Thick curtains covered the tall windows, just like at Antonio's parents' house, so a controlled environment could protect the artwork.

"Sam, do you like art?" asked Cesca.

"I do." Part of me wanted to tell her I'd studied art history, but the less I told them about myself, the better. Not that I could have carried on a conversation at the moment—I was too busy drawing it all in.

How was their such beauty in this horrific place? Two more cameras in this room, globes at opposite corners to capture every movement. It was like being in an old movie, with secret passageways leading behind the artwork and eyeballs peering out from portraits.

The wall to the left was jam-packed with paintings. Most were two- to three-feet wide, with barely six inches separating the frames. Post-modern, Folk, Impressionism. There was little rhyme or reason to their order, other than an apparent need to pack the space like a Tetris game.

I drifted toward the wall, scanning signatures, heart leaping into my throat. A Picasso next to a Renoir, then a de Kooning above a Chagall. Were they all legal purchases?

But as I swept my gaze across them, I didn't get that eerie feeling like I had the night Antonio and I went to the auction and found a stolen painting in their lot. I didn't recognize anything from a news article or a stolen artwork database. That was something, at least.

Cesca was talking behind me, telling Antonio about a painting she made of the ruins. Antonio responded about light, complimenting her. She giggled and continued talking, her words lost on me.

"Which one's your favorite?" asked Giovanni, suddenly next to me.

I'd almost forgotten about the other people in the room. *Keep up the ruse, Sam. Pretend you don't know as much as you do and don't give Leonardo more fodder for his suspicions.* "There's a lot to choose from. Are any of them by famous painters?"

"Some of them are, but it's not about fame. It's about spirit. The soul of the art." A smuggler who believed in the soul of the items he sold off to the highest bidder? Hardly. He smiled and touched a light hand to my back, guiding me along the wall. We stopped in front of a muted piece, showing waves lapping on a beach under a dreary sky. A solitary figure walked on the sand. "This is my favorite of my daughter's. Do you like it?"

The figure melded with the scene behind them, as though they weren't really there. Nothing but a ghost. "It's sad."

"Do you think so?"

"The dark colors, the ethereal figure, the waves washing away their footprints. There's nothing left of them."

"No legacy," he whispered and turned to me. "The plans I shared last night, that's exactly what it's about. What's left of us when we're gone?"

"Memories." I stepped closer to the painting, taking in the brushwork and the light impasto texture, and read the artist's signature. "'Francesca Ferraro.'"

Giovanni came even with me, squinting at the figure in the painting. "My girl is talented."

"She is."

"Now speaking of talent," he said, ushering me to the end wall. The shelving was built around the smaller painting I'd noticed when the doors opened, only a foot and a half wide and under a foot tall. Also muted colors, with a woman reading a book by a dark river, draped in loose blue fabric.

Holy shit. Goosebumps shot up my arms.

I knew this painting.

"This is by Antonio da Correggio—" began Giovanni.

"What's this?" asked Antonio, the use of his name no doubt catching his attention. Everyone gathered around us to admire the piece.

Giovanni beamed, staring at it as reverently as he'd stared at Cesca's painting. "I purchased it two months ago from an art dealer in Brazil."

When I joined the FBI, my first—and only—posting was Boston, with the Art Crime Team. First day on the job, I had a stack of assignments waiting for me, in addition to my primary case, the Isabella Stewart Gardner Museum heist. The top in that stack was a stolen Correggio, taken from a wealthy woman's home in 2012. Correggio had done several small works of Mary Magdalen in the early sixteenth century, and that case was for one of them.

Giovanni continued, "I fell in love with how focused she was on the book and first asked to buy it three years ago."

"She's stunning," said Antonio. "Don't you think, bella?"

She was worth five million dollars and did not belong to Giovanni Ferraro. Bought it two months ago, he'd said? That answered the question: He was not telling the truth about switching to the straight and narrow path. If he was really working on turning his business around for two years, he wouldn't have a stolen painting here.

Cesca said, "I'm doing a copy of her. Just sketches so far. I'm not sure how to get that look on her face right."

Then again, I could have been mistaken. Maybe the original was stolen, copied, or this was a forgery. Stranger things had happened. I'd fallen in love with Antonio over a fraudulent copy of a Chagall, so why not? "Brazil, really? Do you go there often?"

"Not often enough. The last time was Carnival two years ago." He turned to Cristian. "We should go again."

The original was a framed panel, although this frame was different. If I could take it off the wall, I could check the back. The real one had inscriptions and a gallery tag on it, but anyone shipping it across the Atlantic illegally would have removed or concealed those. Infrared would show the change in direction Correggio took when he was painting the water, which originally included an abbey in the distance.

Leo muttered, "A lot's changed in two years."

Giovanni's easy manner melted away. Without looking at him, he said, "Leonardo, go get Johann. There's more artwork to show them on the second floor and you have an early morning."

I turned to see Leonardo behind me, crimson flushing his neck. His eyes narrowed when they met mine, and he walked out.

Two years. Antonio said that was when Gio had his brush with death and started changing things. Which matched the timing Johann mentioned about the reduction in staff.

"What's his problem?" asked Antonio, watching the door. "He was never particularly pleasant, but—"

Cesca spoke at the same time. "He's not usually like—"

Giovanni raised a hand, cutting them both off. His posture and voice relaxed. "Samantha, I apologize for Leonardo's behavior. He gets overly confident in his role sometimes and forgets his place."

"Papa..." Cristian touched Gio's arm and gestured to the door. "We have business to take care of."

"Of course." Gio turned his watch over. "Cesca, you said you wanted to show your cousin Antonio your art studio?"

Her eyes lit up. "Yes, Papa."

Giovanni inclined his head toward me. "I'd intended to show Samantha the artwork on the second floor, so take them there first, once Johann arrives."

"Thank you," she said.

I returned my gaze to the painting in front of us. If we had limited time, I had to make the most of it. "What's she called?"

"*Saint Mary Magdalen Reading by the River.* But I prefer to call her simply *The Magdalen.*"

I nodded, stepping closer to take in every detail. The name was right. The figure, the book, the blue clothes. All of it. When I saw Elliot, I'd tell him about this piece and had to be sure I could answer any question. I could use his cell phone to look up details on the painting and compare to the original.

No, wait. Cesca had a cell phone I could use for that. Even if they monitored hers like they did Vin's, searching for close-ups of a painting she was copying would be reasonable. Expected, even.

Giovanni placed his hand on my back again, and I startled. "You love her as much as I do, don't you? She's so lovely the world disappears around her."

I stood straighter, scanning the pieces on the shelves. Fragments from frescoes and mosaics. Ancient leather-bound books. A set of dog-faced canopic jars to house the Egyptian dead's organs. How many of these things genuinely belonged to him? And how many had been taken from their homes, whether from an actual owner or dug up and secreted out in the middle of the night?

Giovanni's gaze followed mine. "I used to help people navigate red tape so they could take ownership of the beauties they purchased."

"Papa," said Cristian, forcefully. Were his words about where they were supposed to be or the direction of Gio's speech?

Cesca drifted away from our conversation, pulling Antonio with her.

"But then I see a piece like *The Magdalen* and realize she belongs at home, not in some collection in South America. She's Italian. Too many of our treasures have been pilfered for the enjoyment of other cultures."

I gestured to the canopic jars. In the early 2010s, a wave of pro-democracy protests swept across the Middle East and North Africa. That led to an increase in looting of antiquities, a problem Egypt suffered from almost as much as Italy. "Those aren't Italian, are they?"

Antonio's voice echoed in my head, *No snooping. No investigation.* But what was I supposed to do? Let him talk like he was the savior of his culture while ripping apart others? And what about everything else? If he masterminded smuggling activities for decades, why should I believe any of the pieces were legitimately his?

"My wife bought them for me on our fifth anniversary." Giovanni walked over to them and chuckled. "She said they're a reminder that if I step out of line with her, I'll meet the fate they were designed for."

Cristian snorted a laugh.

"How long have you been married?" I asked.

He picked up a framed piece of stained glass, predominantly blue, with yellow and white sections. "She gave me this for our thirty-eighth anniversary last year. An earthquake destroyed the chapel we were married in and the church decided to sell some pieces to help raise funds to rebuild it."

"This is from one of the windows?"

"It was." He handed it to me. "This long golden section had been Saint Gabriel's trumpet."

The angel Gabriel was often depicted carrying the trumpet that would announce Judgment Day. The Resurrection. The end of time on Earth.

Cristian, still stifling laughter, said, "This was to remind him that if he stepped out of line, she would be the one blowing the trumpet announcing the end of days. For him."

I forced a laugh with them, restraining the bubbling anticipation vibrating in my belly. This wasn't snooping if Gio invited me directly to the stolen piece. And Antonio didn't believe his uncle was changing, anyway. These two were not good people, no matter how polite Gio's daughter was or how many funny anecdotes they could tell.

Cristian put the glass back as footsteps sounded from the doorway. Johann was there, as Giovanni had requested, to take us—

But it wasn't Johann. As I turned to the door, I saw Vincenzo. He said, "Leonardo asked me to come down and join Samantha on a visit to Cesca's studio?"

Did he know about *The Magdalen*? Had he communicated the contents of this room to his handler before the messages stalled?

Antonio broke off from his conversation with Cesca and returned to my side, putting an unsurprisingly possessive arm around me. "I'm her escort within these walls."

Things *did* change when Antonio found out Vin was TPC.

Vincenzo put up his hands in conciliation. "Surely he meant only as Cesca's art history teacher. I understand you're an artist and conservator, Dr. Ferraro. I would love to hear your opinion on my student's work."

CHAPTER 20

SAMANTHA

"Here, like this." Antonio took the charcoal from Cesca and traced a line underneath where she'd been focusing on the lower lid of Mary Magdalen.

I'd never watched him draw or paint before—been in the same room, sure, but I'd been on the wrong side of the canvas. The sketching process prior to picking up brush was a kind of magic I'd never figured out. Stick figures were about as good as I could do.

Cesca's studio was on the main floor of the tower with double doors leading out, like so many other rooms on the ground level. Hers opened into a garden with a path that meandered out to the larger one Johann had shown me yesterday.

The room itself was as large as my bedroom three floors above with the same cream-colored walls and bathroom, but devoid of furniture other than a couple of rolling chairs, a drawing table, and two easels.

Rain and thunder continued to jostle her terrace doors and windows. Flashes of lightning sparked from behind the closed curtains. I scanned the paintings on the walls, very few of them framed. Tightened canvases and some pieces of paper held up with tape. Some were as good or better than her beach scene Giovanni showed me.

Before coming to Cesca's studio, she'd taken us up the wide marble staircase from the great room to the second floor of the villa for a tour of the paintings lining the walls. None as spectacular as in the gallery, but beautiful pieces, nonetheless.

Vin had walked quietly behind, playing the guard instead of art history teacher. She looked to him several times as she told us what each piece was, and he answered with only a nod.

An obvious war had raged in Antonio's mind the whole time. If Vincenzo spoke, Antonio's hand clenched on mine. If Cesca spoke, he smiled and engaged her in further conversation.

When we arrived in Cesca's studio, Vincenzo had talked with her and Antonio for a few moments, discussing similarities between her work and earlier attempts by modern masters. She watched Vin move, clearly infatuated with the man, which inspired a need deep inside me to hit him.

After she began working on her copy with Antonio, he transformed into proud uncle and art teacher, as Vin and I faded to the background.

Vin said, "Samantha, you look as though you've caught a chill. Do you need to fetch a sweater?"

It wasn't cold. It was actually fairly warm in the room. The Roman winter was practically tropical for me—compared to the bitter cold of Michigan the last few weeks—with its temperatures closer to what I would have expected in spring. I turned to look at him, about to tell him I was fine, but he widened his eyes, giving me a sign. He wanted to talk.

"Yes, you're right, it *is* cool."

Antonio put down the charcoal and placed a hand on Cesca's shoulder. "Scusi, but I need to take Samantha—"

"No, no." Vincenzo held the door open for me. "I can take her. We'll only be a few moments, and Cesca's learning so much from you. You're as talented as Samantha told me yesterday."

Antonio was slow to pick up the charcoal again. He looked at me, ignoring Vincenzo, as if to ask whether I was alright. He knew he could trust me, at least he kept saying he did. But the way he dropped his arm around me in the gallery said differently.

I crossed the distance to him and placed one hand on his chest and my lips on his cheek. "I love you, bello. He's right. We'll just be a moment."

We walked in silence up the two flights of stairs to my room. If he needed to talk, it would have to be out of earshot of the security cameras or microphones. Sure enough, when we reached my room and I opened the door, he followed me in.

Being alone with him felt eerily familiar, but also wrong. Pins and needles pricked my fingers, reminding me of the role this man had played in my life. How happy he'd once made me. How miserable I was when he left me. How I'd never really forgiven him for what he did.

I walked all the way to the opposite wall where the terrace door was being pummeled by rain and turned to him. "I'm assuming this little act is because you need to talk to me?"

"I can't bear to see you with that man. Do you know who he is?" He gripped me by the upper arms. "Who his family is?"

I shoved him away. "This had better not be why you pulled me up here. My relationship is none of your business."

He came closer again and I sidestepped.

"Touch me one more time and your nose will be broken before you have time to flinch."

His head pulled back. "I know I said it yesterday, but you really have changed."

"Vincenzo Romano, I'm sure some vision of the girl I was the last time we saw each other is cemented in your brain, but that was almost ten years ago. I've been married, divorced, had more than one job, and have spent six years traveling the United States. I've met a lot of people—both good and bad—and I see our old relationship for what it was."

"And what was that?"

I folded my arms, hiding the fact that I was rubbing my fingers together to get the blood flowing again. As uncomfortable as I was in my bedroom with him, it was the anger I was having a hard time controlling. And the bitterness.

But I'd moved on, and I was in love with a man who was perfect for me. Vincenzo didn't deserve a moment of my regret. "A distraction. Temporary. Nothing more than a summer fling or a conquest that I thought was more."

Vincenzo clasped his hands together in front of himself, turning them over, rubbing his palms, staring at them. Maybe my words stung, but sometimes the truth did. Besides, he was the one who made the fool of me, not the other way around. "Did you see any crates in the gallery?"

I blinked a few times at him. Asshole. Nothing to say about the relationship? No *It was more than that, Sam*, even just to make me feel better? Just straight on to business? And why the crates when *The Magdalen* was there? Unless he didn't know about her? "I saw a lot of things in the gallery, but no crates."

"Damn." He stopped rubbing his hands and shoved them into his pockets, clenching his jaw. "Teaching Cesca was supposed to gain me access to the gallery, but Giovanni has her so protective of her passcode that I've never been able to see it so I could get in on my own. They've even trained her to block the view from the security camera. There's a painting being delivered that the TPC is looking for. I thought it would be here already."

I opened my suitcase and withdrew a T-shirt and sweater. If we were up here so I could get changed, I couldn't be wearing the same blouse when we went back downstairs, no matter how much I knew Antonio loved it on me. "I thought you said you hadn't spoken to your handler in some time?"

"I can't use my phone unless it's safe for my message to be overheard." He pulled his phone out to stare at it a moment, then shoved it back in his pocket. "It's something they've been discussing for a year—since before the communications got this difficult. I've heard snippets of conversations about a shipment coming this week. Three crates via delivery company. If it's what I think it is, there's a painting in one of the crates we need to get out of here."

"What do you mean get out of here? Isn't your job to find information that will allow the Carabinieri to arrest Giovanni? Or make him hand over details about his associates?"

"It's not so simple. I'm sure you understand that sometimes recovering a piece of art is more important than prosecution?"

That was the mantra of art crime squads around the world. There were certain pieces of art that you didn't risk. "Why are you telling me this?"

He approached me again, one hand as though to grab my upper arm. When I glowered at the hand, he left it hanging in the air next to me. "Giovanni likes you. I have a feeling if you ask to go to gallery again, he'll take you. I need you to get me the code from that door."

"You work here, why don't you have it?"

"I told you already. Things are difficult right now. From what I understand, Giovanni is making a lot of changes and some people don't like that. He's had to... let some staff go. Others, like Henri and me, who haven't been here long are under closer scrutiny. I can take you down to the cave because it's on the villa's property, but they wouldn't let me take you to town."

The TPC needed my help. I could do good work here. And it would get back to the FBI and help make the case Elliot and I were working on, for me to become a consultant. "Do you know about *The Magdalen*?"

"That new painting Cesca's copying?"

I bit my tongue, heart racing against my ribs. I'd promised Antonio no investigating. But Elliot told me they weren't after Giovanni—there was someone else they wanted more. So if they knew he had this piece, it wasn't a danger to him, was it? "It was stolen from a private residence in Boston in 2012."

"How do you know that?"

Because I was in the FBI for all of one week. "I remember seeing it on a TV show or in a magazine or newspaper or something."

"Well, your memory hasn't changed." A faint smile tugged at his lips and—damn it all—that smile made me proud. "I can do a dead drop tomorrow and provide that information. Maybe they'll respond to that, maybe not, but the least I can do is try. You're sure?"

Was I though?

I was. I always was with this sort of thing. That's why Elliot had been after me to rejoin the FBI since I left. I was certain, all the way down to my toes. "I am."

"I knew it was my lucky day when I saw you here." The faint smile grew and he clasped his hands, shaking them as if in thanks. "Now get that sweater on, so we can go back down to your adoring boyfriend."

I scowled at his back as he walked toward the door.

Before turning the door handle, he looked over his shoulder at me. "And by the way, Johann's working tonight, but Leo's scheduled for the morning. You two need to be stealthier with your sneaking around while he's on duty."

CHAPTER 21

ANTONIO

I met Samantha behind the bathroom door that night. My hand drove into her hair without a word, our bodies and mouths crashing together. She'd slipped into my room again, as Johann opened my pill bottle. It would be an easy act to repeat each evening for such an intense payoff.

She pulled back with a shuddering breath, lips already swollen. "Johann knows."

"Knows what?"

"Vincenzo warned me about our sneaking between rooms." Her fingers laced together behind my neck, playing with the hair at my nape. "And he said Leo's working the tower in the morning."

My eyes slid shut as the energy seeped out of my body. Not as easy an act as I'd expected.

"I can't stay the whole night." Her ankle rose around my calf, rubbing up and down. "Johann will let us get away with it, but—"

"There's no way Leonardo would." I let my head roll forward so I rested my forehead against hers. "I'd hoped my uncle was keeping his promise about decreasing your guards."

"Probably smart of him not to."

I straightened to see her clearly, good hand frozen in her hair. "Scusami?"

She sucked her bottom lip between her teeth. This was not her *I'm not investigating* face.

"You learned something else from Vincenzo, didn't you?"

Her foot fell from where it had been wrapped around my leg. "He says there's a painting that's going to arrive in a crate that he needs to get out of here."

"And...?"

"He doesn't have the passcode to the gallery, so he wants me to get it."

My hand dropped to her shoulder. "You're not thinking about doing that for him, are you?"

The lip-worrying continued. She *was* considering it.

My stomach began to churn. "You come up here with him for twenty minutes, now all of a sudden you believe his story?"

"It makes sense." She gave a half-hearted shrug.

What did he say to her in her room? What did they do? Did he touch her? Did she still have feelings for him? Of course, she felt something, but was it clouding her judgment?

Trust her. "You're different when he's around." *That was hardly trusting, you fool.* "And I don't like it." *That was worse.*

The bitten lip vanished and she gave a quick tug on a chunk of my hair. "Don't go there."

But I went there. "He's lied to you before. What if he's using your past together to conceal another lie? What if he's not the TPC agent and it's someone else?"

"Like who?"

"Why not... why not Henri? He's out to the town every day for groceries, has access to everyone, wanders the villa and tower at night delivering food to people? Who does that?"

"Don't tell me you're still on this jealousy thing? I thought we were past that?"

Jealousy? It was hardly jealousy that reminded me every time I saw Vincenzo that he'd made love—no, it was only ever sex between them, sì, that was it—to my girlfriend. Or that he'd had her foolishly flying across the Atlantic to be with him, when he was lying to her about his level of commitment?

"Take a breath," she said, the corners of her lips tightening. "Your face is turning red."

"He's taking advantage of you."

"You've got that backwards." More than the corners tightened and her fingers released my neck. One landed on my good shoulder, the other on my chest. She pushed, not hard enough to separate us, but making her displeasure clear.

"I don't. You're angry, irritable—"

"You aren't?" She pushed harder, but I held my lower body against hers, keeping her pinned against the wall. Her voice raised in decibels beyond the whispers we'd been using. "I haven't talked to my sister in two days. She's got radiation tomorrow. I haven't missed a single appointment until now, and I can't even call her! Plus, your project's getting behind. Every day you aren't working is another day—"

"Shh." If she got any louder, the camera in the staircase finial would pick her up and no matter how lenient Johann was, he'd have to escort her back to her room.

"We're cooped up in this damn house and can't go anywhere without someone watching us. And even if we could, there are still eyes everywhere!"

I'd warned her about this place in the airport, but she'd been too stubborn to listen. "It's not just that. You're—I don't know. Shy? Nervous? Something's not right with you. And it happens every time he comes into the room." It differed from the way she used to act when she was afraid of her initial attraction to me, but close enough it hurt my heart whenever I saw it.

Her jaw clenched. "Because he's an asshole."

"One you're considering betraying my family to help."

"A family who practically kidnapped you."

"Giovanni just wants to make the Ferraros whole again."

She rolled her eyes so dramatically, her head tilted back. "Who's the one believing the liar now?"

"It's not the same."

"It's exactly the same. You're normally the big man with the personality everyone flocks to. But here? Every time Giovanni steps into a room you shrink and become compliant, willing to do anything he tells you."

"He's my uncle."

"He's a smuggler."

"You don't understand."

"I'm not stupid, Antonio. You say you love me over and over, complain I don't talk to you about things, then you refuse to tell me about all of this."

"All of what?"

"What you did here. It's just vague stories about getting in-volved, wanting to please your uncle, and somehow getting shot in the process." Her arms relaxed, the hand which had been pushing on my shoulder trailing down to my hand and bringing it to her lips. "You have a lot of demons, and I suspect most of them are here."

I'd had so many reasons to tell her not to come, and this was one of them. I didn't want her to see the man I was with them. Nine years had brought about vast changes in me, but even seeing Cristian the handful of times I had in September had me falling into old patterns. Always deferring to him, letting him take the lead on everything. Asking him to deal with my problems and not worrying what that meant.

My head fell beside hers, so I could avoid her gaze.

If she knows, she'll leave.

She let go of my hand and lifted my chin, her voice soft. "For the record, I also threatened to break Vincenzo's nose while we were up here."

"That's my Samantha." The churning in my stomach rose into my throat. I *could* trust her. If I was to have the future I wanted with her, I had to learn how. "I was only ever on the fringes of his business."

Her hands slid down my torso, lifting the hem of my shirt to circle my waist, and she pulled me tighter to her.

I stared down at her chest, at the white sweater she wore and the Foster Mutual logo on it. Her ex-husband's family company. One more man from her past who wouldn't leave us alone. "Collecting money and delivering messages, primarily. Most of the fights I got into were people who didn't want to pay or who didn't like the warnings or threats I delivered. I'd always had a way with words, so my fists rarely came into the equation."

A week ago, I'd told her about Giovanni for the first time, forced into the conversation by Elliot Skinner. That day, she'd pulled away when she learned too much. But this time? She held on tighter and whispered, "I still love you."

I scanned her face, searching for any doubt or second guesses. But they were absent. Honesty and trust were the way to her heart—she'd told me this from the early days of our relationship and it continued to amaze me how true it was. My bad arm inched out slowly, finding her waist, while the other combed through her glorious hair. "There was one man who'd always given us trouble. A jeweler who..."

Samantha's head cocked when my words faded away, and her fingers traced up and down my back. No words. No interruptions. Just all the time in the world to tell her the truth.

"How did I get so lucky?"

"Lucky?" She raised a doubtful eyebrow at me. "I'm pretty sure this discussion started with how shitty our current situation is."

I pressed a kiss to her temple. "At least I'm here with you."

"There *is* that." Her fingers skirted the waistband of my pants and a pressure built deep inside me. A glint flashed in her eyes and her hands ran lower, over my backside. "Finish your story first."

"You play dirty," I said, rubbing my growing erection across her front.

"No dirtier than you." She lifted her hands and cupped my face, an unwavering level of openness shining from her. "I'm not going anywhere. Just tell me."

Good God, but I loved this woman. She'd been so uncertain about us since the start, but on New Year's Eve, she gave in. Told me she loved me. The barriers were almost gone.

Why did I leave the engagement ring at home instead of bringing it to Napoli? Probably because I was not sure she'd come with me.

"Who's the one staring and blinking now?" Her grip shifted back to my waist, ghosting gentle fingers across my skin.

I'd never even told Mario the full details, and he was the one who saved me. "Leonardo normally dealt with him—this was long before he was the head of security—but the man had fallen behind in his payments. Giovanni suspected it was intentional, so sent me to work some sort of magic. If I failed, Leonardo and Cristian were with me, as well as another man."

She opened her mouth, as if to ask a question, but snapped it shut. *Finish your story*, she was clearly saying.

"I sat down with him, the other three watching over my shoulders. I made friendly, talked about his business, his clients, his family—all the standard things—making it clear that his agreement with Zio Gio was not just about himself, but about all the people who depended on him. He knew this, but I think he'd grown tired of Leo's ways, and responded positively to me."

Samantha's brows drew down, head pulling back slightly in confusion.

"The jeweler said he'd pay everything, but needed a couple of days. Leonardo flew into a rage. Said it would be right then and there or he'd have to hand over diamonds as collateral." I closed my eyes and inhaled her scent, calming my heart. "I argued with Leo, in front of everyone, and he backhanded me."

"Leo did?"

I nodded. "Cristian slammed Leo up against the wall, telling him he was never to touch anyone with the Ferraro name. Threats were hurled, the volume rose, until the jeweler's son rushed in with a walking cane. From the golden handle, I assume it was something they were designing for a customer."

"He didn't know what his father was doing?"

"No." I looked at her, into a face which held more curiosity than accusation. "It's always been a blur what happened. Cristian told me the man who was with us—Dario—pulled his gun as soon as the son came into the room. However, I'd charged ahead, thinking to take the cane away before someone got hurt. The son hit me, I stumbled back, went after him again, and Dario shot."

"Shot you?"

"It was a small space. Apparently, it was a warning shot that deflected off some piece of machinery in the office and hit me."

"Apparently?"

"It's not like the police investigated." My right arm throbbed, as though reminding me of the pain of being shot, and I withdrew it from her waist to hold it against my stomach. I should have worn the sling. "I called Mario from the hospital, while I was still high on whatever painkillers they'd given me. He was there four hours later and didn't leave my side until I was at his place in Napoli."

I didn't even know if the jeweler ever paid.

"So…" She was distracted, watching my bad arm tremble. She slipped one hand under the forearm, under the guise that she was caressing my abs. My nurse, yet again. "Why would Leo react like that? Do you two have some sort of past before that?"

"We do." He and I had been friends until a woman came between us. I couldn't remember her name, let alone her face. I removed her hand from my arm and brought it to my lips, then my neck. "Man stuff I'd rather not discuss."

"Long term man stuff?"

"Very short term and not one of my wisest decisions."

She ran a hand over her cheek and forehead. "I don't think I want to hear it."

"You don't seem as bothered by this as I expected."

"I'm not happy about it, but you already gave me the broad strokes, so it's not like any of it's a surprise." She blew out a long breath. "It's part of what made you who you are, right? Like you said Monday night on the balconies—my past with Vin is part of what made me who I am."

"For better or worse?" I said with a grin I couldn't hold back.

"It's funny." She leaned her weight against the wall, rather than continuing to press into me. "On the plane, Elliot told me it's okay to be angry with Jimmy and the Scotts for what happened in Brenton, while still feeling sorry for all of them."

"Meaning, I need to appreciate the man I became because of my experience here, even though I'm still holding onto the anger for how it happened—let alone how it ended?"

"Yeah, something like that."

"This is rather perceptive for someone who spends so much energy bottling up her feelings."

She scrunched her nose. "Just because I don't talk about them doesn't mean I don't have them."

I dipped my head closer, running my nose along her jaw. "I have some other wonderful feelings for you to experience, if you're interested?"

She pushed back gently, and I straightened to see her. "After I share my other news."

CHAPTER 22

ANTONIO

"More news about Vincenzo?" For all her patience and understanding through my story, it was unlikely I'd react as well to news about the handsome art historian and bodyguard.

She shook her head slowly, frowning. "I recognized *The Magdalen*."

"What do you mean? You saw it in someone's house or in a museum at some point? At an auction?" I knew none of that was true, but I'd hoped Zio Gio was telling the truth about changing. If she recognized the painting from a stolen art database, that was a mark against him.

"Do you want me to get your sling?"

The trembles in my arm had grown stronger and a bead of sweat rolled down my temple. "It's fine—I'm just—"

"Stubborn."

I threaded my good arm between her and the wall, pulling her against me again. "I'm taking lessons from a master."

With a shake of her head, she slipped out of my grasp and out of her sweater. "It was one of the case files I had on my first day."

I cradled my bad arm, taking the weight off of it. Perhaps I should have done that ten minutes ago. "I thought you were in Boston for the Gardner Heist?"

She chuckled. "If only the FBI actually worked that way. One case at a time? But no, Elliot saw to it I had a pretty deep stack." A darkness formed over her, the same one that always did when she spoke of that period in her past.

"And I assume the case file was not about it being purchased legally by a Brazilian art dealer?"

"Giovanni said he bought it two months ago. If he's really been trying to turn things around for the last two years, he wouldn't have that painting."

This was what I'd feared most about her going in there. She spent a great deal of time reviewing art crime cases, and when combined with her amazing visual memory for art, the odds of her finding something were too high. "Just because he has it does not mean it was obtained illegally."

She folded her arms, a scowl creasing her face. But she didn't argue the point.

"Every country has laws about this sort of thing. If he didn't know it was stolen property... If he purchased it in good faith, then it's legally his. Plus, if it was a case file on your desk, I'm assuming the insurance company already paid for it?"

"True, but he said he first saw it at the art dealer's three years ago. That was before his little brush with death and decision to change things around. I'd bet money that art dealer was part of some other shady deal Giovanni was there for, so he would have at least suspected anything in their possession was not there legally. That eliminates any good faith argument." She withdrew one hand from the fold and waved it through the air. "Plus, if he's been in the smuggling business for so long, he would have picked up on clues or something from this art dealer. A simple internet search for that painting would have brought up its stolen history."

Of course she wanted to believe the worst of my uncle, considering everything she knew about him.

Marone, after what I told her about him and how I'd reacted to his news about the changes, I could barely believe *I* was considering his words to be the truth.

"Antonio, his entire speech about returning items to the country where they belonged—he's not wrong about that. I mean, the woman it was stolen from deserves it back, but like you said, her insurance company already paid it out. It doesn't even belong to her anymore. If the authorities recovered it, the insurance company would just sell it to recoup their money."

"What are we going to do, then?"

She tucked her fingers under the hem of the white Henley Cristian had loaned me. "Get naked, have sex, and forget about it until morning?"

"Amore, we've been spending too much time together." I laughed softly, helping her ease my shirt off. "You're starting to sound like me."

"Seriously, I *am* listening to what you said, to your warnings about this place. I've been biting my tongue about practically everything I know around Leonardo. After we're gone, I'll call Elliot and tell him it's here." She took the hem of her shirt in both hands, about to lift it over her head, and she paused. "I did tell Vincenzo about it, though."

Of course she did.

When she'd snuck off to her room with her ex-boyfriend and told him secrets about my uncle.

I sucked in a slow breath. *Stop being a jealous fool.* Just because he was now a white knight, placing himself in front of the dragon that was my uncle, didn't mean he was any better suited to be with her than before her discovery. "What did he say?"

Samantha was my soul mate, my future, and no one could ever change that—not even a handsome TPC agent, and especially not one who broke her heart, made her distrust all Italian men, and who begged me at every moment to slap his handsome smile off. She finished pulling off the shirt and held it in front of herself. "Just that he's going to let them know about it."

"Sounds good." I took her shirt from her and dropped it to the floor. "Now, can we get on with the rest of our priorities? Or did you have other news?"

"That's all I've got." She let out a sigh, fingers tracing up the bandage on my arm. "Do you need help with this?"

"Will it make you feel better?"

Her gaze lingered there, the fingers gentle along the edge of the gauze. It *would* make her feel better. She didn't have to say the words for me to know.

"Please do." I remained still, watching her roll the bandage with practiced efficiency. "None of that when we get to Mario's villa, though, sì?"

"Need to remain the big tough guy who took a bullet for his girlfriend?"

"What better way for Mario to understand that he can't move in on my woman?"

"Trust me, I made it very clear to him when I was there in September." A twinkle shone in her eye.

"Did you also threaten to break his nose?"

She smiled to herself as she worked. "Actually, yes."

I kissed the side of her head. "I suppose I should consider myself lucky you never said that to me."

A rumble of thunder shook the tower. Before dinner, Johann advised us a tornado had touched down earlier in the day, but fortunately, it dissipated almost as quickly as it had formed.

She paused with the bandage. "Whether the storm clears and we can meet Elliot tomorrow or not, I intend to get the passcode for the gallery. Giving it to Vincenzo is a separate decision, but one step at a time. Cesca might be the key—I bet I could get her code."

"Cesca?" I urged her chin up so she'd look at me instead of the bandage. "We talked about this last night. She's a child with no idea what her father does. You can't involve her."

"Like it or not, she was born in the middle of it." Samantha pulled her chin out of my grip and finished removing the bandage. "I don't like this anymore than you do, but Vin's already targeted her. That's why he's teaching her."

As if I couldn't dislike him any more. "Taking advantage—"

"Don't say it like that."

"You've seen how she looks at him. The girl's infatuated."

Samantha placed the bandage on the counter, staring at it for a long moment, then looked up at my reflection. "He's an undercover agent and he's using the tools at his disposal to make the world a better place."

"What would you say if someone did that with your niece?" Little Emma was only three years old, but the argument remained valid.

Her head fell forward and shoulders sagged. She stayed like that for so long, I stepped over to her and placed a hand on her upper back.

"Bella? Is there more going on here that you've not yet told me?"

"This is all so much easier in theory. When the world is black and white, good and bad, and there's no one stuck in the middle." She turned slowly, leaning against the counter with her ankles crossed. "I *like* your uncle. He's so different from your father—and I adore your father—but he's got so much of that same passion inside of him. It's hard not to admire."

I stretched my bad arm out, flames erupting through the spot where the bullet had ripped through my muscle, and took her hand. The other rose to her cheek. "I understand. This is how I fell in with them."

She slid a hand around my waist, pulling me closer. "I think I should talk it over with Elliot tomorrow."

My lips found her cheek, and I whispered through tiny kisses, making their way toward her ear, "You'll have maybe three minutes with him, unless I can pull off a miracle. Your earlier plan was the wise one. Talk to him once we've left."

She sighed, uncrossing her ankles to allow me to step between her legs. "Alright. I'll ask Giovanni to take me to the gallery and get the—"

"No." I pulled back to look her square in the eyes before she could object. "Let me do it. They're less suspicious of me, so it will be far easier. We can ask to go to the gallery together, if the opportunity comes up. If it doesn't, I'll say it's related to the discussions I'm having with my uncle about his future."

"I can't ask you to do that."

"You don't have to ask, bella. This is what partners do for each other."

CHAPTER 23

SAMANTHA

We strolled along a narrow sidewalk in Cittavera on Thursday morning. The weather had cleared, but pools of water dotted the street and flooded soil-filled flowerpots. At least a dozen cats watched us from various vantage points. Cristian and Leonardo walked ahead of Antonio and me, granting us a welcome sliver of privacy. Antonio took full advantage, with the arm around my waist regularly dipping lower to sweep over the curve of my ass.

True to Vincenzo's warning, Leonardo had been pulling a guard duty outside of our rooms in the morning that would have made the Secret Service proud. Good thing I'd snuck into my own room just after midnight, before Johann's shift ended. There would have been no fooling Leo, and he would have moved me to a different floor to ensure we weren't breaking the rules.

I was a little worse for wear. The bad dreams had started a few times, but they didn't follow their entire course—dream-Antonio made it through to live another day. Wearing his pajama shirt helped my sleep our first night here, so last night he'd given me the shirt he'd worn that day, as well.

How long would that work once I got home and the scent of him faded? Waking with a scream or a sob in my sister's house would scare the kids. On the upside, if I woke at two in the morning, it would be eight in Naples and I'd be able to call Antonio.

"What do you think you'll try this morning, bella?" Antonio wore khaki pants paired with a black Henley and light gray jacket, along with the sling. The clothes belonged to Cristian, and none of it fit him properly—snug in the shoulders and across his ass, too short at the hem and ankles. Considering how fashionable Antonio normally was, it was no surprise he acted like it was intentional and was as sexy as ever.

Cristian looked over his shoulder at me. "Johann swears by the apple cakes. Did you try those?"

Antonio chuckled. "We only bought three of those Tuesday and he ate two in the car."

"Cesca ate the other one." I laughed and Cristian did the same.

I had to stop laughing. Stop letting Cristian's charm and pleasantries pull down my defensive walls. He was a smuggler. There was no space in my heart, my brain, or my soul to be friends with a man like that. No matter what Antonio said last night and no matter what the relationship between the two of them was, Cristian and his father were exactly the type of men I'd sworn to fight against when I joined the FBI.

But how did I reconcile that with the fact that Cristian was the one Antonio called when things got bad two weeks ago? And for all the information he gave us about Parker Johnson and what he was doing back home in Brenton?

"Maybe a custard cornetto," I snapped, annoyed at myself for even debating that I might like the man.

Tiny cars crawled along the narrow road, which made a sharp right angle turn just past the stairs down to the square where the bakery was situated. There were more people out than vehicles, many bundled up as though they were in a snowstorm—probably locals. Still, there were others, wearing lighter jackets and speaking English, with American and British accents. Some French. A few in a foreign tongue I was unfamiliar with.

Antonio hummed. "I want something with whipped cream this morning. And custard sounds good."

Elliot said he'd be in the bakery at ten and two. It was only nine thirty, so I kept alert, in case we met him on the way. There was a seawall at the far end of the square; we could talk there, but with both Leo and Cristian keeping an eye on us, the odds of me getting away so easily were low.

"Yeah, custard sounds good," I said.

Antonio squeezed me, pulling my attention back from what I could see of the square between the last few houses along the road. "You already said that."

"Something interesting over there?" asked Leo, more accusation than question. His gaze followed mine, out to the seawall.

I was thinking too much. Elliot was an expert, in the business far longer than Leo, but I couldn't give Leo any hints about what Antonio and I were up to.

Cristian looked toward the water, as well.

A squealing noise broke through the hum of the town—the chattering voices, squawking gulls, and breaking waves—and my attention tore away from Antonio. A tiny car came barreling around the corner onto our street. A mop of black hair was barely visible over the steering wheel. Could the driver even see?

The car careened out of its lane toward the sidewalk.

"Cristian!" I bolted straight for him before the car reached us. My shoulder slammed into his side and all the air rushed out of him at once. We fell hard onto the sidewalk as the sound of smashing metal echoed behind us, competing with screams, yells, and a great deal of swearing in various languages.

Before I could check on Cristian, two large and very strong hands hauled me up into the air, practically tossing me across the sidewalk.

I collided with the short wall separating the walkway from the square down below.

Antonio rushed to my side. Leo—gun out and head on a swivel—knelt over Cristian, who was still on the ground, clutching his head. Leo must have been the one who threw me.

The little green car had rammed into a parked one, but the driver had slowed just enough that the damage would be minor. If I hadn't gotten Cristian out of the way, though, he could have been seriously hurt.

"Are you alright, bella?" Antonio's good hand prodded at my head, my shoulders, my elbow.

I waved him off. "Who was that?"

As if in answer to my question, Leo shouted for Antonio and stood, readying an all-out assault on the car. But just then a kid, several years younger than Cesca, jumped out from the driver's seat and ran down the road.

That explained why I only saw the top of his head.

"Go," I waved Antonio over to Cristian, who seemed to need him more than I did.

A black-clad local policeman on a motorcycle came speeding around the corner. Leo's gun was back in his waistband immediately, and a man in jeans and a sweater vest approached him, saying in French that he was a doctor.

"Are you alright?" A familiar voice next to me. Elliot.

"Yeah." I looked at him and then intentionally flicked my eyes to the scene. Other than the surprise and probably a tear in my clothes, I really was fine. But I pressed a hand to my head and hauled myself onto the separating wall, feigning shock. "I just need to sit for a minute or two."

The officer parked his motorcycle and took off his helmet.

Elliot sat next to me and patted my back, playing the role of concerned bystander, but keeping his voice low. "We don't have a lot of time. First, are you safe?"

"Yes. But they've got a guard detail on me pretty much twenty-four-seven."

"Think you can do a job for me?"

I kept my eyes forward, watching Leo argue with the officer, gesturing wildly down the road. With the help of Antonio and the French doctor, Cristian sat up, clutching the shoulder he landed on.

"Get that little troublemaker back here!" Leo yelled. The way he'd stashed the gun in his belt, I wouldn't have expected him to call attention to himself with the officer. How much did he interact with the local police? If they were running a smuggling operation out of a villa next to this tiny town, they probably all knew him well.

"What kind of job?" I asked.

He pulled out his phone and pressed it to his ear, pretending to take a call, but keeping his voice down. "We got a tip about a new acquisition. I need confirmation."

I twisted from my waist, touching my back like I'd hurt it, as well.

"Alright. Talk to you later," Elliot said in a louder voice. He brought the phone in front of him and scrolled through apps. I glanced at the final app as I straightened out of my stretch.

I flinched, which I quickly covered up with a moan of pain. It was *The Magdalen*.

Elliot swiped the image away and slid his phone into his pocket. "It's called—"

"Already seen it." So much for good faith purchases. At least I didn't need Cesca's phone to confirm any details on it. If the FBI had a tip about its arrival, it was most likely the real thing. And Vincenzo wouldn't have to risk a dead drop, either. "But I don't have a phone or camera."

"I heard. I have something for you." He leaned back, stretching one arm behind me. "Magnetic back. Double-tap it to take photos."

"Why me?" I pulled up my arm, running a hand over it as though checking for cuts.

"Inter-organizational disagreement." He looked at my arm and shook his head, maintaining his Good Samaritan ruse. "Plus..."

"More fodder for our portfolio?"

"Precisely. Will you be in Naples by the weekend for me to pick it up?"

"Should be."

"Just be careful. I heard he's getting out of the business, so we're looking for leverage to turn him. Don't push yourself farther than I'd be comfortable with you doing. I'd rather you flush that thing down a toilet than get into—"

"Samantha!" hollered Leo. "We're leaving."

I waved to Leo and nodded, giving him my most convincing grimace. As I stood, I turned to the low wall I'd been sitting on and placed my hands on it, stretching out my back, sliding Elliot's small black disc into my palm. Three-quarter inch diameter by quarter-inch thick. "I figured out your source inside."

Elliot's façade didn't crack. "Not surprised."

"We went to school together."

Elliot blinked twice. Rapidly. The only hint he hadn't known that part.

"Yeah, in Ameli—"

"Calm down," Antonio said from behind me, closer than where he'd been with the other men. "She saved Cristian's life."

A rough hand landed on my upper arm and Leonardo spun me to face him. "I said, we're leaving. Don't turn your back on me."

I pulled free—biting back every instinct to ram my palm into his nose.

Antonio growled, "Don't touch her."

Elliot stood, feigning a cower. In a British accent he didn't normally have, he said, "Sorry, sir. She was complaining she hurt her—"

"I don't care what she hurt," Leo snapped in English.

Elliot nodded, hunching his shoulders down so he appeared shorter than Leo. "Put some ice on it, alternating with heat."

"This place is full of fucking doctors." Leo huffed and stormed back toward Cristian, who was standing now, cradling one arm.

"Thank you for looking after my girlfriend, signore." Antonio bowed his head to Elliot. "We need to go."

I gave Elliot a small wave over my shoulder as we left, then turned to Antonio. "No bakery?"

"Mi dispiace, but Leo's shaken. He was afraid it was an attempt on Cristian's life."

"By a kid?"

"It's unlikely, but stranger things have happened. The officer said that boy steals a car at least once every couple of weeks, but this was his first collision. It's such a small town, the officer's heading to the kid's house to speak with his mother instead of pursuing him." Antonio leaned in to kiss my temple and whispered, "Plus, I think Leo's angry you're the only one who acted."

"This isn't going to make things easier for me, is it?"

"No, bella. Not in the slightest."

CHAPTER 24

ANTONIO

"That girlfriend of yours—" Leonardo snarled at me.

Giovanni knocked on his desk. "Saved my son's life."

Leo's mouth opened to protest but cut off when Gio glowered at him.

We were in the game room, Cristian and I sitting in the armchairs, while Giovanni sat behind an ornate desk normally used for cards. He riffled through papers, occasionally looking to his laptop. Leo stalked back and forth, eventually stopping by the carom table to roll a yellow cue ball from cushion to cushion.

Cristian said, "The boy was only—"

"Shh," said Giovanni, returning focus to his work. He had a private office upstairs, but Leo was too antsy to move discussions to the second floor. He wanted as many escape routes as possible.

So much had changed over the last nine years. Zio Gio was the aggressor in most things back then, from protection and extortion to smuggling, but I couldn't remember him ever sitting at a computer or in front of his files, checking on someone before deciding how to act. In this case, both the police officer and the young boy. Where he got his information, I'd never known, but a person didn't build his kind of wealth without a vast network of whisperers.

Cristian stood and crossed to the shelf where they kept the other two carom balls and pins, shooing Leonardo away. "Bouncing that thing is making me more anxious."

"We should have gone after him," muttered Leo.

It was a kid. I kept my mouth shut. Giovanni would finish his research soon enough. Arguing with either him or Leonardo would bring more attention to Samantha than I wanted. Sitting down in broad daylight with Elliot was a stupid risk. What if someone recognized that he'd been lingering around the bakery twice every day? Gio could have had him followed. Perhaps all the way to TPC headquarters in Roma. Then what?

What had he said to her? Their conversation had lasted longer than mine with him, so it was not simply to ask if she was alright.

And then there was the sparkle in her eyes afterward. The joke about the bakery after tackling Cristian out of the way of the car. She didn't seem hurt and was more excited than stunned despite the near miss.

Elliot had said something important to her. And I needed to know what it was.

Giovanni closed his laptop. "I've asked Henri to prepare a special dinner for Samantha in thanks."

"What?" My head snapped toward him. That meant she was safe, unless my sudden reaction triggered questions from Leo, so I responded, "She likes all foods, especially Italian."

Leo made a shot, hitting Cristian's cue ball, bouncing off two cushions, and knocking over a white pin. He straightened, a smile finally crossing his face. "What about the boy?"

"Everything the officer said was true." Giovanni stood and rounded his desk to sit next to me. "I have four stories backing him up."

I ran a hand through my hair and clasped the back of my neck. Visiting this place was harder than I'd expected when Samantha and I discussed it at the airport, for more reasons than my past.

Cristian and Leo continued their game, marking points on a chalkboard on the wall.

Giovanni leaned toward me. "We're safe, Antonio. No need to worry."

The throbbing through my arm reminded me that our lives had been in more danger at home in sleepy little Brenton, Michigan than they were here. I let out a long sigh, curving in my injured shoulder. "It's not that. It's being separated from her. Three months apart, then two weeks together, being shot, now so close to her yet so far away."

He smiled and pointed upward. "God is watching."

"God was watching when that boy almost hit Cristian, too. But Samantha was the one who saved him."

"We have a chapel downstairs," he chuckled. "I can have your rings blessed."

Cristian and Leo continued their game, Cristian's numbers climbing faster.

"Sì, have your priest marry Samantha and I without my parents here." I rolled my eyes heavenward. That would only ensure Mamma never allowed Papa to speak to Zio Gio again, no matter how much effort he put into reconciliation. "Splendid idea."

"You'll have plenty of time together this evening. We'll have our special dinner, visit the gallery once more, maybe even a tour of the wine cellar. Or the top of the tower? It should be clear tonight and you can see all the way to Sardegna."

"No, you can't," said Cristian, as the red pin toppled on the table. He winked at Leo. "That's my game."

Leo frowned and wiped the board. "How are you so calm? Someone almost hit you with a car."

"You heard Papa." Cristian set the pins back up and grabbed his cue ball. "The boy's nothing more than a troublemaker. We'd be better off recruiting him."

"No more games." Leo hung his cue in the rack on the wall. "I need to check in with the men. Increase patrols."

I looked at Zio Gio, who nodded to Leo. Did he think it was necessary? Or was he deferring to his security head's overabundance of caution?

At least we only had one day left here.

CHAPTER 25

SAMANTHA

Why didn't Elliot realize Vincenzo and I went to school togeth-er? He was too sharp to forget I'd gone, but maybe he didn't know Vin's background? Of course. He wouldn't have had access to the TPC's employment files, especially not for their undercover agents.

Then again... maybe I misread his reaction when I said I'd gone to school with the TPC contact. Was I misremembering it now? Was it just the adrenaline and chaos of the car accident that clouded what I saw?

Or could Antonio be right? Could Vin be lying to me? It wouldn't be the first time.

"Alright, Samantha."

I startled. "What?"

Henri stood with a pen poised over his notebook.

Right. We were preparing for dinner.

"Tell me what your favorite meal is."

Good question. What *was* my favorite? "Italian?"

I settled onto a stool at the long marble kitchen island and took in the details of the room. Like the rest of the villa's main floor, the coffered ceilings were sixteen feet high, made of warm wood. White and blue tiles lined the back splash behind Henri, pairing beautifully with the yellow walls.

The appliances were a mix of old and new worlds. A microwave and stainless double wall oven sat next to a gas stovetop and an open-front brick oven. Marble sinks and enough cabinet space to house every ingredient on the planet.

"Do you cook for all the staff?" I asked.

"Sometimes. The staff village has their own kitchens, so I mostly prepare food for those staying in the villa and any guests."

Johann stood just inside the door, a reminder that the word 'guest' only meant so much here. "Or when we come begging."

Henri laughed. "But you always help cleanup, which is more than I can say for the rest."

"I think she'd like your lamb."

Henri lifted his eyebrows to me in question.

I nodded. "Lamb's good."

He directed Johann to the stainless industrial refrigerator behind me. "Can you check how much we have? Shoulder or leg, either will work."

Johann nodded, humming once the door was open.

"How does this work?" I pointed to Henri and then over my shoulder at Johann. "He seems to be a bodyguard, but also knows his way around your kitchen?"

Henri plucked a corkscrew and a bottle of red wine from underneath the island. He opened it and set it aside. "I've only been here a year, so still have an escort when I go into town. The first time Johann came with me, it was clear he knew how to cook and how to choose ingredients."

"I put in a request to Leo to be the exclusive grocery helper." Johann placed a tray of wrapped meat on the island, and the chef nodded. "Leo went once, complained how boring it was, and the job was mine. I help him shop, put everything away, and he shows me some recipes when we have time."

Henri cocked an eyebrow at me. "Something wrong?"

I was frowning. Hadn't noticed it. "Nothing. It's interesting, that's all."

What was going on? I was in the center of a smuggling empire, with a stolen painting on the other side of the house, let alone anything else that could have been hidden away. My mentor asked me to take photos as evidence so they could gain leverage against the homeowner.

And here I was, hanging out in the kitchen, chatting with a French chef and a German bodyguard like old buddies. Like we were going to trade recipes.

"Johann," said Henri as he fetched some red wine glasses from a cabinet behind him. "Could you get the smoked salmon and bocconcini out? I feel like crostini."

Mmm. "That sounds good."

"So, no more advice on dinner other than something Italian?" asked Henri, placing the glasses on the island.

I pulled the glasses to me and poured. It smelled faintly of strawberries and sparkled with tiny bubbles. Odd for a red wine. "To be honest, I eat pretty much anything put in front of me. You should ask Antonio. He'd be able to list off a ton of delicious things, I bet."

"Ahh, but the instruction was to make your favorite." Henri leaned forward on the island and said in a mock-whisper, "I was told burgers and fries were popular in the United States."

"Very true." I laughed, almost spilling the wine I was pouring. "And French fries are French, like you, so clearly that's your specialty."

Johann arrived next to me with the ingredients he'd been asked to retrieve. "And perhaps some bratwurst?"

I handed the glasses to each man. "Here's to—wait. Can you drink while on duty, Johann?"

"I'm off today." He raised his glass. "To international cuisine."

Off duty, but escorting me around the villa since we got back? "Why isn't someone else watching me?"

"Antonio asked me to stay with you until he's done with Giovanni." He took a sip of his wine and shrugged. "Plus, it lets me avoid Leonardo roping me into some other less interesting task. I have a feeling we're going to be locking down soon."

Henri paused mid-reach for the cheese. His gaze cast across the kitchen, then settled on Johann. "Locking down?"

Johann put down his glass. "I shouldn't be talking about this."

"But...?" I prompted.

He shook his head. "There's a lot going on right now."

Henri turned from the island and busied himself with something on the far counter. "Do you think we could go into Cittavera later today?"

"Leonardo's shaken over the incident in town," said Johann, rounding the island to see what Henri was doing. "Tomorrow might be better."

Henri grunted in ascent. The lockdown concept didn't seem to sit well with him. He looked up at the corner of the room. To one of the security cameras. "I'll need to get more supplies."

"They're being delivered," whispered Johann, whose back was to me. "Tonight."

"Groceries being delivered?" I asked.

Henri paused, his back stiffening. I wasn't supposed to hear that. What were they talking about if it wasn't groceries or kitchen supplies? Stolen artwork? It made sense that Johann would know about something like that, but why would he tell the chef?

The hairs on my neck prickled. Could Antonio have been right when he was throwing names around? Was Henri—or both of them—with the TPC? No, they were French and German. Interpol, maybe, but not Carabinieri.

Although that could have been why Elliot seemed surprised when I told him I went to school with his man inside.

Could they be informants?

Or wait—Johann had a sick sister. Needed money. Could he be a spy for a competitor who used that as leverage?

Johann turned to smile at me. "I ordered some special bottles of wine as a thank you to Henri. The delivery company said they'd be coming today."

Wine? If that was all it was, why the whisper?

The bodyguard returned to my side and leaned closer to keep his voice low. "Leonardo complains about French wine all the time, but you should hear him rage over American wine."

Henri, still facing away from me, said, "Johann has an exceptional palate and tastes similar to mine."

I took a sip of my wine, the strawberry scent mingling with a hint of chocolate. It was delicious. I raised the glass toward the camera but directed my words to Henri. "There are a lot of cameras here."

Johann chuckled. "Keeps us safe."

"And honest." Henri turned from where he'd been cutting slices of bread. "It's no different from working in any big kitchen. You either have cameras or an executive chef breathing down your neck. I'd choose the cameras any day. They don't think they know your job better than you do."

"How did you wind up here?"

Henri knelt behind the island, rummaging for something.

"He was working at the bakery in Cittavera." Johann pulled out the stool next to me and sat. "When the old chef..."

"Left." Henri stood suddenly with a kitchen torch in his hand, his expression serious. "When the old chef left."

What did that mean?

"Bella!" Antonio appeared in the doorway, a broad smile on his face that caused my heart to flutter. His hand flew dramatically to his chest as he approached me. "You're having wine without me?"

"What else am I supposed to do when you go off to the game room with the boys?" Just having him nearby eased the knot in my stomach that I'd barely noticed forming. There were so many secrets in this building, it was nauseating.

He pressed his lips to my cheek, holding them there long enough I got a hit of his cologne, which went very well with the wine. "Henri, I understand you're crafting something special for dinner?"

"Trying to," Henri said.

"I'm not very helpful." I pointed to the lamb on the island. "That's as far as we got, and it was Johann's recommendation, anyway."

Antonio shook his head and crossed to the refrigerator. "She'd live on microwave meals, if she could."

"And takeout," I added with a grin, turning to watch him rummage.

He closed the refrigerator and gestured to a short, narrow door next to it. "Do you keep the root cellar stocked?"

"I do."

"Carrots? Maybe go with a Middle-Eastern flair? Harissa and honey-roasted carrots? Or some roasted onions? Rosemary potatoes?"

Henri joined Antonio and opened the door, a cool draft seeping through it. "I'll see what we have. What about roasted sweet potatoes? Maybe with a pistachio and chili pesto?"

Johann nudged me. "Are any of these your favorites?"

Antonio and Henri descended a set of stairs behind the door, randomly naming various ingredients and foods.

"I don't know, but they all sound good." I took a gulp of my wine and stood, looking down the staircase, so steep it was practically a ladder.

"Want to see?" Johann joined me. "It's original to the monastery."

"Really?"

"Same as the wine cellar at the base of the tower." Johann rounded the island and picked up where Henri had left off with the crostini while I returned to my seat. "That's a real highlight."

"I'll have to find someone who's allowed to take me down there."

"Antonio probably knows the way, but Henri knows the inventory." Johann grinned. "He hides things down there sometimes."

I paused, wine glass almost to my mouth. Hides things?

"Like the wine I was talking about. The last time Leonardo found a bottle, he..." Johann cut off, eyes flicking to the side where the camera was, but not up. He waved a clove of garlic he'd been rubbing across the bread. "Never mind."

He paused mid-sentence a lot for someone who claimed he didn't mind having cameras on him.

Henri's voice grew louder and I turned to see him and Antonio climbing from the root cellar. "We've decided and you'll love it."

"But is it my favorite?"

"Trust me?" Antonio gave me a wink and a sly smile.

"When it comes to food? Yes."

He laughed and came closer, kissing my forehead. "I was thinking—after your snack, do you want to see the ruins? You said your trip yesterday was overwhelming, so perhaps we can take our time?"

Yes! Vincenzo's warning last night and Leo's harsh reaction to the car accident meant the odds Antonio and I would sleep together tonight were low. Going to the cave would give me a chance to tell him about Elliot and the camera. And he could tell me what happened in his secret meeting.

CHAPTER 26

ANTONIO

Samantha and I strolled along the walkway toward the cave, through the ruins of the ancient merchant's villa. Hand in hand, sun shining above, cool but not cold.

She'd told me that Vincenzo only revealed his truth once they were in the cave and he'd turned off the camera. If he wouldn't tell her anything out here, then there must have been more devices to capture movements or conversations. Security had grown so much tighter over the years.

When I lived in Roma, they had cameras, but only watching the outside, not the inside. Was it Leonardo's paranoia or related to the changes Giovanni spoke of? Was he now more afraid of spies than direct assaults?

"I'm sorry, bella." I pulled her hand to my lips.

"For what?"

"Being distracted. So many people around." I let go of her hand and walked ahead of her, down the narrow walkway, into the cave. "And not enough us time."

She patted my back. "This reminds me of our first hike together."

"Good view back there?" I said over my shoulder, recalling one of my early flirtations with her.

"Almost as good as that day." She swatted my bottom. "I liked watching your legs."

"And kept that fact to yourself?" I paused as we reached the entryway to the cave and the carved path opened wide enough for three abreast. "Have you thought more about Matt's job offer?"

She grimaced and shook her head. "A permanent position's awfully..."

"Permanent?"

"I like the statues. Especially this one." She halted in front of the Venus statue, reaching around Venus's head and pointing upward. The sudden change in subject was either her avoiding the question—which wouldn't surprise me—or a hint that the device to disable the camera was hidden here.

"You know Venus is the goddess of love, sì?" I turned her to face me, pressing her against the wall. If we were going to have a moment without anyone watching, it would be best to convince them we didn't know there was a camera there. I ran my good hand down her side, resting it against her hip, sliding around to her ass.

"Stop," she whispered with a chuckle. "It's against the rules."

"I've missed you so much." My nose traced from her temple to her ear. "Not being able to sleep next to you is a sin."

She tapped my chest and I pulled back only enough to see her face. *Stay there*, she mouthed and turned to plant a foot inside the alcove. She lifted up, fished around above Venus's head, and hopped down. "Done. You're not going to believe what—"

"Hold on." I pulled her against me. "Not even a little bit of fooling around?"

She frowned. "Vincenzo says we've got less than ten minutes. And I'm betting Leo won't wait that long, given the whole car fiasco."

I held her tight. "We can talk while I caress your ass."

"Antonio!" She smacked my chest playfully, but didn't move away—that was something, at least.

Shifting into a more serious mode, I gave her a summary of the conversation I'd had with Giovanni, Cristian, and Leonardo. "The head of security when I was here before was nowhere near as paranoid as Leonardo. But based on Vincenzo's presence, it's justified."

"How much danger do you think we're in just staying here?"

"Honestly?" I ran my fingers absently up and down her back, staring into her stunning blue-green eyes that were muted inside the cave. "I don't think we are, so long as we follow the rules. The security system is over-the-top, but it keeps the place safe."

"And we're still staying for whatever your surprise is tomorrow?"

"I think so. Maybe we can sneak you into my room again tonight?" I nipped at her bottom lip. "That was fun."

"Not dangerous?"

"The only danger is that they move our rooms." I shot a look heavenward. "Come now. What did Elliot have to say?"

She flagged away from me, far enough for one of her hands to scrub across her face. This would be bad. "He wants a photo of *The Magdalen*. Gave me a spy camera kinda thing to take it."

I froze. This was exactly what I'd told her not to do.

"I know." Her hand shifted to my cheek. "I have a necklace it can attach to, so I could—"

"No." I snatched her hand from my face. "That *is* dangerous. Not the moving rooms kind of danger. Injury and death danger. I'm serious, Samantha."

She pulled away from me. "You encourage me to follow my passion, my true path. That's working with the FBI, either as an agent or a contractor or whatever the hell this is. You can't tell me to go forward with it and then balk at the first sign of danger."

"First sign?" I spluttered, throwing my good hand into the air. "How many times were you and I nearly killed over the last two weeks?"

"They're just looking for information, not to arrest—"

"Marone, this has nothing to do with what's going to happen to my uncle. This is about you!" I dragged my hand through my hair, the muscles clenching in my bad arm so much I winced. "I told you no snooping."

Her eyes narrowed and she jabbed a finger into my chest. "And I told you questions are what I do."

This debate was getting me exactly where it always got me—nowhere. I closed my eyes and stretched my arm in its sling. She was right, but so was I. "Nathan Miller said you were reckless."

She wrinkled her nose. "What does that have to do with this?"

"He thinks you would have gotten yourself killed in the FBI because you take foolish risks. That's what you're doing now."

Her shoulders drooped, mouth falling open. This truth hurt her, but was it because Miller said it or because he'd said to me?

"We're running out of time, bella." I pulled her closer, so her face rested against my neck and I didn't have to see the pain in her eyes. That look was my fault. How was I supposed to protect her and support her at the same time, when she continued doing things that made me choose? "Give it to me. I'll take the pictures."

"No." She wrapped her arms around me, holding tight. "What are we going to do if I go to work for Elliot? Hand every case file over to you?"

"Then work for Matt. Or give the camera to Vincenzo."

"He doesn't have the same access I do." She touched her lips to my neck. "Antonio, this isn't foolish—it's my ticket. If I get this done, maybe this is enough for Elliot to get me a contract position that lets me work from Brenton. If you or Vincenzo do it, that buys me nothing."

For her to stay in Brenton and become my chosen family, I had to stand by and watch her risk her life to betray my blood family. "I hate this."

"You don't have to like it." She pulled back, taking my face in both her hands. "You just have to accept it. You can't say you love me while still rejecting this part of me."

"I know." A lump rose into my throat. Everything she was saying was true, but I *did* hate it. "How do people do this every day?"

She shrugged. "You used to do something like this every day when you worked here, didn't you?"

The lump grew. Again, she was right. I'd seen so much violence when I was here, but it never mattered like it did with her.

It hadn't occurred to me how my Zia Giulia dealt with Giovanni's lifestyle. Cristian was part of it, but she was a bystander.

That was likely why she was in Paris.

"How much time to do we have left?"

She looked down at her watch. "We're late. They're probably already on their way."

"No time for a quickie?"

"I love you," she said through a suppressed chuckle. "But quick is not your specialty."

"The only way to get better at something is to practice, you know." I waggled my eyebrows, doing my best to appear like I was alright with all of this, but I couldn't manage a full smirk. "I seem to recall being rather quick in a dance club bathroom once."

She shook her head and left my side, planting her foot into the alcove and pointing to the ground next to it. "There's a blind spot where we were standing. It'll be most convincing if we're still making out when the camera comes back on."

I resumed my position. "Sounds like a perfect excuse."

"Do you really need one?" She looked down at me, a softness in her eyes. There was a moment of staring and blinking, of not sharing her true feelings. She was no longer holding back *I love you*, so what was it now?

Once she was done, I helped her slide soundlessly into my arms. "I love you, bella."

"I know." Her fingers threaded into the hair at the nape of my neck, and she pulled my mouth to hers. Our lips parted together, tongues sweeping across each other. She moaned in the kiss, her other hand wrapping around my waist, running over my ass to pull me closer.

My cock hardened and the prospect of a quickie became more of a priority.

She smiled in the kiss, one of her hands dragging down the front of my pants. "When you say quick—"

"Hey!" said a man, surprisingly close.

We startled and I jumped back from her, both of us snapping our heads to see one of the guards I didn't recognize, standing at the mouth of the cave.

I gestured to him, then to Samantha, giving him a clear *You're interrupting* look.

"The—there's a camera—a security—" he stammered.

"Camera?" I shot back, as though I didn't know there was one in the cave.

He nodded and pointed above our heads. "We had to be sure nothing was going on."

"Well, nothing's going on now, is it?" I took Samantha's hand in mine, hauling her past the guard and out of the cave, completing our ruse. "It's only another day, bella. Then we'll have some privacy."

CHAPTER 27

SAMANTHA

Dinner that night was amazing. Between Antonio and Henri, they'd drawn up a menu that fused Mediterranean and Middle Eastern perfectly. My belly was full and happy.

Henri arrived at the table side with his rolling cart laden with small desserts. Individual servings of opera cakes, tiramisu, stuffed dates, and baklava.

"How did you make all this in one day, Henri?" I asked.

He cleared our dinner plates and placed the dessert trays on the table. "Trade secret."

"Did Johann help?"

"Not such a secret, I suppose." Henri finished clearing the plates with a grin. "He wasn't my only sous-chef today."

Cesca pointed to a couple of the trays. "I stuffed the dates and put together the tiramisu."

Antonio nodded appreciatively. "Then those are the first ones I'll try."

Before we could dig into our desserts, Giovanni stood with his wineglass. "Samantha, we're blessed to have you here. For all the time and effort I spend selecting the men to protect my family, apparently all I really needed was for Antonio to find a girlfriend."

Everyone laughed, but I bowed my head. If only Giovanni's pleasure extended to my sleeping arrangements. "I'm sure Cristian would have gotten out of the way if I hadn't distracted him. I was fixated on the view across the square and everyone thought I saw something."

Antonio patted my leg. We were finally sitting in the right seats at the dining table. I was to his left, next to Giovanni, so his good hand was on my side. The other remained in a sling.

Cesca lifted her glass with the small taste of wine in it. "I'm happy you're both here, too. And I'll have to get the details about what happened later. It sounds really scary."

I clasped Antonio's hand on my lap. He didn't want this part of his family to know about my FBI past or to have any inkling I might ever go back to pursuing art crimes. The easiest way to do that was to appear as weak as possible, and I'd undermined that by tackling Cristian. It would take work to reset their impressions. "It was, Cesca. I was shaking for hours afterward."

One positive had come out of the day's events: Leonardo was working. That meant he wasn't at the dining table and we didn't have to hear a constant barrage of insults and snark.

Giovanni took a swallow from his glass and sat, encouraging everyone else to enjoy the toast.

Henri paused on his way out. "I forgot something. We haven't shown Samantha the wine cellar yet. Johann said she might be interested?"

I put down my fork, a piece of opera cake still on it. "Yes, he was telling me it's from when the villa was a monastery?"

Henri nodded. "There are several casks with wine made from the vineyards here. One that should be ready to bottle. Perhaps you can help me taste it?"

Giovanni clapped Henri on the back. "Better than the colored water you like from France, isn't it?"

"Oui, monsieur, your wine is exceptional."

Antonio picked up my hand and gave it a light kiss. "Samantha was saying earlier that she'd also like to see the gallery again tonight. Is that possible, Zio? Perhaps before the wine cellar?"

Giovanni swallowed a mouthful of wine. "An excellent idea. There are several pieces she didn't get to see yesterday."

"And a movie after that, Papa?" asked Cesca.

Cristian laughed and nudged his little sister. "Not one of those ridiculous American romantic comedies, I hope?"

Cesca's lips clamped shut and she looked down. She did that a lot. This was a girl who wasn't used to getting the things she wanted. Unless it was also what these men wanted for her.

The thought curled my gut. "I really like romantic comedies."

Antonio chuckled. "It's true. Why do you think she's with me?"

A smile danced across Cesca's face, and both her father and brother laughed. What would happen to this poor girl when the FBI and TPC found sufficient proof of what was hiding inside these walls? It was going to destroy her, wasn't it?

I squeezed Antonio's hand, partially in thanks, partially because I needed the support. The fingers of my free hand gravitated to my necklace, but instead of the diamond, the pendant was a large, flat black disc that I'd packed for wearing with my work clothes, which all came with me when Antonio asked me out of the blue to join him.

Affixed to its back: Elliot's camera.

"Bella," said Antonio, releasing my hand and reaching for the pendant. "What's this? Where's the necklace I—"

Shit.

He cut off almost as quickly as the panic spread through me. I'd told him earlier I had a pendant I could attach the camera to, but he must have forgotten.

"Habit. I always wear this necklace with this blouse." It was a robin's egg blue dress shirt, one he loved.

"A habit we'll have to break you of, I think." He gave me a forced smile, which had a hint of *I'm sorry* in it.

I frowned at him and guided his hand to his fork. "About that movie?"

Giovanni said, "No, it's late, tesorina, and you have classes tomorrow."

She stuck out her bottom lip, but the decision was made.

Antonio's foot traveled to meet mine, his eyes still on me. "How about the gallery first, then I'll take you to the top of the tower to see the stars, then we can go down to the wine cellar?"

"That sounds perfect."

· · · ● ●· ● · · ·

Giovanni, Cristian, and I carried our wineglasses through the hallways of the estate until we arrived at the gallery doors. The men continued to tell jokes like they had through dinner while I sipped my wine slowly—ensuring my brain stayed sharp—laughing at the right times.

It was hard to reconcile Antonio with these men, except in moments like this. Antonio's laughter was more subdued, likely because he'd only had one tiny glass of wine. It didn't mix well with his medication, which was far more important.

Antonio walked next to his uncle and cousin, while Cesca and I pulled up the rear. She asked me a stream of questions about my job and places I'd visited. I'd had to remind myself several times that I was not a former FBI agent, rock climber, or adrenaline junkie.

Odds were good Leonardo was in his security command center monitoring everything I said and did.

We stopped in front of the giant wooden door and Giovanni switched his wine to his other hand to reach for the number pad.

Antonio said, "Why the separate security on the gallery door? It was not like that before."

The distraction was exactly what we needed. Giovanni turned his body toward Antonio as he punched in the numbers, letting his guard down. Antonio didn't look down to see the numbers, but given Giovanni's change in position, I was able to see his code.

I headed straight for *The Magdalen*, but Cesca pulled my arm to a painting on the wall next to the tall window, with its heavy cream curtains.

"I did this one a couple of months ago." She stopped in front of a canvas with half its background covered in iridescent blue, which was then crisscrossed with thick black brushstrokes, like she'd used a masonry trowel to apply it. "It's based on a French painter whose work I saw at a gallery last year."

The artist was Pierre Soulages. I recognized the bold style, evoking an almost prehistoric feel. Leonardo was already suspicious of me, so I held my tongue, in case he was watching—or Cristian and Giovanni were putting on an act.

The three men veered toward the Picasso I'd spotted yesterday. Antonio said something about not seeing it before, and his uncle began into a story about the auction he bought it at. At least that one was likely legal—although stolen pieces could find their way into auctions, like Antonio and I had caught last summer.

"Very nice. I love the shade of blue." I smiled at Cesca. "Very different from your work recreating *The Magdalen*?"

"It's easier in some ways, but harder in others. If I make a mistake with something like this one—" She pointed to her black and blue painting. "—it's done. Scraping off the layer of paint creates a big mess."

I swept my eyes around the paintings crowding the walls, up to the coffered ceilings, and lingered on the crystal chandelier at the center of the room. There were only the two cameras I'd noticed yesterday, angled to take in every square inch. No blind spots. This was going to be a challenge. I took a step toward my target, and Cesca walked with me.

"But if I get her eye wrong in a sketch..." We paused together in front of *The Magdalen*, and she sighed. "I can erase it and try again."

"Was Antonio able to help?" I tilted my head, holding my wine glass close to my face, and fiddled with my necklace. How could I turn over the pendant and tap the camera without Cesca or the security camera capturing it? One or the other would have been simple, but both?

"He was amazing!" She grabbed my arm that held my necklace, jostling it in her excitement.

My stomach clenched as I gripped the pendant during the unexpected movement. I'd tested the magnet on the back of it several times, and it held tight to the metal pendant. But the shaking was a risk.

Antonio approached us. "Did I hear my name?"

"You should see how much progress I made after your lesson yesterday!" Cesca grabbed him next. "I wish you were staying longer."

Wineglass blocking my necklace from the security camera. Check. Antonio absorbing Cesca's attention. Check. Giovanni and Cristian discussing another piece. Check.

My heart crashed against my ribs, a subtle tremor running through my hand with the wineglass. It was time.

I flipped the necklace over and double-tapped the camera several times, then rotated to capture more of the gallery. I'd tested it in my room, finding the spot that triggered the shutter. Hopefully, that meant pictures were being taken. It was soundless and no lights flashed, so all I had was hope and a dozen attempts.

A grunt came from behind me, accompanied by a sound like squeaking wheels. I returned my pendant to its normal position, relief washing over me, and spun to see two men in head-to-toe shades of beige, navigating a dolly with three wooden crates on it. One pulled, while the other half-pushed, half-held up the crates.

Were these the ones Vincenzo was looking for? Did one of them hold the key to the TPC's investigation? And if so, did Elliot need the photos I'd taken anymore? Was I taking on a huge risk for something unnecessary?

My stomach clenched. Or it could have been the delivery Johann was telling Henri about. Maybe he'd lied to me about smuggling in foreign wine? Or maybe he timed that delivery to arrive with this one as a cover?

"What's this now?" snapped Giovanni, striding over to them. "The delivery was supposed to be Saturday."

A bodyguard trailed behind the delivery men, holding a sheet of paper. "Sorry, signore, but Leonardo said you were waiting for—"

"Saturday!" Giovanni ripped the paper from his guard and thrust it toward Cristian. His sudden rage left me speechless, showing a hint of the man Antonio often described, which I hadn't seen yet. "Deal with this."

Cristian unfolded the sheet, scanned it, and approached the delivery men.

"Perhaps we should move the tour to its next stage?" Giovanni came to my side, gesturing toward the door, making it clear his question was an order.

Antonio and Cesca nodded, and I moved behind them to leave.

"Wow!" The delivery man responsible for holding the crates on the dolly took off his cap and wiped a sleeve across his brow. He scanned the walls and ceiling. "It's like a museum in here."

One of the crates began to tip. The man pulling the dolly swore under his breath and rushed around to catch it before it fell, and he knocked into me.

My wine glass crashed to the marble floor, shattering and spilling what little was left—thankfully missing the rugs. "Oh my god, I'm sorry!" I knelt to pick up the shards, but Giovanni gripped me by the elbow before I got to the floor.

"I'll have one of the maids clean it up." He gave me a tight smile, as though he were the one apologizing for the interruption. "Go see the stars and the wine cellar. We still have tomorrow morning if there's anything else you want to see."

CHAPTER 28

SAMANTHA

"There!" I jabbed a finger against the window, toward the third shooting star I'd seen. "Did you see that one?"

"I missed it." Antonio stood behind me, arms wrapped around my waist, head on my shoulder. "I was too distracted by my own my guiding star."

The view from the top of the tower was breathtaking. Seven stories up, the room provided an unobstructed 360-degree panorama of the sky, the sea, of Cittavera, and the countryside for miles. The peaked ceiling was low at the edges, with wide, short windows surrounding us.

In that moment, it was easy to forget where we were. No stolen paintings, no smugglers, no sneaking around, risking my life. Just me and the man I loved watching the stars track across the clear night.

"You're a cheeseball."

"But you love it." He tightened his grip with his good arm.

"Sometimes," I chuckled.

"Wait until the sun comes up," he whispered. "This was my peaceful place. I used to spend hours up here, sketching."

"When the tower was built, was there a room here? Or was it open?"

"Originally, there were two more stories and the top floor was open. The roof was added a century or so ago, long after the earthquake that knocked off the top stories. The people in town say the windows were added fifty or sixty years ago."

I rubbed my hands over his arms, let my eyes flutter closed as I inhaled deeply. Vanilla combined with amber from him, plus damp stone from the tower.

His left hand rose, caressing his knuckles up my belly between my breasts to stroke my necklace. "Did it work?"

I'd spied one security camera in the top far corner of this room when we entered, one of the low-profile dome style that were harder to spot. We couldn't speak openly, but Antonio's meaning was obvious to me. "No idea. I hope so."

He lifted the pendant and made a quiet noise of question.

My gaze fell to the flat disc, to the rear of what he was inspecting. I sucked in a quick breath. "Fuck."

Elliot's camera wasn't there.

His right arm tensed around my waist and he let out a low groan, easing his arm back.

Panic splintered like ice in my veins. "It's missing."

Neither of us budged. But both of our bodies had gone rigid.

He tucked his mouth close to my ear to whisper. "Are you sure?"

I turned slowly in his grasp and kissed him. My lips traveled along his jaw to his ear, and I combed my fingers into his hair. They settled right behind his ear to mask that I was talking to him. "It was definitely there when we were in the gallery. We need to find it."

"There you are."

Antonio and I both jumped, spinning to see Henri at the top of the stairs, smiling at us.

"Giovanni suggested this would be a perfect time to show you the wine cellar."

Antonio backed away from me, supporting his bad arm with his good. The muscle clicking in his jaw was no doubt a combination of pain from the arm and worry about the tiny camera. "That sounds wonderful. I need to head back to my room first, though. I threw the sling in there on our way upstairs and I'm paying for it."

Henri nodded. "I'll take Samantha down and you can meet us there."

No, I had to find the camera. Unless that was Antonio's plan? No one would question him retracing our steps the way they'd question me. I had to let him take care of this. I gave him a peck on the cheek. "Take your time. I expect this won't be a quick tour of the wine cellar? Is it huge?"

Antonio forced out a weak laugh. "That's an understatement. I'll see you down there, but it may take me a few minutes. I think I need to sit down."

I gripped his forearm. "Do you need help?"

"No need, bella." He pressed a kiss to my cheek and waved me off with Henri. "I've had worse."

His plan must have been to start with this room. How many security cameras would catch him searching through the estate?

How many people were manning those cameras? Were they always on? Did they rotate?

Losing Elliot's camera put us both in danger.

Being obvious about looking for it put us in even more.

CHAPTER 29

ANTONIO

I slid down the wall until I was sitting on the floor. Leaned forward, cradling my arm. It was sore, but this was mostly a show for the security camera, in case someone was watching me. Our story was that Samantha was off with Henri because my arm hurt too much for me to go with them without my sling, and I had to support that narrative.

Being closer to the floor also gave me a better angle to sweep my gaze across the room and look for Elliot's tiny camera.

My stomach twisted in knots at the prospect of them finding it. Marone, what if they found it and could link it back to her?

I could imagine the consequences.

Bringing her here had been a stupid enough choice, but letting her talk to Elliot? Letting her talk me into this investigation?

It's who she is, Tony. This is the woman you love. Reckless. Passionate. A heart which wouldn't let crimes go unpunished.

I leaned forward, clutching my arm. We'd looked out the windows in each direction, but I couldn't see anything that looked like a spy camera. It could have been on the stairs. It could have still been in the gallery.

Or anywhere in between.

I rolled to my left side and pushed myself up.

If she dropped it in here, the odds of someone finding it were low. People rarely came up here. The upper floor stairs? The guards used them more than anyone else. I should hurry over those spaces. Cursory glances only.

The higher risk areas would be the hallways between the tower at the end of the eastern hall and the gallery in the northern corner of the villa. Few people had full access to the gallery, so the odds of it being found there were low. Unless someone was in the room opening the crates.

The damn crates.

One of them must have been what Vincenzo was looking for. I didn't want him to be a TPC officer. I wanted it to be a lie. Didn't want him to have this thing in common with Samantha that meant so much to her. Didn't want him tied to her anymore.

I took the stairs slowly, keeping my eyes down. It had to look like I was still in pain while I passed by the security cameras. Where were all of them?

And what was in those crates? Surely whatever it was would be proof that my uncle was lying about everything. Some stolen or looted item he would smuggle out of the country.

I reached the fourth floor landing and snuck quickly into my room for the sling, throwing it on as I left. I continued—third floor, second floor.

Niente. I was not going so fast I would have missed it if it were there.

I swallowed hard, battling against the tension in my jaw. It was the only way to stop my teeth from chattering. *Per favore, don't let someone else find it.*

Halfway through the eastern hallway on the main floor, excited voices reached my ear.

None of them were Samantha, who was in the wine cellar with Henri, two floors below the entrance to the tower. He didn't seem as much of a threat as the others did. Only a chef, even though he moved like he fit in with the guards. After a year with Giovanni, that hardly surprised me.

When I'd moved in with Cristian in Roma, I was a joking and teasing young man, just shy of my twenty-second birthday. Within a couple of years, I was so much more. I had a different type of confidence about myself.

Samantha and I first met only two weeks before I moved. I tripped over my tongue, laughed nervously at the presentation she gave in class, and then she shot me down when I asked her out. I'd had a crush on her for months and my friends had harassed me about it incessantly.

But after everything I learned from Cristian, I never had a problem picking up a woman again.

Until, yet again, Samantha, who turned me down repeatedly until finally my sister lied to both of us and set us up on our first date.

Samantha was the only conquest in my life that mattered.

I followed the sound of voices toward the gallery.

Cristian's raised voice was the first one I could make out. "Leonardo will figure it out."

Figure what out?

An unfamiliar voice spoke next. "They're long gone."

One of the gallery doors was propped open, and when I entered, the sight halted my heart. Giovanni, Cristian, and two guards stood around the small round table at the center of the room. As always, a vase with a beautiful bouquet sat at its middle, nothing else to detract from the inlaid wood pattern on its top. But now?

Next to the vase sat a tiny black disc.

Elliot's camera.

"What's going on?" I asked slowly, trying not to betray the terror pulsing through my veins.

The men all turned to look at me.

Giovanni's nostrils flared and he bared his teeth. He picked up the tiny camera and shook it in his fist. "Betrayal!"

I stepped closer, approaching my uncle, despite every instinct telling me to turn around and escape. There would be no out-running this. Head-on it was. I tilted my head and pursed my lips. "I don't understand. What is it?"

"I'm sure it was them," Leo said from behind me.

Che cazzo, my breath caught in my throat. Was he accusing Samantha and me? I spun to face him and the other men did the same.

As Leo swiped a hand over his cheek, he said, "The crates arrive two days early, those fools have an accident, then this shows up. And they're nowhere to be found."

"Would someone tell me what's going on?" The throbbing in my head and my arm were almost too much to bear. My knees grew weak, and I placed a hand on the table.

I should have gone to Mario's.

Cristian wrapped an arm around my waist, like he was about to catch me. "Are you alright?"

No, I was not alright. Far from it. I ground out through clenched teeth, "My arm is killing me."

"Go lie down, my boy," said Zio Giovanni, placing the disc back on the table.

"It's just an arm." Leonardo huffed and shouldered past me to pick up the tiny camera. "When the cleaner came in after your girlfriend broke her wineglass—"

A shiver ran through me. That's when she dropped it.

"—they found this next to the crates. It looks like a small camera."

I swallowed hard, both from the truth and the pain. "The crates?"

Giovanni snatched it from Leonardo, curling his fist around it. "Let's go to the security control room. Check the videos and find out which of the delivery men brought it. Then we track him down."

Acid churned in my stomach. That video would surely show Samantha taking photos and dropping the camera. I had to do something. But what?

CHAPTER 30

SAMANTHA

Two floors below the main level of the tower, Henri held the thick oak door with its iron bands open for me, granting access first to a wide stone staircase. As we stepped through, he flipped on a light, illuminating a wine cellar that looked a great deal like the cave below us.

Rough-hewn arched ceiling, wooden casks lining one wall, and terracotta coves for bottles along the other. My hand glided along the cool metal railing, descending into the most stunning wine cellar I'd seen in my life.

Henri walked two steps behind me. "The casks in this room are all from Signore Ferraro's vineyard."

"This room?" The floor was smooth stone, a layer of sand dusted across it to absorb moisture.

Once Henri was off the stairs, he came next to me, pointing down the long, narrow room. "It takes a turn at the end to a tasting room with table, chairs, and more wine."

Unseen lamps lit the casks from behind, casting an eerie glow, while wall sconces flickered with electric lights. "Just imagine—this place is old enough that those sconces would have been torches once upon a time."

"You can almost feel the history, can't you?" He walked next to me, gesturing toward the end. "I'll get the wine thief once Antonio gets here for a barrel sample, but there's another a bottle I want to pull for you to taste. You can keep going and I'll be there in a few minutes."

I cast a glance over my shoulder. How long would Antonio be? Was his arm really bothering him that much? Had he found Elliot's camera? My gaze flew around the room, attempting to appreciate the moment and calm my raging heart. I maintained a look of awe and wonder, while pinpointing a single bullet camera, trained on the door. Antonio had warned me the place had eyes, but I'd never expected so many. "Should we wait for Antonio?"

"No need, he knows where we are."

I nodded, something not sitting right with me. It wasn't Henri. It was this space. There was a scent in the air that was off.

A good wine cellar had no smells in it, other than those you wanted to seep into the wine. I'd worked a few insurance claims for sommeliers in restaurants and estates, but nothing this grand.

"Does it always smell like this?"

Henri paused in front of a row of bottles and raised his nose, inhaling deeply. "Wet stone. Red fruit. Cranberries. Cork. A hint of salt."

All those scents were there, but there was something else. I sniffed. Quick bursts. Something musty. Or it was frayed nerves. "I must be imagining things. You nailed everything."

He smiled and returned focus to the rows of stacked bottles. How did anyone find anything down here?

"I'm going to head further back."

Henri inched a bottle out, turning it slowly to see the label. "I'll be right there once I find my bottle. Johann may have moved it as a joke."

At the bend in the cellar, an arch of flat red bricks formed the transition into the next room. More casks, more bottles, but instead of being long and narrow, the room widened into a circle. At the center, a ten-foot round table with six chairs around it.

Two barrels sat on their ends by the far wall, next to an ancient free-standing cupboard. Ornately carved wooden doors in the bottom and top hid unknown treasures, while a row of crystal bottles held liquids in all shades from clear to amber to dark brown.

Prickles skittered up and down my spine. Something wasn't right. I moved slowly, scanning the casks lined up in rows on their sides, looking around for more cameras—but there were none. Why no cameras back here?

"I think you'll like this one," said Henri behind me. "I snuck it in. It's French."

"This is an awful lot of wine."

He placed the bottle on the giant table. "They'll ship out half the casks for bottling and to be sold around the country."

A legitimate endeavor? Or cover? Send out fourteen casks full of wine and one full of antiquities?

"Could you get out three glasses?" Henri pointed to the upper doors of the cupboard. "Signore Ferraro is in negotiations with a company in America to distribute there."

I ran my fingers over the grape and vine carvings around the edges of the door, the shapes so worn I suspected they were easily a hundred years old. Dozens of wide-bodied glasses crammed the interior, next to glasses for scotch, martinis, shots, and white wine. I pulled out three red wine glasses and closed the door, but something on the floor caught my attention, half-hidden behind the two barrels on their ends.

A thick-soled boot.

A black-clad leg.

With shaking hands, I put the glasses down and inched closer.

A body.

A blond beard.

A wave of heat flashed through me. My brain clawed back to New Year's Eve and David Scott's body after Jimmy shot him.

I clamped a hand over my mouth and took an unsteady step backward, running into something solid. Strong hands gripped my upper arms.

A high-pitched whirring sounded in my ears, drowning out the man's words.

I spun to face him, connecting the heel of my palm with his chest. Jimmy stumbled back. I wouldn't let him—

Fuck.

It was Henri, drawn into a defensive posture, one hand up to catch another strike, the other rubbing at the spot I'd hit. "Are you alright?"

I'd just punched him, and he was asking if I was alright? My knees were weak and my stomach roiled. "It's Johann."

Henri's outstretched hand pointed to the nearest chair. "Samantha, sit down."

The weight of the moment crashed down on me. Foreign country. Surrounded by criminals. And a chef, who'd been Johann's friend.

Two weeks ago, I would have handled this like a job. Like I'd been trained to handle it. Jimmy ruined so much more than his marriage, our town, and David and Olivia's lives.

He'd ruined me.

And I wasn't about to stand for that anymore. All I had to do was push forward. This was a crime and Henri didn't need to deal with it.

I rushed back to the body and told Henri, "Go call security. Get someone down here."

He came with me, calmer than I would have expected. "What should we tell them?"

We tipped the nearest barrel and rolled it out of the way, fully revealing Johann's body, slumped against the wall, his head at an awkward angle.

"Exactly what happened." I knelt and felt for a pulse. Nothing. "You brought me down here and we found him."

"We shouldn't touch the body. It might con—"

I craned my neck to look at him, standing there with his clenched fists. What was he going to say before he cut off? Contaminate the scene? Be something contagious? Confuse me? I cocked an eyebrow, but he turned on his heel.

"There's an intercom by the door. I can call the security desk."

"There aren't any cameras in this room, are there?" No cameras meant no evidence.

Henri paused, head dipping forward. "No, there aren't. I suspect Signore Ferraro holds meetings down here, so there's security monitoring the first room to watch comings and goings, but... but that's it."

"The perfect place to kill someone."

He turned his head to the side, showing his profile, but not looking back at me. "There are too many of those places here."

As Henri disappeared around the corner, I did a cursory review of the body without disturbing it. No obvious scratch marks, visible puncture wounds, or tears in his clothing. The angle of his neck wouldn't have been comfortable for a live person, but it didn't appear broken. His eyes and mouth were closed, as were his hands.

I scanned the length of his legs, one curled up, the other twisted to the side. Not broken, but—

A flash of white caught my attention, underneath one of his shoes. I got down on my hands and knees to get a closer look in the dim light, which I was mostly blocking out. I reached for it, fingers wrapping around a scrap of paper and I pulled it out.

One inch by two, with words written on it.

Delivery complete. Pickup requested tomorrow.

Was this Johann's? Tied to the delivery he and Henri were discussing in the kitchen? Were they spies? If it was even a possibility, I couldn't let Henri know I'd found it. And I couldn't stay down here alone with him.

I shoved it into my pocket and gave Johann's body one last glance before following Henri to the exit.

Chapter 31

Antonio

The wall of screens showed every corner of the estate—except inside the bedrooms, just as Cristian had promised me on our first night. Some remained constant, others flipped between cameras. Two men worked the desk, a dramatic change from my days when there were half as many cameras and twice as many men working for Zio Giovanni.

Leonardo pointed to a screen. "That one. Bring it to the center and back it up an hour. Find the timestamp where the crates arrived. I want to see him plant the device."

The camera was tiny and, if we were lucky, it would be too small to make out. If it was clear, what could I do? My heart thundered in my chest. I'd warned her but given in to her excitement and went along with the scheme.

"Now scan forward," said Leo.

The video showed the group of us in the gallery, Samantha carrying her wineglass as she and Cesca moved through the room. She had one arm folded up to hold the glass, the other playing with her necklace. The video fast-forwarded, went past the crate delivery and we watched everyone head out.

"Back it up to before the crates arrived," said Leo.

I could delay this search, but Leo wouldn't give it up forever. I could declare we were leaving at that second, but it would be too suspicious. If they discovered she'd been taking photographs, was it best to tell them she was FBI? Cristian had asked if she was with the authorities over and over, so they might believe it. We could contact Elliot and have him whisk her away.

Not just her—both of us. If they knew I'd been part of the plan, my presumption of safety might be incorrect.

Surely they wouldn't kill an FBI agent.

Marone, hopefully they wouldn't hurt her.

Cristian said, "Stop there."

The two men arrived through the doors of the gallery, and the dance began. My eyes stayed on Samantha. Her back to the camera, nearing the men with the crate while Giovanni railed against them for their arrival. He gestured for everyone to leave, and she began walking toward the exit.

Rapid movement on one display competed for my attention, but I kept my eyes on Samantha's movements.

"I need help in the wine cellar!" came a voice over an intercom. It was Henri.

I slammed a hand down on the controls for the main display to pause the video and hit a button to open communication with the wine cellar. "Is Samantha alright?"

"She's safe," said Henri.

Safe? What did that mean?

The operator switched primary displays so we could all see Henri. I wavered toward the door, my first instinct to run to her rescue. But I couldn't leave the video review in case they continued.

"It's Johann. He's dead."

Leonardo barely glanced at Cristian, and the two sped out, along with one of the men who'd been at the desk. The other calmly worked the computer system in front of him, sending out a priority message to the entire team.

"Lockdown initiated, signore," he said.

"Lockdown?" I said, dragging my hand through my hair. "What's going on, Zio?"

"Send a message to Cesca," said Giovanni, ignoring my question. "Tell her to get to her room and lock the door."

"Zio!" I said, clamping a hand on his arm. "Samantha was in the wine cellar with Henri."

My uncle nodded. "Send a message to Vincenzo. Have him escort Samantha to her room and stand guard at her door. No one in or out."

"Vincenzo again," I spat. "She should have been with me in Napoli all along. Coming here was a mistake."

Gio's lip curled. "Pick your battles wisely, boy."

"Are you threatening me now?" I growled, the first time I'd ever raised my voice to Giovanni. "Go ahead. Prove that all your words have been empty. Prove to me you've not changed an ounce."

"I'm under attack and you make this about you."

"No, Gio, it's about you, like it always is." About his need for power and control. His need to own and consume. "*You're* not the one who's dead. Johann is."

"Get out." He smacked the chair in front of him, and the man launched from his seat, making a hasty escape. Once the guard was out of the room, Giovanni sank into the chair, his hands easing over the control board. He swapped videos and resumed play on the gallery display. "It *is* about you, Antonio. You, your father, and the rest of the family."

On a video to the side, Leo, Cristian, and two other men charged into the wine cellar. They burst past Henri, running the length of the room.

"Samantha and I are—"

"Not leaving." He hit a button to pause the main video of the gallery and pointed to a spot on the floor at Samantha's feet.

I froze, the excuses dying on my tongue. It was the camera, near the shards of her wineglass, plain as day.

"You're a terrible liar, Antonio." He swiveled in the chair, looking at me with impassive eyes. "How the others all missed this on fast-forward, I'll never know."

"It wasn't her—"

He raised a hand to cut me off. "Don't insult me with your pathetic excuses. Leonardo was right about her all along."

Some combination of keys or buttons would delete that video, then there'd be no proof. No one would come after her. But Giovanni had this information to hold over us, and his word was the only one which mattered here.

He stood slowly, raising himself to his full height, tilting his head back. Still shorter than me, but his spirit took up all the air in the room. "Do you know what happens to people who betray me?"

"What's it to be, then?" My stomach churned, anger battling with terror. If he'd known the camera was ours, why play this game? "You hand us over to Leo? Torture us? Have us beaten?"

"You were once part of my family. I trusted you with my life." He stepped closer, but I gave no ground.

"I took a bullet for you, Zio." Years of rage bubbled up, pouring over the edge. "And you had nothing to say about it. No regrets, no apologies, no kind words. Nothing."

"How could I?" he shot back. "That Napolitano stole you from me."

"That Napolitano *saved* me from you." Moving to Napoli with Mario after that event was one of the luckiest things that ever happened to me.

"He's not here this time, is he?"

A man's voice came over the intercom. "I have Samantha."

"Vincenzo, where are you taking me?" she asked, voice quavering.

I looked to the screen before they vanished then reappeared on another display as they made their way to the stairs. "If you hurt her, I swear, you will never see the rest of your family again."

Giovanni's cheeks pinched and the vein in his forehead pulsed, a sign his rage simmered just below the surface.

I tensed my muscles and braced my jaw, preparing for a blow. But I wouldn't back down. Samantha's life depended on it. I glared at him, displaying as much strength and confidence as I could muster. That was my woman and I'd give my dying breath to protect her.

One of his hands balled into a fist, but instead of backhanding me, he slammed it down on the desk. He paused for a moment, head hanging over the keyboard, then hit several keys.

Delete file? the display read. And he hit *Accept*.

My breath caught.

"Tell me who she's spying for."

"She's not." I continued clenching my muscles to fend off the tremble. What was going on? "I'll be sure nothing like this happens again."

Giovanni nodded. "Leo's convinced the men who delivered the crate were responsible, so he can continue believing that."

His breaths were deep, a similar war no doubt waging inside of him to the one inside me. "You say I concede nothing. Take this as my show of good faith. I'll keep your secret, but in return, you stay and accept the gift coming tomorrow."

"Fine." I should have dropped to my knees in thanks, but instead, I pressed my luck in case he changed his mind and decided to take Samantha in the middle of the night. "Samantha's staying with me tonight."

He navigated the security displays showing Samantha and Vincenzo arriving at her room. Her shoulders caved in and tears streaked her face. She spoke frantically with him, but no sound came through from the secondary displays.

This was not my Samantha. Before New Year's, she would have faced this threat, but that night had scarred her. She'd refused to see a therapist or grief counselor for more than five minutes. Told me she was fine.

But this scene told a different story. I gestured to the screen. "She's no threat."

"Or she's simply a better liar than you." He straightened, turning to look at me. The vein in his forehead had calmed, but his nostrils remained flared. "My dream was clear, St. Peter said—"

"That *you* had to change because of what you've done in your life." This was a hole I shouldn't have dug, but if he was so desperate to have me there, I'd take what I needed. "His decision had nothing to do with me, my girlfriend, or our relationship. I need to be sure she's safe."

"It's my house and there are plenty of guards to protect her."

"One of your men is dead, Zio! That means either one of your employees is responsible or someone snuck into the estate. If she's not safe here, we're leaving." I turned to go, but he grabbed my arm.

"I'll allow her to stay with you." His eyes glinted in the light of the displays. "But only so you can keep a closer eye on her. If I get any hint she's working for the authorities—"

"You won't."

Chapter 32

Samantha

I stared out the terrace door, into the dark night, then spun and walked to the front door of my room. Back and forth, over and over. Leonardo had arrived in the wine cellar first, hurling every accusation at me. I was behind this. I was party to a conspiracy. I'd killed Johann myself.

But his rage made it clear they either hadn't found the camera, or they had and couldn't link it to me. So I did the only thing I could think of: I played the helpless victim, crying and asking for Antonio.

He had to return eventually. The men wouldn't say anything about him, instead having Vincenzo whisk me away. Then he confined me to my room like the prisoner I was.

I should have gone to Mario's.

But would Elliot have asked Antonio about *The Magdalen*? If he had, what would Antonio have said? Would Giovanni have taken him to see the gallery? And would Antonio have even noticed it among all the other masterpieces stuffed in there?

I shoved open the terrace door, into a much warmer and more humid night than any of the others since we'd arrived.

Voices floated around me as guards rushed about the estate. My discovery in the wine cellar had thrown the place into chaos.

A dark blue sedan with red stripe and CARABINIERI emblazoned on the side drove up the driveway and vanished behind the corner of the tower, heading to the front door. Behind it, a van reading "Polizia Mortuaria."

They called the police for Johann's death? In some part of my brain, men like this never alerted the authorities of anything. It would risk too much attention to their business. Unless these men were on Giovanni's payroll?

Clear your head, Sam.

I spun back into my room, closing the terrace doors behind me.

We had a TPC undercover agent waiting for whatever was in those crates. An FBI agent asking for proof *The Magdalen* was in Giovanni's possession. One dead body.

Johann's death could have been natural. Maybe it was a heart attack and he simply fell behind the barrels. The barrels were light enough for a single person to move. If someone murdered him, the person responsible should have tucked the body further out of the way or hidden him better.

Then there was the matter of the note. Was it his? Did he drop it when he died? Or did it belong to someone else? Did he surprise someone? It could have been a coincidence, but genuine coincidences were rare, particularly when the death of a young, fit man was involved.

I should have handed the note over to Leo when he arrived, but I was too pissed off from how he treated me to say anything. And there was no telling Henri, given the possibility he was colluding with Johann on whatever delivery they'd been whispering about.

Did we have a killer in the estate? Was it a crime of passion? Did Johann uncover something?

I halted my pacing as I reached the door to the tower. Did he discover Vincenzo was with the TPC? If Johann confronted him, would Vincenzo have killed someone to protect his identity? Memories washed over me. Riding through Rome together on a scooter, throwing coins into the Trevi Fountain, touring the Vatican with him. There was no way Vincenzo was capable of that.

Was he?

It had been ten years since I last saw him. I'd changed in that time, and he would have, too. How much could all those years in undercover roles change a person?

Or could it be one of Giovanni's competitors? Former associates, as he liked to say? Did one of them have an agent inside? I'd suspected Johann was exactly that yesterday, but if he was, and Giovanni's men killed him for it, the estate wouldn't be in this kind of uproar. They'd be cheering that they outed a traitor.

Henri hadn't reacted the way a man with his background should. A man who'd been a chef all his life should have reacted... more like I initially had.

I had to get back down into the wine cellar and investigate this. Figure out the note. Look for more clues. I had to help.

Where was Antonio?

On my next circuit of the room, I heard him nearby. "Get out of my way."

A voice responded, "I can't let you—"

There was a sharp knock at my door, and I tore it open. It was Antonio, with a guard right beside him. Vincenzo was nowhere to be seen.

I flung my arms around him, biting on my tongue to produce some waterworks for the camera beyond them, in case anyone was watching.

He let out a low groan.

"Your arm," I said, breaking off from him, looking down at the arm across his stomach I'd crushed against. "I'm sorry. I was just so—did you hear about—oh my god—about Johann?"

"Get what you need for tonight." He jerked his chin toward my bathroom. "You're staying with me."

The guard behind him said, "I'm under strict—"

"The orders have changed. Talk to my uncle," he snapped. "Go, bella."

I nodded and hurried into my bathroom, grabbed a toothbrush, and returned to present it to him.

Antonio's brows furrowed, I gave him a slight shrug, and he stepped back to usher me toward his room. "You can pack the rest tomorrow."

The guard had moved to the far side of the floor. He spoke into a phone, flipping his free hand in a circle while he talked, appearing agitated.

"What's going on?" I whispered as we made our way the few steps to Antonio's room.

"Quiet, woman," he said, more loudly than needed. Apparently, I wasn't the only one playing to our audience.

CHAPTER 33

ANTONIO

The door clicked shut behind me and I spun Samantha to face me. "Are you alright?"

"Did they find the camera?" she whispered.

"You first." I ran my hand over her cheek and into her hair, tears still clinging to her lids. "You were so upset. Did Leo hurt you?"

"You saw that?"

"I was in the control room with Giovanni. The only thing I couldn't see was the room at the back of the wine cellar."

She took my hand and brought it to her lips. "I'm fine. I was a little shaken when I found Johann, but—"

"Only shaken?" I'd read so much more into her reaction than that.

"It was an act." She waved a dismissive hand, something she normally only did to tease, but then paused. "Okay, mostly an act. But I really don't want to talk about it. What about the camera?"

"Giovanni found it."

She sucked in a sharp breath and covered her mouth. "No idea it was mine?"

I grit my teeth, easing my bad hand forward until it rested against her hip. "He knows it was yours, but he destroyed the security video proving it."

"He what?"

"Che cazzo, bella. This whole night..." I kissed her salty cheek, wanting nothing more than to sink into her and never leave. So many ups and downs, panic, relief, and then more panic. And the overwhelming fear my uncle could change his mind about her at any second. "Tell me what happened."

She combed her fingers into my hair and pulled me closer. "Henri was pulling a bottle of wine while I went into the tasting room. After I grabbed some glasses from the cupboard, I saw Johann's body, half-hidden behind some barrels."

"Dead?"

"It was clean, whatever happened. Maybe natural causes, but the way his body was shoved against the wall... I don't know." Her eyes were clear and the tremble I'd expected was not there. "I looked around some before Leo and Cristian arrived."

Of course she *looked around*.

"And I found this." She pulled a scrap of paper from her pocket and placed it in my good hand. "It was underneath him, so it was either his or already lying there when he fell."

I read, "'Delivery complete. Pickup requested tomorrow.' What does this mean?"

She shook her head. "It might be related to his death, it might not. But I found his body after the crates were delivered to the gallery, so maybe that's the delivery."

"Vincenzo told you he was waiting for a crate delivery to get some painting out of here. You think it's his?"

"Maybe?" She stared at the paper, raking her teeth over her bottom lip. "Before you arrived in the kitchen this morning, Johann said something to Henri about a delivery coming tonight. He claimed they were talking about some American wine they were trying to hide from Leonardo, so it might be that, too."

I shoved the paper into my pocket. "Did you tell anyone about it?"

"If Henri was involved, I didn't want him to know I'd found it. And then Leo..." She shook her head. "He was so *Leo* when he arrived, I didn't tell him, either."

"He's always been his own worst enemy."

She drew in a deep breath, her shoulders and chest rising, and let it all out slowly. "I didn't get any time in private with Vin to find out if it was his."

"You kept it a secret because you were protecting him, didn't you?" I could have punched him in his pretty little face.

"I can't help it." Her head lowered to my shoulder. "I met Jimmy thirteen years ago, and I still can't process what he did. It's like the good times are frozen in my memory and I can't adjust. I see him in my dreams every night. I don't think I could handle another person from my past changing into something so evil."

"Don't you lose a second more sleep over that. It's not your fault, either directly or in some misguided universal sort of way. Jimmy chose his path. They were poor choices, stacking on top of each other, and he made all of them."

"I talked to Johann several times. For all my suspicions he might have been hiding things, he was a good man. Nice to me, played with the cats outside, worried about Cesca." She straightened, blinking, eyes scanning my face. For how close we'd become over our time together, and despite everything we'd survived in the last weeks, something still held her back. Hopefully, it was only pride, rather than any continued doubts about our relationship.

"Don't shut me out, amore. Keep talking through it."

She brushed a hand up my arm, over the bandage. Light fingers, betraying that she was thinking about seeing me fall that night. "For a moment, I saw David. Like it was New Year's all over again. I know I shouldn't, but I want to help them figure out what happened."

"You want to regain control?"

She nodded, her hand skimming up to my neck. "Tell me about Elliot's camera and Giovanni."

"I stood up to him."

Her brows furrowed. Lightness surged through my chest, a ridiculous excitement at the prospect of telling her what I did building inside me.

"You were right. He's always been the one in control of everything. Eight years ago, I told him I wouldn't work for him. But that was easy. It was over the phone." I bit my lip, taking in the gorgeous, strong creature in front of me. Many of my own doubts about us were deeply rooted in the sins of my past—about not being worthy of her because of them—and being here put me in full contact with those sins. "For the first time in my life, I stood toe-to-toe with him and didn't back down."

"You made him destroy it?" Her head cocked, a smile emerging. That we could have this moment after all the danger this evening was nothing short of a miracle.

"We were alone in the security control room after Henri called in. He showed me the video of Elliot's camera at your feet after you dropped your wine glass and he said destroying the video was proof that he wants to change."

"That's—" She shook her head slowly, as though unable to believe what I was saying. "—wow."

"Sì." I dragged my hand up her side and caressed the side of her breast. "I told him you were staying with me, even after he said no. Told him..."

Heat flared in her eyes, a look I'd only seen once before, in the VIP bathroom at the club in Napoli. A curious level of lust inspired by challenge. She'd once told me she was attracted to men with big personalities who took control of things, even though she was always battling for control herself.

Samantha would never admit it, but she needed a man who could take charge, but also respected when she did. This was the fine line it took to win her heart.

"I told him our relationship was not the cause of his misfortunes and I promised there would be no more spying."

She frowned, the heat diminished. "I told Elliot—"

"It was a threat, bella." My hand wound its way into her hair. "He destroyed the video footage under the condition that we stay for his surprise tomorrow. He still has one day with your secret hidden inside him. Don't even try to tell me Elliot would encourage you to press this now."

She stared up at me, blinking away at least fifteen different arguments.

"Samantha, I let myself get wrapped up in your adventure, but we need to put a stop to this one. Partners means sometimes I go along with you when I'm not sure, and sometimes you go along with me. This time is my turn to take the lead."

"Hear me out. What if we work with them to find out—"

"No." I stepped closer to her, nudging her back to the wall.

"No?"

"This is usually the moment I pull out some joke to snap you out of things, but not today." I leaned against her, pressing into her softness. "It's time you listen to me."

"Oh, really?" The corner of her lips twitched, and she took my hand out of her hair. Fluttering her eyelashes, she said, "You gonna make me?"

Nathan Miller had explained that she found control by throwing herself out of the very thing she was seeking—control. Jumping out of planes, climbing mountains, sleeping while suspended from a cliff face. Poking her nose around in my uncle's business. It must have been the adrenaline rush.

I intertwined our fingers and pinned her hand against the wall above her head. She needed a distraction. "I am."

"Good," she whispered. "Just be careful with that bad arm."

I shot my most potent feigned glower at her. "No discussion of my arm, woman."

"Woman?" One eyebrow cocked. "That's rather barbaric of you."

"I can do worse." I pulled her hand down and used it to push her toward the bed.

It caught her off guard, and she laughed as she stumbled across the room. "So you're a tough guy now."

"Shut up and take your pants off."

Her eyes flicked toward the door, but she closed them and took a slow breath. This was the *Calm down and enjoy the moment, Samantha* breath. I knew it well. She didn't want the guard to hear us, but we could be quiet. "Just my pants? Is that all I am to you?"

I planted my palm at the center of her chest and pushed her to the bed. "Sì, what else are you good for?"

"Certainly not cooking or cleaning."

I bit back the chuckle before it escaped my lips. "This is true."

She undid her pants and lay back, shimmying out of them and her underwear. "What if I want to take off more?"

My cock throbbed, demanding I agree to her counter-offer. "I'll allow this."

"But what about you?" she asked as she hauled her shirt over her head. "You get to stay fully dressed?"

"I get to do whatever I want," I said as I kicked off my shoes. "Remember how we're doing things my way now?"

She threw her shirt and bra over me and crawled backwards up the bed. Marone, that body was awe-inspiring. Long lines of lean muscle, defined obliques, perfectly formed breasts that matched the size of my hands. "Not sure I agreed to that."

Bad arm tight to my body, I knelt on the bed and ran my tongue across my upper lip. "You'll soon be begging to do things my way."

"I still want to follow up on Johann. Check the wine cel—"

I traced one finger along her opening, and her words came to a shuddering halt. My job was to keep her safe—from herself, if from no one else. "Shut it, Caine."

"At least take your shirt off," she gasped.

"When I'm ready." I eased down with my face between her legs, propped on one good arm. The other fell forward and for half a second I leaned some weight on it. Cazzo Madre—I shot up and got off the bed.

"Are you al—"

"I said no discussion of my arm," I growled, and hauled on one of her legs to bring her to the edge of the bed. Being shot would not prevent me from showing my woman how much I cared.

That look crossed her face. The one of sympathy or pity which I was already sick of.

I sank to my knees at the side of the bed and threw her leg over my left shoulder. My good arm rounded her hip and brushed against her swollen clit as I leaned close enough to taste her.

"Do you think—" She drew in a rough breath and threaded her fingers into my hair. "—your uncle's telling the truth?"

That brain never stopped churning.

"We'll talk about it in the morning." I blew gently across her sex and she squirmed under the attention. "Tonight we dodged a bullet."

She moaned when my tongue darted between her folds, and she clutched my head tighter.

"And we're going to celebrate that victory first."

CHAPTER 34

ANTONIO

The next morning, I sat at the dining table with Giovanni and Cristian. Leonardo was overseeing security and the investigation into Johann's death. They'd ordered Cesca to her rooms for the day.

"How's Samantha?" asked Cristian. "She was rather upset last night."

I nodded, fiddling with the espresso cup in front of me, consciously keeping my hand away from Johann's scrap of paper I'd tucked back into my pocket. "Still in bed. Discovering Johann was a shock. It took her a while to fall asleep."

In truth, it had taken us both quite a while, but that was our own doing. When we woke, I'd insisted she stay in bed longer, to maintain the ruse of distraught woman. She'd frowned, and I'd reminded her that this was not like visiting each other's families over Christmas. We didn't need her to impress these men. What mattered here was that no one pointed any fingers at us.

Unfortunately, that statement had only increased her displeasure. Some part of her brain agreed with me, but it was a much quieter part than the side wanting to do more than lounge around.

Henri came out from the kitchen carrying a tray laden with breakfast pastries and cookies.

"Not like our remarkable chef," said Cristian. "Henri didn't miss a beat after all the excitement."

"Work's the best distraction," said Henri.

Giovanni took a sip from his cappuccino, as though we were discussing moving on after our football team lost, not after one of the men died. Or was killed. "Good man."

The chef placed the tray between the three of us and stepped back. "Can I get you anything else?"

"Privacy," said Zio Giovanni.

Henri nodded and withdrew, closing the door to the kitchen.

I surveyed the pastries, finding nothing appetizing. My stomach had been doing somersaults the entire morning. What if Giovanni changed his mind about the camera? Had he told Cristian? Was there a backup of the video showing her drop it?

"Did you discover anything about Johann, Zio?"

Cristian responded. "We have video of him entering the wine cellar, but no one else between that and when Henri arrived with your girlfriend. Leo's slowly eliminating candidates, such as the obvious ones like Papa, myself, and you. We know when he was last seen alive, so Leo's tracking down proof for each other person, confirming their whereabouts. It's slow going."

"And—" Giovanni scowled. "—nothing for sure about the spy camera. Leo suspects it was one of the crate delivery men, and I'm inclined to agree. They were not supposed to be here yesterday, so it makes sense to suggest they had ulterior motives."

Relief unknotted the twists in my stomach. He hadn't changed his mind.

"As Henri said, work is the best distraction." I raised my espresso to my mouth, inhaling the deep roasted scent, attempting to find calm. "Samantha was hoping she could join in the investigation into what happened to Johann. She's not with the police, but her insurance investigations provide her with skills, which may help."

Giovanni looked at Cristian, face impassive. "What do you think?"

"You're leaving today, aren't you?" asked Cristian.

"After the surprise arrives, whenever that is." That was the limit of my promise to Giovanni. And once it was done, Samantha and I would finally escape to Napoli.

Gio placed his cup on the table and plucked a maritozzo from the tray, coated in powdered sugar and filled with some sort of cream. "Do you think she can work with Leonardo? His experience in leading the team is different from this job."

Another surprise from my uncle. Samantha had insisted I offer her aid, and the only reason I'd agreed was because I was certain they'd say no.

"She's more accustomed to using words to discover the truth, rather than her fists," I said. "However, if he can control his tongue, I'm sure she could be of some assistance before we go." Perhaps I'd return the note to her, so she could produce it as evidence, proving her worth.

Giovanni looked toward the archway behind me, and I turned in my seat.

Vincenzo nodded to Giovanni and approached the table, looking at me. "Pardon the intrusion, but I heard Samantha didn't come to breakfast this morning. Did you see her? How's she feeling?"

"I did see her—she stayed with me last night." I lifted one eyebrow, making my message clear: she was in my bed and we did far more than sleep. It was petty, but every time this former flame of hers came anywhere near her, all I wanted was to shove him into a wall.

Vincenzo looked at Giovanni and back at me, a polite smile decorating his irritatingly attractive face.

Giovanni knocked on the table, and everyone turned to him. "She wants to help Leonardo with his investigation into Johann's death."

"A generous offer." Vincenzo's head cocked. "Does she have some idea of what happened?"

"She seems to be a smart woman." Giovanni's gaze met mine, and all I could see was him destroying the video of her dropping the camera last night. "Another set of eyes never hurts."

I patted my mouth with a napkin, wishing to escape my uncle's scrutiny. Even though I'd stood up to him once, it clearly would not become a habit. "I'll wake her and let her know."

Vincenzo placed a hand on my shoulder and gestured toward my cup. "Don't worry, Antonio. I'll go so you can finish your breakfast."

"Good idea," said Giovanni, cutting off my argument before I could voice it. "You need your strength, my boy."

CHAPTER 35

SAMANTHA

I'd packed most of my things into my carry-on, ready to finally leave, as soon as Giovanni's mysterious surprise arrived. Antonio had already seen the first surprise—the new conservation studio. What else could possibly be so important to keep us in this hellhole for so much longer?

My room was too damn small. I stepped out onto the terrace, the damp morning air invading every cell of my body. The chill was no match for my Michigan-winter-ready jacket, but I hadn't been able to shake the prickles at the back of my neck since I woke.

It wasn't the cold; it was the wrongness.

Antonio had warned me before we left the airport that there would be lies, but the sheer weight of them was overwhelming. And more than the lies were the secrets.

An undercover agent, a stolen painting, my stupid ex-boyfriend, and a murder.

Four stories below me, a dozen men made slow circuits of the property, walking in pairs with their M4s. Last night's chaos had transformed into an organized response. From what Antonio told me, it was all under Leo's careful watch.

Now here I stood, unable to leave my room until Antonio gave me the all-clear. He was still nervous over Giovanni's promise about the camera. I should have been, too, but what about Johann? What if he was murdered and there was a killer on the loose? They'd found my secret camera, so that was done with. The bigger question was who would—who could—kill the huge German?

If he was killed, I reminded myself for the hundredth time.

I re-entered the room, closing the door and throwing my jacket onto the bed on my way to the bathroom.

The mirror reflected a woman as tired as I felt. The bruising around my neck had faded enough it didn't stand out. No one had mentioned it when we arrived and no one's eyes had lingered on it, so hopefully no one was silently wondering what had caused the bruises. Or whether Antonio had done it, for that matter.

Calm down and put on some makeup. Antonio will like that. I didn't have much in my bag, but anything would be a nice surprise for him. And a way to celebrate our freedom.

By tonight, we'd be in Naples. It was Friday, so Mario would probably force us to go to La Fiamma together and dance the night away. I paused with the eye shadow brush over my lid. Maybe I'd wear that Versace dress Antonio bought me in September. It would be chilly outside, but Mario would have us past the bouncers fast enough, I'd barely notice. And Antonio would definitely put his jacket around me.

God, I love that man.

A light knock came at the door.

"One sec," I called, finishing the eye shadow. Unfortunately, when I opened the door, it wasn't the man I'd hoped for. "Vincenzo. What can I do for you?"

His mouth tensed, eyes crinkling at their corners. "Can I come in?"

No. But someone was watching, always watching, and he'd been into my room before. I stepped back and waved him in. Anything else might raise suspicions.

Once the door clicked closed, he turned and took me in his arms. "I haven't stopped thinking about you and what happened last night."

The embrace just increased the awkward feeling in my neck. I broke his hold and pushed him away. "Don't do that."

It was as though Vin expected we could still be friends. "I thought you were staying with your boyfriend?"

"His name's Antonio, and yes, I am." I returned to the bathroom, to applying makeup that would make my boyfriend happy. Did I have to continue with the fake face in front of Vincenzo? Pretend I was the weepy woman who was distressed over finding a body, rather than the one who wanted to do something about it? "I was still upset this morning, and Antonio thought a little extra sleep would help."

"But instead you packed?"

"We're leaving today, so I should be ready." Next came eyeliner, which I'd never been able to put on straight. Miraculously, this time, it came out perfectly. Maybe I should rage-decorate my face more often. "Are you really here to see how I'm doing? Or was there something else?"

"I'm worried, Sam." He leaned against the doorframe, inspiring memories of getting ready in the mornings when I stayed at his apartment. "I heard the crates arrived yesterday?"

"They did." Next, mascara, which drew out the color of my eyes. Yeah, Antonio would love this. "Giovanni was pissed, too. Said they weren't supposed to arrive until tomorrow."

"One of them must be what the TPC was waiting for."

"What's inside?" I capped the mascara and moved on to blush. It always reminded me of war paint, preparing me for battle with a man, with a museum curator, with a repair vendor.

He shrugged. "All I know is there's a painting forty six centimeters by sixty-one. They gave me some rough notes on what's on it."

"There were three crates. I looked but couldn't see details on the shipping labels. One was smaller than the others and might hold something that size." I stepped back from the mirror. Before the New Year's Eve ball, my sister and I had gone to a professional for hair and make-up—she hadn't gone to the ball, it was just a fun sister's day—and I looked nothing like that. Femme fatale I was not.

"You're so beautiful."

I flicked my eyes toward him, catching the full-body scan in progress. "I said stop that, Vin."

He'd had his chance a long time ago. "I wish you'd left yesterday. Things are getting bad here and I'm worried something might happen to you."

Business. I could always do business. "Have you talked to your handler about the crates?"

"I left a message in my dead drop location this morning. Now I wait."

"And if you don't hear back?" I packed up my toiletries bag and leaned a hip against the counter.

"I'm not sure. Part of me thinks I should take the painting and get out. At least we've saved it that way."

"Is there any chance the TPC doesn't want it anymore? Or that the one they're looking for isn't in those crates?" Elliot had told me Giovanni wasn't behind the smuggling ring. Involved with it, but he wasn't the one they were after. Maybe Vincenzo had been cut loose when they realized that? No, they would have gotten him out. They were still monitoring messages coming out of the estate, so the operation remained active.

He shoved his hands into his pockets, staring down at the floor. "I'm glad you're here. It's been tough since the communications slowed so much. I know I keep making you uncomfortable, but..."

There was no *but* about it. He did make me uncomfortable. Our history had made me keep Antonio at arm's length for longer than I should have. And I wasn't about to let Vin off the hook for that just to make him feel better. "I can pass a message along after we go, if that might help?"

"Did you hear they found a camera in the gallery last night?"

I nodded. Antonio and I agreed it would be best to acknowledge he'd told me about the camera, but that I knew only that. "Antonio mentioned it."

"Between that camera and Johann, I may have to leave as well. I'm not sure if I want to risk them pinning either of those things on me."

Antonio and I had been worried enough about what they'd do with me if they discovered I was talking to an FBI agent. What would they do if they found someone was undercover? "How many positions did you have before this one?"

"I originally worked in an office in Tuscany. They had me pose as a bodyguard four years ago during a sting operation. My job was to identify the painting a thief was trying to sell, but they felt my appearance suited a bodyguard better than a buyer." He folded his arms and shrugged. "It's a long and winding story, but I did a few more of those and it landed me here two years ago."

"Before or after Giovanni's big change?"

"After. Protecting the family and property is simple work, but if I'd had to get involved in..." His gaze fell from me to the counter and he gave a little shudder. "From what I've heard, I don't think I could have handled it before. Your boyfriend's family is dangerous."

No kidding. "But that's the job you signed up for, right?"

He nodded slowly, still not looking at me. Avoiding me because of his worries or because Antonio was right and he was lying to me again?

"How did you get in here? What was the cover story?" I picked up my bag, ready to leave the bathroom.

"It was another undercover job where I was working as a security guard for an antiques dealer in Rome, one with a lot of looted antiquities moving through his store." He shoved off the door and walked further into the room, letting me by. "Giovanni was supposed to arrange transport for some pieces, but his illness delayed the process and someone else took care of them."

I stopped by the bed where my suitcase lay. "Someone else?"

He waved it off. "The original plan was to gather information about the dealer, but when the Ferraros declared they were getting out of the business, they had a lot of turnover and it was too good an opportunity to pass up."

The story sounded true, but Antonio had me doubting every word coming out of Vin's mouth. I had to find out if I could trust him or not, so I pressed for more. "Why, if he was getting out of the business?"

"He didn't stop everything right away and we were hoping he'd be more willing to give up information on the other organizations he was working with."

"I don't understand. You've been here for two years, and you barely hear anything from your handlers. Why haven't they moved you somewhere else?"

He settled against the small desk under the television, watching as I moved items aside to fit the toiletries bag into the suitcase. "The first year, I was under too close of scrutiny to learn much. This past year's been more fruitful. I drop information, names, and whatever else I discover. If none of it was useful, I expect they would have pulled me out a long time ago. Then word came that this new painting—the one we suspect is in the crates—was being delivered, and I received the message a month ago that they want it."

"So you wait in silence?"

"Security's tricky here, especially now, making communications difficult on either side." Vin looked up at me, his gray eyes piercing deep into my soul, before they dropped to the floor again. "None of this is what I expected, but I'm doing the best I can."

He was so alone.

Vin kept his arms tight to his body, barely looking at me. "I might take you up on that offer of getting a message out if I don't hear anything before you go. Just to be certain the right people receive it."

He reminded me so much of Antonio at that moment. Both were men of intense emotions, underscored by an almost unshakable confidence. With Antonio, I glimpsed moments when that slipped, like when he gave me the promise ring or when he talked about wanting to impress my family. Every moment around his uncle was like that, too. Not a lack of confidence, but more a muting of his giant personality.

Vincenzo had never revealed that side to me. Until now.

"Hey." I drew closer to him and placed a hand on his forearm. "You've got this. Let me know if you want my help. No guarantees, but if there's something I can do..."

He unfolded one hand and placed it on top of mine. "Thanks, Sam. That means a lot."

I withdrew and turned to zipper my suitcase. There wasn't any heat when he touched me or when I got close to him, just more of that wrongness. If I was honest with myself, I wasn't fully over what happened between us. I'd gotten past it enough to admit I was in love with Antonio, but it was likely I'd always carry some resentment. Or, like Antonio said, maybe it was a blessing that he helped make me who I was, and I should thank him.

"I did come up for a reason, though." He stood, giving his head a shake, like he was clearing the stress and anxiety of his undercover position and resuming his pretend guard role. "Giovanni said you're going to help Leonardo investigate Johann's death."

"Really?" I spun so quickly, he startled. I'd expected Antonio wouldn't even bring it up, let alone have Giovanni agree. This was fantastic news. I'd gladly deal with Leonardo to escape this little room and feel useful.

He nodded. "I'm to take you down to the wine cellar now. Antonio will meet you there."

"Are you helping, too?"

"I'd like to, but Leonardo has me patrolling the shore and the cave area today." He came to my side, lifting my suitcase to the floor, despite it weighing all of twenty pounds. "In the end, it's good, since my dead drop is down in the ruins, so I can keep an eye out for my contact."

"That works out."

Vincenzo stood too close to me. From my position between the bed and the wall, there was only so much space I had to back away from him. His eyes dragged slowly up from my feet, and his hand reached for me, but it stopped before he touched me. "Promise me you'll be careful? I'm worried about you getting involved with these men."

"I can handle myself." It was an instinctive response, the one I always gave when people told me that. Most people looked at me and saw nothing more than an overly serious insurance adjuster. Only a handful understood my core—my need to investigate things, my experience with the FBI, my regular training in the gym and on the range. Being underestimated was a benefit to me, but it still pissed me off every time someone treated me like I needed a man's protection.

"Of course you can, but let me worry about you." His hand finished its trek toward me and he squeezed my arm. "It gives me something to think about, other than how deep I've gotten."

I didn't move out of his grip. The way his eyes crinkled at the corners, he looked older than when we'd been together, more than the ten years it had been. He'd been through too much in that time, just like I had.

"I have another distraction for you, then. I—" Should I tell him? Did I believe his story? Maybe he could poke around and find out a piece of the puzzle. "I found a letter on Johann's body last night."

He released my arm and took a half-step back. "You what?"

"It said the delivery was complete and that pickup was required tomorrow. Well, tomorrow from whatever day it was written."

Vin turned, hands landing on his hips, and he paced to the terrace door. He spun to face me. "Do you think he was working for someone else?"

"Possible."

"What if he was and they're after the same painting?" He clenched one fist and brought it to his mouth, eyes scanning back and forth. "If I don't hear from my handlers soon, I'll have to act. What could be so special about it, you think?"

"No idea. Do you know who it's by?"

"Like I told you, I only know the dimensions." He shook his head. "Thanks for this, Sam. That helps, but if there's another player involved in this game, it means you need to be even more careful."

CHAPTER 36

ANTONIO

I descended the wide stone staircase to the tower's bottom floor and the entrance to the wine cellar. Vincenzo stood next to the grand door, smiling as I approached.

"Where's Samantha?" A jolt of pain ran through my injured arm, reminding me I was less a man than he was. *You're not. It will heal.*

As though he noticed my flinch, he used both arms to heft open the heavy door. "She's inside. Will Leonardo be down soon?"

"He will. He's upstairs confirming perimeter assignments first." I paused, looking him up and down. Taking in his lean form, fitted black shirt, and bright gray eyes. "Why aren't you working with him?"

"I have other duties today." He shrugged and gestured into the wine cellar. "I suspect Samantha's in the tasting room. Have you ever been down there?"

"Of course. I used to work here."

He nodded. "I heard stories about that."

"Stories?" I stopped myself before snapping more words at him.

"I'll be working down in the cave and around the ruins today. Samantha quite liked the tour I gave her on Tuesday." His head tilted back slightly, as though he was challenging me. Or baiting me.

"I expect she enjoyed the tour I gave her yesterday better."

"Perhaps." He took a half-step toward me, smiling an irritatingly handsome smile. "Is it true you haven't been back in nine years?"

What business was that of his? "I'm here for Samantha, not for small talk with the staff." It's possible the last came out as a snarl.

His smile reverted to a smirk, and he lifted one eyebrow. More challenge. "She's all yours."

I hummed my assent—perhaps it was more like a growl that time—and shouldered past him. She *was* all mine. I'd proved that to her last night. Three times.

The lights were dim and I squinted to adjust as the door closed behind me. The scent of oak, red fruit, and wet stone invaded my nostrils, reminding me of all the times Zio Gio had brought me down here. "Samantha?"

No response. That woman had an intensity about her and was undoubtedly too focused on a search for clues to have heard anything outside of two feet away from her. I made my way through the dank space, running my fingers along the terracotta-lined shelves and over dusty bottles which waited until they were perfect before being chosen.

Living in my condo was convenient, particularly when I had to leave for months at a time and the staff could look after it. But it also lacked. My parents had a proper wine cellar, although not as extensive as Giovanni's, and theirs smelled more of wet earth than stone and more of cherries than the mix of red berries.

Last week, Samantha and I posed as home buyers as part of an investigation. I'd told the real estate agent that Samantha wanted a yard. But returning to this villa brought back memories of my time studying for my architecture degrees, and all the plans I'd had for the house I'd design for myself.

Long ago, those plans had been for a bachelor's pad, focused more on entertainment—game room, small cinema, and a cellar to store a vast array of alcohol.

Priorities change.

The condo was large, with a massive studio for my painting and research, gourmet kitchen, and four bedrooms to accommodate a family. And yet, it no longer felt right.

"Bella?" I called as I neared the turn into the tasting room. "Are you down here?"

Still nothing.

I brushed a cobweb from my hand, which I'd collected from the top of one of the oak barrels my fingers had trailed over. The cleaning staff must not work down here. Although the sand on the floor appeared fresh, fully dry rather than having captured any of the moisture in the air yet.

As I rounded the corner into the tasting room, the most extraordinary sight greeted me. Samantha, on hands and knees at the far end of the room, beside the cupboard. She had a flashlight pointed between two barrels, head down to the floor, looking into the small space.

That magnificent ass, high up in the air, faced me.

I leaned against the archway into the room and gritted my teeth through the effort required to fold my arms. Kicked one ankle over the other to add to the casual effect. "Not right now, bella, we have other priorities."

She huffed, dropping her forehead to the floor. No doubt, her eyes were rolling. She turned off her flashlight and pushed herself up to dust sand and dirt off her gray long-sleeved T-shirt and black cargo pants. "Took you long enough."

"So this little display—" I flicked my fingers toward her, intending to tease about her outfit and her position, but she came closer and my heart skipped. Despite the dirty clothes and long braid confining her luxurious hair, she was stunning. "Makeup for a murder investigation? That hardly seems like you."

Her lips clamped shut, fighting against a smile. "They cleaned the room already, so I thought I'd check for whatever they may have missed."

I straightened from my flirtation pose—it hadn't accomplished much, anyway. "Find anything?"

She came close enough to give me a peck on the lips and returned to the spot where I'd found her. "There's something odd next to these barrels. Scratch marks on the floor that you can't see unless you—" She knelt and brushed away some of the sand by the barrels. "—look closely enough."

The cellar was carved from the rock the estate sat upon, so scratches would be reasonable if the room weren't centuries old. I sank to my knees beside her, running a hand over the grooves. "Interesting. Are there marks like this anywhere else?"

"Not in this room." She sat back on her haunches and pointed to where two barrels sat on their ends nearby. "He was next to those, against the wall, and I didn't see any drag marks in the sand yesterday. Three options: That's where he was killed and the killer had a short distance to cover their tracks; it happened somewhere else and they did a lot of tidying; or they carried him."

Johann was a large man, easily passing two hundred and fifty pounds. "Not likely to carry Johann very far?"

"Nope."

"So you didn't search the first room?"

She frowned and shook her head. "I didn't want to be on camera if I wasn't sure what I was looking for."

This was one more thing we had in common—too much pride.

Last night, Giovanni and I had seen Cristian and Leonardo arrive in the wine cellar via the security displays, but lost sight of them when they entered the back room. "I don't think there are cameras in here."

"Yeah. I couldn't see any, and Henri was under the same impression." She ran her fingers over the scratch marks in the floor. "They feel fresh. Everything else down here is worn down and has soft edges."

"Do you want me to check the other room?"

Her eyes traveled to my bad arm. I'd forgone the sling again, choosing to brace the arm against my abdomen or stretch it out far enough to keep the hand in my pocket for support. "No mention of—"

"I know." She winked at me. "My big, tough boyfriend is invulnerable."

"You're one to talk." I dropped my voice. "Who's insisting she return to the scene of a murder?"

"Could have been natural causes." She flicked the flashlight on. "Plus, it's no different from investigating insurance fraud. Something wrong happened and you can either try to set things right or sit back and watch someone else do it."

"What's wrong with watching?"

She cocked an eyebrow at me.

"I know, bella. Who would trust anyone to do as good a job as you'll do?" I chuckled as she swung her hand at my chest. "But it is different. Your fraud investigations involve people stealing money. This is life and death."

"Vincenzo said they don't know why Johann would be a target. Until we're certain of that, everyone's at risk. This isn't just a fortress, it's a home. What if Cesca's the next one who's in the wrong place at the wrong time?"

I smiled at my lovely girlfriend. There she was, protecting the world again. "I admire your conviction, bella."

She gave me a tight-lipped smile, always uneasy under genuine praise. "Don't admire me too much, yet. I haven't found anything conclusive."

"I'll go out to the other room and look for more scratch marks. Then we can figure out the rest."

Samantha pushed up to standing and held out a hand to help me up, which I waved away. Vincenzo didn't need that help from her. He could have picked her up and carried her anywhere.

Stop it, you fool.

I was not less a man than Vincenzo. But I continued to experience the petty pangs of jealousy. Samantha had warned me that I had to let it go. Surely she'd feel the same if Faith, my former fiancée, was the one whose face was everywhere.

"If there are no cameras..." Once I was standing, I drew closer to her. "How about you get back down on the floor and..."

Her cheeks flushed crimson and she sucked in her bottom lip. *Stop*, she mouthed.

I blew a raspberry and rolled my eyes. "Get your mind out of the gutter. I was going to say you should get down and finish inspecting those marks."

She laughed and smacked me again, this time connecting with my bad arm. I bit back a grimace and she bit back an apology I could tell she was about to offer.

· · • • • • • • · ·

I crawled on my knees to the next batch of casks and leaned toward the floor. Che cazzo, this would have been easier with two good arms. One to hold me up, the other to check the floor. Crawl forward. Continue.

No, instead it was lean down, flex my abs tight to keep my torso up, run fingers along the floor, sit up, move forward on my knees. Lean down. Repeat. All while trying to prevent from my bad arm swinging around and causing more pain.

"Find anything?" hollered Samantha.

"A great deal of sand," I muttered.

"What was that?"

I rose my volume so she could hear me properly. "Nothing yet. You?"

"I don't know. There's... something..."

A muffled boom sounded, and darkness fell upon us.

"Shit!" said Samantha. "What happened?"

"Did you hear the thunder? Maybe the power's out."

She groaned loudly, full of irritation. "It's like this entire house is against me."

I held onto the casks next to me to stand, laughing. "A little melodramatic today?"

"Very funny, Ferraro."

Making my way toward her, feeling along the wall of wine barrels, I said, "You didn't hit a switch or anything, did you?"

"You don't suppose the security camera can see through this darkness?"

"I don't think so." I scanned the space behind me, in the general direction of the door. "There are no lights coming from the intercom panel. Do you remember if there were any?"

A low, rumbling noise sounded, shaking the entire room. Perfetto.

"They don't have backup power?" she said.

"Where's your flashlight?"

"I put it down... somewhere."

I held back my laughter, imagining her glowering around the pitch black room with her hands on her hips. "Are you sitting or standing?"

"What kind of question is that?" Another rumble and the world shuddered. "It feels like the whole place is about to come down."

"We could take advantage of dark, amore." I reached the last barrel and felt for the archway leading into the tasting room.

"Whose mind's in the gutter now?" She chuckled, then cut off immediately. "Hold up. I found... there..."

I paused, waiting for her flashlight to come back on instead of risking damage to a leg in addition to my arm. "Bella?"

"C'mon," she muttered.

"Samantha, what—"

The sound of stone grinding against stone accompanied a gush of cool air. And Samantha's excited cry of, "Yes!"

"Bella?"

"Antonio, you're not going to—Ahh!" she cried, followed by breaking glass, a loud smash, and another scream from Samantha.

I lunged forward, ramming my knee into one of the casks, making the turn into the tasting room. "Samantha, are you alright?"

"Ow, shit!"

Just then, the lights came back on. Samantha lay on the ground, next to the overturned cupboard which had held all the glasses, their shattered remains strewn all around. I ran, skidding to the floor next to her. "What happened?"

She rolled to her side, only one cut visible on her neck, just below her ear. Her shaky hand rose, and she pointed to the wall behind me. "I'm no expert, but I think that's a lead."

Next to where the cupboard used to stand, the wall had moved to reveal a passageway beyond. "The scratch marks must have been from it opening?"

"Samantha?" It was Leonardo, far later than I'd expected him. "Antonio?"

"We're back here." I helped Samantha sit up and checked her over for injuries. Nothing visible other than her neck.

A wicked gleam danced in her eyes.

"What happened?" I asked. The ancient cupboard had been here as long as I could remember and it was likely decades older than I was.

"I found a lever behind a cask and I backed up when the wall moved. It happened so fast—I don't think I ran into the cupboard, but I guess I must have."

Leonardo arrived in the room. "What have you done, Antonio?"

"Giovanni sent us down here." I turned to glower at him. "He wanted Samantha's eyes on this place."

He gestured at the open door and the rock face.

Samantha stretched her shoulders, cleaning dust and sand off her clothes yet again. She'd been lucky the glasses fell away from her. "Leo, this is right next to where I found Johann. I heard there was nothing on the video in the wine cellar of his attacker. What if they came in this way?"

I helped her stand. "Where does it go?"

"Or..." She paused, evaluating the door and the wall. "If he collapsed from something natural and the door opened, it could have pushed him into the corner. But that would mean someone opened it."

Leonardo glowered at each of us. "It leads to the cave. We had it excavated five years ago to help move shipments which came in by water." His glare turned to Samantha, growing colder. "This is not something for her to see."

"Little late for that now." She rolled her eyes, in a manner far different from how she normally rolled them at me. "Let's see if there are any clues."

Leonardo approached the hidden door. "Only people we trust completely know this is here."

"Only people you trust have been told about it." Samantha fell into step next to him. "I hate to break it to you, but if I found it, someone else you don't trust might have, too."

He stared at her for a long moment, fists clenching and un-clenching. But this was my Samantha, and she was in her ele-ment. I'd seen a change in her last night, as though she was finally overcoming what happened on New Year's Eve. This confirmed it. The old Samantha was on her way back.

"Listen, Leonardo," she said. "You don't have to like me to accept I'm right. The three of us can work together on this, then you can go right back to calling me a harpy. Frankly, I don't care. You and I may have different reasons for wanting to find out what happened to Johann, but our goal is the same."

He didn't respond, just walked through the doorway into the cramped, narrow stone hallway.

I grabbed Samantha's flashlight from where she left it on the table and inclined my head. "Shall we?"

CHAPTER 37

SAMANTHA

The hidden doorway and dank steps down to the cave didn't yield any clues. We walked the length of it twice with my flashlight and the one Leonardo had brought. There were no cameras in the stairwell, just like the tasting room. They must have assumed the only ways into those two rooms were from the cave and the wine cellar's entry, so why monitor the entire thing?

The base of the staircase was hidden from sight, requiring a person to know exactly which tiny offshoot from the cave was the right one to follow in order to find it. My first time down there with Vincenzo, I'd found the entrance, but hadn't explored further.

"This was the last place we spotted him on the recording," said Leo, as we walked into the kitchen. "After this, he went to the wine cellar and was killed."

We were tracing Johann's last steps. No one knew why he'd gone to the cellar and the kitchen was our last stop.

"Or died," I said, as I'd been following up to Leo's comments over and over. There was no proof either way, and the in-house doctor hadn't been able to make a determination before the body was taken away. "Where's Henri? Did you question him?"

Leo's jaw ticked again. It seemed to be even more difficult for him to be nice to me than vice versa. "He's been busy preparing for our guest this afternoon."

"Shouldn't Henri be busy in the kitchen?"

"He's getting something at the market."

That wasn't right. "Didn't you ban all travel to and from the estate?"

Leo frowned, not that different from the look he'd been providing me with since he joined Antonio and me in the wine cellar. "The only exception is for special guests with..." He waved his hand toward Antonio. "Special surprises."

Antonio's head tilted. "Do you know what it is? Samantha and I have been here all week waiting for this big occasion. And no clue why."

A hint of a smile ghosted over Leo's lips. What was that about? "We should continue looking around. If this was Johann's last known location, perhaps he was on an errand for Henri."

If I mentioned how calm Henri had been when we found Johann, would that focus too much suspicion on him?

How far would Leo go with a suspect? I had to get more information first.

Thunder rumbled outside and the lights flickered.

Antonio asked, "Were the lights out in the entire estate earlier? Before you arrived in the wine cellar with us?"

Leo shook his head. "What do you mean?"

"The lights were out in the wine cellar," I said. "I found the lever for the door, it opened, the cupboard fell, then the lights came on before you got there."

"I turned them on with the switch." Leo folded his arms, emphasizing the breadth of his chest and shoulders. He probably thought we'd had them out to fool around—although Antonio did suggest that, so maybe those suspicions were valid.

"Neither of us turned them off," I said.

"Did you hear any movement before the cupboard fell?" asked Leo.

It was hard to tell. The tasting room had been mostly silent just before the door ground open. "All I could hear was thunder. It's possible the sound of the door opening masked some—you think someone was in the hallway behind the secret door? Snuck in and shoved the cupboard over as a distraction?"

"You said it yourself," said Leo with a frown. "The door is right next to where Johann was found. What if someone who knows about the door used it to sneak up on him or to sneak out after?"

Antonio ran a hand through his hair. He was frustrated, no doubt thinking the same thing I was—that if Leo's theory were true and Antonio weren't with me, whoever it was might not have settled for a distraction. "But how did they get the lights off? How did they get into the wine cellar or into the hidden staircase without being caught on camera?"

"There's a switch for the lights on the other side of the door." Leonardo's gaze rose to the ceiling, to one of the cameras. "We should review the footage again. Maybe there's something before or after Johann, or perhaps when you two were in the cellar?"

Vincenzo appeared outside the kitchen's door, far enough away and at an angle to ensure I was the only one who could see him. He beckoned me to join him, but I gave a subtle shake of my head. Leonardo and Antonio continued speaking to each other, their words lost, while I focused on my silent conversation with Vin. He used his eyes and a sharp flick of his head to ask again.

Antonio's arm shot into the air. His temper was flaring this time, and I'd missed why. "Have you not listened to anything Giovanni said? Don't you care how much she's helping?"

"Helping what?" Leo unfolded one arm to wave Antonio's comments away. "All I see is a woman snooping around in business that's none of her own."

"Here!" Antonio pushed his hand into his pocket and withdrew something, thrusting it at Leonardo. "She found this."

"When?" Leo snapped, studying it.

Shit! It was the scrap of paper with the note. I glanced at Antonio, my irritation with Leo and this conversation hopefully masking my irritation with my boyfriend for handing it over without discussing it with me. "This morning."

Leo's eyes bored into me. "Where?"

"Next to where Johann was," I said.

Vincenzo appeared in my line of sight again, waving with a hand.

"Not possible," Leonardo said slowly, tucking it into his pocket. "We went over every inch of that room last night and laid down a fresh layer of sand."

"It was behind the casks." A muscle in Antonio's jaw clicked. More lies, but lies designed to protect me. "That's how she found the lever to open the door."

"She needs to go back to her room."

I drew in a breath through my nose, my head falling back, so I stared at the ceiling. *Count to five, Sam.* "I do not."

Leonardo pounded a fist on the counter. "The security of this estate is my responsibility. I refuse—"

Antonio raised a finger to Leo's face. "Giovanni said she could help and that you were supposed to work *with* her, not against her."

Leo balled both of his hands into fists, raising them to his face, muttering a string of profanities about the Mother Mary, pig's balls, and a few colorful ones about the private parts of cows. "Johann was Interpol."

My head snapped toward Antonio, and his did the same toward me. In unison, we said, "What?"

Leonardo lowered his hands, resting them on the counter in front of himself. "We got word from one of our men in the pol—" He glowered at me before continuing. "One of our men this morning. They ran his fingerprints as part of the autopsy and came back with a lot of unanswered questions."

It may have raised several for him, but it answered some for me. The men who picked up Johann's body were obviously on Giovanni's payroll. Undoubtedly, they'd concocted a story which wouldn't link the death to the Ferraro family.

But it added two questions to my list: One, was his note for Interpol? Two, had Vincenzo been working with him all along?

I held up my hands as if in surrender, a move that didn't seem to calm Leonardo, but maybe it would satisfy him enough to get me out of there. I needed to talk to Vin. "Why don't you two go up to the control room and review the footage I have no idea exists. Maybe I'll take a tour—"

"No!" said both Leonardo and Antonio at the same time. At least they could agree on that.

"Bella, there's a killer on the loose."

"It might be natural—"

Leo cut me off. "And I won't have you snooping around on your own."

Vincenzo joined us in the kitchen. "Did I hear that Samantha needs an escort?" He smiled at each of us, a move which wasn't reciprocated by anyone.

"I think this should satisfy both of you?" I nodded to Antonio, surprised at not receiving any argument. Leonardo wouldn't have been happy unless I was locked in my room, while Antonio's snarl every time Vincenzo came near was becoming more and more pronounced.

I couldn't wait to get out of this damn villa.

As soon as Vin and I were out of earshot, I whispered, "They're heading up to the control room. They'll be reviewing some old videos, but I have a feeling they'll be watching us."

"Then we have to be quick." He pointed me down a hallway, which led to the family room with access to the outside. "I received a response. You said you'd help if you could—well, I need it now."

• • • • • • • • • •

Vincenzo and I stood next to each other in the family room, staring out at the gardens and path beyond. Like almost every room on the main floor, it was plush, with a giant carved fireplace. Red velvet covered the sofas and four gilt wing chairs sat facing a piano. Underneath thick brocade curtains, heavy rain pelted the windowed door.

"I don't think going out's a good idea," I said.

He slid an arm around the small of my back and leaned close to whisper in my ear. "The weather's a perfect cover."

I held in the cringe, an awkward need to shove him away settling deep inside me. How focused on searching for clues were Leonardo and Antonio? Would Vincenzo and I standing like this cause them to stop their work? I whispered, "You're too close."

"Leonardo's been pushing us together. This helps our chances."

And Antonio would be furious. He'd been trying to prove the entire time we were here that he wasn't jealous, but I'd never dated anyone with as many doubts as Antonio. If he could keep his wits about him, he wouldn't try to stop us from talking, because he knew who Vin really was.

"But if we go out there, they'll know something's up," I said. "Even the men working are inside guard buildings."

"My apartment is over there." He pointed out the window, past the garden and the pool, to a low stucco-covered building. "If we head in that direction, we can visit my place."

"And Antonio would come after us and snap your neck." I sighed audibly and half-turned to him, keeping my back to the only camera I'd spotted. My words came out barely above a breath. "How good are the microphones on the security cameras?"

"If they have us on the primary display, they can pick up almost anything, but probably not this conversation."

Probably wasn't good enough. I crossed to the piano and pulled out the bench to sit. "Do you play?"

He chuckled and sat to my right. "No. Do you?"

My fingers hovered over middle C. "Not even 'Heart and Soul?'"

He shook his head.

I began the top part, simple but distracting. Face toward the keys, like I was focusing on the only thing I knew, I mumbled, "What do we need to do?"

Vin put his fingers on the keys two octaves above me and mimicked my play—fumbling once or twice—and my volume. "Get to the cave. I have a delivery coming."

Delivery of what? From whom, I could guess. "I know another way. There's a passage in the wine cellar."

He laughed, resuming a normal voice. "You're much better than me."

"My sister tried teaching me, but I didn't have the patience." I tapped the last key three times. Piano required too much sitting still. "I don't suppose you want to go to the wine cellar? I could use a nice glass of something strong right about now."

He nodded and stood, offering me a hand, which I ignored.

CHAPTER 38

SAMANTHA

"Have you ever worked in the security control room?" I asked Vin as we approached the hidden door in the tasting room. Someone had cleaned the glass from the floor and stood the cupboard back against the wall.

"I have."

"So you know we're in a blind spot?"

He nodded. "The outer room is monitored, but not this one. Giovanni brings people down here for privacy."

"If Antonio and Leo are still up there, they know we're here." I leaned over the casks at the far wall. What was I doing? This place was dangerous enough as it was. If either of those men got suspicious or jealous and came down here, Vin and I were done for. "Pick a bottle of wine. Look like you're putting some thought into it and ask me what I think of whatever vintage you choose."

He nodded and left for the racks of wine. I pulled the lever. Leonardo said only trusted staff knew about this door—that was probably another reason there were no cameras in here. While the door opened, in case the camera could make out the noise, I hollered to Vincenzo, "I'm partial to Chianti, if there's anything like that. Or maybe a Valpolicella?"

If they *were* listening, hopefully Antonio would pick up on my hidden message. He'd prepared a from-scratch feast for me the night after he arrived home a couple of weeks ago, and those were the two reds he'd served with the meal.

"Found a bottle of each," replied Vin. "We'll try both?"

"Sounds good, thanks."

"Giovanni's selection is truly magnificent." He strolled back into the tasting room, seeming without a care in the world, but his gaze fell to the open door in the rock wall, his eyes widening. "Do you want to be alone with your thoughts?"

"No," I said, speaking loud enough to keep up the ruse, just in case. "Antonio wouldn't approve—nor would Leo. You know how it is."

"I'm sorry for how this has to play out, Samantha. I'm sure it's not easy to have someone looking over your shoulder nonstop."

I gestured to the hallway. "Think we can raise a glass to Johann, then have a few moments of silence?"

He neared the door, nodding. "That sounds good."

"How long do we have?" I asked after we were through the short hallway and halfway down the stairs.

"Did Leo show this to you?"

"No, I found it."

Vincenzo walked ahead of me, scanning the low ceiling and rough walls. "What's it for?"

"Shipments." I shrugged, even though he couldn't see me. "It ends in the cave. I'm not sure if we'll be in a blind spot when we get down there, but it's close to the Venus statue so we can turn off the camera. I don't know how much time we'll have."

He checked his watch and I did the same. "They said three o'clock because the weather could hide them."

That gave us ten minutes. "How did they get in touch with you?"

"I checked my dead drop location while I was working the perimeter this morning, and there was a reply. It's been so long since they returned anything..."

"But someone always picked them up?"

He shrugged. "Could have been an animal eating the paper for all I knew."

"You told them about *The Magdalen*?"

Elliot said he needed me to get the proof because of an inter-organizational disagreement. That must have meant it wasn't on the TPC's priority list, so maybe they ignored it? Maybe they went straight to Elliot about it being brought up? Did I just get Elliot into a heap of trouble for acting outside their agreed parameters? It could get the FBI kicked off the case and Elliot thrown out of the country. Maybe that was a bad call.

"No response on that part," he said.

Probably for the best.

Vincenzo said, "You turn off the camera—stay as close as you can to the back wall, which may keep you hidden, since the security is focused on the entrance. I'll run out and signal them once you're done. They should be able to make it into the cave and drop off my things, then out again."

"What are they delivering?"

"I don't know yet."

"Before we get down there…" I put a hand on his arm midway down the stairs. "I need you to tell me the truth."

He turned to look at me, his face dim in the corridor, reflecting the scant light from above. "Focus on the job, Sam."

"Were you working with Johann?"

His head twisted slightly, eyes narrowing in the darkness.

"Leonardo told us Johann was Interpol. Just now, in the kitchen."

He took my hand from his arm and stared at it for a beat. Without looking up at me, he continued down the stairs, pulling me behind him. "I can't reveal operational information to you."

"You've told me so much, though."

"About me, only."

"Is anyone else involved?"

Antonio had suggested Henri. Could any of the other guards be in on it? Why did Vin complain about being so shut off from his handlers if there were others here?

"They keep us in the dark, so there's no chance we can reveal each other if we're caught." He stopped, turning enough to see the hand he still held in the dim light coming from the cave.

I pulled it away from him.

"Come on, Sam. We need to hurry."

· · · · · · · · · · ·

It was chilly and damp in the cave, with the rain pelting down outside. A shiver ran through me as I watched the seconds tick by on my watch. It had been four minutes since I disabled the camera. "Six minutes left, Vin."

He stood at the entrance to the cave, the low rumble of a boat engine approaching.

This was good work. Important work. I was helping the TPC fight an antiquities smuggler. It was the right choice.

Wasn't it?

The sympathy and regret for betraying Antonio's family was nothing more than Stockholm syndrome. It didn't matter Giovanni was being so nice, that I liked his daughter, or that someone had died mysteriously inside the walls of the estate. Or that Giovanni destroyed the evidence of the camera Elliot gave me. They were bad men doing the things I wanted to combat.

So why did this feel so wrong? I was still all turned around. My heart was the one stopping me when my brain told me to move forward.

A rib boat appeared, with its high roll bar in the back and a single occupant—a man in a black rain jacket pulled taut over muscled shoulders and chest, water pouring off him as he entered the protection of the cave. "The storm's good cover, but absolutely miserable."

"Five minutes left," I said.

The man in the boat looked at me, eyes narrowing. "Who's this? You're supposed to be here alone."

"She's a guest who supports the TPC." Vin stepped closer to the water's edge. "I needed some help to meet you."

The man nodded and reached under the boat's controls to a cabinet, pulling out something black and cylindrical. "It's waterproof and the right size. The tools you should need are inside."

"Four minutes," I said.

The man tossed the item to Vincenzo and piloted the boat around the statue at the center, water sloshing up over the edge of the walkway. "I'll be back when I hear from you."

"Three."

He left as quietly as he'd entered, the rain masking any noise long before he was out at sea.

Vincenzo urged me back to the staircase and disabled his security jammer before rushing into the stairwell with me.

"What is it?"

"You remember I told you about that painting? I think it's a case to get it out." He nudged me from behind. "Hurry up the stairs."

I took the steps two at a time until I was in the tasting room again. At the top of the stairs, I looked back at Vin. "You'll have to dry off before anyone sees you."

"Good point." He pulled a bar towel from the cupboard and used it to dry his hair. "We'll have to stay down here for a while."

What were the odds Leo or Antonio would be on their way? How long could Antonio tamp down on his jealousy before he came after me?

Chapter 39

Antonio

Leonardo and I sat together in the security control room. He knocked on camera thirteen's display, which had gone fuzzy. "This camera's been acting up the last couple of months. It needs replacing."

It was the cave's display.

Before we lost the signal, I'd glimpsed something brown at the edge of the frame. It had to be her braid. Samantha must have taken Vincenzo down there, using the tasting room door. But why? What were they doing there? Why was she spending so much time with... he was a TPC agent. That was why she was with him and I knew it, but after everything else which had happened, could she consider her safety over her need to put things right? Just for one day?

I pointed to the screen we'd been focused on prior to the cave monitor going haywire. "Johann went into the wine cellar an hour before Samantha and Henri did. No one else came in or out of the space during that time. And neither did anyone come in or out of the cave, and potentially through the secret passage."

"And no one knows why he was down there. Nothing on his body that would provide any clues, other than the note. But it may only be a clue pointing to him being an Interpol agent, which we already know."

"What about the small camera you found in the gallery? Giovanni said you suspect the men who brought in the crate?"

"Considering how fast they disappeared after the delivery, I do." Leonardo stared at the fuzzy monitor. "Giovanni's gone soft over the last two years. That's led to many of the men doing a poor job, because he forgives almost everything. I spoke with the two who welcomed the delivery men, and no one wanded them, let alone checked the crates. It would have been too easy for them to smuggle the camera in."

"Nothing on the recording?" It was a dangerous business bringing it up, in case Leonardo noticed something off in my actions or my mood, but I had to know if he had any suspicions about us.

He flung his hand in front of the monitors. "I've been telling Giovanni that this system needs to be updated for at least three years now. Too many cameras malfunctioning, files corrupting, and too many blind spots if you know what you're doing. It wasn't too bad originally, but now that he has this newfound respect for—" He threw his arms up in the air. "—all of humanity, he won't listen to reason. He trusts too much."

I'd gone back and forth every few hours while we were here, doubting Giovanni, believing the claims that he'd changed, wondering what secret game he was playing. Leonardo's frustration was obvious and not something he'd do to try and win me over for his boss. "He's really changed that much?"

His lip curled. "In case you forgot, I'm in charge of security, so it's my job to doubt and worry about everything. Giovanni thinks people will believe he's changed so long as he says he has. The world does not work that way."

"It would be a blessing if it did." I tapped a button on the control panel and switched to the wine cellar video from just before the lights went out on Samantha and me.

Leo scanned the other screens, also performing the duty of the man he'd chased away when we arrived.

I made a note of the timestamp when the lights went out, then switched to the cave camera, lining the times up. "There are only so many ways the lights could have gone off. The switch at the entrance, but it's clear on the video no one was there. The breaker could have blown, but you turned the lights on with the switch, so that's not it. That leaves the switch in the passage."

"But no one was down there." Leonardo stared at the cave display. "The breaker is possible, if someone else corrected it at the same time I arrived. It would be a big coincidence, but we should check the video of the electrical room."

"There aren't any other secret passageways I should know about?"

"Wait." Leo hit a button, switching another display to primary. "Look at this..."

Vincenzo walked into the frame in the wine cellar's live feed, his voice clear through the monitoring system. "Henri hides French wine down here underneath the Italian. There's a Jean Foillard Beaujolais somewhere. Maybe that will help your mood?"

Was it my imagination or did his hair look different from when he escorted her away from the kitchen? Messier? Her fingers had not been running through it. They hadn't.

Leonardo cocked his head. "They seem to get along quite well, don't they?"

Samantha appeared on the screen, carrying a glass half-full of red wine. "Sounds good."

"That's enough." I hit mute on the display. "What's your problem?"

"Me? Problem?" He hit the button to resume sound.

Samantha's laugh filled the room and I hit the mute button again.

"Is this still about that woman?"

He folded his arms. "It's always about you, isn't it? The amazing Tony Ferraro."

"I go by Antonio now."

"I remember Fat Tony wandering around these halls, slack jawed and drooling over what we did here." His jaw clenched. "I also remember you following Cristian everywhere. You were his little pet back then."

And I remember the boot licker you were, nothing more than Cristian's bodyguard.

"Now you're *her* little pet." He unfolded his arms long enough to point at the screen. "She's not much to look at, so she must be impressive in be—"

My fist headed toward his face faster than my thoughts processed the movement. But he was ready for it, countered with a dodge and swept my hand to the side. I stumbled forward, my right arm flinging out to catch myself on the desk before I fell. Pain screamed up my arm, even worse than when I'd been shot. "Vaffanculo a chi t'è morto!"

Leonardo shoved me into the wall and bit back, "She was my girlfriend!"

"Any woman who'd leave you that easily—" I spun to face him, bracing my bad arm, attempting to mask the agony. Preparing for him to come at me. "—was not worth your time!"

"What's going on here?" snapped Giovanni, hidden behind Leonardo's broad form.

"Nothing." Leonardo rolled his shoulders and straightened. Once he was facing my uncle, he'd have been sporting an expression of innocence. "We were remembering old times."

Gio scoffed. "Put on your best faces. Our guests are arriving."

"She's here?" asked Leo. Who was *she*? Unless this was my surprise?

"They just passed the gate. I want you out front to greet the car." Gio sighed. "They're guests whom I trust. Wand them but be polite about it."

Leo hummed in assent and left without another word.

Zio Gio looked me up and down. "Did he hurt you?"

No, like the adult I was, I attempted to hit him for insulting Samantha. Perhaps I should tell her what Leonardo said and let her deal with him. "No, Zio, I'm fine."

He smiled and nodded. "Let's go to the reception hall. Henri is preparing food and drinks to celebrate our big moment."

"My second surprise?"

"Exactly." He stretched an around my shoulder and ushered me out of the security room, as the guard who'd been there originally returned to his seat. "I'll send someone to fetch Samantha. She'll want to see this, too."

· · · ● · ● · ● · ·

The sound of voices carried down the hallway as Giovanni and I made our way toward the reception hall.

"Exiting a business such as mine comes with risk. Between the car nearly running over Cristian and Johann's death, we've seen two of those in as many days. Some of my associates trust me to step away quietly, while others don't. There's one pushing harder than the others, who's overstepped his bounds—by a lot."

"You mean Fiori?" How did any of this tie into the mysterious surprise?

"He's tried to hurt me more than once since I began discussing my withdrawal into private life, but last summer, things escalated. How much do you know about the stolen painting which surfaced at your uncle Andrea's studio last summer?"

Papa had told me the news on Christmas Eve. The TPC had accused Andrea of working with the thieves who delivered the painting to his studio in Roma. They had just learned that the woman behind the theft from my worksite in Pompeii had also been the one to sneak the painting into Zio Andrea's studio. "Only that it was linked to a theft from Pompeii in September."

He nodded, withdrawing the arm from my shoulders. "Sending me messages, reminders to stay quiet—that was expected. I never thought he'd go after my family and their business. That I cannot abide."

I stretched my bad arm downward so I could stuff my hand into my pocket. Every movement felt as if it was on fire. Arguing with Leonardo had been a foolish decision—not a decision at all, really. No one insulted my woman like that.

Gio stopped short of the archway into the room. It was cavernous, with exposed dark oak beams making up the vaulted ceiling. Arch-topped windows lined one wall, looking out toward the sea, while simpler windows on the other side looked out into the gardens. This room was distinct among those on the main floor. It had been built into the hill, rather than on top of it. Jagged pale rock dominated the rear of the room, the stucco wall following its edges. A meeting table of more dark wood took up the center with a banquette and pale green sofas beyond.

Henri straightened serving trays with a variety of sweets on the banquette, while Cristian inspected the work. Three guards maintained watch by the windows, while a slender man I didn't recognize stood staring out a window.

"Antonio!" Cesca shot up from one of the sofas, a half-eaten eclair in her hand. She started in our direction, but Gio gave a near imperceptible head shake and she nodded before sitting again.

"My wife and older daughter in Paris are unaffected, but Francesca was here when Johann died." Gio let out a long sigh. "I understand you don't just know Pasquale Fiori's name? You met him?"

"Sì, he helped Samantha and I after she hurt her ankle on a hike in Napoli."

"And you understand he was the one who took the fresco from your site?"

"I do."

"My goal was a clean break, not a war." He looked up at me, an honesty shining in his dark brown eyes. "I know you doubt all of this, but I hope you can appreciate the risk I've taken to prove it to you."

I scanned the room. No clues anywhere.

But a very excited Cesca practically bounced on her seat, so I joined her and her almost fully eaten eclair. "Henri normally only makes Italian meals, but these French pastries are amazing!"

"So we're here for something French?"

She made a motion like twisting a key over her lips. "I'm sworn to secrecy."

"There she is!" announced Giovanni from outside the room, in English.

"I narrowly avoided getting washed away in the deluge, but I'm here," replied a woman, in a smooth, unaccented English.

Giovanni appeared with a beautiful woman on his arm, slightly taller than him in her high heels. Dark brown hair and cream skin. Her clothes were impeccable, a long black wrap-style dress and a small blazing red top handle bag on the crook of her arm. Behind them walked Leonardo and a man the same size, with eyes and a gait which spoke of a more calculating danger than Leo's.

Cesca and I stood while the slender man at the window turned, and everyone made their way to the table at the center of the room.

"You didn't tell me Dr. Ferraro would be here," said the woman to Giovanni. She looked me up and down, smiled, then inclined her head toward the slender man. "I went to all the effort of securing an expert and you already had one."

"Mi scusi." I gritted my teeth through pulling out my right hand to shake. "You have me at a disadvantage."

"I normally do." She unthreaded her arm from my uncle's elbow and shook my hand, a surprisingly strong and confident grip. Fortunately, she only squeezed, rather than shaking.

"Antonio, I'd like you to meet Scarlett Reynolds. She and..." Giovanni paused and gestured to the man who'd come in with her.

"Her associate," said Scarlett, whose eyes flicked to the big man and then to the table.

The man nodded and placed a hard-sided black case on the surface.

"Of course." Giovanni approached the case as the man fell back into position behind Scarlett. Gio placed a hand on the case and extended his other toward me, a beaming smile on his face. "They've brought your surprise, my boy. Would you like to wait for—"

His gaze shifted to the entry into the room, and I turned to see Samantha and Vincenzo enter. She sported less of a frown than I'd hoped to see after she spent that much time with her ex. Regardless, at least that time was done.

Chapter 40

Samantha

A bead of sweat rolled down my back. No one had grabbed Vincenzo and me since our secret rendezvous with the TPC agent in the cave, so we must have avoided detection. He'd run the tube over to his room during a momentary break in the rain, only leaving my side for ten minutes, and getting wet enough to mask that his shirt hadn't dried fully from signaling his contact outside of the cave.

As he'd returned, he said there was a message on his phone that he was to deliver me to the reception hall. And here we were.

Antonio stood next to a slender woman with gleaming dark brown hair, wearing shoes as tall as the ones Antonio had bought me for New Year's Eve. His posture was rigid, right hand shoved deep in his pocket. When he'd turned to look at me, the pinched expression on his face made it clear he'd hit it on something and was in pain.

Fool man.

Bella, he mouthed, a smile sliding across his face.

No matter how much stress I was under, it vanished for a heartbeat. It was the same every time Antonio looked at me in that way. My world was complete and I couldn't help but smile, which caused his to grow.

Giovanni came to my side and slipped his arm around mine, pulling me into the room. He seemed too happy for the circumstances, with Johann's death just last night, plus discovering he'd been working with Interpol. Given Giovanni's history, he must have been good at hiding his intentions and emotions. "I'd like you to meet—"

The woman turned to face me and a memory flashed through my brain. It was the woman who'd sat next to me on the flight to Naples, when I'd run off to see Antonio. "Scarlett?"

Giovanni's face fell, while Antonio's eyebrows rose in surprise.

Before I could rescue her from not remembering my name, she held out a hand. "Sam, right?"

"Right." I scanned the room. Antonio, Giovanni, Cristian, Cesca, Leonardo, and three armed men I recognized. That meant the tall, scary-looking one and the slender, bookish one were likely with Scarlett.

Leonardo spoke up. "How do you two know each other?" His tone was accusatory, not conversational, as usual.

Before I could snap back at him, Scarlett fluttered her eyelashes. "We sat next to each other on a plane in August, when I came for our first meeting."

She'd slept most of the flight, while I'd been too stressed to do the same, reading and re-reading the letter Antonio wrote to me after I dumped him.

Scarlet touched my arm. "We'll have to catch up once the unveiling is finished."

Giovanni steered me toward Antonio and placed a hand on his nephew's back. "Go ahead. Open it."

This was the grand moment. This black case was the reason we'd been subjected to an entire week here, rather than just the day they needed to show him the conservation studio plans. The tall man with Scarlett placed his thumb on a security pad and there was an audible click.

Antonio undid the latches and slowly lifted the lid. Every eye in the room was on the case.

Except for the man with Scarlett. He would have known what was inside, and his eyes were trained on the men with the guns. He wore a Glock at his waist. How had he gotten that past Leonardo?

Antonio sucked in a deep breath and I returned my focus to the big surprise. Inside the case, encased in a protective foam lining, was a fourteen- by ten-inch piece of limestone fresco decorated with yellow flowers. Next to it, a small terracotta pot.

My stomach flipped. My eyes met Antonio's. Oh my god, was Giovanni telling the truth about everything? Cristian had told Antonio that Pasquale Fiori stole this fresco and pot—had Giovanni gotten them back?

Antonio breathed, "The stolen fresco. From the Casa di Marte. How?"

Giovanni's smile was as wide as I'd ever seen from Antonio's father. At that moment, the similarity between the two men was uncanny.

Antonio said, "I don't understand. Did you buy this from him?"

Giovanni inclined his head toward Scarlett. "This has been in the works for months. After Fiori tampered with Andrea's work, I knew something had to be done. So when he stole this from my family, I decided to take it back."

Antonio leaned closer, inspecting the fresco. Without looking up at me, he said, "Is it the right size? It feels like it is."

I'd taken a measurement of the missing piece and this matched the size and shape perfectly. I joined him to look at the edges. "Looks like the same tool marks, too. What about the pigment pot?"

"It's yellow, which is what the missing one was, but I need to take it back to the lab." He straightened, peering at Giovanni. "I can take it back to the lab, sì?"

Giovanni spread his arms wide. "This is a gift from me to you. Do with it as you will. But I assume you'll return it to the Archaeological Park."

The slender man withdrew a sheet of paper from an inside pocket of his jacket. He unfolded it, producing a rough rectangle with irregular edges. It was an exact tracing of the piece stolen from the Casa. He laid it on top of the fresco, lining up the edges. "The size is exactly right. I have a portable Raman spectrometer that we can use to confirm the pigment."

Antonio looked at the man. "Do I know you?"

He nodded at Antonio. "We met at a symposium in—"

"Munich? Three years ago?"

"Daniel Weber." The slender man's face lit up, seeming excited Antonio remembered him. "I spoke about preserving the frescoes in—"

"—in Saint Mark's Cathedral in Alexandria!"

"Yes, exactly! Ms. Reynolds invited me here to verify the authenticity of the pieces."

As the two men reminisced and went about setting up the spectrometer, I faded to the edge of the room. It was too much to process. The tube Vincenzo's contact had delivered, the painting he was going to take from the crate, and now Giovanni returning the lost pieces from Pompeii.

Scarlett joined me, while her associate hovered nearby. "Don't tell me Dr. Ferraro is the one you were flying to in August?"

I kept my voice low, rather than inviting further scrutiny from Leonardo. Although whispering probably did exactly that. I looked at Antonio, hand still clutched in his pocket, explaining to a rapt Cesca how the spectrometer worked. A giddy energy flowed out of him and my heart swelled to see it. "He is."

"Good looking man. Something wrong with his arm?"

"He was shot a week ago." I shook my head to clear the memories before they came over me again. It was in the past. I was stronger than those memories. "I thought you said you were in tech security?"

"Good memory. You could say I'm *tech-nically* in security." She smiled, raising an eyebrow and shifting her gaze toward Leonardo. "Well, technically... in *bypassing* security."

I stifled a gasp. "You're a thief?"

"Oh no." She swiped a hand through her hair. "I'm a recovery agent. I find and return lost things. As I understand it, that fresco and pot were stolen from the Pompeii Archaeological Park and Dr. Ferraro works there. I can't stand when people steal cultural treasures like that."

"We should've talked more on the plane. You and I apparently have a great deal in common." Except no matter how she dressed it up, she was a thief. But did stealing from the man who stole it make it less wrong? And did it even matter? Because wasn't that the same thing I'd helped Vincenzo with earlier? Getting the tools to steal something from Giovanni?

Unless the TPC was wrong about whatever was in those crates. What about *The Magdalen*? Why not take her back? She was worth a lot of money and didn't belong to Gio either.

What was in that crate that was so important?

And why did I care so much? I should have been rejoicing that the surprise was revealed and we could leave. Antonio would return to Naples a conquering hero—who couldn't tell anyone how he got the items back.

And Vincenzo would recover the painting from the gallery. Except I hadn't given him the passcode yet. I'd have to find another private moment with him.

"Everything looks right," said Antonio. "Zio, I can't thank you enough for this."

Gio tipped his head, the unspoken message clear: This was something he wanted his brothers to hear about. How much of a risk was it for him to have this stolen? Would Antonio suffer Fiori's revenge over it? Or would Giovanni be taking the brunt of that?

"It was good seeing you again, Sam." Scarlett squeezed my arm. "I'm glad things worked out for you."

A bright flash of lightning forked across the sky outside the seaside windows. The rain—which had eased to a steady drizzle while Vincenzo and I were in the wine cellar—resumed the downpour.

"Rav," said Scarlett, and her associate joined her. "We need to get going."

He nodded, shaggy black hair falling onto his forehead.

Before they could leave, Leonardo was at her side. "Are you sure you don't want to stay for snacks or a meal? Our chef is preparing a feast to celebrate."

A feast sounded like Giovanni was expecting us to stay the night. A boom of thunder cracked overhead.

"You're persistent, Leo, I'll give you that." Scarlett blinked slowly at him and patted his chest. "Maybe next time."

Leo grinned at her, a hungry look coming over him. For all the barbs and insults, it was almost dizzying to think of this man as a human, but the lust in his eyes made it clear he was not a robot. "I'll have to be sure we contract with your company again."

"You do that," she said with a wink. Without asking for permission, she and Rav left, two of the guards moving quickly to catch up with them.

A strong arm wrapped around my waist from behind and picked me up. "Can you believe this, bella? The Casa will be complete again!"

I settled on my feet once Antonio's excitement was over, and I turned around in his grasp. "It's unbelievable."

"It's a miracle." His eyes slid closed and his head fell back.

"We're still leaving tonight, though, right? It's almost six o'clock already, so we'd be rolling in pretty late, but—"

"What?" said Cesca. "But Henri's making a celebration meal. How can we celebrate the fresco or you guys if you leave?"

Antonio pulled close to me, his nose finding my ear, and his voice dropping so only I could hear him. "I'll do whatever you want, amore. Stay, leave, go back to the airport and fly to Australia. I don't care."

"Australia?" I leaned back to look at him. "What's in Australia?"

He shrugged, barely able to hold back his laughter. "Then Vegas?"

I smacked him, his excited energy invading my cells. "Stop with the Vegas."

"I've always wanted to see Vegas," said Cesca.

Cristian said, "When you're twenty-one."

A prickling at the back of my neck reminded me that everyone's attention was on Antonio and me. He may have been fine being the center of everything, but I wasn't. I stepped out of his grasp and he feigned a pout. "You want to stay, don't you?"

He nodded. "We can leave tomorrow morning."

"It's settled!" Giovanni clapped his hands and turned to Daniel. "Dr. Weber, would you care to join us? There are plenty of guest rooms and food."

"Yes, that's very generous," the slender man said as he finished packing up his spectrometer. "I'd appreciate some time with Dr. Ferraro."

Antonio grabbed my waist again, but with only one good hand, I could have easily spun out of his grip. That would make more of a scene, so I stayed close. "Tonight, we dine, my love. For tomorrow, we return to the bakery for breakfast and head to Mario's."

CHAPTER 41

ANTONIO

"And then he said—" Cristian laughed, long and loud, slapping the dining table.

I finished with him, tears streaming down my cheeks. "—in case I get a hole in one!"

We raised our glasses and took another mouthful of wine.

Samantha sat stone-faced next to us.

"Bella, he was a golfer. Two pairs of pants. You know, what if he got a hole in—"

"Yeah, I understand," she said with a yawn. "I just can't believe you two are still going at this hour."

"What?" I flipped over my watch and squinted at it. "It's only..."

"One in the morning and you're drunk," she said. "Giovanni and Daniel left an hour ago. Cesca left four hours ago."

"I'm not drunk." I grabbed for her, but she moved far too quickly for me. "I've only had three glasses of wine."

"Three too many with your codeine." She nudged me, and I tipped backward against the chair.

I waved a hand to toss her silly comment aside. "Amore, I grew up with red wine in my nursing bottle."

Cristian chuckled. "And I probably put it there."

That threw us into another fit of laughter.

Samantha cracked the barest of smiles and stood. "I'm going to bed. Can I have the key?"

"Don't leave me, Samantha." I dragged out the middle syllable of her name, the trick that caused goosebumps to crawl up her arms and made her purr.

"You could choose to come upstairs now, and I wouldn't have to." She was so serious.

I waggled my eyebrows at her. "Are you inviting me to your bed?"

"We don't allow that around here, you know." Cristian shook his head and took another drink. "Papa's silly rules. Look where it's gotten us."

"Here..." I dug into my pocket, searching for the key. It was there somewhere. I'd had it earlier.

She sank her hand into my right pocket and withdrew the key. How did it get on that side? "Next time, we make sure we both have keys to *our* room."

Cristian hollered toward an exit from the dining room. "Hey! Who's out there?"

One of the guards with the ridiculous gun at his hip poked his head in. "Do you need something?"

"I need an escort to our room." She rolled her eyes and kissed me on the cheek, then pulled back to look at me eye-to-eye. Her giant pupils practically swallowed her stunning irises whole. "Don't stay up too late."

"Your eyes are the most beautiful shade of green. Have I ever told you that?"

She gave me a tight-lipped smile and kissed my forehead. "Love you, you drunken fool."

"I love you, too." I snatched her hand before she could go and brought it to my lips. It had a hint of sugar and chocolate from her dessert. "You taste so good."

With a shake of her head, she was off with the guard.

As soon as she was out of earshot, a chuckle burst out of me. "She's right. I need some water."

Cristian laughed and stood, grabbing a pitcher from the end of the table for me. "You seem quite taken with her."

I accepted the glass and chugged it down. "I thought I'd known love before I met her, but she's something special."

"Thought about settling down?"

"Thought about it?" I passed the empty glass across the table and Cristian refilled it for me. "I intend to grow old with that woman. Play with our grandchildren together. I can't imagine anyone more perfectly suited for me."

Cristian's smile faded, and he stared at the glass for a long moment before passing it back to me. He was clearly the more sober one. "This whole thing with Papa after the heart attack—it was a big change. Not everyone was happy about it. But if it means I could sit at your wedding or meet those grandchildren someday, it's worth it."

"Money and power don't buy happiness?"

He shook his head. "It's been so long, I almost forgot how much I enjoyed your company."

"And considering the circumstances..."

"I should go check on Leonardo. He's probably still at the security desk reviewing videos."

"Does the man ever sleep?"

"He's a pig's ass sometimes, but he's doing his best to keep everyone safe."

"He doesn't think we're at risk at all?"

"With patrols doubled and monitoring increased, we're as safe here as anywhere."

"Good. I worry about Cesca wandering around the house." I drained my glass and stood. Perhaps a little too quickly. I braced myself against the table and let out a groan when my right arm moved too fast. "Have you ever been shot in the bicep? It hurts a surprising amount."

Cristian laughed. "Shoulder, twice in the leg, one that nicked my waist, and a grazing shot across my forearm. But no biceps."

"As much as I enjoyed your company—" I walked out of the room with him. The hallway swayed, but only slightly. "—I don't miss all of that. The violence."

"I thought I would." Cristian pointed to the turn ahead of us. It's all I've ever known. "But I don't. I even started seeing a woman in Terracina."

I came to an abrupt halt and grabbed his arm. "As in a relationship? More than a few nights?"

"Would you believe Papa won't even allow *me* to have overnight visitors?" He inclined his head in the direction we'd been walking and continued. "I don't know how you changed his mind on that."

"How long have you been seeing her?"

"She was Papa's real estate agent for the conservation studio building. It's been six months now."

"Are *you* going to settle down?"

He gave me a sidelong glance. "She has children, two and five, who both like me."

"Marone, no!" I laughed, focusing hard on the door ahead of us, which led into the security control room. "That's wonderful news."

He spluttered a laugh. "Just don't tell Leo. He'd never approve."

"What was going on with him and the recovery woman?"

Cristian paused, hand on the door, failing to control his laughter. "I think she identified the biggest threat here and neutralized him. How do you think her man got his gun past Leo?"

• • • • •• • • •• •

Leonardo barely acknowledged us as we came in. With the lockdown in place, he had two long-term men working the security displays at all times, but at the moment, he took one of the seats, its normal occupant hovering behind him. Leo's brow was furrowed and his lids looked heavy.

Cristian slapped him on the back, still in the laughing mood we'd carried with us from the dining room. "Find anything new?"

Leonardo grunted. "I did." ·

He worked the controls, bringing a view of the wine cellar to the larger central display. Johann entered the frame in fast forward mode, walked past the casks and wine bottles on their shelves and made his way into the tasting room. We'd watched this several times before, searching for clues or for someone to wander through the video. Leo let it play a few seconds longer, while the time stamp scrolled by.

"We watched all of this already." I cast a sidelong glance at Cristian, who rolled his eyes dramatically. We should have stayed at the table for another glass of wine. "What did you see?"

Leo held up a finger to silence me—eliciting suppressed laughter from Cristian and me—and hit a button which brought the speed to normal. He increased the volume to its maximum. A faint noise came across the system and we all leaned closer, the jokes and teasing forgotten.

It was the sound of stone grinding on stone.

I hit rewind and played it again. "The door down to the cave?"

Leo shooed my hand from the controls, keeping his finger up. There was another noise. "I can't make it out."

Cristian said, "A voice?"

"Choking?" I asked. "Difficulty breathing?"

Leo gestured to the two guards. "We've listened to it at least fifteen times. I don't know what it means."

"This adds more questions to the pile, doesn't it?" I ran a hand through my hair and gripped the back of my neck. Thoughts swam through my brain, and I'd had too much wine to make sense of most of them. "Chief among them, who closed the door without telling anyone Johann was lying there? Unless it's on a timer?"

Leo's focus remained on the screen in front of him. "It's not. The mechanism is very strong. If it was natural causes, perhaps he collapsed as the door was opening, and it pushed him against the wall. Heart attack? Stroke? Aneurysm? We haven't received any of those details from the autopsy yet. But his body would have been hidden when the door was open, so someone could have closed it and never known."

"But..." I closed my eyes, trying to shake some sobriety into my brain. "No one else came in or out before Samantha got down there, and the door certainly was not open when she arrived."

Cristian massaged his temples. "I've had too much to drink to figure this out tonight."

"I feel the same." I clapped a hand on my cousin's shoulder. My brain was not processing properly, but my gut told me I was being foolish wandering around the estate drunk. Samantha sometimes confessed to the hairs prickling at the back of her neck the instant her subconscious realized something bad was happening; this was similar. "Have you found out why he was down there?"

"Henri mentioned Samantha's tour to him. It could have been a thank you to Henri for all the time they spent in the kitchen together. Or..." Leo leaned back in the chair and glowered up at me. "Johann liked your woman, so perhaps he went down to make sure everything was ready for her little visit?"

I let out a sigh. Attempting to punch Leo earlier had been stupid. If nothing else, this week reminded me I'd grown beyond these men and our petty squabbles. Had he been nicer to Samantha from the get-go, things would have gone far smoother. "Leo, I'm sorry."

His lip curled. "You're drunk."

"Sì, but this is beside the point." I pressed a hand to my heart. "About our discussion earlier, I was in the wrong. I'd like to move past that."

The two guards working became suddenly rather interested in a display at the far end of the control center. My gaze snapped to it but saw nothing. They were avoiding the conversation.

Leo's snarl lessened slightly. That was an improvement.

"Mi dispiace," I said. "This is not the time to discuss it."

A knock came on the window inset in the door, and we turned to see Vincenzo. He entered the room, two small cups balanced on a tray, the scent of coffee filling my lungs. "I didn't expect all of you here or I would have brought more."

"Grazie," said the standing guard as he took a cup.

"You're supposed to be working the tower," said Leo. "Where's Henri? He normally delivers the food and drink."

"Asleep, I think." Vincenzo shrugged his pretty little shoulders. "He had a long day with the visitors and dinner."

The smell of the beans overwhelmed the small space. I turned to Cristian. "We should go for some coffee."

"It might help you get into your room tonight," he chuckled. "I don't think she was impressed with your condition."

"Samantha's already upstairs?" asked Vincenzo.

Leonardo stood, taking up more space than was comfortable in the room. He looked down at me, grinding his teeth. My apology must have impacted him, as he neither made a barb at me, nor did he encourage Vincenzo to visit her. "I could use a coffee, too."

"Perfetto." Cristian navigated his way around Leonardo and held the door open. "Let's all go, like old times."

"Except this time will be coffee, not more alcohol," said Leonardo.

CHAPTER 42

SAMANTHA

I stared at myself in the mirror as I brushed my teeth. Bloodshot eyes, drooping lids, and limp hair. What a sight. Despite that, Antonio's last words were about how beautiful he thought I looked. I spit the toothpaste into the sink and washed it down the drain.

He was hopeless.

And how long would he be up with Cristian? It was late and I was tired, but I didn't want to fall asleep while he was still out there without a key. The smart thing would have been to force him upstairs with me. Or at least have him walk me up here so he could have kept it.

There was a knock at the door, so I dropped the toothbrush into its holder and ran my fingers through my hair to liven it up. Almost pinched my cheeks to add a rosy glow. He'd still be too drunk to notice, anyway.

He was sober enough for me to tease, though.

I stopped in front of the door. "Go away. There's no one here." I bit back a chuckle, which mingled with a yawn.

"Samantha!" came a hushed voice. Not Antonio's.

"Who is it?"

"It's Vin. I need to talk to you."

My hand reached slowly toward the lock. Why would he be here at this hour? Did he know I was alone? "What do you want?"

"I need help. It's time."

Time for what? I'd already helped him with one task today. What could he possibly need? And what would Antonio say if he saw Vin at our door? The last time he'd been drunk and saw my big brother stand-in kiss the top of my head, he'd grown so jealous he flew from Naples to Brenton the next day.

But Vincenzo wasn't a big brother. Wasn't a friend. No, he was a former lover. He'd broken my heart. Antonio would probably break his face.

Get over it, Sam.

I unlocked the door and pulled it open, mouthing, *Camera*. The finial camera was right behind him. This was risky.

"It's off. Don't worry about it."

"What do you mean?"

He pushed his way past me and closed the door.

"Vin, you're not welcome in—"

Behind him, lightning flashed around the edges of the curtains to the terrace. The weather had shifted as Scarlett left and another storm had rolled in.

Vincenzo lifted his shirt, revealing toned muscle.

My breath caught. Wrong. This was wrong. "Vin, stop—"

But he also revealed the black tube the man in the boat had given him. He pulled it out of his waistband and let the shirt fall back into place. "I can't do this alone. You're the only one I trust. The only one the TPC can trust."

"There are guards everywhere."

He waved his hands. "We don't have time for this. Did you get the code for the gallery?"

"Yes, when we went to the gallery earlier, but Leonardo has the place—"

"Everything's coordinated through the security control room. I took care of the guards and—"

I stepped away from him, clenching my muscles to get the blood flowing and to wake myself up. "Took care of?"

"Don't worry." He closed the distance between us, but didn't touch me. "They're asleep and the security cameras are all disabled."

"Vin..." I backed against the door.

"Sam, you said you'd help. We need to get that painting out of here before Giovanni hands it over to its buyer. If he does that, we'll never see it again."

"He returned the fresco." It was a stupid response, but all I could come up with. Antonio and I had doubted everything Giovanni said about his change of heart and business. There was no way a smuggler with as much success and money as him would give it all up. But he had Scarlett get the Casa di Marte fresco back. That meant something.

Didn't it?

Vin's face hardened. "He paid a thief to steal it."

"From another thief." My throat tightened. Was I defending Scarlett and her methods, solely because she returned the fresco?

"You don't believe that." He came so close I could smell his cologne, bringing with it all the memories of when we were together. Confessing our love, making plans for when he moved to the States, dreaming about shared careers tracking down criminals. "You believe in law and order, Sam."

"I believe in doing in the right thing."

He raised the tube. "Then put on something you can slip this under—it's too obvious in my waistband—and help me do the right thing."

I looked into his eyes, the light gray invisible in the shadows. This was the sort of thing I was always doing to Antonio. I'd get a harebrained scheme in my head about solving an art crime and he'd counter with all the reasons we should report it to the authorities and go about our lives. Now Vin was asking me to get involved in his scheme, and I was the one resisting, even though he *was* the authorities. "I don't know when Antonio will be back."

He smiled and his shoulders relaxed, like he recognized my resistance was over. "I was just talking to him. He's heading to the kitchen with Cristian and Leonardo for coffee. I think they'll be there a while."

"With Leonardo?" I hurried past Vin to my suitcase and pulled out a pair of lounge pants. The tube was only two inches in diameter and two feet long, which could easily be concealed against my thigh. I ripped a hole in the deep pocket to feed the cylinder through.

"It sounds as though they used to be friends."

"How long will this take?" I went into the bathroom to get changed and closed the door over, so we could still talk.

"Gallery, cave, and done in under thirty minutes." He handed the tube in through the open door when I reached for it. It was a lot heavier than I'd expected and something inside clanked when I moved it too fast.

"He'll be at least that long downstairs, won't he?" *Please*. I didn't want him coming up here to find me gone. The doubts in his head would consume him.

Vin's voice softened. "He will. And my contact in the boat will be there in fifteen, so we need to hurry."

Elliot Skinner and I had discussed a plan to get me working as a consultant with the FBI Art Crime Team. We were building a portfolio of cases, proving I didn't have to be stationed in a field office. So I could work from anywhere I wanted to. Surely securing this painting would go a long way toward that goal. It would prove I could do important things.

Then I'd be able to settle down in Brenton with Antonio and my family around me. And if Antonio and I weren't really meant to be together, I could move. Maybe back to Boston to help with the Gardner Museum case again. Maybe to Texas or Florida with warmer winters than the Midwest.

Or maybe even back to London for the occasional case the FBI coordinated with Scotland Yard.

But I wanted it to work with Antonio. I wanted to live in Brenton with my family and new friends, whether I stayed on with Foster Mutual Insurance as an adjuster or switched to Special Investigations like they offered me last week.

No matter what it was, I could still be with Antonio.

I blinked at myself in the mirror, just as haggard as earlier, but with a different light shining from inside. I could do this.

And I could have everything I wanted.

· · · · ● · ● · · · ·

Vin pulled a screwdriver and a small pry bar out of the tube I'd carried to the gallery. We'd only seen one guard on our way down, but Vin and I smiled and said he was escorting me to the kitchen for a late-night snack. The man waved us on and I got us into the gallery.

I held the tube while he worked on opening the crate as quickly as he could. It was three feet tall and wide, two deep, made of pale wood, and it would open from the top as soon as the screws were out. "A drill would have been easier."

He put his weight into unscrewing the lid, shoulders bouncing slightly. "I'll tell them that the next time I have to do something like this."

"Or send two screwdrivers. I feel useless."

"Listen at the door. We shouldn't have any company, but it's best to be certain."

I nodded and crossed to the gallery door, pressing my ear against it.

"So, you never told me—why didn't you join the FBI?" He grunted as he started on the third screw. "I'm sure you didn't fail any of the application process."

"Long story. Not interested in talking about it."

"Do you still follow the news on frauds and robberies?" He chuckled, moving at a remarkable pace. He was on the fourth already. "I remember you talking so much through our art crime classes, like you knew half of what any of the instructors were going to say."

"Sometimes." More like all the time. That's how I'd identified the stolen painting at the auction in August. "I have other hobbies now."

Before moving to the fifth screw, he pointed at *The Magdalen*. "That's the one you said was stolen?"

"Yeah. Giovanni said it came from a dealer in Brazil and started talking about bringing pieces home to Italy." I brought the pry bar over when he was on the last screw and loosened the tight-fitting lid. Once he was done, we lifted it off, revealing a framed painting stored in cellophane wrap, cushioned with blocks of wood and pink Styrofoam.

"Give me a hand." He gestured to the end of the crate, and I held it steady while he withdrew the painting. He took a quick peek, then laid it on its front. "That's the right one. We're running low on time. We need to get it out of the frame and rolled up. There's a staple remover in the tube."

I nodded, heart accelerating. Waking me up. He split the cellophane with the screwdriver as I pulled out the staple remover. We worked in silence, as quickly as possible. Unscrewed the offset clamps holding the painting in its frame. Worked in concert with the staple remover and—as cumbersome as it was—the pry bar to remove the tacks holding the canvas to the wooden stretcher that held it taut.

Antonio would kill me for handling a painting so indelicately, but Vincenzo's frenzied movements were contagious.

Vin lifted the stretcher out. "Put that back in the crate and redo the screws. If we're lucky, they'll assume they were cheated."

"Don't have enough time to do all of it." I secured the stretcher in the frame with half its clamps and slid it into the crate with the shipping blocks.

"Leonardo believes one of the men who brought it—" He scooped up the tacks and placed them inside a bag he lay next to the tube. "—also brought that secret camera in here."

"So it would be a reasonable assumption on his part that they didn't actually bring the painting—just used the crate as a ruse." I began screwing the lid back onto the crate. That theory would only hold if Giovanni didn't tell anyone the truth about the camera.

Antonio and I needed to get out before the crates were opened.

"I wish I knew who they were," he said. "What were they hoping to get pictures of?"

I paused, watching Vin for a moment. Elliot had implied going after *The Magdalen* was an FBI-only operation, so Vin still didn't know I'd brought the camera in. *Should I tell him the truth?*

Vin didn't look up, just began rolling the canvas, preparing to place it inside the tube.

I glimpsed a flash of yellow on the front. My breath hitched. Then green.

The painting was of yellow flowers.

No, no, no. It had to be a coincidence. Pasquale Fiori's yacht was *The Five Sunflowers*, named after the only lost painting of Van Gogh's *Sunflowers* series. Fiori had stolen the yellow flower fresco from Pompeii, plus the yellow pigment to go with it.

The screwdriver slipped and fell out of my grasp, my palm jamming down on the screw I was working on. I grunted in pain. "Do you know who Giovanni was going to sell it to?"

Vincenzo shook his head. "All I know is that it was coming from Cape Town. There were a few buyers on the short list the last time I got that report."

The fresco wasn't recovered. It was traded. Fiori had sent it to Giovanni as payment for this painting. And Giovanni used it to manipulate Antonio.

Giovanni had lied about everything.

"Give me your phone," I said.

"I can't do that. We have to—"

I finished the last screw, tossed him the screwdriver, and held out my hand. "Give me your fucking phone."

His head jerked back, but he withdrew the phone from his pocket and handed it to me. He'd said they monitored communications, but if the security systems were down, it was the perfect opportunity.

I walked over to *The Magdalen*, snapped a photo of it, and texted it to Elliot Skinner, with a message: *E - Inside Giovanni Ferraro's house per geocode data attached. Don't respond to this number.*

Behind me, I heard the tools drop into the tube. Vin was ready.

I handed the phone back to him, snatched the tube, and shoved it through the bottom of my pocket, holding tight to the end. "Let's get this painting out of here."

CHAPTER 43

ANTONIO

Leonardo entered the kitchen first, heading straight for a lower cupboard by the sink to retrieve a disassembled moka pot, large enough for the three of us. "I'll make the coffee. You two will just hurt yourselves."

Cristian elbowed me, knocking me—and by bad arm—into the doorframe.

"Che cazzo," I hissed under my breath. Apparently we didn't need to deal with boiling water to hurt ourselves.

"Be careful." Leo filled a kettle and put it on to boil, while Cristian opened and closed various cupboard doors.

"The beans are down here," said Leo, withdrawing a stainless canister from underneath the island. "You've never made your own, have you?"

I pulled out a stool on the opposite side of the island from him and sat, while Leo scooped out some dark beans to fill the grinder at the back of the counter.

"Why would I?" Cristian hollered over the grinder as he took the seat next to me. "There's always someone working here who can make it for me."

Leonardo shook his head and placed the pot on the island. He went about filling the basket with grounds, leveled it off with a finger, and sat it down in front of us. He yawned, reaching for his neck and stretching it out. "Johann's file is clean."

"What do you mean?" I asked.

"I mean there's no sign he could have been with Interpol. No gaps in his history, excellent references from other people he worked for..." His eyes were bloodshot with dark circles underneath. "But I didn't hire him, so there are questions I would have asked that I can't find answers to."

Cristian leaned closer to me. "We only promoted Leo to the security head position a year and a half ago. After Papa's incident, his predecessor was exhibiting symptoms he may have been involved in the conspiracy with the old chef."

"And I said we should have gone through everyone's backgrounds again." Leo crossed to the stove and removed the kettle, returning to fill the moka's base. "I'm starting that tomorrow."

Cristian only nodded, no retorts or jokes to be had. That was as close as he'd get to acknowledging he made the wrong decision then—assuming he was the one who'd made it.

No doubt he'd discover something in Vincenzo's history, if he looked closely enough. I'd have to tell Samantha about that, so she could warn him. As much as I hated having her ex-boyfriend around, I could hardly leave him to whatever fate Leo would have in store for him after discovering he was with the Carabinieri.

"And I found something else on the video recordings earlier." Leo dropped the basket into the moka's base, then held the base with a towel to protect his hand from the heat while he twisted the top on. He pointed at me with the towel-clad hand. "When you and your little investigator were down there."

Her name is Samantha. The room swam for a moment and I held the counter's edge. Definitely too much to drink. "What was it?"

Cristian chuckled next to me, gripping my good arm to steady me.

"Nothing helpful." Leo moved back to the stove with the pot and placed it on a burner, dialing the flame to low. "A blur on the cave's camera. The best I could figure was that it was the sleeve of a black shirt, but all the men here wear black shirts."

I swallowed hard, needing the coffee in my system immediately. "I don't understand."

Cristian leaned an elbow on the counter. "One of the men snuck through the cave, up the stairs, and pulled the cupboard down next to Samantha?"

"I think so," said Leo.

The alcohol churned in my stomach. That was it. I was never drinking again. At least, not while I was on medication. Stupid choice. "I talked to Vincenzo before I joined her in there. He said he was—" No. It couldn't be. "—he was assigned to the perimeter by the cave."

Leo shook his head. "I suspected him at first, too. I checked the recordings from the other cameras down there, and he appears to have followed his prescribed route. There are moments at which he was not visible, but it's unlikely he could have done it without missing his checkpoints."

"But possible?" I said, sliding off my stool, ready to dash up the stairs to her. Except I'd probably trip and break my nose.

"I doubt he'd do it." Leo scoffed. "I've seen the way he looks at her."

"You son of a—"

"Bad timing, but I need to piss," muttered Cristian. He stood, pressed my shoulder to force me back onto my stool, and headed for the door. "Don't kill each other while I'm gone."

I pointed a finger at Leonardo. I'd attempted to apologize to this man, and this was what I got for it? "Don't you speak of her—"

"Calm down." He leaned forward on the counter, taunting me with the nearness of his jaw. Fortunate for him, he was far enough I couldn't reach him without embarrassing myself again. "I don't know why, but it would appear his lust is no comparison to her feelings for you."

"Why did you do it?"

"Do what?"

"Push them together." It was a guess, based on how often Vincenzo showed up when Leonardo handled the guard assignments and how often he mentioned the two of them were together. Based on the sly look which crossed his face, I was right.

He turned to the stove, to monitor the moka, which didn't need monitoring other than to keep his ears open. "You don't deserve her."

I snorted. "I hear that a lot."

"There!" Leo rounded on me, finger jabbing in my direction. "There it is again. Never taking anything seriously!"

I waved his comment aside. "Says the man who takes everything *too* seriously."

"Not seriously enough!" His arms flew wide, eyes scanning the room. "I had an Interpol agent inside these walls and now he's dead."

"Neither of those are your fault."

"I should have had this position five years ago, but you—" His hands landed on the counter, his eyes narrowing. "—ensured that didn't happen."

Either I was even more drunk than I thought, or he was making no sense. "What did I have to do with it?"

"You and that stubborn jeweler almost ruined everything."

I squeezed my eyes shut, scrolling back to the day I'd tried to forget for nine years. "Me? I was in hospital for a week. I nearly died and you blame me for your job?"

"Always running your mouth, thinking you were such a gift."

Running my mouth? "So, it's not about the woman?"

"Anna Maria. Say it."

It was late, I was growing tired, and he was babbling. "Fine. Anna Maria."

"You don't even remember her, do you?"

I shrugged one shoulder, rather than biting back at him. All I could remember was that I was as full of myself as he accused, high on my ability to charm anyone into doing anything. After Leonardo... what did he do? Something that pissed me off. Either way, I charmed his girlfriend into my bed. It was a petty, selfish move that I'd already apologized for.

His shoulders rose, like he was about to launch over the counter, a vein pulsing in his neck. "An hour before we left for the jeweler, she told me everything."

"The moka's spluttering," I said, as much to avoid his gaze as to save the coffee. "It's going to burn."

He grabbed the pot and spun to the sink, running cold water over the base to stop the brewing process. Dropping it onto the counter, he leaned over it with his back to me. His breaths were deep and ragged.

The drunken haze was still there but easing its way to the edge of my consciousness, rather than veiling the entire thing.

Leonardo was my friend when I moved to Roma. He would come into town to stay with Cristian, we'd party on the weekends, and he'd tease me about my studies. 'You're a Ferraro,' he'd say. 'You don't have to get all these degrees. Just work for your uncle.'

I'd go to the gym with him and Cristian, and I transformed from Fat Tony into Antonio. Learned to use my charisma for picking up women instead of only making them laugh and admiring them from afar.

Most of it, I even hid from my parents. They chastised me for spending too much time with Cristian, but they knew only a fraction of what I did with him. They didn't know about the weeks I'd spend at Giovanni's, the work I did for him, nor did I allow Mario to tell them about the shooting. As far as they were concerned, moving to Napoli for the last year of my master's degree was a sign of great accomplishment.

Other than Mario and the men here, none of those close to me knew about my time working for Giovanni. Until Samantha dragged it out of me. And she was still by my side.

And she was right. I had to find a way to reconcile my anger over what happened with the appreciation for it making me a better person. It took years until I recognized how wrong I'd been for betraying Leonardo's friendship—the truth only dawning on me after I found my own fiancée in bed with another man.

This moment with Leonardo might be my only chance to heal this old scar and let it go. "I blamed you for the shooting."

He let out a mocking laugh. "Of course you did."

"I was in the wrong with Anna Maria."

"You were." His shoulders fell an inch, the edge leaving his voice. Who could blame him for overreacting to my success with the jeweler's negotiations, if he'd just heard about my betrayal? "But rest assured, Dario was punished heavily, as was I. Then after your other cousin whisked you away, I thought they'd throw me out. Every day without you here, they reminded me it was my fault."

"You lost your woman and their trust."

Leonardo pulled three small cups from a cupboard and poured the coffee into them. He pushed one across the counter to me. "I was under consideration to lead the security team five years ago, but they were still angry over you leaving. They hired someone else, now look where we are."

We both took a slow sip, savoring the thick, rich flavor. Almost as good as Mario's coffee.

"Leo, there have been many things I've wanted to say to you over the years."

He grunted. "Same."

"But I think the most important is that I'm sorry." I'd taken some slight he'd made toward me—which I couldn't even remember—and thrown our lives into chaos for it. I'd broken up his relationship and ended up shot when his jealousy erupted at the jeweler's shop. "And I forgive you."

I'd expected him to throw the coffee in my face for having the gall to forgive him, but he put the cup down and went about rinsing the moka pot.

When he turned off the water, he faced me again. "After our chat last night, I asked around. Apparently, she's on her third husband."

I nearly spit out my coffee.

He frowned and picked up his cup, raising it to me. "So thank *you*."

Cristian sauntered into the room, eyes lighting up when he grabbed his cup, inhaling deeply. "Not killing each other, I see. This is progress."

CHAPTER 44

SAMANTHA

Vincenzo and I hurried down the hallway toward the tower and the wine cellar. The estate was quiet in the middle of the night, no guards to be seen.

"Sam?" came a small voice behind us.

We turned and were met by Cesca's wide eyes.

"What are you two—"

"Cesca. What are you doing up at this hour?" I walked over to her and put a hand on her arm. "And wandering all by yourself? Didn't Leo tell you to stay—"

"Sometimes I go—when I can't sleep—" Her chin trembled. "Why are you with him? In your pajamas?"

Of course. She had a crush on Vin and thought I was sneaking around with him.

"I was hungry and wanted a snack. Antonio's still awake somewhere in the house with Cristian, and Vin was posted in the tower." I rubbed her arm, trying to soothe her. "That's all. You know I'm not allowed out by myself."

"Then you should have asked him to get something for you." She sniffled and yanked her arm away, her cheeks flushing crimson.

Guilt churned in my stomach. The photo I'd sent Elliot would lead to big changes around here. Changes that would hurt Cesca. *But Giovanni lied about everything, Sam. Don't forget that.*

"Sam," hissed Vin.

I leaned down to look her in the eyes. If she didn't trust me, she'd run straight to someone and tell them about this. "We're going down to the wine cellar first to grab a bottle of wine. Do you want to come with us? Then we can walk you back to your room?"

She shook her head. "No."

What was I going to do now? Vin didn't need me anymore. He could take the painting to his handler and be done with it. I could walk Cesca back to her room and no one would know I was involved in any of this.

"Vin, you go ahead. I'll see Cesca to her room." I turned my body to the side, to sneak the tube out of its hiding spot under my pants, and Cesca tore off down the hallway.

Vin grabbed me when I started after her. "Leave her."

"But she could alert someone." I stared after her, the sounds of her crying ringing in my ears.

"It's a perfect cover."

I turned to look at him, taking in his drawn brows and tense jaw. "What?"

"If someone catches us..." He neared me, pushing my arm down so the tube wasn't visible. "We can say we were sneaking off together. She'll vouch for it, and I'm guessing Leonardo would, too."

What would Antonio think? Would he trust me? Would his continued doubts overwhelm the logical parts of his brain like they normally did?

"Plus, you didn't show me how you opened that door downstairs. I need you with me."

If Antonio didn't trust me, what future could we have? If there was a chance of me working with the FBI on art crime cases, going undercover, we'd have to deal with these moments. This was who I was. I couldn't dedicate myself to a man who wouldn't let me do what I was meant to.

"Okay." I nodded slowly, starting back in the direction we'd been headed.

We increased our speed, slowing on the stairs to the wine cellar, when one of the guards appeared on his patrol. I leaned into our act, averting my face while Vincenzo spoke to him.

No doubt there were knowing smiles exchanged between the two of them, but the words were no more than, "We're just taking a walk. Don't tell anyone."

· • · • · ● · ● · ● · • · ·

At the bottom of the rough-cut steps down to the cave, Vin pulled a portable headlamp from one of his pockets, donned it, and lit the area.

"That's a strong light," I said, attempting to smother the nervous energy zipping around inside me. Stupid comment.

He took my free hand—the other still clutching the tube against my thigh—and led me along the walkway edging the cave's pool, past the Venus statue. "Wait here."

"I guess we don't need to shut off the camera?"

"We don't. Let me signal my contact." He smiled and squeezed my hand, then followed the pathway to the outside of the cave without me. The rain had stopped and the sky must have cleared, because a sliver of moonlight danced across the water at the mouth.

I held up my watch and pressed the button, which illuminated the face. Two in the morning. Our half hour was up. I was supposed to be back upstairs in my room by now. How accurate was Vin's timing? When would the guards wake up? Soon?

Fuck.

A boat motor started up close by, and Vincenzo returned, using his headlamp to illuminate the water and the rib boat's path. Small waves lapped against the walkway in the cave and the scent of diesel flooded the space. Once the boat was next to me, the motor stopped.

Vin turned to me. I held up a hand to shield my eyes from the headlamp. It was really bright. "Let's have that painting, Sam."

"Can you point that thing somewhere else?" I pulled the tube out from my pocket, practically blinded. I looked toward the boat, but my corneas needed to recover. "And it's been a half hour. We need to hurry."

He pushed the headlamp up and approached me. "We're home-free, Sam."

"No, we're not. We still have to get upstairs."

"Hurry up," came a low voice from the direction of the boat.

The voice was familiar, tugging at a memory trapped deep in my brain. An accent, a tone, a something. I blinked, trying to clear the spots from my eyes, but it was too dark.

Vin eased the tube from my hand and said, "Come with me."

"Yeah, as soon as you've handed it over."

"I'm not going back upstairs." He took my hand, which had still been hovering by my eyes, and whispered, "They'll kill you if you they find out you helped me."

I pulled back, blinking wildly, my eyes finally adjusting to see him. There was such pain on his face, that pinched look he'd had all night. "They're getting you out?"

He nodded. "I don't want to leave you behind. Not again."

My stomach lurched. Every time we'd been together over the last week, he'd tried to hold me, touch me, protect me. He wasn't still in love with me, was he?

"Vincenzo, get in," said the man. "We don't have time for this."

My gaze snapped toward the boat, and I saw the helmsman. A single man. A large one in a dark black jacket and pants.

And I knew him.

My heart all but stopped.

"Oh my god, Vin. What's he doing here?"

CHAPTER 45

ANTONIO

I waved to Cristian and Leonardo at the bottom of the staircase and crossed the distance to my door, while they went off to their own rooms. Samantha had my key and Dr. Weber was staying on our floor, so I knocked quietly. "Bella?"

Coffee with Cristian and Leonardo had been practically pleasant. Maybe my apology meant a lot to Leo. Or he thought my half-drunken state—far improved after the coffee—left me too weak to defend myself. Or he was simply too tired, like the rest of us.

I leaned against the door and tried the handle. Locked. I knocked again, louder. "Bella?"

She knew we only had one key, so I'd expected her to stay up waiting for me. What time was it? I turned my watched over—two in the morning. She'd come upstairs an hour ago. The nightmares continued to invade her sleep every night— although she handled the daytime better than just after the New Year's incident—so at the very least, she should have been sleeping lightly.

Another knock, louder again. Still nothing.

Those prickles she described began along the back of my neck.

Visions of New Year's flashed through my brain. To when the Scotts had held her at gunpoint in our hotel room. To my breaking down the door to see Olivia Scott with a scarf knotted around Samantha's throat, choking the life out of her.

I pounded on the door, yelling her name. "Samantha! It's me! Open up!"

It was locked, but it was only wood. I rammed my good shoulder into it, pain screaming through the injury in my right arm and the still healing cuts across my back. But none of that mattered. If she was in there and needed my help, nothing would stand in my way.

I slammed into the door again, greeted by the sound of splintering wood.

Leonardo came running up the stairs. "What are you doing?"

"She's not answering!"

He grabbed me before I could continue my assault. "That doesn't mean you can destroy the house."

"You don't understand!" I wrenched my arm out of his grip and lunged again. "She wouldn't leave me out here."

Leo's gaze swept the floor, from room to room, jaw set firmly. "Are you sure she was even up here in the first place?"

I stopped before I hit the door this time. "She left dinner and said she was coming up here."

"Who escorted her up?" He was already on his way toward the stairs.

The goosebumps grew stronger, competing with the rapid thrum of my heart. I searched for the face, for the name of the man who'd walked her from the dining room. "I don't know his name. He had... dark brown hair and... marone, he looked like half the men who work here!"

Leo paused at the top of the stairs when I didn't follow. "Antonio, Vincenzo is supposed to be working this floor tonight. Do you see him anywhere?"

"What are you implying?"

"Wherever he is, I suspect she is, as well."

I flagged against the door, the room spinning. Between the alcohol, my medication, and the caffeine hit, my heart was beating too quickly. She was not with Vincenzo. And even if she was, it was not in the way Leonardo was saying.

He was her past.

I was her future.

· · · ● · ● ● · · ·

Leonardo tore out of the security room before I reached it, cell phone in front of his mouth. He yelled into it as he passed me, "We're looking for Vincenzo and Antonio's girlfriend, Samantha! Everyone report where you are so I can coordinate the search!"

I froze in place, unsure if I should follow him or find out what caused this. He was at a sprint, heading toward the tower. There was no way I'd catch him, so ran to the control room.

One guard lay on the floor.

The other slumped over the desk.

All the screens were off.

I charged in and checked pulses, finding both men simply unconscious. The security displays were another matter. I hit buttons, attempted to cycle the power. Lights flashed on the keyboard, but the screens remained blank.

Leonardo and the entire security team were working blind.

Had Vincenzo... the coffee. Of course! Both cups had been drained. Was this a TPC action?

Or was it Henri? Had he left the coffee for Vincenzo to deliver as a cover for... for what? Another murder?

Oh, marone, Samantha, where are you?

I couldn't do this again. Couldn't live knowing she was in danger. There had to be something I could do.

Think, Tony.

The lights were on, so it was not the breaker. The security system was hard-wired into the wall, so there was no plug to come loose. I squeezed as far behind the desk as I could, but the wiring was intact.

I knelt next to the slumped-over man and looked underneath the desk, spotting a removable panel. When I took it off, my heart jumped. Three of the wires hung loose. I snapped them into place and leaned back to check the monitors. Everything flickered to life.

The cave's camera was still on. And there she stood, with Vincenzo, talking to a man on a rib boat, whose face was not visible.

She *was* with Vincenzo. Body-to-body with him, her hand in his.

Bile burned its way up my throat.

It's not what it looks like, Tony. She's planning something. Look for the truth.

Vincenzo pointed to the boat with a tube, which looked like it was used for transport. He'd asked her to get the passcode to the gallery so he could get a painting out. Could that be what it was? Had he drugged the men here to cover this operation?

A moan sounded from the man on the floor.

The other in the chair slowly lifted his head. "What...?"

I had to get downstairs before anything happened to her. But should I have them call Leonardo or not? If the man in the boat was Vincenzo's contact and they were recovering a painting of Giovanni's, I couldn't tell Leonardo.

If he caught them, she'd be dead. I had to get her out of there.

Chapter 46

Samantha

"He's my contact with the TPC, Sam." Vincenzo remained precariously close to me, but I couldn't rip my eyes off the man in the boat.

"No, he's not." I stepped away from Vin, but he held tight.

Last year, when I was visiting Antonio in Naples, I'd hurt myself on a hike and couldn't walk back from the grotto where it happened. An art-loving Corsican man named Pasquale Fiori had swooped to my rescue, picking us up in a rib boat. He and his two bodyguards had taken us to his superyacht where his doctor had looked after my injured ankle.

And the man I knew only as Bodyguard One stood in front of me, maneuvering his boat closer to the edge.

I lowered my voice. "He works for Fiori."

"No," said Vincenzo. "We work for the TPC."

My eyes flashed back to him. "Who's your handler?"

He stepped closer again. "Sam, don't you trust me?"

"Who's the FBI agent coordinating with the TPC?"

"Vincenzo, leave her and get in the boat," snapped the man. Corsican accent. That's what I remembered.

"What I told you about Tuscany was true. I did join the Carabinieri before we broke up. And it wasn't a lie that my path between then and now has been a crazy one, nor even the story about the antiquities dealers I worked for." Vin scanned my face, his hand releasing mine to trace the line of my jaw. "I've regretted what happened between us ever since. I was young and had no idea how lucky I'd been to find someone so perfect for me. So when I saw you..."

Every muscle in my body flagged.

Scarlett really recovered the fresco. She wasn't merely a delivery person. She'd snuck past Fiori's security to get it so we could take it home.

Giovanni wasn't trading it for some painting. He'd paid Scarlett—risked Fiori's retaliation—to make a gesture to his brothers. Just like he'd sworn.

And Vincenzo was nothing more than a thief who worked for Fiori.

"You son of a bitch." I swiped his hand away from my face. He'd toyed with my emotions, reminding me of our past at every moment to keep me off guard. "You used me."

"No. When I saw you at the dinner table on Monday..." He shook his head and tossed the tube to Bodyguard One in the boat. "I thought you were with the FBI. It was a blessing because I thought you were only posing as Antonio's girlfriend and maybe we had a chance. But a curse all the same because I wouldn't get a second chance with an FBI agent, considering who I work for." At least he'd given up the lie.

I looked at Bodyguard One, securing the tube under a bungee cord on the boat's edge.

"You hesitated that first day down here. Do you remember? I asked when the FBI got involved and you were confused. I knew you weren't working for them, so that was my in." He reached for the helmsman's hand, and between the two of them, they pulled the boat next to the walkway at the edge of the pool. Vincenzo stepped in. "I remembered how passionate you were about art crimes and thought telling you I was still with the TPC would get me some extra time with you."

Extra time? Or extra resources? How many things had he said that were a lie? And how much was I responsible for him taking this painting? "Did you actually know the passcode already?"

The rib's motor started up.

Vin put his hand on the man's arm to stop him. "No, I didn't."

"What about the secret door in the tasting room?"

He drew in a slow breath, looking to the ceiling, the light of his lamp climbing high above us, to illuminate the entire cave.

Vin said, "Yes, I knew about that. But I knew you wouldn't come down if I didn't need your help. And I was hoping... that you'd remember how good we were together."

Antonio had told me I was letting my old feelings for Vin get in the way. He was right. I had to learn to listen to that man more often.

What to do now? He had the painting that I'd help him get. I'd sent the photo of *The Magdalen* to Elliot. Everything I'd done tonight was for the wrong side. I had to fix this.

I took Vincenzo's hand and pulled him closer, so he had to balance himself in the boat, but I didn't get in. "If I go with you, will I be in more danger than I am here?"

"No."

"If I were, would you protect me?"

"Of course."

I caved in my shoulders, making myself appear as weak as possible. That was how he knew me before, as the naïve young woman, wide-eyed and full of hope for the future, rather than the constantly irritated investigator I was now. I could use that to draw out a confession. But to what end? The cameras were off, Antonio was drunk wandering the villa. Maybe if I delayed them long enough, I'd figure out a way to get my hands on the painting. But then what? "Antonio jumped in front of a bullet for me. Am I worth that much to you?"

"More." He pushed the headlamp higher on his head. "I'd kill for you."

Oh god, that meant... "You killed Johann?"

He nodded. "I got careless and he found my dead drop location."

My heart lurched. *Stay calm, Sam.* "The note about the delivery was yours?"

He nodded once more, putting one foot on the walkway next to me. "Come with me?"

I ran a hand over Vin's cheek, trying to imagine Antonio's kind face, so I could give Vin the smile that would make him believe I wasn't sick to my stomach. "And you were the one who knocked over the cupboard?"

The bodyguard revved the boat's engine, keeping her in neutral. "Hurry up or I'm leaving you here, Vincenzo."

Yes, that's it. Get frustrated. It'll lower your defenses.

"I didn't want to, and I'm sorry." His words tumbled out. "But I didn't know what to do. If you found the note, what if you found something else to tie me to it? If you knew the truth, I was afraid you'd leave."

"You're quite talented—" At lying. "How did you get from the cellar door all the way up the hidden staircase without anyone noticing?"

The boat's driver engaged the throttle and the boat inched ahead, causing Vin to stumble back into it and out of my grasp. "Last warning."

I didn't have a plan yet. How could I get the painting off the boat without them grabbing me? Kidnapping me all over again? And then what would I do? How long could I keep up this game with Vincenzo to save myself from that?

Movement to my right caught my eye. Someone was at the base of the secret staircase. Someone holding their right arm against their body.

Antonio!

My heart took a leap and I had to hold down the smile.

That changed things. Changed everything.

No more victim.

My partner had arrived.

I stepped closer to the edge and held out my hand, slipping it inside Vincenzo's when he reached for me. "You're right. We were always stronger together."

Vin's brows drew down. But my words hadn't been for him. Those were special words between Antonio and me. They were as clear a message to him as I could manage: *I know you're there. Wait for my signal.*

Chapter 47

Antonio

Stronger together.

Warmth—tinged with more than a modicum of abject terror—bloomed in my chest. This incredible woman of remarkable strength chose me to be hers.

I'd recognized the man in the boat as soon as I'd settled in my hiding space. Two of Pasquale Fiori's bodyguards had helped Samantha to his yacht after she injured her ankle in September. One of them was on Zio Giovanni's payroll.

And this was the other one.

Now I had to figure out her plan.

On New Year's Eve, her unspoken plan had been for me to duck when her old friend Jimmy had his gun trained on us. Instead, I'd barreled headlong at him, the only choice I saw to ensure she was safe behind me.

Tonight, no one held a gun, but from Vincenzo's headlamp light, I could see the bodyguard at the helm carried one strapped to his thigh, below his rain jacket.

Taking them straight on them was not an option. I only had one good arm and there was too much distance to cross. At least twenty or thirty feet, not to mention the water of the natural pool. And it was clear Vincenzo was still in love with her, so he wouldn't hurt her.

But would he try to kill me?

I'd arrived in time to hear Vincenzo's admission about Johann—if he'd killed the German over that note, he'd wouldn't likely have any qualms about killing his rival for Samantha's affections.

"I missed you," Samantha said to Vincenzo.

My heart nearly shattered. *Calm down, man. She's using his feelings to get to the truth.*

Whenever she spoke to me of important things, there were delays. Blinks. Stares. Deep breaths. But with Vincenzo, she barely paused. There was no honesty behind it, just a crusade to uncover the truth. And since I'd repaired the security desk, it was all being recorded.

She stepped into the boat with him, and the warmth gave way to the terror.

I clenched my jaw tight. Where was my signal? When was I supposed to move? *Tell me, woman.*

A voice erupted behind me, and I heard footsteps. I spun to see Leonardo tearing down the stairs.

I waved my hands frantically to stop him before he alerted them to our presence.

He bellowed, "Where are they?"

"Go!" yelled Vincenzo, pushing Samantha down against the back of the boat.

Leonardo collided with me, stumbling into the cave. He called over his shoulder, pulling his gun, "Down here! Spies!"

Fiori's bodyguard piloted around the statue, withdrawing his handgun at the same time.

I launched myself into Leo's back as the bodyguard fired, pain erupting through my arm, radiating out through my entire body.

Leonardo fired as we fell.

Samantha screamed and tumbled into the water.

No! I had to get to her. I began to stand, but the bodyguard fired again, his second, third, and fourth shots ricocheting off the rock Leonardo and I had fallen next to. "Samantha!"

"Don't leave her!" Vincenzo pulled on the pilot's arm, but he continued out the mouth of the cave and they vanished.

A wave of nausea hit me, and I retched, nothing but coffee and wine spilling out on the walkway. Samantha was in the water. She was hurt. No matter how much pain I was in, I had to get to her. "Leo?"

"Cazzo Madre. Fucking hell," he groaned. Clearly shot, but alive. And not my priority.

I crawled to the edge and rolled in, holding the walkway with my good arm and sinking my head under the water to look for her. Without Vincenzo's light, it was pitch black. I couldn't see anything. I crested the surface. "Flashlight!"

Leo made a noise and flicked on a flashlight, shoving it in my direction.

With a yell in agony, I took the flashlight in my right arm and shone it into the water, driving my head underneath again.

Nathan Miller's last words on New Year's flashed through my brain. 'If she comes away from one more visit with you with more scars, we're going to have a problem.'

Che cazzo, but if she didn't come back from this trip, I wouldn't be able to live with myself. She was my world and I couldn't—

But out of the darkness, she appeared. Swimming toward me. Blowing bubbles out through her nose, a smile growing across her face.

I pulled myself up, tossed the flashlight onto the edge, and wiped the water from my eyes.

She rose from the water face first, taking in a calm breath. "Wow, that's a lot deeper than I was expecting."

"You're not..."

"Shot? Nope!" She treaded water effortlessly, pausing only to push some hair back from her face before swimming closer to me. Of course—this was my diver. She lifted a black plastic tube out of the water and grinned broadly. "He stole this painting. I stole it back."

Footsteps sounded from the passageway.

Leo groaned again, the sound trailing off.

"Shit!" Her eyes went wide and she took one stroke to get to the edge before pulling herself out of the water. She rushed to Leo's side and hauled her shirt off to press it against him. "Jesus, it's cold in here!"

I remained in the water, the temperature overcoming my initial panic. "In here, too."

"Then get out." She didn't spare me a look, focused on wrapping her shirt around Leo's arm. "Part of me wants to laugh at the irony. He was shot in the arm and passed out."

I chuckled. "That's what he gets for making fun of me?"

"Exactly." She looked back at me, the flashlight casting deep shadows against her face. "You can't climb up, can you?"

"No," I laughed, continuing to hold on to the edge. "Although the temperature of the water is reducing the pain somewhat. How long does it take for hypothermia to kick in?"

She shook her head and rolled her eyes. "In this water? Probably hours."

Someone burst through the bottom of the secret passage, and I craned my head to look. A man with another flashlight and a gun.

"Henri?" said Samantha.

The chef carried a gun?

"Cazzo," he muttered. Everyone spoke Italian here, but he'd always sworn in French. He ran around the edge of the pool, to Leo's side. "E says thanks for the photo."

Samantha's head snapped up, as did mine. "What?" we said in unison.

"Say no more," he said.

"How did you know—" Samantha began, but Henri made a slicing motion across his throat. She looked over at me, the discussion between us clear: Elliot Skinner had told her the TPC had someone inside. Vincenzo had told her it was him, so she easily fell into his trap. And we'd misread every suspicious moment with Henri. He was the undercover TPC operative.

"Vincenzo was working for Fiori," I said.

Samantha inclined her head toward the black tube, lying next to Leo's flashlight. "I helped him take a painting from the gallery and he was meeting someone here so they could take it to him."

Henri nodded, looking pointedly at her. "He forced you? Held you at gunpoint?"

I said intentionally, "Sì, that's exactly what happened."

"But I retrieved the painting before they made it out," she said.

"Good. That will help when this one wakes up." Henri took over pressure on Leonardo's injury.

Samantha whispered, "Vincenzo killed Johann."

Henri's body went rigid. He closed his eyes and took one long breath. "He's not getting away with that."

Facts clicked into place. Henri and Johann spending so much time together in the kitchen. Johann, his constant companion to the village. Add to that Henri's intense reaction and it was clear they'd been working together all along.

Samantha came over to help me out of the water. When I was out, lying on the walkway and shivering, she kissed me. Soft, gentle, and brief. "You know I was making up all that stuff with Vincenzo, right?"

More voices sounded from the passageway. This time, several of them.

Henri said, "The reinforcements are almost here."

"Stronger together, amore." It took more effort than it should, but I sat up, stripped off my wet shirt, and handed it to her. "Although I'd rather you were in more than your bra and lounge pants when they get here."

CHAPTER 48

SAMANTHA

The next morning, I finished braiding my hair and wrapped the end with an elastic. My eyes were sore and skin sallow. One short—but very deep—sleep would not be enough to make up for last night.

Antonio's arm snaked around my waist from behind, grimacing at me in the mirror as he lay his head on my shoulder. "No one's come knocking so far this morning, so I suspect we're alright."

I pressed my cheek against his and closed my eyes, inhaling his intoxicating scent. Leaning back against his chest to feel his heart beating. "I hope Leo's okay."

"You're a good woman."

After Henri revealed he was the TPC agent, three guards arrived and transported Leo upstairs to Gio's private physician. Likely on to a hospital after that, but Cristian encouraged us to return to our room.

"Honesty time." I turned in his arms and draped my hands behind his neck. "Did you think I was fooling around with Vin?"

His jaw remained as clenched as it had been since I pulled him from the water last night. We needed to get him to Naples and the doctor he'd been referred to. He could have done more damage to the arm. Hopefully not irreparable. "Total honesty?"

I nodded, stomach twisting in knots.

"I noticed a change in you after New Year's. You were quieter, less sure of yourself. And that got even worse whenever Vincenzo was around. Perhaps you fell into patterns more comfortable to the young woman you were when the two of you were together."

A young woman who hadn't found herself yet. Whose father had left when she was five and whose best friend didn't talk to her anymore. My life's plans were still in reach at that point, but the worst of my days were ahead of me.

Ten years ago, Vincenzo left me. Eight years ago, my mother died. Seven since my divorce. In some ways, I'd seen my breakup with Vin as the first domino in a long line of heartbreaks.

A long line I didn't snap out of until Antonio. And here we stood, on the other side of another one of my scars, which could finally heal. Because in the end, Vincenzo didn't have any power over me anymore.

He squeezed my waist. "I worried more that you'd lose your fire than that you'd cheat on me. So I suppose I worried I would lose that part of you to him."

I ran fingers through the short hair over his ear, then down his jaw, and across his lips. Vincenzo said he wanted me, but he didn't know who I was. This man in front of me—he did. He knew my fears, my hopes, and my dreams. At least, more of them than anyone else did.

He saw *me*.

And I loved him so much for it. "The next three and a half months apart is going to be harder than the last, isn't it?"

"Sì, I expect they will." He gave me a peck on the nose. "Come now. Let's get our bags and leave. A week with Mario will have you begging to go home."

I laughed and nodded, slipping out of his grip.

• • • • • • • • • •

I sat at the dining table for breakfast, tired faces all around. Henri arrived with food and drinks, as though nothing had happened last night, despite some intense initial questions about why he was in the cave with a gun. I didn't know how he got out of that, but if he was in the kitchen this morning, he must have had a good story.

Cesca drew in a deep breath and held it. Her eyes found mine, then fell to her hands in her lap.

Cristian reached over and put his hand on her shoulder.

She finally said, "Papa told me everything this morning. He said Vincenzo was working for a bad man and you caught him. Is that true? Is that what last night was all about?"

I nodded. Between the two of us, Antonio and I had cobbled together a story about my early suspicions of Vincenzo. About how I played along with having an interest in him, so he'd give away his plans, and about how he'd threatened me last night.

Giovanni took a cornetto from the tray on the table. "We're fortunate Samantha was here when he attempted to deceive us. It's just too bad he got away."

"But we know who he works for." Cristian nodded at Henri as the chef placed an espresso cup in front of him. "I didn't think he'd be so bold. Fiori, that is."

Henri's gaze swept the group of us, and he gave me a small smile before retreating to the kitchen.

Antonio sat to my right, next to Cristian, so his good arm faced me. His hand ran along my thigh. "But you were so bold to take the fresco back from him. Do you think last night's attempted theft was retaliation for that?"

"No," I said, forgetting myself and my cover. Vincenzo had told me they were waiting for that painting to be delivered for some time. Although that could have been another lie. "I mean, you just got the fresco back yesterday, right? And I found Vincenzo's note about the painting being delivered two days ago. He knew he wanted to steal it before he knew the fresco was here."

"Good point," said Antonio immediately, helping strengthen my case.

Giovanni's eyes narrowed. "Fiori had a man inside my home for two years, spying and making plans. How much other damage did he do? Did he plant bugs? Had he stolen other things? We're going to have to do the full security overhaul Leonardo's been talking about. And verify everyone's backgrounds all over again."

"Speaking of Leonardo," I said. "How's he doing?"

Cristian and Gio looked at each other, then looked at Cesca. Maybe she hadn't gotten a full update on everything that had happened last night.

"Thanks for helping my dad, Sam. And Antonio, I hope I see you again soon." She stood and plucked three items off the tray Henri had brought, putting them on her plate. With that, she rounded the table and headed off.

Giovanni said, "It was bad. My doctor's dealt with many gunshot wounds, so he could handle most of it. Once he was stable enough, we sent him to the hospital for the rest."

"And," said Cristian, "we reviewed a lot of video this morning. The last thing we saw was Vincenzo in the control room. Then the video feeds all died and came back on when you and he were with the boat. That was clever of you to get the painting back. We caught all the discussion, including when he confessed to killing Johann."

Giovanni's face tightened, his neck flushing red. "Four years that Interpol agent hid under my roof."

"Papa," whispered Cristian.

"It's a test, I know." Gio's eyes went heavenward. "Johann, I'll work on forgiving. But Vincenzo? Working for my greatest enem—"

"Signore!" One of the guards rushed into the room. "The Carabinieri are here."

Giovanni tapped a napkin on his lips. "Who? Specifically?"

"Not one of ours. Three vehicles are at the front gate. They say they're not looking for trouble."

Giovanni waved the guard away. "Probably just here about last night's gunfire."

The guard shook his head. "They have a warrant to search the premises."

Was this related to the photo I sent to Elliot last night? Henri made it clear they knew it was from me. Could they really get a warrant so fast? Probably not, unless they were ready for it.

"It's more likely about Johann," I said.

Cristian shot from his seat, barking out orders to the guard and two others who arrived at a run. "Let the Carabinieri officers through the gate. Monitor their every step. Hide the automatic weapons. Minimal staff visible. Cesca to her room."

"To your room, you two," said Giovanni, finger pointing at us.

Antonio stood, taking my hand. "No. If it's about last night's shooting or Johann's death, they'll want to see the video and speak with Samantha."

His uncle shot him a glare but threw down his napkin and headed out of the dining room, toward the grand hall and the front door.

Antonio and I walked several paces behind him, shouting voices and hurried footsteps all around us. I'd almost grown accustomed to having watchful eyes everywhere, but this flurry of activity was different. They weren't just eyes; they were trained men, getting into position.

I pulled closer to Antonio. "What's going to happen?"

He slipped his hand out of mine and covered his mouth to whisper, "Do you think it's Johann? Or maybe *The Magdalen*?"

"I don't know." Was that painting really enough to come in? End their years of surveillance? Or was this a shot across the bow? A warning? Or was Johann's death something that had to be answered for?

"We could also find the man who was to drive us to Mario's and just leave?"

I chuckled. "I'm too curious about this."

Antonio shook his head and took my hand again, pulling it to his lips. "Why does this not surprise me?"

Giovanni came to a halt at the front door and one of the men opened it to the grand courtyard and the auto court beyond. Sun streamed in around him as he folded his arms, not moving any further. "What can I do for my friends at the Carabinieri today?"

A man approached, rich olive skin and salt and pepper black hair, dressed in a dark blue jacket with CARABINIERI emblazoned across the front in white. Underneath, the letters TPC. Above, the flaming grenade insignia of the cultural heritage crimes team.

Antonio leaned close to my ear. "Is that Bruno Gallo?"

I moved so I could see around Giovanni. "It is."

Bruno Gallo had been Elliot's contact in Italy in the fall. They'd worked with us on the fresco theft.

"Do you think they heard about the fresco?" I whispered.

"Also possible."

"How's your English, Signore?" asked Bruno. "One of the men with me doesn't speak Italian, but I can translate for him if needed." He gestured toward the driveway.

"It's excellent," said Giovanni in English. "We can meet in my office."

A hand touched my arm, nudging me out of the way. Henri walked around me with a slight nod. He stopped next to Giovanni.

"If you don't mind—" A deep voice came from outside the door, one I knew all too well. Elliot Skinner joined the TPC agent in the doorway, along with a woman whose dark jacket read INTERPOL. "—our warrant says we can talk in your gallery."

Henri leaned in and whispered something to Giovanni, who spun to face him. Rage clouded Gio's features, full face flushing red, but Henri didn't flinch. He just gestured to the northern end of the villa, toward the gallery. In near-perfect English, with an Italian—not French—accent, he said, "This way, gentlemen."

CHAPTER 49

ANTONIO

Samantha and I stood outside the gallery to watch her FBI mentor Elliot Skinner, Carabinieri TPC officer Bruno Gallo, and Henri, the undercover TPC agent, leave with the other officers. They carried no guns, left with no paintings or stolen antiquities, and gave no hint the first two knew Samantha or me.

"Taxes!" bellowed Zio Giovanni from the gallery.

The door was open, and Samantha inclined her head. "Should we go in? Or make our escape?"

"What happened to that curiosity?"

She battled to hide her smile, her twinkling eyes giving her away. "It's killing me."

I pressed my hand to the small of her back, and we entered the gallery.

Giovanni paced through the room, flailing his hands in the air. "Do they have any idea how ridiculous this is?"

Cristian sat in one of the antique chairs by the wall, watching his father. His head rolled in our direction. "She's not welcome here."

Samantha opened her mouth as if to argue, but I cut her off.

These words would be more acceptable from me. "You already told us you watched last night's videos. You saw what she did for you. For Leo. For me. Not only did she risk her life to save your painting, but she exposed Vincenzo. How dare you tell her she's not welcome?"

Giovanni diverted his path to storm directly in front of me. His face was deep red, nostrils flaring. "This is more of Saint Peter's justice. You two broke the rules—"

"You broke the law," I snapped. "Whatever they were here for is your fault."

"What taxes?" Samantha's voice was calm, matter-of-fact. As though this were another of her investigations and nothing more.

His hand flew toward *The Magdalen* on the far wall. "They're claiming I owe import taxes on that painting."

"So pay them," I said.

"That's not the point!" yelled Gio, who resumed his pacing. "They think I'm a weak old man? My lawyers are going to eat them alive."

Eat them alive? He was lucky they only had information about a single painting and that they weren't here about a murdered Interpol agent.

Samantha didn't flinch but headed to the door. Was she giving up so easily? No, she closed it over and returned to my side. As expected, she also sidestepped when I attempted to slide my arm around her waist. Professional Samantha had arrived. "It's interesting timing, don't you think?"

"Interesting? It was Vincenzo. That son of a pig sent them a photo of the painting." Gio stopped in front of one of Cesca's paintings, the one of the person walking alone. "They said if I don't pay my taxes and fines for importing her, they'll seize her and throw me in jail."

"Papa," said Cristian. "Calm down. I don't want you to have another heart attack."

"Calm down?" Gio growled. "They come into my house and dare ask me to hand over information about someone? They think I have no honor?"

Samantha nudged me, flicking her eyes toward the two men. *Information about who*, she mouthed.

"About who, Zio?"

"Vincenzo's puppet master."

Fiori? Elliot had told Samantha they wanted someone higher in the smuggling ring than Giovanni. The photo she sent them of *The Magdalen* was all Elliot had asked for. This must have been his play. They likely had the warrant written before the photo arrived.

"You know..." Samantha eased her hands into her pockets, taking a posture of easy confidence. "I don't think us being here was a bad thing, Giovanni. I think Vincenzo saw it as an opportunity to reveal himself and what Fiori was doing. That's a blessing."

Gio rounded on her. "A blessing?"

"Yes." She walked toward him. "You got the fresco back from him and we spoiled his plans to steal the yellow flower painting."

"Blessings?" Cristian stood slowly, his lip curling. "Vincenzo killed Johann, or are you forgetting that?"

"No." She shook her head, taking Gio's place in front of Cesca's painting. "Did you know he was attempting to use your daughter to gain entrance to the gallery?"

"And you were as well," spat Gio. "You brought that camera in here, Samantha."

"I knew it." Cristian grabbed her arm.

Her hands were out of her pockets in a flash, her arm twisting abruptly to escape his grasp. She stepped away from him as he tried again.

"Hands off her, Cristian." I hurried to insert myself between the two of them. Was she capable of playing any game other than a dangerous one? "Zio, you claim you've changed. You want to make up for over fifteen years of silence between you and your brothers? Samantha's right. Hand over whatever evidence you have on Fiori."

"If I do that..." Giovanni pressed a fist against his chest and flagged into a chair.

Cristian was at his side immediately. "Papa?"

Giovanni waved it away but resumed rubbing over his heart. "I told you already. Getting out of my line of work puts a target on my back. And if I help them go after any of my former associates, the target would only grow."

I knelt in front of him, next to Cristian. "Have any of them gone after your family?"

He shook his head.

"Then this is your warning to anyone who finds out." I put a hand on his knee. "You'll keep all your secrets unless they come for you."

Samantha stood behind me, her light touch on my shoulder. "And Antonio tells your brothers about the good work you're doing. That's probably the best step you can take to reconcile with them."

Gio leaned back in his chair, no longer massaging his chest. "It's time for you two to leave."

I looked to Cristian, the worry over his father's health clear. "You said you needed to be sure Fiori was not targeting Samantha."

"What?" she said from behind me, so I put my hand on hers.

"Are we safe?" I asked.

"From what I hear, yes." Cristian's head rolled forward. "But my source didn't know this was going on, so he's digging for more details."

He had a man undercover on Fiori's yacht. If the bodyguard came for Vincenzo by water last night, Fiori might be nearby. Waiting.

Vincenzo certainly would be. Unless he got a better view of what Samantha did, he likely thought she'd been shot and fallen off the boat as well. We'd have to keep an eye out for them until someone put Pasquale Fiori behind bars.

CHAPTER 50

ANTONIO

"Bella," I whispered, rubbing Samantha's hand which had been in mine the entire drive from Giovanni's. Two and a half hours later, the car stopped in front of Mario's. Finally.

She sat up, stretching her arms and neck, yawning while she gazed up at the green gate and the villa beyond. "I missed this place."

None of the flowers were in bloom, but the evergreen olive grove across the road held onto its leaves, almost making me forget how cold it was outside. The gate to the courtyard opened and my favorite cousin appeared.

"Grazie mille." I tapped Gio's driver on the shoulder before kissing Samantha's temple. "Let me open your door."

She rolled her eyes but waited patiently for me.

I got out and rounded the vehicle, giving Mario a tight smile before opening her door.

Samantha wore black cargo pants and the robin's egg blouse that turned her eyes blue. She smiled when she saw Mario.

"Buongiorno, bellisima." He bypassed me to give her an enthusiastic hug. "It's been too long."

"It has."

He clapped me on the back, frowning at my arm in its sling. "I rescheduled your doctor's appointment for Tuesday. Can you make it until then?"

I nodded. "It's just a scratch."

"Good god," muttered Samantha.

The driver placed our bags next to us and tipped his head before getting back into the car and driving away.

Mario picked up my duffel before I could, not even asking. He knew it was far more than a scratch, but he wouldn't mention it out loud unless we'd been drinking first. "I have an important question for my love."

Samantha chuckled as we followed him through the courtyard to the double front doors. "And what's that?"

"Now that you've met the darker side of the Ferraro family, are you prepared to leave my miserable cousin for me?"

She stifled her laugh, picking up her small suitcase when we reached the winding central staircase inside the villa. "Sorry Mario, but I seem to madly in love with him anyway."

"Madly?" I said, patting her ass.

Mario said over his shoulder from the first floor landing, "Your loss."

Samantha laughed again, a sound like music. "Give it a few more months. We'll see."

"Bella!" I smacked her ass as we arrived at the second floor. "All I get is a few months?"

"Smart woman," chuckled Mario.

"Don't make me do something drastic, amore." I'd foolishly left the engagement ring at home in Brenton. That would serve her right if I'd brought it and proposed. I had her trapped in

Napoli with me for another week, so there'd be no way to avoid it that long.

"Okay, okay," she said, waving a hand in the air. "But you have to promise to take me not only to that hotel with the amazing bed and back to the Vista dell'Ovo restaurant, but also up Vesuvius. We didn't do that last time."

"You'll be mine forever if we do all that?"

"Don't get greedy," she said with mock disapproval.

We arrived at my room, and Mario dropped my duffel next to the bed. "You both look exhausted. Should I get food ready or will you be turning in early?"

I looked at Samantha, dark circles under her eyes, just like the last time she'd arrived at Mario's villa. "Sleep?"

She nodded, sinking onto the bed. "Dozing in the car was alright, but I think I need to check my messages, then nap. Maybe a late dinner?"

Mario nodded and winked at her. "It's Saturday night. Late dinner and club?"

"We've been over this." I smacked his shoulder playfully. "No winking at my girlfriend."

Samantha's shoulders shook in quiet laughter. Now that we had true privacy, she pulled her phone out of her bag, which began pinging as soon as it was on.

I walked Mario to the door and he finally gave me a hug, tighter than usual.

"I'm glad you're safe. I don't need to hear the details unless you want to tell me, but Sofia called about everything that happened over Christmas." He held my good shoulder, eyes falling to my injured arm. "And then your call from Giovanni's... I've been worried sick about you."

Nine years ago, Mario had pulled me out of Giovanni's world. His concern was about more than one shooting or one near-kidnapping. It was about my soul. I owed so much to him, including an explanation of what had happened over the last three weeks. "I'll tell you everything later. But for now, let me say this: They didn't pull me back in. They didn't hurt me. And Samantha and I are stronger for our experience."

More than that, I'd finally stood my ground against Giovanni. I'd left part of my soul at his estate all those years ago, proud that I'd left him, yet guilty over being party to what he did. But with the fresco in hand and the hope of Giovanni helping the TPC, I could let it go. My scales were balanced and I could leave that shame behind.

He nodded, searching my face as though he hoped for more. My cousin was my best friend in the world and would know I was not yet ready to explain. "I suppose that will have to do for now."

I closed the door as he left, then crossed to the bed, sitting next to Samantha. "Anything interesting?"

"One sec," she muttered, reading as she typed, "'Phone wasn't working. I'm fine. Text you tomorrow.'"

"Someone worried?"

She flashed the phone to me, scrolling quickly through her messages. "Two hundred and fifty-three text messages. One's from Matt, two from Cass, five from Elliot, and the rest are from Lucy."

A laugh burst out of me. This hardly surprised me. "Were any of them important?"

"Cass reminded me to have a good time." She smiled at the phone. "She's worried about what happened at New Year's but seems happy I'm here with you."

"Before she handed over your passport, she told me you don't relax enough."

Samantha frowned. "I imagine you agreed?"

"Sì, of course! I've told you this many times." I tapped her nose. "And Matt?"

"I still don't know." The offer of a permanent position with the Special Investigations Unit at Foster Mutual Insurance would be perfect for her. But it also meant settling down into one town instead of spending her days on the road. It meant tying herself to Brenton, which she'd been running from for over six years. "He offered to amend my existing contract to an SIU role in place of daily adjusting. Maybe that's a good short-term plan?"

Short-term. She was still thinking until spring, like she had when she originally arrived in Brenton, intending to leave once her sister's cancer treatments were done. I wanted long-term. I wanted forever. But all I could do was nudge her in that direction, gently. "When do you need to decide?"

She huffed out a breath. "When I get home."

"Alright, bella. We can talk about it this week—or not. It's up to you."

She gave me a half-smile. Something else was holding her back, and I was unsure what it was. "Elliot thanked us for all the help and said he's optimistic about Gio's cooperation. Henri's left his undercover role there; sounds like it wasn't particularly fruitful anyway, because of the crazy amount of security. Johann's time produced more intel, but it dried up over the last year and a half."

"That's when Leonardo took over. I guess he really is good at his job."

She hummed absently. "I only skimmed Lucy's, but I think half of them were about Lorenzo."

"Not my brother Lorenzo?"

"Yup." She tossed the phone onto the bedside table. "She's still debating whether to text him. He is single, right?"

"As far as I know."

She ran a hand over her face. "Can he handle a Lucy?"

"Can anyone handle a Lucy? Other than you?"

Her other hand joined the first one on her face, scrubbing over her eyes and cheeks. "The other half were about an apartment she found. Two bedrooms near Foster Mutual. She starts there in the spring."

"Two?"

"I told you her solution to my apartment search problem was to move in with her, right?"

I nodded.

"She's got a one bedroom now and I told her it was too small. So I guess she went on the hunt." Her hands dragged down her face until I could see her lovely eyes. "She has an appointment for me to go see it with her when I get back. From the sounds of it, she's magically discovered a place that fits all my criteria."

"Don't." I took one of her hands in mine, my slung arm begging to hold her other. But after last night, the pain was nearly unbearable.

"I know," she sighed. "I'll kill her if we have to be locked in a confined space every day."

I chuckled, but pulled her hand to my mouth, pressing a kiss firmly to her skin. My heart hammered against my chest, an easy decision forming in my brain. "The worst two things about our visit to my uncle's were being separated from you and then fearing I'd lost you."

She nodded, her free hand finding its way to stroke across my cheek. "It's just three and a half months."

"I know, amore." I turned my body, curling one leg up on the bed to face her directly. "And that separation—that fear—I don't want to go through that again. Not even a moment."

A tremble ran through her hand. She knew where this was going.

"When I get home, I don't want to say goodbye every night. I don't want to lie in my bed, thinking you're ten minutes away from me. I don't want to wake up without you in my arms."

"Antonio..." she whispered, any further debate dying on her tongue.

"Move in with me."

"You're living in Naples for three and a half months."

"Exactly. Consider my condo a loan for those months. Don't move in with Lucy. Don't stay with your sister. Stay at my place. And when I get home, just continue to stay."

She chewed on her bottom lip, staring and blinking, like she always did when the words became difficult. There were no barriers, no excuses, no reasons for her to say no. In my heart, I knew she felt the same as I did.

"Samantha, you've faced your greatest relationship fear head-on this past week."

"Shh." She placed a finger against my lips. "I can't believe my past with that man held me back from you."

"And still you fear you'll look back on our relationship some-day and say the same to another man about me?"

Her eyes glistened as tears collected against her lids and she stroked a thumb over my lips. No words came, but she shook her head. Whatever she was holding back was so close to coming out, and we had plenty of time for that.

I leaned in to kiss her. Soft lips and gentle tongue, our sighs mingling. We were safe. And we were together.

When we separated, I gave her my sexiest, most debonair smirk. "So, does this mean Vegas is still on the table?"

Her shoulders fell and her eyeballs rolled. "You're ridiculous."

"Tenacious, amore. That's the word you're looking for."

"Yes, that's an excellent word for you." Her face relaxed, as though she'd found peace. Or was about to fall asleep. "And also, yes, you'd be a much better roommate than Lucy. But I think the rent's probably out of my price range."

"Good thing I only accept payment—" I winked at her. "—in kisses."

She bit down on her bottom lip, struggling to contain a laugh. "Good thing I have a lot of those lying around."

"So this is a yes?"

"Sì, amore," she said with a silly smile, which rapidly evolved into a yawn. "This is a yes."

Epilogue

Samantha

Two months later...

I glowered at the sparkler-studded cake being placed in front of me and at all the people singing 'Happy Birthday.' When the ruckus stopped, I turned the glower on my sister, who only laughed. "I'm pretty sure I said no staff parades, funny hats, or entire restaurants singing?"

"C'mon, Sam, make a wish and blow them out!" squealed Lucy, my petite and far-too-excited best friend.

We sat around a table at Caruther's restaurant, strangers from every table clapping, even though the song had ended.

Lucy continued, "Although I guess you don't blow out sparklers, do you? You just sort of wait for them to—"

"Shh—" Sofia, Antonio's older sister, put a hand on Lucy's arm. "She can still make a wish."

"You know what I'd wish for?" Lucy said with a giggle.

She'd probably wish for a new computer. Or a second phone.

Lucy continued, "If I were her, I'd wish for my sexy boy—"

Cass, my sister, nudged Lucy. "Quiet."

I stared as the sparklers began fizzling out.

Wish for my sexy boyfriend to show up? He'd canceled our morning video call. Texted me that he'd been out the night before and was nursing a hangover. Sure, he sent another thirty or forty texts in fits and spurts through the day, but the quantity was nowhere near as satisfying as one video call would have been.

Perfetto, as he liked to say.

Our visit in Naples had been wonderful. He went to work the day after we arrived at Mario's, but his team chased him off while his arm was still bothering him. I forced him to endure my nursing skills, he taught me how to make pasta dough—although mine turned to mush—and we simply relaxed.

No danger, no mystery, just us.

I was home a day before the Pompeii Archaeological Park's press conference to celebrate the stolen fresco's return. I got to watch him via a livestream—all handsome and sexy in his new suit—standing off to the side, acting like he wasn't the one who'd brought it home. We'd agreed it was best for both of us to stay out of the limelight, in case I managed to secure that contract position with the FBI.

Our first week apart had been the hardest. My friends and the building staff helped me move my things into the cavernous condo. Matt supported every change to the insurance adjusting workflows I proposed for Foster Mutual, and I was enjoying the SIU job. Plus, I managed to calm Lucy down a little over the whole Lorenzo thing.

Antonio and I had continued our weekly video chats, daily texts, and a lot of calls about where I could find things in his condo. The place was every bit as much mine as it was his, he insisted, except for one spot: I wasn't to open his bedside table unless we were on a video call. Deep in my gut, I knew why. There would be another diamond inside. Not a promise ring or a necklace, but a diamond that would change everything. One that would symbolize a future I wasn't ready for. At least, not while we were living on separate continents.

The nightmares still bothered me every once in a while but sleeping on his sheets—and occasionally spritzing his cologne on the pillows—helped.

"Sam?" Nathan put his hand on my shoulder. I looked over into his deep blue eyes, full of concern. "The sparklers went out fifteen minutes ago?"

I rolled my eyes at him, causing his concern to evolve into a laugh.

Lucy squirmed in her seat almost as much as my three-year-old niece did. "Sam, can you grab me a glass of wine from the bar?"

"Good idea," said my Cass. "Grab me water."

"I'm the birthday girl," I said. "Why don't you go?"

"I'm stuck in the back!" Lucy was wedged between Sofia and her husband on one side and my niece and nephew on the other. "And the server isn't paying any attention to the short woman next to the little kids."

"Fine. Cut the cake for me." I stood, happy to get out from under the spotlight. My phone buzzed with an email. My heart did a little skip. Maybe it was Antonio? But no, I had special patterns programmed into my phone when he called, texted, or emailed.

I pulled the phone out on my way to the bar and read the notification. An email from Elliot with the subject line: 'News'

Good thing I'd left the table.

Without looking up at the bartender, I slid into one of the high-backed bar stools and checked the email. It was short, sweet, and to the point: 'Giovanni is cooperating. Things are escalating with Fiori. Let me know when you're done playing insurance adjuster. -E'

Shit. I placed the phone face down on the bar and leaned forward, head falling into my hands. This was big news. I had to tell Antonio.

I stared at the bar in front of me and ran a hand along its length. August first, last year. That was the day Antonio had asked me if the seat next to me was taken. At this very bar. He'd sat next to me and told me bad jokes, then I turned him down for the first time. My sister was just starting her chemo and I was still bitter about being back home in Brenton, Michigan.

That fool man. A lump caught in my throat. It was my birthday. What was wrong with expecting he'd put up with a hangover to talk to me on my birthday?

"Mi scusi," said a deep voice from behind me.

I startled, spinning around to see—to see Antonio standing there, leaning on the stool.

"But is this seat taken?"

Oh my god, it was him. It was really him!

Don't cry, Sam.

I launched off the stool and spread my arms wide. "Antonio!"

Instead of wrapping his arms around me, he backed away and laid a finger on the side of my jaw, twisting it toward the bar. "No, no, you barely looked at me that night."

"What?" I stared at him from the corner of my eye for a beat. For about twenty beats of my heart, rather, it was running in overdrive.

"I said, 'Is this seat taken?'"

Was he seriously replaying that evening? Right now? When we hadn't seen each other for two whole months?

His brows lifted.

I let out a sigh and climbed back onto the stool. "No, it's not taken."

"You know—" He took the seat next to me and smoothed his black dress shirt. Black tie. Exactly what he'd worn that night. "—I heard a rumor."

"Yes, about the butter." I rested my chin on my hand and glanced over at him. "You shouldn't be spreading it."

"No, no, I'm the one who tells the bad jokes here."

I gave him the most serious look I could, which wasn't very serious. I needed to kiss this man. "And the fish said dam when it swam into the wall."

He tsked at me. "You look like your evening has gone about as well as mine has."

I huffed playfully. "Worse, trust me."

"Fantastico! You're joining my game, finally!" The bartender arrived, and Antonio ordered a glass of red wine for each of us. "So, would you like to talk about it?"

I turned around on the barstool, to where my family sat at our table. They were all watching, laughing, and smiling. Every one of them was in on this. I returned my attention to the gorgeous man sitting next to me. "Well, you see, it's my birthday. And my no-good boyfriend skipped our video chat this morning."

"Mi dispiace." He pressed a hand to his chest in mock sympathy. "He sounds like a horrible man to take such a glorious creature for granted."

"He is." I bit down on my lip to control a laugh. "And what was so terrible about your evening?"

"I've been in this restaurant for five minutes now, and no one has tried to seduce me yet." He leaned close, lowering his voice. "Perhaps I'm losing my touch?"

I gave him an obvious once-over. "You're kinda cute. Don't suppose you want to come home with me?"

"I'll have to check with my roommate." He held out his hand, and I slipped mine into it. To touch him after all this time sent traces of electricity up and down my arm. He brought the hand to his lips and pressed lightly, letting us both savor the moment. "I'm not sure she would approve."

I leaned closer. "How long do I have to play this game before I get to kiss you?"

He took in a sudden breath, feigning shock. "In public, bella?"

I slipped off my stool and cupped his cheek, his soft lips meeting mine. My heart rate sped up as he moaned in the kiss, and I wrapped my arms around him. There was only slight hesitation from his right arm, which he was still working with a physiotherapist on. His delicious scent enveloped me.

This was home.

"Mi sei mancata molto, bella."

"I missed you, too." My face nuzzled against his neck, and I could have stayed there forever. "How long are you here?"

"I fly back in the morning."

"Seriously?" I pulled away, my stomach rolling at the thought. Did he stay somewhere other than his condo last night? Why didn't he tell me he was in town? "When did you arrive?"

"My plane touched down fifty minutes ago." He flew all the way from Naples for one night?

"Do you have meetings or something?"

He chuckled, running a hand through my hair, the golden flecks in his brown eyes dancing in the bar's lights. "The day I told you I would have to stay longer in Napoli, the first thing you said was that I would miss your birthday." He kissed my temple. "I could hardly do that to you."

I stared at him, soaking up the look in his eyes.

That first night in August, all I'd seen was a ridiculously handsome man hitting on me. I noticed the shoulders, the jaw-line, the hair I wanted to touch. But tonight, it all faded away.

It was just him. All of it was him.

His heart, his soul, his spirit. His silly jokes. The way he flew halfway across the world to surprise me for my birthday.

This was the man I loved.

My partner. In all things.

Right, partner. "I need to tell you about the email I just got from Elliot."

He threw his head back, laughing so loudly people turned to stare at him. Once he settled down, he ran a thumb over my cheek. "Can we talk about that later?"

I shook my head to clear my thoughts. This wasn't the right time. My hand flinched, wanting to cover my face for saying it out loud.

Antonio kissed the tip of my nose. "I love you and your brain, Ms. Caine."

"Good." I grinned back at him, then looked over his shoulder at my smiling, troublemaking family. "Screw the birthday cake. I'd like to go home now."

His delicious smirk rose. "My place or yours?"

I pulled his hand from my face and pressed a kiss against his palm before intertwining our fingers. "Ours."

As we walked out together, waving at my family, he leaned close to whisper in my ear. "Did you ever open my bedside drawer?"

"Pandora's box remains closed..." I let go of his hand and snaked my arm around his waist. I'd been tempted at least five times every single day, my suspicion of what was inside it growing a little more comfortable each time I looked at the closed drawer. "We can open it when you're home for good."

His arm landed around my shoulders, and he squeezed me to him. "I look forward to that."

THE END OF BOOK 4

BOOK 5: Antonio's finally home from his time in Italy. Is a quiet life within Sam and Antonio's grasp? Or will a mysterious letter that arrives at the Ferraro's art conservation studio—and a visit from Pasquale Fiori—trigger their final adventure together?

Forging Caine is available for preorder at
https://www.amazon.com/dp/B0BDSDVLK5

FREE NOVELLA: Curious what happens between this epilogue and *Forging Caine*? Check out the free novella *The Phoenix Heist*! It's the prequel to a new romantic suspense series, starring Scarlett Reynolds and her heist crew. It also features cameos by Sam and Antonio (plus Elliot!).

Join Janet's author newsletter and get
The Phoenix Heist for FREE only at
https://bf.janetoppedisano.com/smbari40im

Forging Caine - Excerpt

Antonio

My phone rang and I snatched it, ready to hurl it out the window for the interruption. Unknown again. Who could be calling me so insistently with a masked number? Unless it was my Zio Giovanni or someone from that part of the family?

Samantha rolled her eyes and withdrew her hand from mine. "Someone obviously wants to talk to you."

"It's probably Cristian. I'll deal with it." I answered and snapped into the phone, "What?"

An unfamiliar voice responded in Italian, "Is this Dr. Antonio Ferraro?"

It could be a client, a contact I made in Napoli, or still someone from Giovanni's organization. But I had little patience for it now. "I'm sorry, but who is this?"

"You may not remember, but my name is Pasquale Fiori."

My chest constricted and I gripped Samantha's forearm too tightly. I mouthed, *Fiori*.

Her eyes grew wide and she hauled out her phone, unlocking it and typing furiously.

"We met last September outside of Sorrento. You and your girlfriend visited my boat, moored off Capri."

"Yes, of course," I said. "How could I forget your kindness?"

"Good, good. I'm in Detroit for a few days and I remembered you live in the area. I was hoping to see you again."

Samantha showed me her phone, with a note-taking app open. She'd typed, *What does he want?*

I held up a finger, shaking my head.

Fiori continued, "I know it's short notice, but are you free tonight?"

He sounded so calm, so friendly. It was the same as when we'd met him and his doctor had taken care of Samantha's injured ankle after a hike gone awry. Cristian had told me in January that they feared Fiori was after Samantha as revenge, since she'd brought the authorities down on several crimes he'd been involved with. The last we'd heard, she was safe.

Now here he was.

Samantha's face squirreled up, exaggerating the confused reaction I was having underneath the layer of panic.

If he was truly *after* her and wanted to hurt her, why call in advance?

"Tonight?" I asked, staring deliberately at her. "I'm heading over to a friend's house right now, so I can't—"

Samantha jabbed at her phone.

"Are you sure?" asked Fiori. "I was hoping you could bring your girlfriend. Samantha, yes?"

"Yes, it was—I mean, it is—I mean, we have dinner plans with family tonight. Detroit is too far a drive."

Samantha returned to typing and held up her phone. It read, *He wants to see us? Say yes!* She'd been so focused on getting to her sister's earlier, but Investigator Samantha was taking over from Devoted Sister Samantha.

"How about desserts and drinks after that?" said Fiori. Why was he so insistent? What did he truly want? Surely it was not simply to catch up with old acquaintances. "The Ferraro's business is in Brenton, yes? And you live there?"

Samantha gestured with her hands, with her chin, with her whole body.

I tipped the phone away from my ear slightly so she could hear better. "Tomorrow might be better?"

"No, no, tonight. Is there a place in Brenton you think I might enjoy?"

Samantha nodded vigorously and pointed from the phone to her and back again, as though she wished to speak with him. That was not about to happen. Heaven knew what she'd promise.

"Let me discuss it with Samantha. Do you have a number so I can call you back in fifteen minutes?"

"I'll call you back in twenty." Fiori hung up.

I sat still for a moment, while Samantha's eyebrows climbed progressively higher. Fiori—the man behind Samantha's ex appearing at Giovanni's, whose goon tried to shoot me in January, who my cousin feared wanted Samantha dead—he was nearby. On the very day I returned from Napoli.

"Antonio?" Samantha nudged me and I snapped to attention. "He wants to see you?"

"Us," I said. "He specifically mentioned you and was quite insistent it had to be tonight."

"Why?"

I pressed the phone against my chest, as though he were still listening. "I don't know. It can't be a coincidence that the only day he can see us is the same day I get home."

"I don't like this." Yet she tapped her fingers against her lips, one of so many tells I'd learned from her.

"You're excited. You're planning something."

"Are you kidding me?" Her eyes all but twinkled. "He's on our turf now."

Read the full story (available soon) at
https://www.amazon.com/dp/B0BDSDVLK5

Acknowledgements

Just like *Disarming Caine* was the end to an era (my last book fully drafted before I decided to start publishing), *Enduring Caine* is the start of a new one. It's the first full-length novel conceptualized and written entirely after I published my first book. And it really had no place in my original series concept.

But do you want to know a secret? Once I finished *Disarming Caine*, I had a need in my heart for Antonio to surprise Sam for her birthday. I wrote the epilogue to this book and had fun playing it up against their original meet cute. My first thought was to send it out as a bonus epilogue for my newsletter subscribers.

Then my brain got to thinking (much like it did when I drafted *Chasing Caine*, which wasn't in my original series concept, either)... what did Sam and Antonio do while they were in Naples?

And from that epilogue and that question, this book was born. It's an important hook into the final book of the series, setting the stage for what's to come.

As always, I have to say thanks to my husband and son for their encouragement and the time they support me hiding out in my writing cave.

Next, I'd like to thank my beta readers: Paula, Pat, Colin, Missy, and Kari. They always have helpful feedback, digging into early copies of my books to help ensure I'm keeping the pace and tension up, that I'm not confusing anyone, and they are amazing cheerleaders.

And finally my editor, Miranda Darrow, who helps ensure I kill my darlings (the passages or possibly entire chapters I love too much, but which must be deleted), for the benefit of all. (Confession: The two chapters I deleted are available to my newsletter subscribers)

And finally, I'd like to thank you, my reader. Without you, I'd just be writing stories for myself. As pleasant as that might be, I truly love sharing my words with you. Thank you for reading my books and for all the kind messages and emails you send.

About Author

Janet Oppedisano hails from Canada's East Coast and has lived in five provinces, from the Maritimes to the Prairies. Growing up with a Mountie for a father and marrying a Navy diver, it's no surprise she writes romance with a hint of danger and mystery in it. Not to mention strong heroes and equally strong heroines.

Prior to publishing her debut novel, she won awards for two of her unpublished works, including the Romance Writers of America's 2021 Vivian Award for Most Anticipated Romance, for *Burning Caine*.

When not writing, you can find her... thinking about writing. And indulging in her favorite pastimes, like baking, traveling, hiking, playing with her dog, and watching her hockey goalie son on the ice.

Oh, and it's pronounced oh-ped-ih-SAH-no. Exactly the way it's spelled. Honest!

You can find Janet and all her social media profiles at:
https://janetoppedisano.com

Made in United States
Orlando, FL
13 June 2023

34095895R00236